*homesick creek*

ALSO BY DIANE HAMMOND

*Going to Bend*

# homesick creek

## DIANE HAMMOND

DOUBLEDAY

*New York   London   Toronto   Sydney   Auckland*

PUBLISHED BY DOUBLEDAY
a division of Random House, Inc.

DOUBLEDAY and the portrayal of an anchor with a dolphin are registered
trademarks of Random House, Inc.

*Book design by rlf design*

Library of Congress Cataloging-in-Publication Data
Hammond, Diane Coplin.
Homesick creek / by Diane Hammond.— 1st ed.
p.  cm.
1. Oregon—Fiction.   2. Women—Fiction.
3. Female friendship—Fiction.   I. Title.

PS3608.A6956H66  2005
813'6—dc22
2004063472

ISBN 0-385-50944-8

PRINTED IN THE UNITED STATES OF AMERICA
July 2005
First Edition
1   3   5   7   9   10   8   6   4   2

*To my parents,*

*Bob and Debbie Coplin,*

*for giving me a love of words*

# *acknowledgments*

Much of *Homesick Creek* was written during many long hours spent driving the roads between Bend, Oregon, and Tacoma, Washington. Thus my deepest love and thanks must go first to my husband, Nolan Harvey, for being an endlessly patient driver and silent partner during my mental as well as physical travels. Without his support and encouragement, this book would not have been. Likewise, I extend my heartfelt appreciation to my daughter, Kerry, for embracing my writing life with humor and pride.

My thanks, too, to Julie and Charles Mann and Hailey and Blake Bertuleit for so generously feeding, housing, and encouraging us through unsettled month after month. Their love and support are reflected throughout this book.

As always, my undying thanks to my agent, Jennifer Rudolph Walsh, for her continuing belief in me, and to my editor, Deb Futter, for her unwavering enthusiasm, incredible support, and most of all, all the times she read installments of *Homesick Creek* after hours, over weekends, and during bits and snatches of time that had no doubt been otherwise committed. And lastly, to Karen Ninnis, proofreader and copy editor extraordinaire, I extend my eternal gratitude for her tenacious and unwavering grasp of the small, vital stuff that makes the best books go.

*homesick creek*

*chapter one*

Mornings come hard and mean on the Oregon coast in winter. Trees on Cape Mano between Hubbard and Sawyer have only lee-side branches, twisted old men with their backs to the sea. More than a few casually built bungalows and cabins are chained to the rocks so gale-force winds won't take them.

Highway 101, Hubbard's only through street, runs north to Canada and south to Mexico, edging along the black basalt shore and over a bridge that spans Hubbard's small harbor. Moored there are both sport and commercial fishing vessels, piloted by the handful of skippers capable of navigating the boiling deep-water channel at the mouth of the harbor. Everyone has a story to tell about a boat that's broken up on the rocks within hailing distance of home. In 1983 eight realtors on a sport-fishing jaunt drowned in plain sight when their charter boat turned broadside and sank.

For all its tiny size and appearance of sleepiness, Hubbard in 1989 lit its fires early, and nowhere earlier than at the Anchor Grill, which opened every morning at four o'clock sharp. The restaurant was located at the exact center of town, across the street from Devil's Horn, a rocky blowhole through which seawater shot thirty feet in the air when storm seas were running. The Anchor was that rare hybrid, beloved by tourists and residents alike, an easy place with vinyl tuck-and-roll booths, stained carpet and paneled walls, stuffed trophy fish, and the everlasting aroma of chowder, fried food, and beer. First light belonged to Hubbard's fishermen and pulp mill workers putting in day shifts ten miles away over in Sawyer. From seven o'clock in the morning until the reek of fish guts signaled the return of the boats in midafternoon, the place was nothing but tourists with their hair, shoes, and umbrellas in various stages of ruination. By evening a good-natured polyglot crowd filled the lounge to the accompaniment of Pinky Leonard on the keyboard and owner Nina Doyle playing the bottles.

Bunny Neary had waitressed at the Anchor for twenty-one years, ever since she was nineteen. A couple of months ago old Dr. Bryant had measured a two-and-a-half-inch difference in the height of her shoulders from lifting and carrying trays, but mostly she liked the work well enough. On a good day she could pick up a hundred, hundred and fifty bucks in tips. And from being there so long, she usually got her pick of shifts.

Not today, though. Beth Ann, who normally worked mornings, had called in with strep throat again. This was Bunny's fourth day in a row covering for her, and she was beat. Being on the opening shift meant getting to the Anchor at three-thirty—three, if she did the whole list of things she was supposed to do before she opened up at four. She hardly ever did, seeing as how no one came into the place at that hour of the morning but the boys, and the boys didn't give a crap whether the salt and pepper shakers were topped off or the half-and-halfs were iced down or the sugars were filled, just as long as the coffee was fresh and

hot. At four o'clock sharp they'd be out there in the back parking lot waiting for her, smelling like Dial soap and cigarettes and
yesterday's jeans. They'd slouch in and heave themselves into
their booths, slap down the newspaper, and call, *Hey, Bunny,
where's that coffee?*

The fact was, though, Bunny would have been beat even if she
hadn't pulled the morning shift. She hadn't slept worth a damn
all night, not after she'd overheard some woman whisper to her
husband over the phone, *Just pretend this is about work. Oh, Lord,
Hack, do I feel stupid; I didn't think she'd be home.*

She let an extra half pull of coffee grounds fall into a fresh filter—the boys liked their coffee strong this time of day, weak as
tea when they started coming in off the boats around two—and
punched the brew button on the coffeemaker, touching the
waiting pot first. Once, another time when she and Hack were
on the outs, she'd made a whole pot of decaf without remembering to put a pot underneath, and there'd been fresh-brewed coffee everywhere. The boys had razzed her about it for weeks. *Hey,
Bunny, did you put a pot under it this time? Ha, ha, ha.* Shit.

*Oh, Lord, Hack, do I feel stupid; I didn't think she'd be home. You can't
talk with her there, can you? So I'll hang up now. I guess I'll just hang up.
Here I go.* And she'd hung up. Then Hack had hung up. Then
Bunny.

"Hey, Bunny, bring me that maple syrup there, would you?"
Dooley Burden called from two tables down. Bunny had known
Dooley all her life. He was maybe sixty-four now, and the
stringiest thing Bunny had ever seen; he looked like if you were
to bite into him, he'd be nothing but tendons and gristle and a
little tough meat, like an old dry rooster. When Bunny was little,
Dooley had worked a couple of seasons as deck crew for her father, but then it turned out he was epileptic. He managed to

keep it a secret until he had a seizure forty miles out, fishing for black cod. He'd worked down at his brother's fuel dock after that, until he fell a couple of winters ago and pretended he'd been going to retire anyway. Now he just hung around town razzing all the young fishermen about their joint-venture seasons and their on-board microwaves. The boys let him talk. They'd heard about how he'd flopped around on the deck with the cod and the trash fish so bad they'd finally had to lash him to a hatch cover to keep him from twitching himself clean over the rail with his eyes rolled back in his head. And they knew about how his turd of a brother, Carlin, never once paid him more than fifty cents above minimum wage in all those thirty-eight years of pumping diesel at three in the morning, while Carlin was busy taking vacations in Hawaii and sailing around the San Juans in his forty-five-foot sailboat like some kind of goddamn son-of-a-bitch big shot.

Bunny set down a sticky little pitcher of maple syrup on Dooley's paper place mat. The place mat came right back up and stuck when he went to pour syrup on his sausage links, next to his eggs, over his short stack. He'd ordered the exact same breakfast every day for the last twenty-one years.

"What's the deal with Beth Ann?" he asked Bunny, who was so tired she was just standing there watching him. Beth Ann was one of the younger waitresses, twenty-three. The boys liked to send her for more coffee just to watch her walk away. "She got a new boyfriend? She's sure looking nice these days."

"New perm," Bunny said. "Plus she's on that liquid protein diet."

"Aw, I like my women with some meat on them," Dooley said, like he'd even had a date in the last fifteen years. He took a big bite of egg and slid his coffee cup toward Bunny so she'd top it off.

"Well, if you'd just told her that to start with, I'm sure she would have called the whole thing off. You've got a little piece of egg there on your chin," Bunny said, pointing.

Dooley shrugged, flicked the egg off with his finger, drank some coffee. "Hack going to buy that dirt bike he was looking at?" he asked Bunny. "That two-fifty? It's got beans, that bike. It's a good piece of machinery, and the boy was asking a good price. You tell Hack I said so."

"What dirt bike?" Bunny said. "He hasn't said anything about another dirt bike."

"Aw, hell," said Dooley. "Guess I've stepped in it now, huh? You think he's coming by this morning?"

"Doesn't he always come by?"

"He's late, though."

"Yeah," Bunny said. She had tried the house a couple of minutes ago. The line had been busy. Busy, at five-fifteen in the morning.

*You can't talk with her there, can you?*

And now there was some dirt bike deal he'd never told her about. She set her coffeepot on the table, slid into the booth across from Dooley, and poured herself a cup of coffee.

"You been keeping him up too late?" Dooley said, and winked.

"Don't he wish." Bunny drank half the cup down, picked up a fork, and cut a bite out of Dooley's soggy short stack.

"What's the matter, honey?" he said, sucking a tooth.

But Bunny just finished her bite of pancake, sighed, and hoisted herself up from the table. "Nothing. Just tired of getting up at three in the morning to take care of you boys."

Back at the waitress station Bunny threaded her name tag through the little round name-tag eyelets stitched into the blouse of her uniform. *Bunny.* Her real name was Bernadette. Bunny was something Hack had started and gotten almost the whole town to go along with. He used to say he called her Bunny because she had such a nice tail. That was Hack. He'd been a wild one when they first started going together fifteen years ago. She'd met him his second day in Hubbard. It had been a sunny June morning, and she and her girlfriend Anita had been sitting on a blanket above the bay gossiping and keeping an eye on their kids, Anita's Doreen and Bunny's Vanilla—Vinny— both of them almost four years old. Of course she hadn't been called Vinny then.

Hack had stumbled up, scaring them half to death before he got close enough to show them that easy smile of his. He'd spent the night under the bridge, and he was shivering, still part drunk, his fatigue jacket soaked with old fog. He came right up to them and asked Bunny if he could borrow her blanket for a minute; he was about to die of cold, he said, and if there was one thing he hadn't been able to stand, ever since he could remember, it was being cold. That was one of the things he'd liked best about Vietnam, the heat.

He squatted down next to Bunny, and there was something hopeful about him that Bunny liked, as if he was expecting good things to happen any minute; he had the scrappy, take-me-home look of kids who get away from their parents too young. So she gave him the blanket. He'd meant to find a better place to stay than under that bridge, he said while he wrapped up, but he'd closed the last tavern—did she know that one, the Wayside?— and by then it was too late to find anything, plus he hadn't seen the town in daylight to know where to find a room. Wrapped up in her blanket, he talked for an hour straight, until the kids started getting hungry and they had to go. Bunny was going to let him keep the blanket, which was just an old flannel one with a hole in the middle, but he gave it back with that slow smile of his and said, *Maybe sometime you could show me some other ways people keep warm around here. If I stick around.*

*Oh,* Bunny had said over her shoulder. *I bet you'll stick around.*

Hack. He'd been something special to look at with his big, rangy body, pretty green eyes, neat brown beard, and a tongue that showed pink as a cat's when he yawned; in fact there'd been something catlike and clean about him all over, even that first time. He'd only been back from Vietnam maybe three months by then, so mixed in with the other things was that half-crazy, what-the-fuck gleam in his eyes you saw in vets a lot in those days. But Bunny had seen that same look all her life in fishermen who'd seen a boat or two go down. Her father had had that look as long as Bunny could remember. In a fishing town everyone knows men who've walked right up and hung their toes over the edge.

Meantime, it looked like Bunny's boyfriend, JoJo, had already been gone almost a year, and it looked like he wasn't coming back this time. He hadn't left her any money either, so she and Vinny had to move in with Bunny's folks, and that wasn't working out. Her father was always ragging on her that she should have made JoJo marry her after she'd had Vinny. Plus, no Hubbard man would date her because they knew how crazy mean JoJo would be if he ever came back and found out. And it was true that he'd beat the holy crap out of you if he was in the mood. Bandy little guys like JoJo took up the slack by being twitchy.

Not Hack. Hack was big and slow and agreeable, and Bunny decided right then, on that first day, that he'd be good to have.

She knew she had the kind of looks Hack could live with: okay face, better-than-okay figure, and a walk that said uh-huh. She also knew that even though he still hadn't found the back-home good time he'd promised himself while he was over there in Vietnam, he was ready to rest awhile. And a man like Hack didn't rest alone. So when he started showing up every afternoon at the Wayside with that mouth of his going steady and smooth and her brand of cigarettes stuck in his pocket, she was ready. She let him buy her a beer sometimes but not always, showed up some days but not others, and never explained one way or another. And she ignored him. Nothing drove Hack crazier than being ignored. He'd come sit down next to her, and she'd pretend she was busy reading in the newspaper about something going on over there in Poland or Africa or someplace. Pretty soon Hack would start talking, some little pay-attention-to-me foolishness, and when that didn't work, he'd bump her barstool or throw little balled-up napkin bits at her, and she'd ignore that too, until he'd finally grab the paper completely out of her hands and lay half his body across the bar in front of her. He moved her and Vinny into a nice rental with him before the end of the first month.

For a couple of years after that he'd done odd jobs around town, and on weekends he raced stock cars over in the Willamette Valley with some buddies he'd met. He liked to race, but it was mostly so he could be around the cars. He talked to Bunny about them all the time, even though she didn't understand one thing he was saying. He referred to the cars as "she," and if he was anywhere near one, he'd stroke and pet its sides and hood and inspect it all over for little hurt places. Bunny had seen him stare at some piece of junk in his hand for an hour trying to figure out a new thing to try, and there would be love in his eyes.

She went with him when she could get Anita or someone to watch Vinny, and on the way home they'd usually pull into the Patio Courts or the Hi-Time Motel and screw on the thin, scratchy sheets for hours. More than anything, more even than cars, Hack loved to screw. His touch was so good Bunny sometimes thought that if God Himself did it, He would do it like Hack. *Oh, pretty lady,* he used to say to her. *The way you make me feel.*

After a couple of years Hack was still in Hubbard and he let Bunny marry him. He got a steady job managing the service department at Vernon Ford over in Sawyer, until old Marv noticed Hack was a born salesman and tried him out on the used car lot instead. He did so well they let him sell new cars after only a year. He bought them a house and then a better one. He bought them a sectional sofa and an electric organ. When Vinny's permanent teeth started coming in gray, he found a special dentist for her, and when Bunny crashed her car into the back of a motor home that time and they got sued, Hack found an attorney who got them out of it.

But the whole time that was all going on, there was this other thing Bunny knew. Hack had come to Hubbard on his way to someplace else, and he had never meant to stay, just to stop and rest awhile. Right from the start there were times when he got sad, got lost-looking and homesick for someplace he'd never been. The spells hadn't lasted long, and when they were over, he'd been glad to be back. But in the last few years the sad times had started coming more often and playing out meaner, and even though Hack still wouldn't talk about them, she knew it was because he was trying to figure out what to do. And whatever he chose, he meant to do alone. One day, Bunny knew, he'd just take her and Vinny and Vernon Ford and everything else about their lives and pitch them over the side and rise up like a big hot-air balloon and be gone. You couldn't keep a man like Hack. The best you could hope for, if you were lucky and you played your cards right, was to get the use of him for a while.

Hack finally walked in the Anchor's back door at six, half an hour late. Joelle Burden, Dooley's sister, was with him. Joelle worked the six a.m. shift. She was wide-mouthed, small-eyed, and tough as all hell. She'd been tough even when she was fifteen and used to baby-sit for Bunny and her sister, Fanny. She used to tape their mouths shut with duct tape if they gave her any flak. Sometimes Fanny went around with tape marks on her face for days. Now Joelle was fifty-seven, but she was walking real close to Hack anyway, the way women always did. Even Beth Ann, who had plenty of boyfriends her own age, liked to come over and flirt when Hack was around. Hack would tell her jokes and talk in that sweet dirty way of his, and Beth Ann would blush and giggle and make a fool out of herself.

Bunny was setting up some tables in the back for when the tourists began to come in. Paper napkins, paper place mats, forks, knives, spoons. Sugar, Sugar Twin, Equal. Upside-down coffee mugs, upside-down water glasses, fake carnation, fake greens, fake crystal bud vase, real water. Joelle gave Hack a little see-you-later punch on the arm and signaled Bunny to meet her over at the waitress station.

"That man sure can tell a story," she said when Bunny got there. She poured herself a mug of caffeinated and turned her back so Bunny could tie her apron. Joelle had bursitis so bad in both shoulders she couldn't do up half her clothes anymore.

"Do you think Hack's going to buy that Leonard kid's dirt bike?" she said while Bunny worked the bow. "He just asked me what I thought, but shoot, I don't know anything about it. What did you tell him?"

"First thing I heard of it was from Dooley fifteen minutes ago," Bunny said grimly, giving Joelle's bow a final yank.

"Shit. Oh, honey—"

"I'll tell you what, if he gets that thing, he better buy me a new washing machine first," Bunny said. "Mine walks all over the house on the spin cycle. Look at that. See that guy at table seven? Every two seconds he's putting his damn hand up for something like this is the goddamn Ritz."

"You go ahead and talk to Hack, and I'll take care of His Majesty," Joelle said.

"I don't want to talk to him," Bunny said, but Joelle had already hustled out of range.

Hack had been out the front door at the newspaper machine. He passed Joelle on the way back, with the paper tucked under his arm so he didn't get any of the print on his hands. While Bunny filled a mug of coffee for him from the dregs of the oldest pot, he stood real close and slipped his hand over her backside. In a minute, she thought, he'd be talking dirty to her. Last night, after he'd hung up from that phone call, he'd been real nice too, bringing her beers with the tops already cracked open, watching TV in the living room with her instead of working on his pickup out in the garage like she knew he'd planned to. He probably knew she'd overheard something last night. He was being good until he could figure out how much trouble he was in. He didn't even know yet that she knew about the dirt bike.

"You should've stayed in bed another minute or two," he whispered in her ear. "I was warming up something nice for you, but you were too quick."

"Something nice for you, you mean."

"That too." He grinned.

"Go talk to Dooley," she said. "He was asking about whether you're going to buy that boy's dirt bike or not."

Hack didn't miss a beat. He just nodded like he assumed she'd known all along, like maybe he'd even mentioned something about it to her himself once or twice. Joelle must have given him a heads-up when they passed. People were always saving Hack like that. They never did it for Bunny.

"It's a hell of a good price," he said. "I don't know, though. I guess I'll probably let it go. We could use the money for some things around the house."

"Just go talk to Dooley. He had some things he wanted to tell you." Ten years ago she might have been fooled, but not anymore. She knew Hack would buy the bike. There wasn't even any point in talking about it. He'd probably already bought it and just slipped the kid a little extra to keep quiet about it until he could break Bunny into the idea. His agreeing with you about something didn't mean he wouldn't turn right around and go off in the opposite direction, with nothing more between him and your conversation than the hope that you wouldn't find out until he'd had a chance to work on you.

"Listen," Bunny said. "Don't you work me, Hack. I bet you just paid the boy not to tell anyone for a while."

Hack's face closed up, and his eyes froze over. "Now, I come over here to be nice to you," he said, quiet and deadly. "I came over to keep you company. I didn't come over here to take crap. You talk to me when you're sweeter." He turned around and walked away from the waitress station and out of the Anchor. In another minute she heard his pickup roar out of the back parking lot.

*Just pretend this is about work. Oh, Lord, Hack, do I feel stupid; I didn't think she'd be home. You can't talk with her there, can you? So I'll hang up now. I guess I'll just hang up. Here I go.*

Bunny didn't know for sure if Hack had ever cheated on her. He flirted with everyone, but he was always home when he was supposed to be, and he never went anywhere alone on weekends, not even when Bunny had to work a shift at the Anchor to cover for someone. Of course he was always home now too, and there was that phone call. And a few years ago Bunny had suspected a little cotton-haired girl who tended bar at the Wayside Tavern for a couple months and was always having car trouble and catching a ride with Hack to get it fixed over in Sawyer.

It was hard to know what to think. Hack still laid hands on Bunny whenever she'd let him. Bunny wasn't much for sex herself anymore. Somewhere along the line, in tiny bits and pieces, she'd lost her appetite. Every time Hack tried to con her, every time he promised not to do something and then went and did it anyway, every time he dished up some little bones and gristle of truth and tried to sweet-talk her into thinking it was a meal, she'd lost the taste for another little part of him. His sex parts went first, of course, but they were followed by other parts that she missed a lot more. The backs of his thighs. His neck, between his ear and his shoulder. The meaty part of his chest below his collarbone, where the hair made a hurricane shape. The pale insides of his wrists and elbows. Finally, one morning four or five years ago, she woke up and found she could look at him all over and not get the urge for a single bite. Except for times like now, when he might be leaving her; when he might have already left. Watching him walk out of the Anchor Inn, Bunny thought his whole body looked just like a picnic.

When she got off work at ten, Bunny drove by Anita's house. Anita had an edge on her like a razor lately, but Bunny didn't feel like going home. If Hack called to sweet-talk her, she didn't want him to find her that easily, and if he didn't bother to call, she didn't want to know. At least it had stopped raining.

Anita was standing in the lee of her carport, hanging out laundry. She'd been real pretty when she was younger, but you couldn't tell now. Bunny used to cut out diet tips from the newspaper, but she didn't even bother anymore. Anita was up to 190, and she carried most of it on her hips and thighs. Today she was wearing blue sweatpants and a pink checked blouse that gapped at the buttons. Bob hadn't been bringing in much money lately, so she'd had to do the best she could at the thrift shops over in Sawyer.

"You do Bob's," she said, the minute Bunny came around the carport. "Every time I pick up something of his I want to just roll it in the dirt." She snapped a pillowcase, and it sounded like a gunshot. "Last night he came home so toasted he tried to pee in my bureau drawer. He said he thought he was in the bathroom. I had to lead him to the can by his whatsis."

Bunny snickered. Anita looked at her and snickered too. "Jesus," she said, shaking her head. She handed Bunny some underwear and T-shirts and a fistful of clothespins.

Bunny took the other side of the line and started pinning. Bob's underpants were smaller than Hack's. Some of the waistbands were separating from the knit bottoms too, and the elastic was shot. Hack would never wear underpants like that, no matter how broke they were. He'd never even let Bunny try to fix them when they got like that. He always had her keep a package or two of new ones in his drawer. She wondered if the woman on the phone last night understood things like that about Hack, that he wasn't the kind of man who'd wear worn-out underpants. Probably not. When you first started with someone, you didn't notice about his underpants or whether he liked a clean towel every day or what deodorant made him break out. And he didn't notice those things about you; half the time, in the beginning, he didn't even seem to think you peed just like everybody else. Then, when he figured out that you did, he held it against you. That's where men and women were different, in Bunny's opinion. Men went out and looked for women who didn't pee. Women just went out and bought the right deodorant.

But the woman on the phone probably didn't know anything about that yet. She probably only knew about putting on lipstick and body lotion and sexy brassieres to try to fool Hack into thinking she was perfect. And Hack would probably believe her, the way he used to believe Bunny.

"What's the matter, hon?" Anita said, touching her arm. "You need to sit for a minute?"

"What?"

"You looked real bad just then. You were just standing there."

Bunny shook out a T-shirt and pinned it to the line. "Hack wants to buy some kid's dirt bike. He didn't even tell me. Dooley spilled the beans."

"I heard about that," Anita said.

"Who'd you hear it from?"

"I don't— Oh, wait, I know. Roy, down at the Wayside."

"Shit. Hack must have talked about that kid's bike with every single person in this town except me."

"Roy said Hack was real hot on it," Anita said. She stopped hanging laundry. "Actually, I heard he already put money down on it."

"See that?" Bunny cried. "I knew he had. I told him so this

morning, and he got mad like he always gets when he does something sneaky and I find out about it anyway."

"Boys and their toys."

"Well, he's really pissed off this time," Bunny said. She picked up the empty laundry basket and followed Anita inside, where Anita made them a pot of coffee. Bunny had been thinking of taking them both for lunch and a few beers at the Wayside, but she didn't think she could stand hearing from one more person who knew about that damn dirt bike.

"Remember when they used to talk to us?" she asked Anita.

"Who?"

"Bob. Hack."

"Did they talk to us?"

"Hack did. He used to talk all the time. He used to tell me everything, all his plans. When did they stop doing that?"

"Well, Bob stopped about five minutes after we got married, but then, he never was much of a talker."

Bunny stirred sugar into her coffee, making a little whirlpool with her spoon. "Don't you miss it?"

Anita frowned. "No."

"Hack didn't tell me a thing about that damn dirt bike, and then, when I let him know I knew, he lied about it. He said he probably wouldn't get it. Why does he do that?"

"Because you're his mother, honey," Anita said.

"Yeah, well, the whole time he was sweet-talking me, I could just see him trying to figure out how he'd sell the bike back to the kid if I made too much of a stink about it."

"He's always been shifty when you've got him in a corner," Anita said. Anita hadn't liked Hack much ever since he picked Bunny and not her to talk to that first day.

"He doesn't drink, though."

"No," Anita said quietly. "He doesn't drink."

"Oh, Nita, I don't know what made me say that," Bunny said, jumping up and putting her arm around Anita's shoulder. "I'm just mean today. Don't mind me, I'm just tired and strung out from opening the Anchor every morning."

"You sure are," Anita said. "You better go home and get some rest, or you're *really* going to start saying things."

Bunny had no intention of going home. Instead she drove over to Sawyer. It was the first time in a long time, even though Sawyer was only ten miles away. Bunny had gotten out of the habit of leaving town. There wasn't anything beyond Hubbard she really wanted. She wanted Vinny to give her grandchildren and be around to take care of her when she got old. She wanted to have enough money for a new deck and decent wallpaper in the bathroom and a washing machine that didn't walk around during the spin cycle. She wanted to have a wine cooler with her mother, Shirl, in the afternoon sometimes and to get on a later shift at the Anchor. She wanted to be the wife of someone who planned to stick around. Those weren't the kinds of things you could get over in Sawyer.

Bunny parked around the back of Vernon Ford, next to Hack's pickup, and tried to fluff up her hair in the rearview mirror. She'd been trying it short lately, even though Hack liked it longer. It didn't look very good. She started to take off her name tag and then decided to leave it on so she wouldn't have those two round holes in her blouse showing naked like some kind of vampire bite over her left boob.

As soon as she walked in, she saw Hack working in an office at the far end of the showroom, tipped back in a big chair with his boots up on his desk. Big smile, little chuckle, phone receiver snuggled into his shoulder. Selling.

He looked happy. It had been a while since she'd seen him look like that.

At the near end of the showroom, in a dinkier sales cubicle, a young woman was also smiling and talking on the phone. So they had women selling cars now. Bunny wouldn't buy a car from a woman if her life depended on it. Not that she'd ever bought a car in her life. Hack did that.

The saleswoman saw Bunny, hung up the phone, and walked over. Bunny saw good legs, good dress, good jewelry, perfect lipstick like she thought she was better than you. She was probably only a few years older than Vinny. Bunny wished she'd changed out of her uniform before she'd driven over here. Those uniforms would make anyone look bad.

"Hi," the saleswoman said, smiling at Bunny. "Can I help with anything today?"

*Just pretend this is about work. Oh, Lord, Hack, do I feel stupid; I didn't think she'd be home.*

"I'm Hack's wife," Bunny said.

The saleswoman was good. Not much showed. A tiny flinch around her mouth, pupils getting a little big, but that was all. "I'll go tell him you're here."

But Hack was already on his way over, and the saleswoman walked away, looking a little shaky. Hack didn't. He smiled. He was the most coolheaded man on earth when he thought he had something to lose.

"So you must be less ornery. Did you come to buy me coffee? You can take me to the Bobcat." He and Bunny used to go to the Bobcat Diner sometimes for lunch, before she stopped coming to town. He cozied his whole body up to hers and steered her that way toward the door.

"I don't want to go to the Bobcat," Bunny said. "Let's have coffee right here."

"Here?"

"I want to see what you do."

"But it's boring."

"I bet it's not. I've been thinking about it all morning."

She walked straight into his office, sat in his visitor's chair, turned it slightly so it faced the showroom, and folded her hands in her lap. "Just go on and do whatever you usually do," she said. "Pretend I'm not even here."

She had him. She knew he wanted to get her away from the saleswoman, and he knew she knew it. He sifted change in his pants pocket. "I guess I'll go get us a couple cups."

While he was gone, Bunny looked around. Mostly there were good salesmanship awards and junky little plaques on the wall, Ford promotional trash, but on Hack's desk there was a little ceramic teddy bear planter with an ivy growing out of its stomach. Vinny and Bunny had bought it for him last year, after he'd paid off Vinny's Ford Fiesta as a surprise. Bunny noticed there was a lot of dust on top of the teddy bear. The ivy was dry too, like no one ever watered it. Then she noticed a fancy day planner on his desk with a different photograph of Vietnam or Cambodia or someplace for each month. So he'd told her about being over there, how much he'd liked it, all the danger and no rules.

Hack came back with two styrofoam cups of coffee from the service department. For the next half hour Bunny drank her coffee and Hack made phone calls. He kept trying to get her to talk, so he could get a hint about her frame of mind, but she just shushed him and went back to doing what she'd been doing: watching the saleswoman, who had tiptoed back to her office and was staring at papers on her desk and fooling with one of her earrings. She didn't seem to be getting much done. Hack was better at this than she was. Her phone rang once, and she jumped about a foot.

"Well," Bunny said at the end of the half hour, "this was real interesting." She set her empty coffee cup on Hack's fancy day planner and stood up.

"What was interesting?" Hack said. Bunny saw him flick his eyes across the room to the saleswoman's cubicle. She was blotting her face with a Kleenex. "Hearing a bunch of boring phone calls?"

"Oh. Well, that too."

"What else?"

Bunny shrugged. "Just getting a chance to see some things."

"Things?"

Bunny made a big deal out of finding her car keys in her purse. "Oh," she said. "You might as well bring that dirt bike home. I called the Leonard kid from work. I said you asked me to drop off a check, and he said he couldn't figure out why, since you already paid cash."

Hack stood up and sifted pocket change.

"Most people don't keep secrets worth a damn, Hack," Bunny said, pulling out her keys. "It's really pretty easy to find things out if you want to know them. It's even easy to find things out when you *don't* want to know them. Like there are probably a lot of things you could tell me right now that I don't want to know about."

Hack clenched his fists inside his pockets.

"There's really just this one thing I want to know," Bunny said. "I want to know if you're leaving."

"Here?"

"Here." Bunny stabbed her finger into her chest just above her name tag.

"Aw, *crap.*" Hack looked at her and then turned to look out over the showroom floor, over the glossy new cars, over the saleswoman, over the entire town of Sawyer, at someplace so far away not even Bunny could see it. His arms were crossed over his chest so tight Bunny could see his shirt seams pulling. And watching him Bunny thought, *He's getting older. He's got a little gut and he sits down heavy and he gets up heavy and half the time when he goes dirt bike riding anymore he gets hurt. All this time, and I never noticed.*

"Jesus, Bunny."

"Okay." Bunny nodded and slung her purse over her shoulder. When she got to the door, she said, "The kid says he's waxed it for you."

"What?"

"The bike. He said to tell you he put a coat of wax on it for you and got it all polished up. I told him you'd stop by after work."

He nodded at the window.

"See you at home," Bunny said.

"Yeah."

She left the showroom without looking back, even though she could feel Hack turn around, finally, and watch her go. She knew he'd keep watching until she drove completely away, and then he'd go talk to the saleswoman. Bunny didn't know what he'd say after that, what she'd say back, how they'd feel, what they'd decide to do. All she knew was she had to buy a can of wax, go over to that kid's house, and make his dirt bike shine until it was perfect.

# chapter two

Hack Neary stood in the showroom window, watching the rain lash the string of plastic flags around the car lot and wondering what in hell difference honorable behavior made. No one believed him anyway, even when he was telling the truth, as he often did. People heard what they chose to hear, even when it upset them. If Bunny thought he was playing around, then he was as good as playing around, and it didn't matter what he had to say. Plus now he was catching grief over the dirt bike when she hadn't even heard the details. The kid had made him such a great deal that he could turn around and sell it in a minute for a profit. It had been a business decision. He didn't even ride that much anymore. It beat hell out of his knees, which were trashed anyway from jumping out of helicopters in Vietnam. He'd be forty in another month, *forty*. Jesus.

Last May, when Bunny had turned forty, Hack had bought her a used baby grand, a beautiful black glossy thing polished to a near-perfect shine. Not that any of them played the piano, but it was damn classy-looking and expensive as hell, something you'd have to be earning good money to buy, something you'd have to be successful to own. Dooley Burden still razzed him

about it at coffee sometimes. *Hey, Liberace, you still got that piano?*
*Ha, ha, ha.* Bunny posed some of her stuffed rabbits inside the
open top—a preacher, a doctor, Little Red Riding Hood. A couple of years ago she'd begun selling them, putting makeup on
them and dressing them in costumes: farmers and wizards, doctors and clowns. She sold them at Passionetta's Fudge and Candy
for spending money, so she and Anita could go up to Portland
sometimes, have a girls' day out to shop or, once, to go to a Chip-
pendale's show. For Hack's birthday last year she'd made him a
rabbit dressed in fishnets, garters, spike heels, and a boned
merry widow. He'd found it sitting on the bathroom shelf next
to his toothbrush first thing in the morning, holding a little sign
saying OOH-LA-LA—HAPPY BIRTHDAY! Not that she really spoke
French.

It was Hack who'd started her on collecting rabbits in the first
place—what, thirteen years ago? Jesus, no, fourteen—back
when she'd still had the body of a centerfold and the desire to
use it. That was also before he paid for three years of orthodon-
tia to correct the overbite he'd secretly loved because it gave her
a wistful look. He missed that. Now she had a perfect bite and
teeth that were prettier than she was. She should have just left
herself alone. As far as rabbits went, she'd probably bought about
a million since then, until he couldn't turn around without seeing some of the damn things. There were rabbit lamps, rabbit
light switches, rabbit salt and pepper shakers, rabbit clocks, towels, oven mitts, toilet paper holders. She'd even bought him a
pair of pajamas with rabbits on them. He liked to sleep naked,
but she'd said she was tired of him poking her all the time with
his nighttime erection. What kind of woman gave a man hell
about something he did involuntarily in his sleep? He bet even
men in comas got hard-ons. She'd finally conceded that he didn't

have to wear the pajama tops, just the bottoms. Every six months, like acid in an open wound, she got him a brand-new pair at JC Penney.

Hack absently sifted the change in his pocket, watching the showroom window weep and flex in the wind. When he drove to work this morning, the Hubbard coast guard station had already hoisted the storm flag, a black square on an orange ground, the third storm warning this season, and it was still only just December. When he drove by Hubbard Elementary on his way to work, seagulls were already gathering on the athletic field a block back from the beach. You could always predict the weather by watching seagulls. He'd probably have a hell of a ride going home over Cape Mano, the headland between Hubbard and Sawyer. It didn't matter; he had a heavy, muscular truck that could withstand any wind. He might just stop at the little overlook, see if any fishing boats were making a run for the harbor. Coming through the Jaws on a storm sea was a chancy thing even for experienced skippers like old Nate Jensen or Jordie Nelson. Anyone younger and the coast guard would have its boys out in the surf, fighting like hell to bring the boat in.

A year ago, maybe a year and a half, Hack had spent the night in his truck at the Cape Mano overlook. It hunkered down at the very lip of a thousand-foot cliff; if you looked out instead of straight down, you could almost be flying. He'd tucked himself into a sleeping bag inside the cab and felt every little gust and blow, watched the halogen lights appear and disappear as fishing boats bucked and yawed out near the horizon. He'd told Bunny he was at a regional sales meeting over in Eugene. He still didn't know why he'd taken such a risk; the overlook was screened from the highway by only a ratty fringe of coastal pines. If it had been daylight, someone would have seen him there and recognized him right away, his truck's being one of a kind with all its toys and extras, the winch and Playboy mud flaps, the radar detector and CB antenna. If she'd found out he was really spending the night in his truck just three miles from home, she would have been mad as hell, and he could never have explained it. He'd done it anyway, told his little lie, had his night out, and in the morning he'd gone to work like it was just another day.

As a sudden plague of hailstones overtook the passing traffic, Hack heard Rae pock-pock-pocking up behind him in her expensive high-heeled shoes. Her perfume wrapped itself around him like sin. He smelled it even in his dreams; sometimes at night he buried his head in the dirty laundry hamper in the hope that some of it might be clinging somehow to one of his shirts—not that it ever did. Before he knew her, he'd never known anyone who'd worn perfume like that. Bunny's perfume was some sweet cheap thing she'd gotten in Hawaii two years ago and wore only when she was going out with her girlfriends.

Rae Macy. Rae Macy was the most exotic woman Hack Neary had ever known. Long-necked and white-haired at twenty-nine, she walked straight and tall and light on her feet as though she were connected directly to heaven—the walk of a ballerina, maybe; the walk of a courtesan. She didn't talk like other people either. Complicated words and sentences spilled out of her like expensive candy, and when she told a story, she could have been reading a book out loud. Half the time Hack had no idea what she was talking about, something he found unnerving, him being a bluff talker himself.

She came around to stand right beside him now, the length of her arm lightly touching his. No one else was in the showroom.

"Hi," she said softly.

"Hi." He kept looking out the window instead of at her, but it was a hollow gesture. She had him. He bet she knew she had him.

"You okay?" she asked.

"Sure."

"Yes?"

She did that, asked questions twice if she thought he wasn't answering honestly, or if he was feeling something different from what she expected him to feel. He could sense her looking at him, assessing. "Was she okay?"

"Who?" He knew who.

"Your wife."

He didn't want to talk about that.

"She overheard me on the phone, didn't she?"

"Yeah."

"I'm so sorry. I know I shouldn't have—"

He cut her off. "It's okay."

Rae folded her arms tightly across her chest, sending up a fresh whiff of perfume. Did she fold her arms on purpose to make her silk shirt open up more? He could see some of her bra. It looked expensive—lace and ribbon. Bunny wore plain, cheap white underwear she got at the outlet stores. Not that it mattered. He'd seen her breasts a million times, though she didn't let him touch them much anymore. He loved the creamy slope between a woman's collarbone and breast, glimpsed in the V of a partially unbuttoned blouse. Rae's blouse, in this case. Everything she wore looked good to touch: silk, cashmere, soft leather, soft wool. She didn't have to dress up like that, but she said she had always dressed up in San Francisco and she wasn't about to compromise her standards now, just because she lived in a small town. He thought she was wasting her time, but he enjoyed the view all the same.

Most of the women he saw wore knit pants and blouses. That or jeans. He'd never seen Rae in jeans, but then he'd never seen her anywhere except at work. You'd think he'd run into her once in a while in the Sawyer Safeway or someplace on the weekend, but he never had. Not that he came over from Hubbard much on the weekend. Bunny never wanted to, not even to go to a movie.

"What are you thinking about?" Rae said quietly.

"Nothing."

"Oh, as though I believed *that*." She turned abruptly and walked away. He probably should have given her a real answer, but he didn't know what he was thinking about or if he was thinking at all. He could feel the first gentle pulsing of a migraine.

He grabbed his leather-look jacket from the coat tree in his office and headed out to the service area to shoot the shit a little with Bob. When he got there, though, Bob's service bay was empty again. Over at the service desk Francine smiled at him as he came in. She was a big, friendly girl, the kind built for having babies. You weren't supposed to say that kind of thing anymore, but it was true just the same, and Francine would have probably taken it as a compliment. She and Jerry had just celebrated their first anniversary. Francine still kept a photo album of their Hawaii honeymoon on her desk for people to look through while they waited for their car. First thing you saw after the reception shots was Francine in a tight black bathing suit, posing for the camera like a World War II pinup girl, only heavier.

"Hey, Hack," she said. So far she was the only person he'd seen today who seemed genuinely glad to see him.

"You're looking mighty good," Hack said. "You still on that liquid protein diet?"

Francine flushed with pleasure. "I've lost ten pounds already. Jerry can't believe it. He's so proud."

"You tell him he better watch out. If he doesn't keep an eye on you, some stud's going to try and snap you up," Hack said, because he knew it would make her happy. Even ten pounds lighter, she wasn't a girl who would turn heads. "Did Bob come in at all?"

"No. Anita called in for him." Francine gave Hack a look. They both knew Bob was drinking again.

"Well, at least things look slow," Hack said.

"Yeah. Mr. Vernon isn't coming in today either."

"Good." If the old man did show up, Hack would tell him Bob had just left for a dental appointment. Marv never worried about the service department, though, unless someone complained. It always made money.

"Are you going to call him?" Francine said.

"Guess I'd better."

"Well, be sure and tell him there's a full day of appointments tomorrow. Plus we already got one call from someone whose truck roof was caved in by a tree falling on it."

"Okay, I'll tell him."

Back in the showroom, Hack could hear Rae's long fingers flying over her computer keyboard. She had the most beautiful hands he'd ever seen. She was always writing something, poems or stories and shit. She'd shown him a few, and he'd pretended to like them so he wouldn't look unsophisticated. One was something about a bird with a broken wing, and another had some kind of chorus that kept repeating, *We're a mystery about to unfold / We're a morality play about to be told.* Whatever the hell that meant. Maybe she'd write about him one day. Now, to keep her spirits up, he winked at her as he walked by her cubicle, but his heart wasn't in it. Where his peripheral vision was supposed to be, there was nothing but wavy lines. It was his third migraine in a month.

He picked up the phone on his desk and speed-dialed Bob over in Hubbard. Anita picked up.

"He get lit again last night?" Hack said.

"Yeah. He spent twelve dollars on beer, and all I've got in the refrigerator are two eggs and a bottle of olives."

"At least it's nutritious, though." He absently flipped the pages of his fancy daybook. He'd never use a thing like that, a foo-foo thing, but it was nice of Rae to give it to him. She'd given him a few other things too: a letter opener Bunny hadn't noticed, a fancy pen he'd already lost but was hoping to find before Rae asked him about it. Actually, he wished she'd stop giving him things unless they were edible. What was he supposed to do with them? It wasn't as if he could bring them home. Come the day Bunny really got suspicious, he was going to have to make one hell of a dash to the nearest Dumpster.

"Yeah, right," Anita was saying.

"Look, I'll talk to him tomorrow; just make sure he gets here." Bob usually drank himself under the table for a couple of weeks, maybe a month, but he always popped out of it sooner or later. Hack liked to drink too, but he didn't get blind drunk like Bob. He didn't disappear like Bob either. Bob would just pick up and go. He never told anyone where he went, not even Hack, but he always came home after a couple or three days, and it had been like that for years. Anita told Bunny once that as long as he came home alone, she was beyond asking questions except whether he'd be leaving her permanently or not. And Bob always said, *Darlin', I love you. Only way I'll leave you is if you ask me to.* So far Anita hadn't asked him to. Hack didn't expect she ever would. Anita was like that: all blow and no rain. That was one of the things he liked best about her. Hack and Anita had had their differences over the years, but he gave her full credit for sticking by Bob the way she did. Not that he really understood why, but it was a generous act just the same.

"Look, the old man's not coming in today," Hack told Anita now over the phone. "I'll punch the time clock for him. That'll give him five hours anyway."

He picked a dead aphid off one of the dead leaves on his plant, ivy or whatever. He guessed he hadn't watered it enough. He wondered if he'd ever watered it. Bunny and Vinny were good at stuff like that, but Hack never remembered until it was too late.

After he got off the phone with Anita, he looked out the showroom window from his office. There was hardly any traffic now; no one was going to buy a car with the weather like this. He stood up, fished his truck keys out of his jacket pocket, and told Rae he was going out to the bank. It wasn't true, but he said it anyway so she wouldn't want to go with him. Lowering his head and leading with his shoulder, he pressed through the rain and wind and made it into his truck without too much damage to his hair, which was thinning more than he liked to admit. Every morning he arranged it carefully and sprayed it with Bunny's Aqua Net, which helped some.

He pulled out of the Vernon Ford lot with his wipers on high, pushing sheets of water aside with each pass. Down a couple of blocks the Sentry Market sign had cracked right down the middle, and the left half was lying in the road. Hack steered around it and drove on, past the Dairy Queen and Burger King and Fred Meyer store, past the social services agency and state employment office, and pulled into the parking lot of the Flower Blossom.

Agatha Thompson was in the window, putting more fake snow on her nativity scene, a plastic one she lovingly cleaned with a toothbrush and faithfully repainted once every five years. Hack could see that baby Jesus had His eyes painted shut in the manger and felt an instant of vicarious panic. He had a horror of being killed when his eyes were closed. If he was going to die— and there had been a number of times when he thought he might—he wanted to see it coming. Probably the baby Jesus could see, though, right through the painted eyelids. Hack wasn't personally acquainted with either God or Jesus, but he usually cut them a wide berth in case they really were up there doing miracles and damnations. You never knew.

When she saw him coming, Agatha backed out of the window display and pushed the door open for him against the wind. She was in her sixties now, small and round, fluffed up and bright-eyed as a chickadee, always generous with a smile now that she'd had her dentures refitted. She lived just a couple of blocks away from Hack and Bunny in Hubbard, up on Chollum Road.

"Hi, honey," she said, clapping him on the back in greeting, making a shower of raindrops. "You in trouble again?"

"Yeah."

Agatha shook her head fondly. "What did you do this time?"

"Hell, I don't know. Nothing. Got a phone call at the wrong time of day."

"Aw, honey," Agatha said, seeing his face. She'd always had an eye for him, called him a long, cool drink of water. Hack set out her garbage can every Tuesday, plus he hauled away yard junk and did heavy lifting for her four or five times a year. Sometimes she'd call him in between too, if she was having trouble with a stuck window or jar lid.

"You want roses again?" she asked him now. "She liked those ones last time, didn't she?"

"Yeah, I guess." He might as well send a bouquet of stinkweed, for all the difference it was going to make.

Agatha fussed inside her refrigeration case. "How about we send her these peach-colored ones, honey? They're real unusual for this time of year. You want me to just put it on your account?"

"Yeah." Hack sent flowers home so often Agatha just kept a running tab and billed him whenever it reached a hundred bucks. Not that it ever helped much. Bunny knew how to hang on to a snit.

"Okay. I'll have Jimmy deliver them so they're there before you get home. That should sweeten her some."

"Thanks, beautiful." Hack gave Agatha a one-armed hug. "When do you want to do Christmas lights?" Hack put them up for her every year and then took them down when Christmas was over.

"Aw, you don't have time for that, do you?"

"Are you kidding? When have I ever not found time for a beautiful woman?"

Agatha blushed and fussed like a teenager. "Go on, you shouldn't be saying something like that to a woman my age."

"Saturday?"

"If you're sure. I don't want to get you in trouble, honey, especially if Bunny's already on you about something."

Hack winked. "She's always on me about something, you

know that. I'll see you Saturday. Are you going to want that big sled up there on the roof again this year?"

"Only if you think you can manage it."

"I'll manage it. Santa's reindeer have to hitch themselves to something. It wouldn't be the same if they were just hauling some big garbage bags full of gifts."

Agatha tittered. "You're one of a kind, honey."

"Well, thank God for that, huh?"

"Naw." She squeezed his arm. "You just keep your chin up. Whatever it is, she'll get over it."

Hack pushed through the door backward, out into the freshening storm. Over at the Texaco station across the highway, the huge canopy above the pumps was rippling like a bed sheet. Hack wouldn't give two cents for its lasting out the hour. Bits of fir trees were scattered over Highway 101, and an occasional seagull sped overhead, blown sideways toward God only knew where. Hack fought his way into his truck and back to Vernon Ford, pulling into Bob's empty bay so he wouldn't have to go outside again. As he came through the showroom, he tapped on the wall of Rae's cubicle to say he was back. He heard her jump but kept on going to his office. There were no phone messages. When he looked up after checking, she was in his doorway. Her eyes were red, as if she'd been crying.

"You okay?" he said.

She nodded, but her eyes teared up.

Hack said gently, "Look, it's a dog of a day. No one's going to be buying anything until the weather clears. Why don't you go home?"

She looked away.

"No?"

"I hate this," she said. Hack had no idea what it was she hated, but he couldn't stand the thought of hearing any more misery right now. He nodded thoughtfully, as though he'd known exactly what she was talking about. "I know, but it's going to get better. You'll see."

"Do you think so?" She smiled bravely.

"I know so, pretty lady."

Rae nodded and walked back across the showroom. A minute or two later he heard her close the desk drawer where she kept her purse and then fight her way out the front door without saying good-bye.

Hack picked up the phone and speed-dialed his house. No one answered. He called Francine's extension, and she answered on the first ring. When she said no customer had driven in or called in the last hour, he sent her home. She drove a little beater car, and he didn't think she'd be safe on the road much longer. Then he taped a sign to the inside of the dealership's door, saying the showroom and service department would open as usual the following morning. He tried Bunny again to tell her he was on his way home, but there was still no answer. That was okay; now he could pick up the dirt bike without her convincing herself that he was off screwing Rae Macy between leaving the dealership and arriving at home.

He fought his way up and over Cape Mano, rejecting the idea of stopping at the overlook; the wind was too strong for him to see more than a few feet ahead through his windshield. Instead he drove straight to the kid's house on Adams Street and left the truck idling. Dickie Leonard answered his knock. Hack could see four or five toddlers behind him in the living room, playing with bright plastic toys and making enough noise to raise the dead. Myrah Leonard, Dickie's mom, must be doing day care again. She took in kids during the winter, when Pinky's tips were too light down at the Anchor.

Dickie ducked outside and opened the garage door. Inside, even from a distance, Hack could see the bike glowing in the dark like a jewel. When they went in to inspect it, he asked Dickie if he was still sure he wanted to sell it.

"Yeah," the kid said. "I got a speeding ticket that's going to cost me a hundred and eighty-five bucks."

"Piece of shit," Hack said sympathetically.

"Yeah. Mom said my insurance is going to go up again."

"She's probably right. That's the way it usually works. Any accidents?"

The kid shrugged. "Just a fender bender, you know."

"Your fault?"

"Yeah, I guess."

"Did the driver file a claim?"

"Uh-huh."

"So, you're fucked."

"Yeah," the kid said gloomily.

Hack ran his fingers over the finish on the dirt bike. It was a beauty. "You did a fine job with this, Dickie. You could be a detail man at Vernon Ford, if you're ever looking for a job."

"No kidding?"

"Sure. The old man's always looking for somebody to do detailing."

"I didn't detail it, though."

"No?"

"No." Dickie looked confused. "Your wife came by. She spent a good hour and a half working on it. She didn't tell you?"

"Nah. That Bunny—always one for surprises," Hack said.

"Yeah. My mom, she'd never do that for my dad."

"Yeah?" Hack backed the bike out toward his truck. "Well, it's been a pleasure doing business with you. If you come across a good bike again, just let me know."

"Okay."

Hack secured the bike with cargo straps. By the time he was done, he was wet through and his head was pounding. On the spur of the moment he pulled off at the Wayside Tavern for a quick shot of whiskey. Maybe it would soften his migraine a little bit or at least numb the pain. He knew from experience that nothing else would help. Bunny had been after him for years about going to a doctor, but he didn't believe in seeing doctors unless a limb was falling off. After Vietnam he had a dread of them, last-minute bastards who came too late and did too little, like high-functioning angels of death.

Hack plunged gratefully into the Wayside's muggy, dark interior. The outside world got no toehold here; there were no windows, not one, except for a little salt-crusted porthole by the door that no one could see through. The paneling was the color of cardboard boxes, and so was the shag carpet, chosen to hide the traces of a thousand spilled beers. The old fir tables were deeply notched and gouged, full of cigarette burns, dart wounds, and graffiti.

As Hack's eyes adjusted, he spotted Bob in the far back corner. No one else was in the place besides Roy, who was standing behind the bar polishing glasses with a cotton diaper. Hack got a shot of Jack Daniel's from him and brought it over to Bob's table.

"Hey," Bob greeted him. He seemed fully absorbed in blotting up the condensation on his beer bottle with a paper napkin.

"How's it going?" Hack said, dragging up a chair.

"Going great." Bob smiled congenially, leaned forward, and stage-whispered, "I'm stinko."

"Yeah, I could have guessed that." Hack threw back his shot of whiskey. Stars replaced the wavy lines in his peripheral vision, and the pain took his breath away. After it had subsided, he said, "Who gave you the money?"

"Found a little bit extra in Nita's purse."

"She know you're here?"

"Naw. Hell, she's so pissed off at me anyway, I didn't think it would be nice to tell her."

"That was damned thoughtful of you."

"Tha's me," Bob said. "One thoughtful son of a bitch. You ask anyone, they'll tell you that. Hey, Roy," he yelled. "You think I'm a thoughtful son of a bitch?"

"Sure, Bob."

"See?" Bob subsided, frowning at his beer. "I got some friends who aren't so thoughtful, though. Gave me a present, a fucking nasty little present."

"I'm not following you," Hack said.

"Nobody better follow me," Bob muttered. "I don't want anybody following me."

"You going someplace?"

Bob nodded seriously, canted to one side in his chair. Hack positioned himself so he could catch him if he started to fall. "Yeah, I'll be going someplace. Could be real soon."

For the second time this afternoon Hack found himself in a conversation he understood not a single word of. On the other hand, his head hurt so much he didn't care. "Okay, traveling man, I've got to get home," he said, punching Bob on the shoulder lightly. "You want me to drop you off?"

"Nah. You got any money, though? A five, maybe?"

"I'm all cleaned out. Anyhow, bud, you better get home. This storm's a bad one."

"Yeah," Bob said, nodding glumly.

Hack drove through blowing gobs of spindrift the color of tobacco spit and turned up Chollum Road. Five blocks uphill, and he was in his own driveway, surveying the wreckage of a spindly pine that had fallen across his roof. It looked messier than damaging; he'd cut it up once the storm had passed.

Hack was proud of his house. It was a double-wide manufactured home, but he and Bob had raised the pitch of the roof last summer and put new, expensive cedar shingles over the old cheap factory stuff. The only way you'd know it was a factory-built house now was if you went back to the county and looked at the deed. When he was growing up in Tin Spoon, Nevada, he and the Katydid—Katy, his kid sister—had never had a decent house to live in.

Bunny opened the garage door for him, so she must have been listening for his truck. He could see that she'd cleared a place for the dirt bike. He backed up the truck and unloaded it as fast as he could, then closed the garage door and dried his face on a rag from a neat pile of them he kept on his workbench. Most of them were old pajama bottoms.

"Did you have any trouble coming over the cape?" Bunny asked.

"Nah. Wind's blowing pretty damn hard, though. I wouldn't want to be out tonight driving around. Has Vinny called?" He'd heard the weather was going to be bad in Portland too. Vanilla lived up there now, but she kept in close touch.

"About an hour ago," Bunny said. "She said she was going to stay in tonight."

"Yeah. Good." Hack regarded the bike under the fluorescent lights. "You did a real nice job shining it up," he said.

Bunny looked startled. "How did you know?"

"Dickie."

"Shit."

"Now, don't blame him. You did good, and he wanted you to get the credit for it, instead of him. No harm in that."

"Still," Bunny said. "You want a beer?"

"Nah," Hack said. "My head's splitting."

"But you told that woman not to call anymore," she said softly.

"She won't call," Hack said. Their eyes didn't quite meet.

"It's important," Bunny said.

"Hell, Bunny, I know it's important. You think I don't know that?"

"Okay," she said.

But it wasn't okay, not really. It wasn't, and it hadn't been in a very long time.

# chapter three

Something was wrong with Bob. Moored to her kitchen table but drifting, Anita lit her forty-eighth cigarette of the day from the burning tip of her forty-seventh. They were generics, and they tasted like shit, but she had stopped noticing that a long time ago. What she did notice was the fact that when this pack was gone—and at this rate, it would be gone before the end of the day—she would be out of both money and cigarettes. Ever since Bunny had quit smoking a couple of years ago, Anita had lost a mooch buddy. Before that she could call Bunny day or night and run over for a pack in her slippers. Now her only hope was to go through her underwear drawer again and see if she'd missed one the first time, but she knew damn well she hadn't.

For as long as she and Bob had been married—and they'd been married for more than twenty years—Bob had been taking his little mystery trips to someplace he never gave away. *Darlin', I've got this life with you, and then I've got this other obligation, goes way back, something I've got to handle alone. It isn't another woman. Hell, honey, how could there be another woman after you? Anyway, it don't mean a thing as far as you and me goes. Not a thing.*

Anita had fought these disappearances at first, thinking it

might be a bastard child, maybe, or a mistress, but he always came home, he was always sober, and eventually it just got normal for him to go away now and then. Some men hunted; with Bob, it was this. Except that this time he wasn't sober when he got home and he hadn't gotten sober in the three days since. Even more peculiar, he didn't want sex. He always wanted sex when he came back, sometimes twice a day. She went along with it, knowing it would wear off within a few days and they'd go back to the occasional lackluster hump just before they went to sleep. Either way, she didn't enjoy the sex particularly, but the attention was nice. But worst of all, Anita had heard him crying twice. No one, at least no one she knew, cried for joy; sadness, even in a drunk, came from some deep and honest well of sorrow. And he was normally a happy drunk, everyone's long-lost friend and biggest fan. He slapped backs, kissed cheeks, cooed at babies, danced the mambo. If he was at the Anchor and Pinky Leonard was playing the keyboard, he'd grab the mike and sing a sloppy song for the folks. If he was a lousy provider—and he *was* a lousy provider—it was nevertheless true that everyone liked having him around, drunk or sober. There was a sweetness to him, a fragility.

Squalls beat on the little piece-of-shit house that she and Bob had rented ever since they were evicted from the place on Adams Street a few years ago. Anita's fantasy life wasn't about sex but about housing; in her dreams there was a brand-new double-wide with a lawn that was mowed, hedges that were trimmed, and not one single car part in the yard. Bob was always hauling home some oily piece of junk and dumping it in the back to work on later, except he never got around to it. Anita figured they could probably put together a stretch limousine by now with all the parts that were out there rusting in the rain. In the meantime, they drove a sprung Chevy Caprice with blown-out upholstery and a mildew problem.

Every few minutes the wind found a vulnerable place in the gutters, and the resonating metal screamed like something cornered. Places in the rotten exterior siding were so saturated with rain you could drag a butter knife through them without even bearing down. Anita pictured the whole place folding up like a waterlogged cardboard box. She'd call and yell at the property manager at Century 21 again, but it wouldn't get them anywhere; it never did. The landlord was some rich bastard over in Salem who used the place as a tax write-off. Anita figured he'd put a total of maybe eighty-five bucks into the house since they'd moved in, and that was to change out the pipes under the sink so the subflooring didn't get flooded every time they turned on the hot water. The garbage disposal hadn't worked in five years, the four-burner stove was down to two, and four months ago she'd found a rat in the toilet. The property manager had told her to just put something heavy on the toilet lid and give it an hour. That was when Anita knew she might as well stop waiting for her real life to begin, the life that included a nice yard and a man who could maintain it. This was her real life, right here, right now, waiting in a piece-of-shit dump for a rat to die in her toilet.

You'd never know it now, but in high school Anita had been prettier than Bunny. Everyone used to say she looked just like the Breck girl. Her senior year she'd been the Miss Harrison County runner-up, beat out only by LeeAnn Sprague, whose folks had paid for tap dancing lessons since she was born. Anita had sung "If I'd Loved You" from *Carousel*, but her background tape had jammed, and she'd had to start over, which would throw anybody off. She still had her competition gown in a dry cleaner's bag in her closet, champagne taffeta and chiffon, strapless because everyone agreed that her shoulders were one of her best features, with a huge bow in back that fanned across her shoulder blades like the wings of an angel. She'd worn satin pumps dyed to match, and she'd smiled and smiled even through the mistake with the music, her teeth coated with Vaseline so her lips wouldn't stick. She had glided down the runway like a queen.

But somewhere between that day and now she'd ballooned and hardened. A lot of people didn't think you noticed when you lost your looks, but that was crap. Anita saw every single thing: the doughy skin; the weight; the stringy hair, the messy center part, the gray. She knew exactly what she looked like. She looked like someone who was circling the drain.

She and Bunny had started heading in different directions right out of high school, Bunny mostly up and Anita mostly down. Anita tried not to notice how many things Hack bought Bunny, or Bunny bought herself, and not just the piano and the rabbits. Over the years he had bought her and Vinny lots of nice things: a top-of-the-line microwave, new cars, dental care. Several years ago he had given Bunny lizard-skin cowboy boots with flames up the sides. He'd even given her panties with little jewels that spelled SEXY, though that was probably a gift for himself as much as for her. Hack was like that sometimes, could turn even a present into the chance to come away with something for himself.

Anita and Bunny had both been there that day when Hack first came up to borrow a blanket. He could have chosen either one of them, and he had chosen Bunny. If he had chosen her instead, what would Anita be like now? She pictured everything she'd become being swept off the table to float away on the wind like milkweed: the awful house, the beater car, the ugly clothes that were never new, the smoker's cough, the squint, the lines in her face, all of them pointing down.

She picked a piece of tobacco off her tongue and looked at the clock. It was four thirty-five, black and oily as creosote outside. Bob had risen like the dead from his hangover three hours ago and gone out. She knew he was at the Wayside. Whenever he went farther away, he took his toothbrush, his comb, and a fresh change of clothes. All of them were still in the house.

The old wall phone went off in the corner of the kitchen like a bomb. She figured it was Roy calling to tell her to come get Bob, but it was her daughter, Doreen, instead, sounding hysterical.

"Slow down, honey, I can't understand you," Anita said, squeezing her temples with her free hand. She'd been telling Doreen to slow down ever since Doreen could talk. The girl started crying, and in the background Anita could hear her three-year-old granddaughter, Crystal, sobbing too. Anita gave her a minute. "Honey, just take a deep breath. Breathe."

The girl drew a shuddery breath. "They just arrested Danny."

"Crap."

"Yeah."

"What for?"

"Meth. Apparently his fucking buddy Bruce has been running a goddamn meth lab in his basement, and they say Danny was helping him. Crystal, *shut the fuck up.*"

Anita could hear Crystal whimper. She made her voice low and soothing. "It's okay, honey. She's just scared. You want me to come over there and get her?"

"Yeah ... no. I don't know. I mean, how are we going to make bail? We're broke. Plus if he can't work tomorrow, they'll fire him, and then we're fucked, we're just totally fucked." Danny was a stock boy at the Sentry Market over in Sawyer. It was his fourth job in a year and a half, fifty cents above minimum wage. "I can't believe this. If he did do it—the meth thing, I mean—*then how come we never have any goddamn money?*"

"I don't know, honey. Have you called that attorney he had last time? He'll tell you what to do."

"Yeah, right. He'll tell me to go to hell is what he'll tell me, because we can't come up with a thousand bucks in cash like we had to last time before he'd even talk to us. We still owe nine hundred dollars from the trial, and Danny got convicted anyway," Doreen said bitterly.

"Well, then the court will give you somebody for free. They have to do that, honey. Danny's got rights."

"Yeah, they'll give us some broken-down old guy who doesn't give a shit." Doreen started to cry again, in an odd, flat way. From what Anita could hear in the background, Crystal was still crying too.

"Listen to me, honey," Anita said. "Are you listening? You need to call the police station and find out what's going on. That bondsman you got last time, see if you can find him again. Do you remember his name? Wasn't it Larry something? Those people must have listings in the yellow pages. I'll be there as soon as I can to get Crystal. Has she eaten yet, because we're real low on food right now, honey? I've been too busy to get to the store."

"Yeah, she's eaten. I got her Burger King a couple of hours ago."

"All right, then put some clothes in a bag for her and a snack for later, and I'll be there as fast as I can. If they tell you to come down to the jail, just leave me a note on the door."

"I can't fucking believe this is happening," Doreen said.

"Well, it's happening, honey. Just keep your chin up."

Anita hung up with a sigh. The girl had always been high-strung. Patrick had been an easy baby, fat and placid, but Doreen had screamed and fussed and demanded, and no matter how much Anita did for her, it wasn't enough. When she was three and a half, Anita had cracked and hit her on the side of her head with a heavy glass ashtray. It took a while for the bruise to fade, but Anita just said Doreen had fallen down the stairs. Whenever Doreen was naughty after that, all Anita had had to do was look in the direction of that ashtray, which she made a point of keeping out on the coffee table, and Doreen would shut right up. Anita had never had to do anything like that with Patrick. He'd been her dream child, still was. She had a picture of him in his army full dress uniform on a table in the living room. It was still hard to believe he was over there in Germany. When he enlisted three years ago, she'd cried for hours. A couple of times he'd sent home money, forty, sixty dollars, but Anita had sent the money orders right back. She wasn't going to take money from her baby boy. There might come a time when she had to, but she was damned if it was going to be while Bob could still get out there and work.

Anita dialed the Wayside number from memory. When Roy answered, she asked him to put Bob on the phone. A minute later she could hear the receiver being fumbled on the bar, and then Bob said, "Honey?"

"Listen, Danny's in trouble again. I told Doreen I'd come over and pick up Crystal."

"Jesus," Bob said sympathetically.

"So you need to come home," Anita said.

"I wouldn't be any help."

"Honey, I need the car."

"Shit! Course you do." Bob put down the receiver, and Anita could hear him yell at Roy, "Wife needs the car. You seen it, by any chance? Big blue Caprice, lots of rust, needs a new front left tire real bad, but the others still have a few miles on 'em, muffler's a real piece of shit—"

"Bob," Anita could hear Roy say, amused, "you drove here. Go look in the parking lot."

"Oh! Hey!" Bob raised the receiver and with jubilation told Anita, "Honey, it's okay. It's right here."

"I know it's there. It needs to be here."

"No shit?"

Anita set her jaw. "Look, honey, put Roy on the phone."

Another bunch of fumbling, and then Roy said, "Yeah."

"Who's there who could drive the car home and pick me up? I've got to get over to Sawyer. Danny's in some kind of trouble again."

"Dooley's here. You want me to ask him?"

"Yes," Anita said, relieved. Odd or not, Dooley Burden was somebody you could rely on. "Would you, Roy? I'll wait."

The phone clunked down on the bar again, and when it was picked up this time, Dooley was on the line. "I got Bob's keys right here," he said. "You want me to come now?"

"Yeah, I've got to get over to Sawyer and pick up Crystal. Danny's in trouble again."

"No problem. What do you want me to tell Bob?"

"Tell him whatever you want to. He won't remember it anyway."

"Will do. I'm on my way."

But when Dooley arrived five minutes later, it was in his own

47

little Subaru instead of the Caprice. He held the passenger side door open for her.

"Uh-oh," Anita said once she was inside. "Where's the car?"

"You didn't have much gas," Dooley said, heading back to the Wayside. "I didn't figure you'd want to bother filling it up right now. You take this one and just drop it by on your way back through town."

Anita felt the backs of her eyes prickle with shame and gratitude. They wouldn't have money for gas until Bob got paid again. She pretended to look out the window until she could trust herself. "That was nice of you, to think about that, Dooley. I'll take good care of it," she said.

"I know you will. You tell that girl of yours to take care of herself. I've always had a soft spot for Doreen, ever since she was tiny and used to wear that majorette outfit everywhere."

In the Wayside parking lot he left the car idling while Anita came around to the driver's side. "You be careful. Wind's a son of a bitch," he yelled as he made a dash for the Wayside front door.

Anita hauled the seat belt across her lap, flipped the wipers on high, and turned the car toward Sawyer, cursing Danny for the millionth time. He'd been trouble from the minute Doreen had started going with him five years ago, but try telling that to the girl. When she got pregnant at sixteen, they got married for Crystal's sake, but you could tell it was never going to work out between them. Then last year he'd gotten in trouble for stealing tools from a body shop over in Sawyer where he'd worked for a couple of months. He said he'd been given permission to take them home for a night or two to work on his old Mustang, but the owner testified in court that that was garbage. Danny had been sentenced to two years' probation. If he really was involved in this latest thing, he could just hang, as far as Anita was concerned. She'd move Doreen and Crystal home with her and Bob if she had to. She'd figure something out. She always did.

Anita drove over the cape, fighting every gust of wind. Dooley's car was nice, though, even if it was small. It had been a long time since she'd driven such a new car. Bunny had a good car, of course, a nice midnight blue Thunderbird with a white landau roof. When they did things together, they never went in Anita's car. In her next life Anita was going to have a new-model car every two years like clockwork and park it outside her new double-wide, just see if she didn't.

At Doreen's apartment Anita pulled into the parking space next to Doreen's car. The asshole manager would probably give Anita hell again for taking up someone else's designated parking place, but that was just tough shit. She was tugging her purse out after her when Doreen opened the door. Her eyes were bloody-looking and puffy from crying, but her makeup was fresh, her mascara as thick and black as iron filings. Her hair was all poufed up too and pulled back into a ponytail. She'd always had thin hair like Anita. The back-combing wasn't fooling anybody.

"How come you're driving Dooley's car?"

"Daddy's got ours." Anita pulled the apartment door closed behind her. The place was spotless at least. Doreen was a good housekeeper. Crystal came dashing over in footie pajamas and plowed into Anita's legs. Anita swung her up and gave her a big kiss. The girl giggled and wrapped her legs around Anita's hips, put her arms around her neck.

"Hi, sweetie," Anita said. "You glad to see Grammy?"

"Uh-huh," the girl said around a big wad of bubble gum.

"She shouldn't be chewing gum," Anita said. Crystal already

had four steel teeth because Doreen used to put her to bed with a bottle of juice every night.

"Don't start with me," Doreen said.

Anita sighed and gave Crystal a loud, smoochy kiss and let her down. "How about you go and get Mister Bear? Gram's going to take you home for a visit."

Crystal skipped off, looking for her ratty teddy bear. Doreen shuffled a paper shopping bag full of Crystal's clothes across the floor toward Anita.

"Did you call the police station?"

"Yeah," Doreen said. "They told me I had to come down there in person. I've been getting ready."

Usually Doreen didn't get dressed until late afternoon anymore. Sometimes she didn't get dressed at all. Whenever Anita brought it up, Doreen just said what difference did it make when no one looked at her anymore anyway. Anita had to admit she had a point, but it wasn't healthy all the same.

"Do you want me to come down there with you?" Anita asked.

"No. I called Teresa, and she said she'd go." Teresa was Doreen's best friend. She was three months pregnant with her second baby.

"How's she feeling?"

"Like hell. You should see her, she's already gained fifteen pounds," Doreen said with satisfaction.

Crystal came back dragging Mister Bear, a filthy teddy bear with a bow tie, checked vest, big feet, and one eye. For the last four months she had refused to go anywhere without him.

Anita picked up the shopping bag with Crystal's clothes. Crystal struggled into her pink plastic Barbie raincoat. Anita reached down to do up the zipper, but Crystal pushed her hands away.

"I can do it," she said, and with infinite care zipped up the zipper all by herself.

"Well, I'll be," Anita said. "When did you learn to do that, hon?"

Crystal slipped a sticky hand into Anita's hand. Anita turned to Doreen and said, "Call me when you know something." She gave her daughter a strong one-armed hug. "Love you, baby."

"Yeah, you too," said Doreen.

Anita buckled Crystal into the passenger seat, working around Mister Bear, and piloted Dooley's little car back onto Highway 101, feeling the gift of a tailwind for the first time all day.

"You okay, honey?" she asked, reaching over and patting Crystal's leg.

"Yes," Crystal said gravely. Anita wondered how much she understood of what went on around her. More than any of them gave her credit for, probably. Doreen didn't watch her mouth around Crystal enough, and neither did Danny; the child was growing up in the cracks and margins of the lives of other people who were needier than she was. It shouldn't be like that. In Anita's opinion, it took a certain amount of joy to raise a child right, just the same as it took vitamins and milk and warm clothes and kindness. Anita and Bob had had that once, when Doreen and Patrick were little and it looked like Bob was going to make something of himself in auto mechanics, maybe even have a shop of his own one day. Doreen and Danny had never generated joy in any amount, from what Anita could see.

"What did you do today, honey?" Anita asked Crystal, preferring to fill the car with talk rather than with bitter thoughts.

"We watched TV."

"*Sesame Street?*"

"The Home Shopping Channel."

Anita glanced over. Crystal continued to gaze out the window solemnly, looking tiny even in the Subaru's small bucket seat. Anita probably should have gotten Crystal's booster seat from Doreen, but she hadn't thought of it. "Did Mommy buy anything?"

"She wanted to, but her car was rejected."

"What?"

"Mommy said her fucking credit car was rejected."

"Oh."

"She cried," Crystal said.

"Aw, honey." Anita found her hand and squeezed it. "It was a sad day at home today, wasn't it?"

"Yes."

"Well, you'll just have to let Grammy read you some stories and maybe you can color a nice new picture for us to put on the refrigerator door."

"Will Daddy come home soon?"

"I don't know, sweetie. We'll just have to wait and see. Mommy's going to find out."

"Yes." Crystal nodded. She knew about waiting. She'd spent a lot of her young life waiting in the Adult and Family Services office for shots, waiting for Danny or Doreen or someone to come get her at Head Start over in Sawyer; waiting for someone to notice that none of her clothes fit; waiting for someone to give her steel teeth. What kind of life was that?

"Will Granddad be there?" Crystal asked.

"I don't know. He could be."

"Okay."

They drove the rest of the way home in silence as Anita tried to think of how to get her hands on enough money to buy cookies or ice cream. The child certainly deserved it, after the day she'd had. Anita couldn't ask Bunny for help again, not so soon; Bunny had treated them to lunch at the Anchor just last week, and when Anita got home, she'd found twenty dollars stuffed into her purse. Bob didn't get paid for another week, and old Marv Vernon made it very clear he didn't give pay advances.

She steered Dooley's little car into the Wayside's parking lot. Their Caprice was still there, but with luck Roy had cut Bob off or he'd run out of whatever money he'd scrounged and was already home. She helped Crystal out of the car and brought her inside.

"C'mon now, Anita, you know I can't let you bring a kid in here," Roy said with embarrassment. He knew how things were with them.

"Is Bob gone?" Anita retreated to the open door, as though their being on the threshold would do Roy any good if an Alcohol, Tobacco, and Firearms agent came by.

"Yeah. Hack took him home." Roy held out the Caprice's car keys.

"How bad was he?" Anita asked, taking them.

Roy shrugged. "He was walking."

"He didn't leave any money behind by any chance?"

"No. I'm sorry, Anita."

Anita shrugged, trying to look like it didn't make a difference. Roy knew it made a difference, but she had her pride. "That's okay. Would you give these to Dooley?" She handed the Subaru keys to Roy. Dooley was nowhere in sight, but Anita figured he was there someplace; his habit of spending huge amounts of time on the toilet working his crosstiks was legendary.

"Sure thing," Roy said. "You be careful out there."

She led Crystal over to the Caprice. It looked like there wasn't going to be any ice cream this evening. Anita would figure some way to make it up to the child. If they were lucky, Bob would already be passed out in the bedroom, sleeping it off. Anita reached over to fasten Crystal's seat belt, bowled over by the smell of mildew. The fucking car leaked like a sieve, and the air freshener hanging from the rearview mirror was pure wishful thinking.

Anita drove up Chollum Road, past Bunny and Hack's house, past Adams Street and Washington Street, then turned left into the spotty gravel and deep potholes that passed for Franklin Court. In their side yard she yanked on the emergency brake with all her strength. Two days ago the car had slipped out of park for no reason while she was under the carport hanging out laundry. The Caprice had rolled halfway down to the corner before she could catch it and haul up on the hand brake. It might be a piece of junk, but they sure as hell couldn't afford another one if something happened to it. Bob was supposed to take a look at the transmission, but there was an excellent chance hell would freeze over before he got to it—that or pigs would fly. For some reason the thought made Anita smile. She must be getting punchy.

Anita hurried Crystal to the kitchen door, and when she opened it, a gust nearly blew it off its hinges. Anita yanked the door closed as fast as she could, but the floor was scattered with pine needles she'd clean up later. A needlepoint sampler hung on the kitchen's far wall, GOD WATCH OVER THIS HOUSE AND ALL WHO LIVE WITHIN. It was a wedding gift from Anita's grandmother. Privately Anita had her doubts about whether the Lord was keeping up His end, but she wasn't about to voice them; they had problems enough as it was. Her mother used to tell her,

*If you don't see the Lord's handiwork in everything around you, for heaven's sake keep it to yourself.*

But maybe there was something to it after all, because there were four overflowing grocery bags sitting on the kitchen table. Bunny or Hack had been here. Anita's eyes teared up, and she reached blindly to help Crystal take off her raincoat so she wouldn't break down right there in her own kitchen.

"I can do it, Grammy," the child said. She removed her coat with the greatest care and handed it to Anita to hang on the peg by the door.

Anita cleared her throat and said, "Look, honey, I think the Food Fairy's been here."

Crystal clapped her hands and helped Anita unpack two roasts, potatoes, carrots, celery, apples, oranges, Saltines, coffee and coffee filters, Oreos, pudding mix, rice, Potato Buds, milk, Campbell's soups, hot dogs and hot dog buns, Life cereal, oatmeal, raisins, brown sugar, Kraft dinner, margarine, a dot-to-dot book, a Cinderella coloring book, a fresh package of crayons, and—here Anita broke down entirely and wept—a carton of Marlboro lights.

Crystal stood beside her, patting her hand over and over. "It's okay, Grammy," she said gravely.

"How did you know?" Anita said when Bunny answered the phone.

"Dooley talks."

Anita clutched the receiver between her shoulder and chin, setting a plate of Oreos and a glass of milk on the table for Crystal. "I'll pay you back," she said.

"Sure," Bunny said, as though Anita ever had. "So is Doreen okay?"

Anita lit a Marlboro and inhaled deeply with closed eyes, as discerning as a connoisseur of fine wines. God, but she'd always loved Marlboros. She let the smoke leak out her nose. "Danny got arrested again," she said.

"Shit."

"Yeah."

"For what?"

"Drugs. Meth lab. Apparently he's been helping a buddy do some cooking."

"She ought to just get out before he involves her."

"I know, but try telling her that," Anita said.

"Did you bring Crystal back?"

"Uh-huh. She's right here, eating the cookies and milk the food fairy brought us."

"Is she okay?"

Anita shrugged, as though Bunny could see her. "You know."

"Yeah."

"You opening up again tomorrow morning?"

"No," Bunny said. "Beth Ann's better."

"Thank God for small mercies," they both said in unison.

"All right," Bunny said. "Let me know if you need anything."

"Yeah. Love you, honey."

"You too."

After Anita had hung up, Crystal said, "Is Granddad here?"

"Can't you hear him snoring?" Anita said. "Holy cow."

Crystal giggled. "He's loud."

"Yeah, he's loud. Sometimes it makes the walls shake."

Crystal looked at the walls in alarm.

"Gram's just pulling your leg."

Crystal looked at her leg.

"It's just an expression, sweetie." Anita sighed. "It means Grammy's just teasing you." Didn't Doreen ever talk to the child?

"Oh." Crystal wiped her hands on her shirt. Anita let it go. Crystal had had enough to deal with today, plus the shirt was a rag anyway; it looked like it had belonged to six other kids before it came to Crystal. Doreen would never wear secondhand clothes herself. Her things all came from Wal-Mart, fresh off the rack and in the latest style. She'd always been like that, too good to wear other people's things. She was appalled that Anita got most of her things from the thrift shops. Anita didn't know where she got such a high horse.

She took three cookies from the bag, dunked them in Crystal's milk, and savored the taste, her head blissfully empty of thoughts for the first time all day, even thoughts about Doreen and Danny. A kitchen full of food could do that. She smiled at Crystal. "Good?" she said.

"Good," Crystal said, licking milk off her last cookie before popping it whole into her mouth.

"Let Gram clean your hands and then how about we go into the living room?" Anita said, getting a dish towel wet and mopping at Crystal's hands. Crystal bounded into the living room before Anita had even hung the towel back up, running straight to the toy chest Bob had made for her. Inside, it was packed with toys Anita picked up at Goodwill: dolls with both eyes and most of their hair, stuffed animals, a toy school bus with two toy children, wooden puzzles with only one piece missing, a plastic pork chop, plastic slices of bread, plastic peas, and a wedge of a plastic banana cream pie.

Anita switched on the television, grateful that the cable was still hooked up. Their bill had to be at least twenty days past due, and the cable company would be cutting them off anytime now. She turned to *60 Minutes*. She loved Morley Safer, thought he was the most gentle-looking man she'd ever seen, not like that Mike Wallace, who kept punching questions at people until they either said what he wanted them to or looked like liars, one or the other. She thought Morley Safer probably treated his wife real nice, brought home flowers for her, or gave her diamond earrings as a surprise. Anita had always wanted a pair of diamond studs the size of raisins, sparkling away so everyone could see. She'd bought a pair of zircon earrings at a flea market once, but they hadn't fooled anyone, and then one of them dropped down the drain in the kitchen sink.

"Honey, do you have Head Start in the morning?" Anita asked Crystal. She'd forgotten to check with Doreen. Doreen worked in the hospital laundry part-time.

Crystal shrugged, busy with the school bus.

"Well, we'll ask when Mommy calls."

Meanwhile, Diane Sawyer was interviewing some crook who'd stolen money from a lot of old people by pretending he was a big-deal real estate developer. They'd caught him in Mexico, living in some fancy house with about five swimming pools and a bunch of gardeners and chefs and laundresses. The old people he'd tricked mostly lived in double-wides and trailers. On the other hand, they'd had money to invest, so Anita didn't feel totally sorry for them, except for one old couple who sat all hunched up inside themselves in the very middle of their sofa, holding hands. Anita knew that hunch; it was the hunch of people bound for bad weather with no shelter in sight. Anita had been sitting like that off and on for years.

The phone rang just as the old man started to cry. The old

woman patted his spotted hand to reassure him. Doreen was on the line, sounding sullen.

"I can't get Danny out tonight," she said. "It looks like he's going to have to stay overnight."

To Anita, keeping Danny in jail for a night seemed like a good idea, and keeping him longer sounded even better. Maybe it would make him start taking his life more seriously for a change. "How's he doing?" Anita asked, but it was mostly for form's sake. She didn't really care how he was doing.

"He looks like shit, plus they've got this Mexican guy in with him who doesn't speak English, and he's been talking the whole time even though Danny can't understand what the fuck he's saying. Danny told him to shut up, but it didn't make any difference."

"Well, it would be scary to be locked up in someone else's language."

"I guess." Doreen wasn't interested in that, though. She said, "You and Daddy don't have any money, do you? Bail is ten thousand dollars."

"Give me a break," Anita said—as though they could even get their hands on ten dollars right now.

"Danny's family isn't going to help either," Doreen said bitterly. "He didn't do it, you know. You're all assuming he did, but he said he just stopped off at Bruce's to see if he could borrow his car and next thing he knew there were a bunch of squad cars and police dogs. He said one of the policemen wrenched his arm around behind him so hard he might have torn something in his shoulder. He could sue, probably."

"Honey, my advice is to take a warm bubble bath, open a beer or a wine cooler if you've got one, and call it a night. There's nothing anyone can do until morning anyway."

Doreen suddenly deflated. "Yeah, I guess. I just can't believe this shit, you know? First they accuse him of stealing, and now this drug thing."

"He's fucking up, honey," Anita said quietly. "You better face it now, because it's going to be a hell of a lot harder to face later. The boy is bad for you, and he's bad for Crystal."

"I don't want to talk about that."

"You're going to have to talk about it one of these days."

"I'm going to hang up," Doreen said.

"Did you want to talk to your daugh—"

But Doreen had hung up. Anita smoothed the straining placket of her shirt. If Doreen thought she was going to beat the bushes to find someone with ten thousand dollars, she was wrong. Hack could probably come up with that kind of money, but why should he, even if Anita asked him—and she had no intention of asking him? Danny was bad news, and the sooner Doreen figured that out, the better. Anita wished someone had talked to her that frankly when she was Doreen's age. Maybe they would have talked her out of Bob, and she'd be married to someone like Hack now instead, someone with money and smarts who gave her nice presents and was only a little unreliable.

"Grammy, it's dinnertime." Crystal approached with a plastic pork chop sandwich on a plate and handed it to Anita.

"Why, honey, that looks just wonderful," Anita said, reaching out and accepting the fake meal that could almost, if you wished for it hard enough, be mistaken for real.

# chapter four

R ae Macy was a born pleaser, a woman who, at twenty-nine, still made a point of smiling at road crew flaggers and postal workers, who exchanged pleasantries with checkers in supermarkets and with fellow shoppers waiting in long department store lines. It was a small act of perfection: the slight, ironic smile, the gentle headshake of collusion that suggested, *at least we're in this together*. Born a good girl, she had become a nice young woman who remembered special occasions with greeting cards, who listened to other people's stories with unfeigned interest, who was well liked by her superiors. She dressed tastefully, did her work capably, was still the straight-A student she had been not so long ago. She held a bachelor's degree from UC Davis and an MBA from Stanford; she was a gifted amateur cellist and spoke fluent Italian. In San Francisco she had held increasingly responsible managerial jobs in US Bank's marketing department, where she was told that her future looked bright.

But here, in this foul little town overhanging the indifferent Pacific Ocean, here in this hell, she sold pickup trucks. A compulsive achiever, she now lived in a place where her accomplishments meant nothing. What was a poem in the *Seneca Review* when no one had ever heard of it? What was an essay, intricately crafted over weeks and sometimes months, when the best-selling periodical here was *Guns*? A year ago Rae would never have guessed that purgatory was a car lot, but now she knew it was so.

Still, she and Sam had moved to Sawyer with their eyes open. Sam Macy had gone back to law school at thirty-two, only to graduate in a time of glut. His choices, they quickly found, were to be unemployed, abandon his new career, or accept work in a less competitive backwater where others were reluctant to go. Eventually the balance of supply and demand was bound to right itself, and as soon as it did, they could return from exile.

And so Sawyer—three hours from a major airport, two and a half from a decent bookstore, two from a shopping mall, and as many from any institution of higher learning. They lived in a condominium on the beach—the pound of flesh Rae had exacted for coming to Sawyer—which turned out to house an ever-changing cast of tourists who assaulted the premises with vigor and noise.

She and Sam had been married for six years, long enough for Rae to know not just the obvious things like how he coughed and the way he read a newspaper but the composition and location of each dental filling. Yet familiarity was not the same thing as intimacy; they had somehow devolved since their wedding from husband and wife to brother and sister. Was this decaying of passion inevitable, like some law of marital physics?

Rae had met him in Stanford's student union, waiting in line for a coffee machine that turned out to be broken. After that he turned up everywhere she went. He was thoughtful to his clients and acquaintances, endlessly patient with the elderly, a gifted extemporaneous speaker much in demand by Sawyer's

Rotary, Kiwanis, Optimist, and Lions clubs as well as the Chamber of Commerce. But for all that, she couldn't remember the fever of an early passion, only a mild annoyance at his persistence. They had never used pet names or terms of endearment, and her heart did not beat faster when she caught sight of him on the street; she at no time longed to be taken into his arms. Was there in her character a deficiency of desire? Yet there was her humiliating longing for Hack Neary, a yearning as strong and confounding as bewitchment.

Through the showroom window she watched Jesús, the lot man, pick debris off the inventory: fir twigs, coffee cup lids, McDonald's french fry envelopes. He was a good man with a gold-toothed smile and many young children in frilly dresses and western wear. Rae liked asking him about his wife, to whom he was devoted. *La reina*, he called her: the queen. The queen was four feet ten, stout, fecund, twinkling with good humor, in possession of not a single word of English. She called Rae Señora Ray.

"Like the ray of the sun," Jesús had explained.

"*¿Como están los niños?*" she asked him now as he cut through the showroom to get a leaf blower from the service department. "How are your children?"

His face lit up like Christmas. "*Muy bien, gracias,*" he said. "They are very good, thank you. *¿Donde está señor Neary?*"

"*No sé.*" Rae sighed. "*Señor está tarde.*" He was ten minutes late. Hack was never late. She felt a sinking in the pit of her stomach. Somehow, in what had to be the joke of an unjust God, she was in thrall to a man of dubious intellect and limited sagacity whose conversations she couldn't remember even fifteen minutes later. Yet there was something winning about him, something deeply appealing, a spiritedness, an almost childlike desire to please, to be liked, that shone unbroken through his shield of glib talk, double entendres, and incessant small lies. Now she had incurred the wrath of his terrible wife, with her nylon waitress's uniform and sagging face, her teeth drawn and claws bared to fight for her man. It was too awful.

*"Aquí. Señor está aquí,"* Jesús said, pointing to Hack's truck just pulling in. Rae turned in time to see him dismount from his pickup, beautiful as any prince, green-eyed, neatly coiffed and bearded, graceful. Jesús smiled at her as though Hack's arrival were their doing, a conjuring act, and removed himself and his gleaming tools into the gloom of the service department.

Bob emerged from the truck's passenger side, looking greenish and frail. Hack said something to him, slapped him on the back, and split off to come into the showroom.

"Hey, beautiful!" he called to her, smiling his best Cheshire cat smile, his normal good mood evidently restored after yesterday's disaster. "And how am I this morning?"

*Señor* was, indeed, *aquí.* Somehow she never remembered the full extent of his obnoxious good nature until he was in her presence.

"Bob okay?" she said.

"Yeah, he's fine."

He hadn't looked fine, but Rae let it pass.

Marv Vernon, the dealership owner, pushed through the showroom door, portly, hale, big-eared, small-time, brimming with satisfaction at the world over which he found himself lord. He held out his hand to give Hack a hearty handshake, then nodded at Rae. She wouldn't let him kiss her cheek, and he refused to shake her hand.

"So, boys and girls," he said. "It looks like a fine day to buy a car!"

He always said that. Rae smiled weakly.

"Is there coffee, hon?" he asked her.

There was coffee.

"Good girl." Then he put his arm around Hack's shoulders and took him across the showroom to the coffee station, talking business in a conversation that wouldn't include Rae if she stayed here until she was a hundred, as might happen. Sam, a native San Franciscan and stranger to any small town, found that the way of life here suited him. He loved knowing everyone and being known by them. He relished the hands-on contact with clients who considered him just one step from God—or, equally gratifying, from Satan. Here, in this town no one had ever heard of, balanced on the lip of the sea, he was a man of learning, a person of station and substance. His clients liked his modest manner and easy handshake, his genuine interest in their families, businesses, and politics, his ability to make sense of incomprehensible laws and legislation. There was a certain Jimmy Stewart ingenuousness about him, a lack of lawyerly smarminess, that they trusted. Several had begun hinting that he might consider running for state representative; the office cried out for a man of his training and temperament. He admitted to Rae that he was taken with the idea of running for an elective office, though even as recently as three months ago it had never crossed his mind. Didn't small towns and provincial backwaters need educated leadership as much as major cities—arguably, *more* than major cities, where the talent pool was already teeming? Here he could make a difference. Rae was forced to agree that he and Sawyer, in the most improbable way, were a perfect fit.

A young couple came into the showroom, stamping the rain off their shoes. They brought in on their clothes the yeasty, sulfurous odor of the pulp mill on the edge of town. Rae guessed the boy had probably just gotten off the graveyard shift. She knew about these things now: swing shift, graveyard, day. The girl whose hand the boy held was six or seven months pregnant and still wearing a regular T-shirt, which strained across her belly. Through the taut cloth Rae could see she was wearing regular jeans too, unzipped all the way and held together by a piece of basted-on elastic. She couldn't be older than eighteen; the boy, twenty, at the most. Both had the pasty, unhealthy pallor of the coast in winter, forsaken as it was by the sun between October and May. In Rae's opinion, the sheer numbers of sex crimes, petty burglaries, assaults, batteries, and alcohol-related incidents supported the reality of seasonal affective disorder.

She smoothed her skirt and stepped forward to greet the couple.

"Is there a salesman here?" the boy asked.

"I'd be glad to help you," Rae said.

The couple looked at each other.

"Oh." The boy broke eye contact. "Well, maybe we'll just look around, if that's okay."

"Of course." Rae made a stiff about-face, clicked into her cubicle in her expensive Italian shoes, and sat staring at her computer monitor. Several minutes later she heard the couple leave the showroom as quietly as they could, so she wouldn't notice. She knew how it would go from here. They would come back this afternoon, and Hack, not Rae, would greet them, and he would joke and schmooze and close their car or truck purchase as easily as you'd slip into an old jacket. The thought occurred to her that the only thing worse than working for a car dealership was being fired by a car dealership. The whole six months she'd worked here, she'd sold only a dozen vehicles, and most of those were when Hack had been away deer hunting for a week.

While she was ruminating, another young woman came in, this time a tough-looking girl with back-combed hair and Tammy Faye eyes. She was holding the hand of a little girl wearing a pink plastic Barbie raincoat. She knocked on Rae's cubicle and, cracking a small piece of gum, said, "I'm looking for my dad."

"I beg your pardon?"

"Bob Simpkins. I didn't see him out in the service department."

"Oh! You must be Doreen. I've heard so much about you."

"Yeah." Doreen snapped her gum deftly. "So have you seen my dad?"

"No, not since he came in this morning."

"Shit. If you see him, I need him to call me."

"Of course. Is there something I can help you with?"

Doreen assessed Rae with sullen eyes. "Do you have ten grand?"

"Not on me, no," Rae said dryly.

"Guess you can't help me then." Doreen reset the strap of her purse over her shoulder and turned to go. Her little girl was playing with a stack of sales literature, pretending the ratty teddy bear she was carrying could read. Doreen pulled her away with a swat at her backside. "*Leave* those. You're not supposed to touch stuff. Didn't I tell you not to touch anything?"

"Oh, she's fine," Rae said. "Really. We have about a million of those brochures."

Doreen looked at her with frank dislike and hauled the little girl out of the showroom roughly by one arm. The child started to cry, and to her horror, so did Rae. She hated this fucking place, hated the weather, the small-mindedness and bigotry, the way everyone thought they were better than she was, hated, most of all, that she was beginning to believe they might be right.

Hack came banging through the showroom door fifteen minutes later, whistling tunelessly. First giving her mascara a quick look in a pocket mirror, Rae walked across the showroom to meet him.

"Bob's daughter, Doreen, was here a little while ago, looking for him. Is he here?"

"Just got back. I took him out to coffee."

"He looked as if he could use it."

"Yeah."

"Well, maybe you should go out and tell him she was here," Rae said. "She seemed on edge."

"Hell, Doreen's always on edge. Anyway, she found us at the Bobcat. Danny's in jail."

"Danny? Is he her husband?" Rae was a diligent student, committing the names of Hack's many Hubbard friends and family to memory. That way, when faced with one of Hack's interminable stories about dirt bike riding or the conversation over that morning's coffee at the Anchor, she could pretend she knew them too.

"Yeah, Doreen's husband." He looked at her, really looked at her, for the first time that day. She stood up a little straighter in her pumps and silk suit, trying to pull the shreds of her dignity around her. With his eyes Hack licked her from head to toe. She could feel a familiar, confused flush begin.

"Hi, baby," he said softly.

"Hi."

"You look so good."

Rae dropped her head in an agony of longing and embarrassment. Hack stood still, perfectly at ease, drawing that look out into a soliloquy of steam and funk, sinking his hands deep into his pockets. She might as well be turning on a pin.

"Don't do that," she said.

"Do what?" His voice was bedroom low, bedroom intimate.

"That. Looking at me."

"I like to look at you."

"Yes, I know." She could feel his eyes burning away, until she could feel the flush between her legs. It was indecent in this workplace, this mundane public fishbowl. "Are things okay at home again?" she asked, having calculated the likely effect of this on his latest seduction.

"Home?" As she'd expected, he shot back to the surface. "Why wouldn't they be?"

"Me. The phone call."

He looked mildly annoyed. "She's fine."

He never referred to his wife by name, at least not with Rae. Just *she*.

"Are you?"

"Am I what?"

"Fine."

"I am now," he said, sliding his eyes around her collarbone, but the moment had passed. He winked—*winked*—and went to his office to answer the ringing phone she'd never even heard.

She walked to her cubicle, dizzy with desire. Urban sophistication, academic degrees, and eloquence counted for nothing here. With all the finesse of a tacky 1960s action hero Hack Neary was leading the lamb of her morality to slaughter, and there didn't seem to be a thing she could do to prevent it.

Out in the filthy service department toilet, Bob vomited up the last of his coffee and scotch. Hack had handed him a flask at the Bobcat, hair of the dog that bit him. Looked like he was going to sober up, though, whether he wanted to or not. And he definitely did not. Anita was watching him all the time with hawk eyes, Doreen was busting his chops because he didn't have ten thousand bucks—*ten thousand*—to bail out Danny, and Crystal was bouncing among all of them like a pinball. Little girl damn near broke his heart, she was so smart and pretty, just as smart and pretty as Doreen had been when she was little, though there wasn't much sign of it in her anymore with that sticky makeup and nasty mouth of hers. The other evening, when Crystal had come out to say good night to him and Anita in her little Cinderella nightgown, he'd seen a ring of bruises circling her arm, and they had Doreen's fingerprints all over them clear as day. He'd hated giving her back to Doreen this morning—Crystal had come over from Hubbard with Hack and Bob, barely able to see over the dashboard of Hack's big pickup, singing "The Wheels on the Bus"—but what could he do? Anita had gotten a call to be a substitute chambermaid at the Lawns Motel and Tourist Cabins, and she'd gone. They needed the money. They were going to need it a fuck of a lot more before it was all over.

But he didn't want to think about that, so he turned his attention to rebuilding Merle Stanley's carburetor. He'd always found peace among car parts. Merle's old Fairlane was obviously terminal, but Merle was so cheap she'd drive it until her ass was dragging on the pavement. And the way the rust was creeping up the chassis, a butt-busting breakthrough might not be too far away. Bob found the thought of Merle's withered old haunches hanging an inch above the asphalt faintly amusing. Not that he wished Merle any harm, of course; he meant no one any harm, never had, tried to give everybody just what they wanted, all of it good. Maybe that was why his life was such a fucking mess. Maybe right there he had the reason. There had to be some reason, and it was the first one he'd thought of yet that made any sense. And he'd been trying to make sense of what he knew since he drove home from Portland four days ago, where he'd been handed the proverbial truckload of shit.

What he found out up there was that Warren Bigelow had AIDS.

Bob didn't know much about AIDS, but from what he did know, it had always sounded like somebody else's problem, him and Warren being sole playmates and all. They'd been playing together—he couldn't say fucking, he didn't think of it as fucking—since they were little kids living in the Eden's View Trailer Park out behind the First Church of God in Hubbard. It was their secret. Nobody needed to know, especially with Warren marrying Sheryl and Bob marrying Anita right out of high school. Neither of them was a faggot, was the thing, or at least that's what Bob had always thought—hell, still thought. Except somehow Warren had come up with AIDS because Bob sure as hell hadn't started it. No, Warren must have lied to Bob all those times he'd sworn that it was just the two of them, he'd never do a thing like that with anyone else. He was a married man, wasn't he? Sure, he liked girls just fine.

But up in Portland this time Warren had lifted his shirt and shown Bob a couple of red spots no bigger than doll's eyes, except Warren said they were cancer. They hadn't looked like much to Bob. He'd had a couple of warts burned off a couple of years ago; he bet you could do the same with those little spots, and he told Warren so. But Warren just started crying, saying once you got those little cancers they spread; he'd seen men covered from head to toe, until it made people puke just to look at you. How was he going to tell Sheryl? What would they do? He'd never get life insurance now, and when the produce company he worked for found out he was sick, they'd fire him on the spot, him being a food handler, even though you couldn't get AIDS from food. So don't tell them, Bob had said, but Warren just shook his head and said it didn't work like that, at least not toward the end, when you were so sick and maybe blind or crazy. He'd already seen men die of it.

"Jesus Christ"—he'd wept—"no one should have to go that way. You think God's punishing us?"

"Nah," Bob had said. "We haven't done anything wrong; we just had a little fun. God don't frown on fun. Besides, you think He sees us down here? Shit, He's too busy to see us, two little specks down here just doing what feels good with what He's given us. Besides, how come He waited this long to strike us down?"

"They say you can have it for ten years before you ever get sick. He could have struck us down in 1980. We'd already done plenty by then."

"Well, you think what you want," Bob had said, "but I don't think God's got a damn thing to do with it."

Except that now, four days later, he wasn't so sure. When his aunt Bets was going through her short-lived religious period, she used to tell him, *God's watching everything you do, kiddo, every little thing. He's just biding His time till Judgment Day. Then He's going to hold you to a full accounting, and you better be ready, you better be clean and pressed and wearing your best suit. He'll forgive you your transgressions, but only to a point, bub. Only to a point.*

Shit. Still, God could wait. Right now what he was worrying about was Anita. What the fuck was he going to do about Anita? Warren had told him he needed to wear a condom from now on if he slept with anyone, so he didn't pass the disease along. *Me and Sheryl, we don't do it anymore, haven't in nine, ten years, so she's okay, thank God,* he'd said. *But you've got to look out for Anita.* Not that it made a hell of a lot of difference now, from what Bob could see. She probably had the disease already, anyway, like him. And how the fuck was he supposed to explain about wearing a rubber, Anita having had her female parts taken out ten years ago, no more birth control needed? Until he figured things out, he wouldn't sleep with her at all, even though he normally liked to after his little play weekends, to remind himself that he was a man, not a fairy. But he couldn't stay away from her forever, and even if he could, she was going to want to know why, him normally being highly sexed and all.

Then there was the question of being tested. He didn't think it really mattered, for him. He'd been playing with Warren right along, for years. If he hadn't caught the thing one time, he'd have gotten it another. Plus Warren had described some of the symptoms to him, so he'd know when he started getting them. No, it wasn't him that needed testing; it was Anita. If she didn't have it, that would ease his mind, even though it still left the rubber question, and if she *did* have it, that would at least solve the rubber question. But how the fuck was he supposed to sneak some of her blood without her knowing? And them without health insurance to cover any of it. They might as well just wait. If she started getting sick, he'd know what was what, and they'd deal with it. It wasn't like you could cure the fucking thing. It wasn't like there was a way out. That was the thing. You couldn't cure it. You died. Warren Bigelow was going to die, and so was he.

Him and Warren had gone and fucking done it this time, they really had. Goddamn son-of-a-bitch bastard.

He sank down beside Merle Stanley's piece-of-shit 1972 Fairlane and wept.

Rae Macy pushed through the service department door. She had fielded a question from one of the dealership's car owners about whether an air filter had been replaced on his Escort. She'd pulled his file, and the most recent job ticket said nothing about it. She took the ticket with her to Bob's work bay; the car had been in just a week ago, and there was a good chance he'd remember. To her astonishment she found him on the floor, keening, pale-faced, crazy-eyed, clammy.

"My God," she said, "are you all right?"

He jumped up and wiped his face with a greasy rag from his coverall pocket. "Yeah. Got something in my eye, burns like a son of a bitch."

Like hell. But since Rae couldn't think of any more appropriate response, she pressed on. "We've got a customer asking about whether we changed out an air filter." She extended the folder lamely. His hands were shaking, but he appeared to be sober, or at least nearly sober. He looked at the folder blankly.

"Guy's a dick," he said, wiping his nose on his sleeve. "Tell him I changed it out. Or, I don't know, maybe I didn't. What the hell difference does it make? He can get along with a dirty air filter; it's not going to fucking kill him. Tell him it's not going to fucking kill him."

"He didn't say it was going to kill him," Rae said softly. "He just asked if the work had been done."

Bob subsided. "Yeah. Well, have him bring the car in, and I'll change it out if I didn't already do it."

"That'll work."

"Yeah." He handed the folder back to her and then stood there, staring at her. There was something going on behind his eyes, something not necessarily friendly.

She shifted her feet uneasily. "What?"

"Nothing. You look real healthy," he said.

"Look, is there something I can do for you? Shall I get Hack?"

"No."

Rae walked back to the showroom and straight into Hack's office, where she closed the door.

"Ooh, this could be nice," Hack said, sliding his eyes all over her. "I like it when you close the door."

"Stop," Rae snapped, sitting in the visitor's chair next to Hack's desk. "Look, I just found Bob out there crying. There's obviously something wrong."

Hack leaned back in his desk chair, folding his arms across his chest and regarding her. "Yeah, well, him and Anita have some financial problems. Things are a little tight."

"He didn't look like someone with financial problems. You don't drop to your knees and weep in a service bay with grease all over you just because you have financial problems."

Hack regarded her with a small, hostile smile. "That depends. Have you ever had financial problems, princess?"

Rae bridled. Did he think she had no problems, that they had money coming out their ears? If they did, would she be working in this hellhole?

"Don't patronize me," she said.

"I wouldn't dream of it. Look, what do you want me to do?"

"I don't know. Go out there, see if he'll tell you what's wrong. Maybe he needs help."

"Always leave a man his pride."

"God, Hack."

"It's true. Look, I already took him to coffee and sobered him up. I'll talk to him on the way home tonight."

Rae nodded, but she didn't buy it. She'd been here long enough to see the way no one asked anyone the really hard questions, like why do you hit your daughter and how could you have chosen that man for your husband. They could talk for hours about meaningless things like motorcycle rallies, motocross races, and beer, but she'd never heard anyone, not anyone, talk about the things that really mattered.

Bob was better by the time Hack dropped him off at the Wayside. For one thing, it was the time of day for drinking, which he fully intended to do even though he'd had to bum some beer money off Hack. For another thing, he'd bucked up, looked the facts straight in the face, and changed his thinking. First of all, Warren hadn't even gotten the results from his AIDS test back yet; he just knew that some guy he'd played with had it. Those little red sores could have been anything, could have been a reaction to new laundry detergent, some new goddamned fabric softener Sheryl picked up because she had a coupon. He'd seen worse sores when he'd fished on the *F/V Giddyup* and guys had been in rain gear and salt water too long. Plus in Portland once he'd seen a guy with cysts all over him, hundreds of them the size of peas, nasty things that looked a fuck of a lot worse than Warren's lousy little red splotches.

And he felt fine. That was the main thing. He felt fine. Last month everyone had had a cold, everyone from Anita and Doreen to the morning coffee drinkers at the Anchor, and had he caught it? No, he had not; he was the only one who hadn't, so don't talk to him about immune system problems, whatever the fuck that even meant. And how about sex? If he had a deadly disease, would he be this horny? Hell, no. He remembered when Billy Johnson got pancreatic cancer and died before he'd even had a chance to finish cataloging his gun collection. He'd told Bob his sex drive had been the first thing to go; cancer had made him limp as an old sock even before the chemo. No such problems here, no, sir. To test himself, Bob had thought about some hookers he'd seen in Portland, thought about some things they could do to him, and sure enough, he'd gotten a hard-on, right there halfway up Cape Mano in a driving hailstorm, bouncing along in Hack Neary's pickup.

Fuck it. He was fine. He was fine, and Anita was fine too.

When he hopped out of Hack's truck at the Wayside, he felt better than fine; he felt downright festive. On Hack's dime he drank Henry Weinhard's Private Reserve on tap, best beer ever made, he'd challenge anyone who felt differently. Nobody much was at the tavern yet, its being dinner hour; Roy was busy polishing glasses for the coming evening, and Dooley Burden was the only other customer, buried deep in the pages of the *Sawyer Sentinel* in the far back corner. That was okay with Bob. It wasn't true that no one liked to drink alone. He'd never minded, as long as the beer was cold and the bartender kept it coming. A man found peace at moments like that, his mind floating easy, touching on the best things there were: the way Anita's hands felt when she rubbed his back; the way Crystal sounded when she had a giggle attack; the first swallow of an ice-cold Henry's.

He and Warren always drank Henry Weinhard in Portland; it was their beer.

Fuck it. Warren wasn't dying either. He couldn't be dying. He'd looked just like normal, hadn't he, except for those two little doll's-eye spots? He was fine; Bob would have known if he wasn't. You couldn't know someone as well as he knew Warren and not know something as basic as whether he was dying or not.

That night, when he climbed into bed beside Anita, not overly toasted for a change but buzzing pleasantly, he rolled toward her instead of away. And she opened herself wide. She was a testy woman sometimes, but she loved her man, that he knew. He sank into her substantial hips and bosom, buried himself deep inside her, comfortable as a man on a beloved old horse. When he was through—and it didn't take long, him being highly sexed—he heard her crying softly.

"What's been going on with you?" she said. "What the hell's going on with you anyway?"

"Aw, baby," he crooned to her in the dark, stroking her thin hair. "It don't matter. Papa's home now. Everything's fine. Everything's going to be just fine."

It occurred to him the next morning that without even meaning to, he'd gone and answered the rubber question: no rubber. Just the way he liked it.

## chapter five

Hack Neary believed that cars have souls. When he laid his hands on the flanks of a car or truck, it sang to him, told him dreams of miles or mountains, of places where it had been or hoped to be going. Not all the stories were good, any more than all souls are good. He remembered a Camaro once that had scared hell out of him. It had had custom paint, custom uphol- stery, custom wheels, immaculate service records, but when Hack laid hands on, it had looked to him like pure evil—and not just because it was a Camaro either. He'd dealt with plenty of Camaros; if he hadn't made his peace with them, exactly, he had at least learned to walk on by. It had taken two years to get that hell car off the lot, and later Hack heard that the kid who bought it crashed the car and died in a nine-foot-deep ditch just south of Hubbard. Hack knew how to read them. He always had.

Rae Macy, on the other hand, had no feel for cars, but then again, that's not what he'd hired her for. He'd hired her because he wanted to look at her some more. She had a narrow waist and a strong back and that fairy hair, fine and white as spiderwebs. If she turned around one day and he saw angel wings, he wouldn't be surprised.

So Hack planted a few car and truck sales a month to keep her spirits up, except that it wasn't working as well as he'd thought it would—not because of her poor sales performance but because it turned out she was ambitious, something he'd never seen before in a woman, especially when she'd chosen a man's job to begin with. He'd have to find something else for her to do, and soon, before she found another job. That nightmare with Bunny and the phone last week had brought Rae down, a long way down; he could see that. He wouldn't have expected it, but then it had never occurred to him that Rae might call the house in the first place; she was naive that way and so had made a mess of his home life for a few days. He'd had to promise Bunny a long weekend at Eagle Crest Resort, over in Bend, and a trip to Cabo San Lucas for their fourteenth anniversary next year.

Hack still remembered their wedding as if it were yesterday. They'd gotten married at the Elks over in Sawyer, and Bunny and Anita and Shirl, Bunny's mother, had spent hours putting up crepe paper streamers and an arch of white helium balloons they walked under for the ceremony. Bunny had made him buy a new pair of cowboy boots for the occasion, and his feet had hurt the whole damn time; that and the rented pants of his blue tux had been too tight, which had given him gas. But Bunny had been in heaven, wearing a long fluffy white dress Shirl had made her that reminded Hack of Little Bo Peep, but of course he'd never said it, just told her she looked beautiful—and she did look pretty, still being in possession of her overbite. Him and Bunny side by side, her in that dress and him in a tuxedo shirt that had looked like one long cascading ruffle, a fussy waterfall frozen in cloth and lace. Bunny had dressed Vinny in a dress that matched her own, only cut down to a six-year-old's size, and she'd also given her a little basket of rose petals to drop along the way to the arch of balloons, like a trail of bread crumbs, only classier.

Even that long ago Vinny had a perfect face and tiny elf bones, which Bunny attributed to Vinny's father, JoJo, who was a small man. She had cried when Hack slipped the wedding ring on Bunny's finger at the end of the ceremony, but Hack had second-guessed that and pulled a little silver ring from his pocket. He'd gotten down on one knee and slid the ring onto her finger, shining in the light of her smile.

Vinny. She'd had his heart that very first day, when he'd first met her and Bunny at the park. He hadn't found much to smile about until then. He'd bummed rides and bounced around and washed himself in plenty of gas station bathrooms, passing through places he'd never been to before and never would return to again, and where he never seemed to find anything to hold him down. His memory was of one long tavern stretching from Seattle to Sawyer, until he'd found Bunny and Vanilla on that hillside like God had put them there to rescue him.

When Hack sat at Bunny's feet that day, still half drunk and watching Vinny, it had taken all he had to keep from breaking down. Little girls had a way of skipping, a way of giggling, eyes as clear and all-seeing as a crystal ball. In her eyes Hack had found reason to hope, after such a long time. Vinny brought him through the Valley of the Shadow of Death as surely as any angel, kept him from the memories that had chased him there, cornering him in a box canyon he hadn't thought there could be any way out of. God, to have a little girl in his arms again after coming through such a wasteland.

So he'd courted Bunny with furious intent; he'd have offered her Venus and Saturn, if she'd wanted them as part of the deal, and then figured out some way to make good. She hadn't, of course, but she'd asked for plenty else: fidelity; a house she could be proud of; a look the other way when she and Shirl drank too much sitting up there on Shirl's deck in the summer sun; all those damned stuffed bunnies, until he'd have joyfully set Elmer Fudd on them, or whoever that cartoon character was that hunted wabbit.

Not that Bunny was a bad wife, not by any stretch. She was tolerant, by and large, and had learned not to ask questions that she didn't want to hear the answers to. Except this Rae thing had thrown her, turned the clock back to the days when he still transgressed from time to time, never infidelity, not really, not to the letter anyway; just a little casual playtime off on one of the logging roads back of Hubbard, a little head, a little hand job maybe, and then home in time for dinner. The thing of it was, none of them had ever loved him, and he'd never even seen any of them again; they were strictly roadhouse booty passing through.

But this time maybe Bunny was right to worry. This thing with Rae was completely different. She was in love with him or at least well on the way down that road. A smart girl like her, a sophisticated girl, made him nervous sometimes, made him afraid he wouldn't understand what she was saying, like those damned poems she wrote and wanted to talk about with him. He hadn't made it through eleventh grade; what the hell did he know about poetry? While pretty boys like her husband Mr. Briefcase had been studying poetry in high school classrooms, he'd been busy taking care of the Katydid, making rent money at Howdy's Market, scrounging up odd jobs to keep some kind of car going.

Like Rae, though, the Katydid had loved poetry. One of her most treasured possessions was an old poetry book she'd bought herself and read to him every night. The one about the gingham dog and the calico cat was her favorite for a long time, a funny choice, its being the story of two nursery toys tearing each other limb from limb in the night. He'd teased her about that, but she loved to read it anyway, night after night in their sucky little apartment behind the Tin Spoon Laundro-Queen.

There it was. With Rae Macy somehow came Katy—now, again, after all these years and all the miles—and it had been like that since the first day Rae had walked in the door. He didn't know what it was about her that made this cave of memory suddenly yawn before him like eternity, except that she was smart like the Katydid, and she seemed to *see* him, to see right through the muscles and bones to his heart. Maybe the Katydid would have turned out like that if she'd grown up and become a woman.

Now, sitting at his desk in a puddle of weak sunlight, he lifted his telephone receiver. "Hi, beautiful," he said when Rae picked up the phone in her cubicle across the showroom.

"Hi."

"Come see me when you can. I want to talk to you about something."

"I'll be right there," she said, and almost immediately appeared in his doorway. She was anxious. Not being able to understand what a woman like her, a woman with money and beauty and options, could possibly be anxious about, he tended to forget how anxious she was. He stood and gestured to his plastic visitor's chair, an ugly orange thing.

"Is everything all right?" she asked, searching his face for clues.

He smiled and said, "Everything's fine."

"Oh," she said. "Whew. Ever since I made that stupid call—"

"Forget it, okay?" he said impatiently. "I'm not kidding. Forget about that."

"Oh, right."

"Anyway, how would you like to be Vernon Ford's new finance officer?"

"You're kidding."

"No. It makes perfect sense. Look, whenever we sell a vehicle, we need to put together financing, right? Ever since Marv's been retired part-time, we've been pretty much on our own to work out loans directly with the banks. Costs us time, makes us look unprofessional having people hang around while we scramble. You with me?"

"Yes." Rae smiled, as though his mind had ever been quicker than hers.

He picked up the pace. "So I was thinking you could stay on top of lender programs, you know, and once we close a sale, we hand customers over to you to work out loans. We look better, and you get a promotion."

"I wouldn't be selling anymore?"

"Only if one of us is out at lunch or sick or something and a customer comes in."

"Huzzah."

Hack squinted at her. "What does that mean, huzzah?"

"It means there may be a God after all."

"Oh." Hack grinned. "Well, I'll still need to clear it with Marv, but I think he'll go for it. There might not be a pay raise, though. He's a cheap son of a bitch. I'll try, but don't get your hopes up."

Rae smiled thinly. "I haven't had my hopes up since we moved here," she said. "I wouldn't even know what hopes to *get* up here. That it will stop raining? That we'll finally get a decent speaker at Rotary?"

"So how's your poetry going?"

"Oh, slow, you know. I just had a piece accepted by the *Kenyon Review*, though."

"Yeah?"

"It has a small circulation, but it's a prestigious journal."

"Oh." Hack cast around for something to say. "Hey, did you ever read that poem about Little Orphant Annie?"

*"An' the Gobble-uns \ 'at gits you / Ef you / Don't / Watch / Out,"* they recited in unison. Rae laughed. "I *love* that poem. God, I'd forgotten all about it. Did your folks used to read it to you?"

"Nah," Hack said. Folks. He'd never had Rae Macy's kind of folks, a mommy and daddy who tucked you into your bed every night, all snug and safe.

Then he heard himself say, "I used to read it to my kid sister sometimes. She always liked that one."

What the fuck was he doing?

"I didn't know you had a sister. You never talk about your family."

"No."

"Why?"

"Nothing to talk about."

"Oh." She looked at him curiously, catching him with that smart-girl lie detector of hers. The cave yawned. Jesus, his heart was pounding.

"So I'll talk to Marv as soon as he comes in."

"Marv?"

"About your promotion."

"Oh! Right."

"Well, I better get some work done," Hack said, shuffling empty file folders around on his desk. She stood—God, that back of hers, like it could withstand even the worst earthquake—and clicked out of his office in her courtesan heels and expensive suit. He'd never seen anyone dress like that before, except on TV. Her husband ought to kneel down every night and give thanks. He'd come into the dealership to pick Rae up a couple of times, narrow-chested guy with a long nose and five o'clock shadow, a Jew, maybe. Not that Hack had anything against Jews; they were good at making money, an ability Hack respected greatly. Guy sure must be doing something right if he could afford to dress Rae in those expensive clothes. Hack could have been a lawyer too if he'd had money like them. Lawyers weren't as smart as they wanted you to think. Guy Ferguson, who'd been a Hubbard lawyer forever, was drunk by eleven o'clock every morning, regular as clockwork. Some days his shoes didn't even match.

What would it take to keep a woman like Rae Macy? More than a baby grand and a million stuffed rabbits, probably.

At his elbow the phone rang, scaring hell out of him.

"Hack?" It was Vinny.

"Hey, sweetheart! Where are you calling from?"

"The house. I've got five minutes before I have to go to work." Vinny sold Estée Lauder makeup at Meier & Frank in Portland. Hack was real proud of her for getting that job; all her friends wanted to sell cosmetics too, but in Hack's opinion they didn't stand a chance, probably never would; they were big, dumpy kids. Not one of them had Vinny's delicate looks, not even close. He still thought the kid should go to college, and he said so to Bunny all the time, but what could you do when they were bubbling over with life and wanted to be grownups *now*? He'd talked to her about taking evening classes while she was up there in Portland anyway, and she said she might, but he was pretty sure she was just humoring him. She knew he hadn't even finished high school and that it was too late for him. Besides, he'd done pretty well on his own, all things considered. But you couldn't always count on that, and he wanted more for her.

"Listen," she was saying, "do you think you can come up here and help us paint the kitchen? We finally got the landlord to agree to let us, as long as we use a neutral color, which is pretty rich coming from him, Mr. Orange Cabinets and Avocado Refrigerator."

"Do you have paint?"

"Not exactly, because to tell you the truth, we're all kind of broke right now, but couldn't you pick some up and we'd pay you back?"

Hack smiled. "So when were you thinking I would do this?"

"Well, see, Heidi and Jennifer and me, we all have to work this Saturday, so no one would be here to get in your way."

"Uh-huh." Saturday was the day after tomorrow. "And what was that part about your helping?"

"Well, we'd clean up after you were done. And you could stay over and take me to dinner. Come on, Hack, say yes, please say yes. You know what a dump this place is."

As a matter of fact, Hack knew what a dump it was *not*; on the dump scale, it was only about a five, ten being hell. He'd lived in hell; he knew. Not that he was going to tell her that.

Vinny was saying, "You could see if Mr. Sykes wanted to come up and help."

Billy Sykes was Vinny's housemate Jennifer's dad. He owned Always Oregon, one of the gift shops on the north end of Hubbard. Generally speaking, Hack didn't completely trust a man who spent his days around figurines and hummingbird feeders and wind chimes and shit, but Billy was okay. He'd been married to fat Janelle all these years, which certainly spoke to the man's fortitude, Janelle having a voice like a dental drill; the woman could strip wallpaper off the walls just by telling a story, which as a matter of fact she was pretty damned good at, even with that voice and all. Yeah, Hack figured he could team up with Billy for a day, might even get a kick out of it. The man had some pretty good stories of his own, having grown up on the Kenai Peninsula in Alaska.

"Did Jennifer talk to him about it?"

"You know they're not getting along right now. We figured if she asked him, he'd say no. He still thinks she should have stayed at home if she wasn't going to college. He might do it if you asked, though."

"Uh-huh." Hack ran the point of his letter opener under his fingernails, mining grease. He'd finally gotten to work on the pickup last night.

"Please?"

"Yeah, yeah. Look, you need to measure the walls so I know how much paint to buy. Call me tomorrow and let me know."

"Oh, thanks, Hack, I told them you'd come."

"Who's the biggest sucker, huh?"

"No, you're the best. I love you tons. Gotta go now."

"Yeah, you too, princess," said Hack, but the girl had already hung up. She'd always been able to talk him into doing things for her. It still pissed Bunny off, seeing Vinny twist him around her little finger. *She's a brat, Hack, and you're just making it worse.* More than a few times Bunny had stormed up to Shirl's house when Hack and Vinny got too silly together, repeating the punch line to some you-had-to-have-been-there joke she hadn't been there for.

Vinny. Her name wasn't really Vinny, or even Vanilla. Hack had made that up, its being the flavor of ice cream she always ordered when he took her out for treats. Her real name was Linda. Not that anyone called her that; not even Bunny called her that anymore, though she'd held out for three full years.

He'd first started making up nicknames with Cherise, his mother. Cherise was a classy name, too classy for a forger and a prostitute, so he came up with Stiletto Jo, instead, for the heels she favored, vicious things that could gouge out eyes and probably had, Cherise being an occasional brawler as well as a drinker, a forger, and a whore. He never called her that to her face, though.

Cherise Neary, his only parent, was a piece of work. She was not only a prostitute but the daughter of a prostitute, second-generation deep trash from Tin Spoon, Nevada, the Refuse State, where, it was true, at least whoring was legal. Cherise's own mother had come by prostitution honestly after she was abandoned by her husband when Cherise was little. Believing that once you started something you might as well stick with it, she gave up the trade only when she was too old to turn a profit. Within four months she was dead of ovarian cancer, progression of the disease having been hastened, no doubt, by the badly broken-down condition of her reproductive organs. By then Cherise herself had been whoring professionally for fifteen years; Hack was twelve years old, the Katydid nearly seven. God only knew who their fathers were. Cherise never even tried to trace them through her appointment book. Anyway she hadn't complained. Her pregnancies were the only vacations she ever got, even her regulars not being eager to have sex with a woman six months, eight months pregnant. The last trimester Cherise had filled a cooler with cold beer, put up her feet, and prayed the babies would be late. Once they were born she was back at work within a month, icing herself during her off hours by sitting on a child's inflatable tube packed in the center with ice chips. In good weather she'd move outside: shop-worn, run-down, cotton-haired; cheap goods in a busted-out lawn chair.

But while Cherise was many things, stupid wasn't one of them. When she was forty-three, tired and waning, she decided to take a lesson from her dead mother and retool for a new career. While Hack looked after the Katydid, Cherise apprenticed with a pickpocket and forger in the next town. Within a year she achieved a fair proficiency and commuted regularly from Tin Spoon to Las Vegas, where she lifted wallets and checkbooks on the streets outside the casinos.

*I'm going now*, she'd tell Hack three or four times a month all the time he was twelve, thirteen, fourteen years old. *You look after your sister till I get back, hon, and I promise I'll bring you something nice.* If she remembered, she'd bring him a T-shirt or some kind of cheap travel game like car bingo that she'd picked up along the way at a Stuckey's—as though she'd ever taken him anywhere, by car or anything else. She arrived home after two or three days—four or five, toward the end—amped on speed and wearing some flashy outfit with her hair all ratted and her eyes as darting and wily as a snake's. *What are you looking at? You think you're so special? You've got no right to say shit to me*, she'd snap at him.

And so he hadn't.

Hack picked up the phone and called Billy Sykes at Always Oregon.

"Hey, I just talked to the kid, and she conned me into painting the kitchen up there this Saturday. Any chance you want to come along and help?"

"Jesus, it sounds great, but we've only got two and a half more weeks until Christmas, and I'm short on help. Can it wait?"

"Can they ever wait?"

"Yeah." Billy chuckled appreciatively. "They can sure talk you into stuff. Shit, they bat those baby blues, and it's like big ammunition coming at you at point-blank range, huh?"

"Yeah," Hack said.

"Look, count me in for anything after New Year's. You need some money for supplies?"

"Nah. You can spring for whatever's next."

"Deal," said Billy, and hung up through a rising tide of female voices, like he was being hied away by a clamoring mob of betties. Too bad. Hack sure would've enjoyed the company, especially on the three-hour drive up and back. Bunny had her regular shift at the Anchor on Saturday, so she was probably out. Normally he'd ask Bob, but he'd been acting too squirrelly lately.

Then he thought of Rae Macy. He'd like to ask her. Not that it made any sense; not that it would be smart in any imaginable way. But the idea that he might have her sitting beside him in his truck all the way up and back wouldn't go away. Maybe he could propose a shopping trip for her. That way she'd have something to do while he painted, and it wouldn't be with him; he'd only be providing the transportation, a small favor. Who could read anything into that? Well, Bunny, for one. But if she didn't know... and why should she know? No one would see them together. It wasn't like he'd be doing anything wrong; he'd just be keeping unimportant information from Bunny that she would find upsetting. It was a kindness, really, that was all.

He might ask her. He might just ask her.

The phone rang, and eerily, it was Bunny, as though she could pick up on the shiftiness of his mind even from over there in Hubbard. Jesus, she kept him on a short tether. But what God giveth, He taketh away again, or some damn thing, because it turned out she was calling to say she and Shirl were thinking of driving up to Bunny's sister Fanny's house in Tillamook for the weekend. Tillamook was more than a hundred miles from Portland, in nearly the opposite direction and along a completely different set of roads.

"So we're thinking we'd leave tomorrow at noon—Beth Ann said she'd cover the rest of my shift," Bunny was saying.

"You mean you'll be gone all weekend?"

"We'd be back by Sunday dinner, though."

"Yeah, I guess that would be okay," Hack said. "We haven't had a lot of time together lately, but if your mom's counting on it—"

"Well, we could try a different weekend," Bunny said doubtfully, "but the thing is, Fanny's birthday is Saturday, so we thought we'd have a little birthday celebration, you know, to take her mind off the divorce." Fanny and her jerk of a husband, Frank, were finally splitting up, after keeping Bunny and Hack squarely in the middle through years of screeching and tears and accusations. The man was the purest form of dick.

"You're right. You go ahead," Hack said. "Vinny called a little while ago and wanted me to go up there and paint her kitchen anyway."

"Are you sure?" Bunny said eagerly. Hack could tell how much she wanted to go by the fact that she didn't blow up about his doing something for Vinny.

"I'm sure."

"Oh, thanks, hon. Really," Bunny said, and hung up.

Some things were just meant to be.

Hack waited a full fifteen minutes before buzzing Rae in her cubicle, to prove to himself that it wasn't that big a deal whether she came with him or not.

She appeared in his doorway. "*¿Sí?*" she said.

"See what?"

"What? Oh, no—*sí*. Spanish for yes," Rae said.

"You're pretty easy," Hack said. "I didn't even ask you anything yet."

"Ask me—" Rae looked rattled. "Look, maybe we just ought to start over."

God, but he loved getting her off-balance. "You taking Spanish lessons?"

"Sort of. Jesús is helping me. Spanish isn't that different from Italian. They're both romance languages."

"Ooh," he said.

Rae shot him an irritated look, so he straightened up. "Look," he said, "how would you like to drive up to Portland this Saturday?"

"But we just had a regional sales meeting."

"No, this would just be for the hell of it. My daughter thinks I should paint her kitchen; she lives up there. So I thought you might like to tag along and do some shopping or whatever."

"Oh. Well—oh!" He watched the blood drain out of her face. "I'll have to see what we have planned."

"Sure," he said. "Whatever. It's no big deal." Little Jack Horner or whoever had probably said that as he pulled his thumb out of the dike.

"Look, I think it's probably not a good idea, Hack," she said softly.

"No?"

"No."

"Yeah," he said. "Well, it just sounded nice."

"It would be nice."

"I wasn't planning on jumping you or anything, you know."

"I know that," she said.

"So how come I feel guilty?"

"Well," she said. "That would be the question, wouldn't it?"

He left the house at six o'clock Saturday morning, the passenger seat in his truck loaded with gear instead of Rae. He'd been hoping she'd change her mind at the last minute, not that he really expected her to, and it was probably all for the best. Still, his heart had jumped when the phone rang yesterday evening. It had been Vinny, though, worrying about the accuracy of her measurements. He'd already figured out that she was pulling the figures out of thin air and had picked up an extra couple of cans, just to be sure. Hack Neary was the King of Paint—not that Vinny or anyone knew it. Every new dive Cherise had moved them into, Hack had painted within the first couple of days. If they didn't have money to buy paint, he stole it. It was amazing what a fresh coat could do to a place, even when the rest was all bugs and drafts and sag. Hack never asked for permission. The landlords were scum. If they didn't like it, they could evict them, a hollow threat since they'd been evicted more times than Hack could count by the time he was fifteen, Cherise not always keeping current with her bills or her earnings.

Katy always helped, once she was old enough. When she was four, she stirred the paint and poured it from the big can into a smaller stewed tomato can he wore around his neck like a noose. Later she got to paint too; by the time she was six and could be trusted, she was the official trim detailer, being more careful than Hack was. She had her own little two-inch brush and tomato sauce can full of paint, and when she painted, she always stuck out her tongue. He got a boot out of that, called her Princess Paints-with-Tongue. She could have passed for Indian too; she had this thick black hair that shone like patent leather and a skin tone you could warm your hands by. Hack thought she was the prettiest thing he'd ever seen, an opinion he held on to right to the end, and he wasn't the only one who thought so.

Traffic was light heading northeast, its being Saturday morning and still early. Hack turned on the radio, as he always did. Normally he enjoyed talk radio, but this morning some asshole was going on about freeze-drying the dead or some damned thing, and it pissed him off. When people died, they were gone, end of story, and it had been that way for millions of years; if you didn't like it, you'd better be praying mighty hard for an afterlife, because short of that, you were just whistling in the dark. He knew. He'd seen a lot of people die in Vietnam, had looked into their faces once they were gone, and he might as well have been looking at an old sock, for all that they resembled the people they'd been when their souls were still attached. Where the spirit went he had no idea, but if it turned out there was an afterlife, it would be like winning the jackpot, pure good luck. Because from the earth-side view of things, all you could count on was when you died, you were gone, period. Harsh but true.

Then there was the overcrowding issue. If there *was* an afterlife—call it heaven or whatever—it had to be getting mighty overpopulated up there. Was there some kind of check-in system? Otherwise, what were your chances of finding your loved ones in that big a crowd, which he envisioned as people standing shoulder to shoulder in every direction as far as the eye could see? Hell, the recent population of China alone was in the billions, and that wasn't counting a single person from the thousands of years leading up to it. You could spend your entire afterlife doing nothing but tapping people on the shoulder and asking if they'd seen a little girl with dark hair or whatever. Or maybe heaven was just a place where you were steered in the right direction by the first person you asked; hell was the very same place, only no one had ever heard of you or yours for all eternity. Could be.

Hack turned off the radio, wondering what he would have been thinking about if Rae Macy had come along. Not heaven and hell. Sex probably. Sex was a whole lot more fun to think about, that was for sure. Maybe he would have told her that he'd started dreaming about her regularly, and in all the dreams she was naked. That would've made her pink up. He'd learned to have his eyes ready on the V of her blouse when he said something dirty to her. Watching the flush rise was better than the dawn.

Maybe he'd marry Rae Macy one day. It wasn't that farfetched if you thought about it. Most couples got divorced anymore; the odds were that he would be free one day, and through no real doing of his own. Bunny might get tired of him, now that Vinny was out of the house and it was just the two of them and they still had nothing to say to each other. Bunny would divorce him, and he wouldn't be to blame for a thing. Rae too; maybe one day she'd realize what an inferior guy her husband was and give him the boot. Then he'd find her, and he was pretty sure he'd marry her. Imagine waking to that every morning. With Bunny, it hadn't ever been like that, not exactly; with Bunny, he'd woken up every morning to Vinny. That had been more than enough.

Although he hadn't planned to, once Hack got into Portland he found himself heading downtown. It was nine o'clock; Meier & Frank must be open by now. He found a parking garage, locked his toolbox in the bed of the pickup, and headed for the corner of Fourth and Morrison. Sure enough, people were going in and out already. He pushed his way past a cripple or two—Jesus, there were always weirdos and beggars by the doors; he wondered if Vinny was safe when she worked evenings—and straight through to the cosmetics counters. He spotted her right away, her blond head bowed over the display case as she rearranged tiny boxes of something expensive. He couldn't believe how much the store charged for some of the war paint they sold. According to Vinny, the better the makeup, the less anyone noticed it. What the hell was that? You spent a fortune on something no one knew you had, or you spent less on something people could actually see and give you credit for. To him, it made no sense, but Vinny just told him he was low-class, and maybe that was true; he liked makeup on a woman. Rae Macy didn't wear makeup, though, or maybe she just wore the good stuff. He'd have to look more carefully the next time. Her other half probably made enough to keep her in Estée Lauder for the rest of her life.

Vinny looked up just as Hack reached the far side of her counter. She wore a white cotton lab coat, as if they made the makeup right there at Meier & Frank. Under the coat she wore a black slinky top, some kind of knit thing, close-fitting. The black made her eyes the intense blue of a swimming pool, or maybe it was her new contact lenses. Who could tell anymore? Once when he'd come up, her eyes had been bottle green; scared the shit out of him until she'd explained it. She said she could put in brown eyes too. That would be too weird, her being so blond but with brown eyes. As a matter of fact, she looked blonder than usual. Black shirt or bleach job? It was a hell of a world.

"Hack!" She ran around the case to give him a hug. "What are you doing here?"

"Hi, princess." He held her tight, then held her off at arm's length. "Didn't you call for a painter?"

"I know, but I didn't think I'd see you. I left the house unlocked, didn't I? You didn't have trouble getting in?"

"Nah, I just wanted to see my girl. You look so grown up."

Vinny smoothed her lab coat, blushing with pleasure.

"They still treating you good? Anyone's chops I need to bust?"

"Not today, Guido." He was Guido to her Vinny. He didn't even remember which one of them had come up with that. "Actually they might be promoting me soon."

"No kidding?"

"Yeah. Joanie told me that."

"You're a star, kiddo."

"That's me," Vinny said, smiling. "So, have you even been to the house yet?"

"Nope, came right here to get my five minutes with you."

"Ten—I'll give you at least ten."

"I'm a lucky guy. I've always said so," he said.

"Can you stay tonight and buy me dinner?"

"Oh, I think I can probably do that. Someplace cheap, you know, McDonald's or whatever."

"Get out," she said, pushing him lightly. He always took her to a nice place. "I'm off at six. You want me to meet you at the house?"

"You still taking the bus? Then I'll come get you. I can't believe you've turned into a big-city girl."

"I know. I love it," Vinny said, and he could tell she meant it. He couldn't see it himself, but it was her life.

She dug around in a drawer behind the counter. "Call me if you need anything." She handed him a business card: "Vini Neary, Sales Associate."

He grinned. "Vini?"

She grinned too. "Hey, at least it's not Linda." She'd threatened to take back her original name, not that she'd ever really do it.

"Yeah. So listen, kiddo, I hear some paint calling my name. I'll see you later, huh?"

"Okay," she said. "I love you."

The glow of her affection warmed him all the way out to the street. She did love him; she always had; it was part of her the way her lungs were part of her, or her heart. When she was little, she'd raced Bunny for the seat beside him at restaurants, had held his hand whether or not they were crossing a street. It was Hack she asked to put her to bed, partly because he knew all the good stories by heart: "Goodnight Moon," "The Owl and the Pussycat," "Rumpelstiltskin," "Beauty and the Beast." He never told her why he knew them, and it had never occurred to her to ask; to her, it was all a part of the personal treasure he brought along with him when he moved in, like his box of ball bearings and the pickle bucket of loose change he'd saved for years and let her count one day to put down on her first car. He never missed a school pageant, spelling bee, awards ceremony, open house. When the PTA elected officers, it was Hack they chose.

*You're a great man,* she said to him at her high school graduation, smiling tearfully over a dozen and a half red roses. *Really, Hack. I mean that.*

Maybe she did, but she was wrong.

# chapter six

Up in Tillamook, Shirl, Bunny, Anita, and Fanny sat around Fanny's living room, tucking into plates of Shirl's home-made triple chocolate fudge cake. Even though it was Fanny's forty-eighth birthday, Bunny had poked in only four candles. It seemed kinder to round down, especially given Fanny's current circumstances. The house looked the same—all blues and browns, plaid upholstery, sculpted shag carpet, her framed coastal lighthouse series in cross-stitch—but only because the divorce was still pending. Once it went through, Fanny would get to keep the house but almost nothing in it. The way she moved around the place, Bunny imagined she was already saying an extended farewell to her furniture. She touched everything, petting the upholstery, dusting a table, rearranging cushions.

"So will you at least keep your bedroom set?" Shirl asked, rubbing chocolate frosting off her dentures with a paper napkin. "You paid a lot for that furniture, hon, and I think you ought to keep it, seeing as how you picked it out."

"I say let him have the stinking bed, you know?" Fanny snapped. "The whole time we slept in it he was cheating. Why would I want to have something around that reminded me?"

"Well, now that's true," Shirl admitted.

"No, I told my lawyer I want the sewing machine, my craft supplies, everything in the kitchen, and one sofa, one chair, and the bed in the guest bedroom."

Shirl clucked. "Still don't seem fair to me. You've made this house a home, honey. It should all stay with you."

"I don't want to talk about it."

Shirl shrugged. "I'm just saying it's not right, Fanny. That's all I'm saying." To Anita, whose cake plate was empty, she said, "You want some more, Nita? I sure do."

Shirl stood up with both plates. She was a tall woman and almost as heavy as Anita, but she carried her weight like a geological formation, soaring and rock solid. Her features were Bunny's, only larger, as though she'd been drawn with Magic Marker to Bunny's felt-tip pen—and with none of the softening overbite.

"I've always loved this recipe," she said over her shoulder from the cake stand across the room. "They say to use one bag of chocolate chips in the frosting, but I always double it. Makes your arteries stand up and take notice, I'll tell you that. And that's without the Cool Whip."

"It's real good, Shirl," Anita said.

"Thanks, hon." Shirl handed her back a laden plate and dropped heavily onto the couch. "So what's up with Danny now? Bunny said he was in some kind of trouble."

"Yeah, he is," Anita said. "They're saying he's been helping some friend make drugs."

"And him with a young child." Shirl clucked. "I call that a shame."

Bunny spoke up. "He might not have done it, Mom. He's a good kid, you know that."

"Do I? I must be thinking of somebody else," Shirl said airily. "You know who he reminds me of? He reminds me of my brother. Howard was always into something too, just like Anita's boy."

"Boy-in-law," Bunny corrected her.

"Whatever," said Shirl.

Anita said, "I didn't know you had a brother."

"Yeah, well, we don't talk about him much. He's been locked up for the last thirty years. Bank robbery, manslaughter." Shirl waved her hand dismissively. "I don't remember what all."

"Mom," Bunny warned.

Shirl looked at her defiantly. "What? Howard was always a bad kid, had trouble written all over him from the get-go. Doreen's Danny, now he's probably a real nice boy who's just got his directions mixed up. Once someone sets him straight, he'll probably settle right down."

"Yeah," Anita said bitterly, taking a big mouthful of cake. "Right."

Bunny, sitting beside her, squeezed Anita's hand. She could just kill Shirl sometimes; the woman had the tact of a land mine. What Anita wasn't saying was that Danny was most likely fucked, according to his free lawyer. Enough of his property and fingerprints had been found in the meth lab to hang him, plus they'd found a couple of people already who'd testify that Danny had sold them drugs on the street. It wasn't looking good. The free lawyer said he expected Danny to be indicted by a grand jury next week.

"So how's Doreen taking it, Nita?" Fanny asked her.

Anita shook her head, scraping the last of the frosting from her plate. "Hard. She's pissed off that if Danny was doing the things they say he was doing, he could have at least brought home some of the money. Turns out the boy probably has a drug problem himself, and that's where the money's been going, right up his nose or whatever." She shook her head again. "Here she's been working as many hours as they'll give her at the hospital, twenty cents above minimum wage, and he's doing that. You know what he told her? He told her he was real sorry and all, but that she was young and strong, and he was sure she'd figure something out. And of course there's Crystal too, my little angel. Bob and me, we're about ready to bring them both home to stay with us until we at least know what's what. Even if Danny's acquitted, he's going to be in jail, at least until the trial's over."

"Well, you just be strong, honey," Shirl said, belching. "You're going to get through this."

"I'm having another beer," Fanny declared. "Anyone else want one? Mom?"

"You have any of those wine coolers left?" Shirl said.

"I think so."

"I'll have that."

"I'm going to have another beer— Nita? You too?" Bunny said. "But you don't have to wait on us, Fan." She followed Fanny into the kitchen with her empty plate and beer bottle.

"So, Anita looks like shit," Fanny whispered to her over the sink.

"Yeah. Bob's acting strange again."

"He's never stopped acting strange, if you ask me. He disappear again, like that other time?"

"Not so much that." There wasn't any point in explaining that Bob had been disappearing right along. "He's asking everyone in town if they have any work for him."

"Doesn't he work for Hack anymore?"

"Yeah, that's the thing. This is for extra, *after*-work work."

Fanny frowned. "Maybe the man's finally discovering he has balls. Imagine, after all these years." It was frankly acknowledged within the family that Bob was worthless as both a husband and a provider. Everyone knew that Anita's working two jobs had been all that had stood between them and the street on more than one occasion.

Bunny snorted. "Anyway, Nita's not complaining, but it's still weird. She says she's found him crying."

"Crying?" Hubbard men didn't cry unless someone died, and even then it had better be a close friend or relation.

"Crying," Bunny confirmed. "And he won't tell her why."

"Huh. What does Hack think?"

"He doesn't know."

Fanny frowned, impressed. Hack usually had an angle on everything, and usually he was right. "Well, anyway, I'm glad you brought her along. Sounds like she was in need of a cat session with the girls."

"Yeah."

Fanny looked at Bunny out of the sides of her eyes. "So what about you—you doing okay?"

Bunny shrugged. "Yeah. No. You know. Hack's got some little girl on the side, I think."

"Again?"

"I don't know. Maybe not."

"You know her?"

"I saw her. She works for him."

"And?" Fanny handed Bunny a cold beer from the refrigerator, set out another on the counter for Anita, then the wine cooler for Shirl.

"And what?" Bunny said.

"She slutty?"

"I don't know. No. She was pretty, Fan. She was young, and she was pretty." Bunny's eyes teared up. "It's been a long time since we looked like that. Maybe we never looked like that. Anyway, he said he wouldn't see her anymore."

"Yeah, right."

Bunny slumped against the counter.

Fanny cracked the top to her beer and said, "I'll tell you something, Sissy. You want it to get better, and they tell you it's going to get better, so you think it's *going* to get better, only it doesn't. At least it didn't with Frank. How many times did he tell me some girl was his last piece of ass, he never loved her, it didn't mean a thing, she came after him first and what could he do?" Fanny laughed bitterly. "That right there is when your bullshit detector should kick in and say, *Yeah, right.*"

Bunny twisted her wedding ring around her finger.

"You think Hack doesn't know what he's doing is wrong?" Fanny said. "He knows. You can bet your ass he knows. They just don't *admit* knowing because if they admit it, then you both have to do something about it. All those years Frank came home to a hot dinner and a clean house, you know? Shit. I'd get up every morning, Sissy, *every morning*, and say, please God don't let me hear anything today. Because every day that I didn't hear anything was one more day I could stay."

Bunny dropped her head.

"You know what you end up asking yourself?" Fanny said. "How little can I live with? You ask yourself how little can I live with, and how much do I need. And the answer keeps getting smaller, and your marriage keeps shrinking. In the beginning it fits fine, you know, roomy enough to keep you warm, and you can move all around in it. Then you have the kids, and when your husband stays away from you, you're mostly glad, because they just get in the way, and who gives a shit about sex when you haven't had two minutes to yourself in five years? And all that time your marriage is getting smaller and smaller, except you don't notice because it hasn't occurred to you to notice, and why should you? You just pull it down and stretch it out, and if you feel a little draft now and then, you ignore it because you don't have time to deal with it anyway. By the time you do, your marriage is this little tiny thing that doesn't cover shit and you're freezing to death out there in the cold."

Bunny just looked at her.

"The thing is, I never knew anyone who could unshrink something once it got small," Fanny said quietly. "And here's the worst part. If Frank asked me to take him back today, I'd probably say yes."

"You're kidding."

"It doesn't matter anyway." Fanny began to cry.

"Aw, Sissy, don't," Bunny said, wrapping her arms around her. "You can do better. You deserve better."

"Yeah, right," Fanny said, pulling away and wiping her nose with the back of her hand.

"What are you girls doing out there?" Shirl hollered from the living room. "You coming back, or do we have to come get you?"

"We're coming back. Just hold your damn horses," Bunny yelled, tearing a paper towel off the roll so Fanny could blow her nose, wipe down her face a little. She grabbed the extra beer and the wine cooler from the counter and brought them to Shirl and Anita in the living room.

"What were you talking about in there?" Shirl said. She turned to Anita. "Watch, she's going to say 'nothing.'"

"Nothing," said Bunny.

"I bet you were talking about Frank," Shirl said. "He's got a new Cadillac, did Fanny tell you?"

"Let's not talk about Frank anymore," Bunny said, jerking her head in the direction of the kitchen, where Fanny was still collecting herself.

"Yeah? Well, you know best; she doesn't tell me anything," Shirl said.

"Well," Anita said supportively, "Doreen doesn't talk to me anymore either, unless she needs something."

"Money," Shirl said. "It's usually money."

"Yeah." Anita chuckled. "It is."

"How's Vinny doing up there in Portland anyway?" Shirl asked Bunny, drinking her wine cooler from the bottle. She'd never learned to do it right, though; she inserted the whole neck into her mouth. It drove Bunny crazy. She'd never seen a wino before, but she thought a wino must drink like that. "You haven't said boo about her lately," Shirl said.

"She's good, I guess," Bunny said. "Hack went up to paint her kitchen this morning."

"Those two," said Shirl, shaking her head. "Thick as thieves all these years."

"Hack thinks she should go to college."

"I thought you ought to go to college," Shirl said.

"Let's not talk about me," Bunny said.

"I'm just saying," said Shirl.

"Well, Martin went to college, and he's got a good job now with Georgia Pacific," Fanny said, coming in from the kitchen. Martin was her oldest and the only college graduate in the family.

"See, now he's done good," Shirl said. "That's all I'm saying."

"Presents!" said Bunny. "Fanny hasn't opened her presents yet. Come on, Fan." She set down a small stack of wrapped boxes beside Fanny on the couch.

"The kids went in together and bought me a real nice color TV," Fanny said.

"That was sweet," said Shirl approvingly. "You raised those kids right, Fanny, I've said it before."

Fanny opened Shirl's gift first, a new pair of Dearfoam slippers. "They're real nice, Mom," Fanny said, giving her a peck on the cheek. "I haven't had new slippers in forever."

Anita gave her a pair of calico potholders. "It's just something small," Anita said apologetically. "I know you like blue."

"Oh, Nita, did you make them? Well, that makes them special," Fanny said. "Thank you, sweetie."

Last she unwrapped Bunny's present, pulling out a stuffed rabbit dressed in intricate silver cloth armor and carrying a sword. Fanny exclaimed, "Oh, Sissy, he's too darling!"

"Your knight in shining armor," Bunny said, watching Fanny closely in case she started to cry again, but Fanny just gave Bunny a hug and handed around the rabbit for closer inspection. Bunny unbuckled his armor to show that underneath he was dressed as a medieval peasant, and everyone gave her a round of applause. In a festive mood at last, they pulled out Bunny's Pictionary game and played it hilariously until dinnertime.

When she got back from Tillamook Sunday afternoon, Bunny put on a roast and potatoes. Normally she didn't cook big meals anymore, there being just the two of them, but it gave her something to do while she waited for Hack to come home. The trip had shaken her. She loved him; didn't she love him? And didn't he love her? Even if they weren't as close as they used to be, who was? After so many years together there were things you'd needed to say at the beginning that you just didn't anymore. *I love you. You make me happy. I look forward to coming home because you are there.* They didn't say these things because they were obvious, not because they were untrue.

And what about all the wedding anniversaries, the Valentine's Days, the Christmases and Mother's Days, every one of which Hack faithfully acknowledged with presents? Could it really just be guilt stirred up by Wal-Mart and Zales? Could these be the things you did for someone you did *not* love? Bunny wouldn't have believed it until yesterday. But Frank had given Fanny a new one-carat tennis bracelet for her birthday just last year. Before that, there had been a watch, a Las Vegas getaway, a car. Was it possible that all this time Hack, like Frank, had simply been buying Bunny off? If they didn't talk much, they never had; Hack was a talker all right, but Bunny wasn't. Even when they fought, it was mostly swift, a series of standoffs, raids, and surrenders. And they didn't fight all that often; almost never, really. Frank and Fanny had fought all the time.

Through her ruminations Bunny heard the garage door open and the low thrum of the truck engine. Immediately she felt a flood of relief. Hack had come home. He'd said he would, and he had. He wasn't Frank; she wasn't Fanny. Grateful that she had something to offer in return, she served up dinner.

"How was the drive?" she asked.

"Okay. Rained most of the way, you know. There was a slide in the Van Duzer Corridor, couple of trees down. Lot of cops out."

"Uh-huh," Bunny said. "How was Vinny?"

"Good. She was good."

"Did she help you paint or make you do all the work?"

"Nah, she helped." He caught Bunny's look. "Hey, she helped."

"You stayed over?"

"Yeah. We didn't finish until nine or so last night. Then there was the touch-up today. How's Fanny?"

Bunny shook her head. "Not good."

"No?"

"She's real broken up."

"Well, sure."

"The thing is, she didn't see it coming."

"No?"

"How could you not see something like that coming?" she pleaded.

Hack shrugged, busy with a potato.

"Well, she didn't."

"No," Hack said.

"Anyway," said Bunny.

They ate in silence.

"It's been a while since you made a roast," Hack said.

Bunny nodded. "I just thought—" She waved her hand vaguely in the direction of the stove. "You know."

"Sure."

After that there wasn't anything left to say. When they finished eating, Hack went out to the garage, and Bunny cleared the table to the distant sound of him moving around his tool bench. If their lives had a sound track, Bunny thought it would be just like that: the muffled sound of activity happening on the other side of a wall. Hack didn't come in until it was time for *60 Minutes*. Bunny stayed in her sewing room, working on a rabbit made up like a fairy-tale princess. When she was done, she would make the princess a prince. Why was it that in fairy tales the women who waited quietly and toiled in obscurity always got rewarded with the prince? They never did in real life. In real life they ended up waitressing or slopping out motel rooms someplace. They ended up like her and Anita; they ended up like Fanny. The forward girls, the grabby ones, got the prince, and the rest of them got exactly dick. Someone somewhere had sold them a real bill of goods, even Shirl. For all her strong opinions and lack of concern about voicing them pretty much as they occurred to her, she'd been fucked too. Bunny's father, Jack, dead these past seven years and not a minute too soon, had been a fisherman and a skipper, gone more than he was home, and a mean drunk when he was there. Shirl used to tell Bunny he couldn't help it; when he got home, he brought with him a whole lot of cares and ugliness he needed to blow off. If he drank, and he did drink, it was just his way of letting go, and they should forgive him for it. The fact that he never spent time with them even when he was in port; that there wasn't a single birthday he'd ever remembered, not even Shirl's; and that he seemed to take a special delight in taunting them: These all were justifiable oversights. He loved them, Shirl maintained; even if it didn't look like that, Bunny and Fanny had to take it on faith that all fathers loved their families deep down. But Bunny wanted to know what kind of love it was that let you treat people the way her father did. His nickname for Shirl was Bigger, and Bunny couldn't remember a time when he'd called her anything else; at the dinner table, when he was there at all, he often singled her out for looks of especial dislike. Bunny and Fanny were afraid of him, the belt he wielded with a heavy hand, and the mouth he had on him, mocking them if they showed fear, and they always showed fear. He hit, he hit hard, and he hit them all. Shirl had had to stay in the house more than once until bruises on her face had faded enough to be covered by makeup.

Seven years ago Shirl had gotten a call from Dutch Harbor, Alaska, saying Jack had apparently fallen off one of the piers the night before. No one saw him go in, or at least no one reported it, and he had drowned. The circumstances surrounding his death were unusual enough to arouse a certain level of suspicion about foul play—he had spent his entire life on the water, after all, and presumably knew better even stinking drunk than to go fall off a high pier—but no one ever came forward with evidence, and with no pressure from the family to investigate further, the matter was quietly dropped. Bunny, for one, had felt he got exactly what he deserved; if someone had pushed him, it was probably no more than he had coming to him. If that made her a worse daughter, and she was sure it did, he had made the bed he lay in. Even Shirl hadn't shed many tears. They didn't even bring his body home, just held a rudimentary memorial with his final crew right there in Dutch Harbor and had him cremated, dumping his ashes into the water from the very same high pier, as though to finish the job. Bunny earnestly believed that even God wouldn't hold it against them, knowing as He surely did how the man had treated his family.

From her sewing room Bunny heard Hack in the kitchen and then the sound of Jack Daniel's being poured into a glass. Hack loved his Jack Daniel's, but he wasn't a drinker, not like her father had been, not like Bob was. She would ask him for more news about Vinny when they went to bed. Bunny had been up to the house in Portland only once, when they'd helped Vinny move in. It was old and run-down, but try telling Vinny that. The girl might as well have been moving into a luxury condominium, to hear her talk about all the amenities: its view of a pocket park at the end of the block; its proximity to a Movietime video store and Fred Meyer store; all utilities included, and for a rent that was already low.

Bunny had never wanted to move to a city or even another town. She figured Vinny must have inherited JoJo's restless feet. But then too the child had always had her own way of seeing things. From the time she was five or six she talked about things she wanted and planned to buy for herself one day: a castle, a life-size doll she could pretend was her twin, a tree house, a pale blue car, underwear in every color but white, an unlimited charge account at Meier & Frank, two cats, a husband, and a daughter—more or less in that order. Hack had petitioned to have a son put on the list, but even Hack couldn't always change Vinny's mind.

Vinny and Hack. Bunny bet Hack had spent every bit as much money on Vinny as he'd spent on Bunny over the years. He'd given her a swing set, built a tree house with a brand-new vinyl floor, cedar siding, and casement windows you could really open; once he'd brought home a Cinderella outfit that came with a jeweled tiara, "glass" slippers, and a ball gown nicer than anything hanging in Bunny's closet. A lot of people told her how lucky she was that Hack was such a good and doting step-father, all of them having a horror story to tell her about some-one whose child had been molested, abused, cut down, or neglected, and of course they were right. Everybody liked Hack, which you could prove just by the fact that he'd gotten an entire town to change the name some of them had been calling Bunny for more than twenty years, never mind changing Linda to Vanilla and then Vinny. It went like that. People liked Hack more than they liked Bunny, and they always had. Even Shirl thought the man walked on water. Of course he'd worked hard to win her over. He still took treats by her house all the time, a nice salmon fillet, a new mailbox. Not that Shirl always sided with him. Sometimes she sided with Bunny, like the time when he wanted to raise Vinny's allowance to twenty-five dollars a week. That was too much, and Shirl had told him so. Hack had backed down and kept it at fifteen dollars, which still sounded like too much to Bunny. In the end it hadn't mattered; Hack just slipped Vinny the extra ten on the side without telling anyone. Bunny had found that out a year or so ago, when Vinny told her by accident. That was just like them; they protected each other from her like two kids.

She was just putting the finishing touches on the princess's pointy hat and veil when the telephone rang. She heard Hack pick up the living room extension and unconsciously tensed—not that woman again—until she could tell from Hack's side of the conversation that it was Bob on the phone.

Hack was saying, "Yeah, at the Anchor. No, the *Anchor*. Have Anita drop you off at the Anchor by seven forty-five. Well, won't she have the car? No, not now, tomorrow morning. Anita. No, *Anita*. Look, is she there? Yeah, let me talk to her. No, now, not tomorrow. Okay. Yeah."

Bob must have gotten off the phone, because Bunny could hear Hack expel his breath in frustration and mutter, *"Jesus,"* while he waited for Anita to pick up.

"Hey," he said. "Yeah, real toasted, from the sound of it. He's going to hurt himself if he doesn't slow down...I know you know. Look, he wants to get a ride over to Sawyer with me in the morning. Can you have him at the Anchor by seven forty-five? I have a meeting with the facilities guy at the electric utility to talk about taking over their fleet management—could be a big deal for all of us. Okay?...Yeah, she's here. Hang on."

Hack set the phone down and yelled, "You want to pick up?"
Bunny picked up.

"Shit," Anita said.

"Bob?"

"Yeah. He's going to find himself wheels up in a ditch someplace if he's not careful. Dooley followed him home again, he
was so bad. Said he was worried Bob might drive off the bridge."

"Aw, Nita."

Anita gave a heavy sigh. "It's okay, he should be passing out
anytime now. Look, do you still have Vinny's old bed?"

"The twin?" Hack had bought Vinny a queen-size bed several
years ago and moved her old twin bed into the garage. "Sure, we
have it."

"Can I borrow it for a while? Things aren't going too good
with Doreen, so I'm moving her and Crystal home, and we just
found out a mouse must have got into Doreen's mattress somehow because there's little bits of stuffing all over the place, and
for all I know the mouse is still inside. I just heaved the whole
goddamned thing into the backyard and said to hell with it. I figure Crystal can have Patrick's old bed."

"Sure, you can even keep ours if you want to. Nobody here's
going to need it."

"Thanks, hon."

"You need any help with Bob, or are you all right?" Bunny
asked. Bob might be a cheerful drunk, but even cheerful drunks
could turn.

"I'm all right. He's pretty much passed out right now in front
of the television. They must have shut off our cable while we
were in Tillamook, but I don't even think he noticed. The picture's nothing but fuzz and snow, and he's just sitting there looking at it."

"Nita, he's never drunk this much before. You've got to get him to stop," Bunny said.

"I know that," Anita said. "Don't you think I know that?"

"I'm sorry, I know you do. I'm just worried for you. Look, when do you need the bed? You need me and Hack to bring it over tonight?"

"Do you think you could? I'm going to pick up Crystal at Head Start tomorrow afternoon and then get a bunch of their things from Doreen's apartment. She needs to be completely moved out by the end of the week."

"We'll just put the canopy on the truck and bring it over. Okay?"

"Yeah."

After they'd hung up, Bunny shut down her sewing machine and found Hack nursing his whiskey in front of the TV, some old Burt Reynolds movie.

"Why is he doing this?" she asked him from the doorway. "How does he expect to get extra work if he's drunk all the time?"

"I don't know, but he's probably trying to get some money together for Danny."

"I don't see why; they've got some free attorney assigned to them."

"There'll still be costs. There are always costs. Plus as long as the man's in jail he's out of work. Maybe they're still trying to make bail."

"I heard his folks weren't doing shit."

"Yeah, I heard that too."

"Well, I could just kick him, is all I know. As though Nita doesn't have enough to be worrying about, with Doreen and Crystal coming back home, and this being the worst time of year for Anita to get work and all. They might need her one day this week at the motel, but they won't commit."

"You can't solve her problems for her, Bunny."

"I know that."

"So we'll help out when we can."

"Well, that's what she was talking to me about. She wants to borrow Vinny's old twin bed for Doreen," Bunny said. "A mouse got into one of theirs. I told her we'd bring it up tonight."

Hack lifted an eyebrow. "You know it's raining like hell out there."

"You can put the canopy on."

"Does it have to be tonight?"

"I want to make sure they're really all right," Bunny said. "It won't take long."

Hack tossed back the rest of his Jack Daniel's, heaved himself out of his armchair, and together they went out to the garage to lift the pickup canopy into position and secure it, then load up the mattress and box spring. Outside, it was oily black and weeping with damp, the kind of night that, for all Bunny had grown up with it, made her feel sorry for the town's stray cats, wet and miserable under some porch or trailer. She took in strays from time to time, and every time it was in weather just like this.

Anita met them at her door, which she held open while Bunny and Hack muscled the bed inside and to the back bedroom. Bunny could see that Anita had brought out some of her old crafts and decorations to try to make the dark little room more cheerful. One of Bunny's early stuffed rabbits, a beauty queen she'd made in Anita's honor, wearing a tiara and a ribbon sash saying "Miss Harrison County," sat on the bureau. A huge stuffed bear, booty from someone's run of good luck at the county fair's ring toss booth one year or another, was on the bed.

Over the bed hung a project Anita had labored over, a rendering of the Last Supper in needlepoint. Anita, despite the bad luck she'd always had, claimed she got some solace from contemplating the Lord, and who was Bunny to tell her she was wrong? In her heart, though, she thought that Anita might want to reconsider, in light of the fact that He had obviously chosen to stand back and do nothing whatsoever while Anita and her family went down the toilet.

After she and Anita made up the bed with Vinny's old twin bedding, they found Hack in the living room. He gestured for them to approach quietly.

"Are you kidding?" said Anita out loud. "He passed out right after he talked to you. He's not going to come to for hours."

They all regarded Bob, still perfectly upright in his chair, though unconscious.

"You think he'll just stay like that?" Bunny asked doubtfully. "He must be really well balanced, to sit right up like that."

Anita shrugged. "If he tips over, I already moved the coffee table out of the way. Only thing he's going to hit is the carpet."

"If you're sure," Bunny said.

"I'm sure." Anita walked them to the kitchen door, turning off the living room lights behind her until the only light left in the house came from the clock above the oven and one small lamp down the hall in Anita's bedroom. Bunny gave her a quick hug at the door, and she and Hack ducked out into the rain.

"Don't you think it's creepy?" she asked Hack as they drove home.

"Think what's creepy?"

"Her leaving him there like that, in the living room."

Hack shrugged. "What else are you going to do with him?"

"I don't know. Leave a light on at least."

"What for? He won't come to before morning anyway."

But that wasn't it exactly; it wasn't Bob she was thinking of at all. It was something else. It was the thought of Anita sleeping in that broken-down old house with Bob bolt upright and insensible in his chair in the pitch dark. It would be like sleeping in a house with a dead man.

## chapter seven

Two weeks after returning from Portland, Bob made the mistake of getting lastingly sober. With sobriety, swifter than vengeance, came the atom bomb truth that he and Warren were going to die, and so, in all likelihood, was Anita. For two weeks he'd insisted they were okay, had let himself *believe* they were okay, but in his heart he knew that was bullshit. Over the last fourteen days, in the privacy of their home and the warmth and safety of their marriage bed, he had knowingly planted the seeds of Anita's death. More than once in the week since then he had looked at her and felt a scream rising from his soul like gall.

It was ten o'clock in the morning of the day his test results would be in. What he wanted to do, ached to do, was drink. What he did do was push himself farther under the Bloom family minivan and concentrate on diagnosing what Faye Bloom had described as a periodic, wracking cough. Faye claimed to hear her engine talking the way other people heard voices. He remembered when she was just a little girl with freckles, baby fat, and a whinny. She'd had something wrong with her that made her run funny, stiff-legged and slower than shit. Thinking on it, Bob realized that she probably had mild cerebral palsy, but back then no one had put a name to it or told them it wasn't her fault that she ran funny. All the kids ragged on her about it. Every year when the President's Fitness Program came around again, Faye Bloom was fucked anew. Plus Bob could still remember the look that came over her when they chose up sides for dodgeball. But she never cried. He couldn't remember a single time when she was chosen anything but last, but she never cried once. No one had thought much about it then, or at least no one except Faye. Bob noticed only because he was usually standing right beside her, since he was invariably chosen next to last, either him or Warren.

Bob and Warren. They had been Bob-and-Warren since almost as far back as he could remember, back to when they were six. They had sat beside each other at school, had eaten from the same paste pot clear through third grade, staunchly defending each other when questioned. *No, ma'am,* they'd say. *If he was eating, I woulda seen him, and I didn't see nothing, I swear.*

They'd both lived in the Eden's View Trailer Park out back of the First Church of God, and it was generally acknowledged that they were the poorest kids at Hubbard Elementary, and that was saying something, Hubbard's being a poor town to begin with.

Everybody had a story. Bob's began when his mother, Vivian, ran away the day before Bob's fifth birthday and his father dumped him on Vivian's sister, Bets, with the promise that he would repay her with a lifetime of free auto repairs. It hadn't been much of a deal to begin with, his father being an indifferent mechanic, but then he died two months later in an accident at the mill involving caustics and a loose valve. People said by the time someone could get to him, he looked like raw meat weeping. It took him a couple of days to actually die, but that was just a technicality.

After that it was him, Aunt Bets, and a one-eared tomcat named Pretty Boy. Bets doted on the cat, fed him choice scraps she brought home from work at the Sentry Market over in Sawyer. Pretty Boy ate pork loin and sirloin and prime ribs of beef, salmon and halibut and albacore tuna. Bob ate Wheaties and milk and occasionally a pork chop when Bets could be bothered to fix one. Sometimes when her back was turned, Bob would sneak some scraps from Pretty Boy's bowl, trading the cat for his leftover cereal milk. He and Pretty Boy generally banded together when Bets was in one of her moods, and she was often in one of her moods, seeing as how her feet were always killing her from standing up at the Sentry, running a cash register all day long. She packed a wallop for someone four feet ten. She slapped and she hit and one time she bit him. Bob and Pretty Boy both stayed out of the trailer most of the time and no matter what the weather.

But when Bob turned six, the Lord must have heard his prayers, because Warren Bigelow and his family moved into the dump next door. Warren's father gambled for a living, but he'd been on a losing streak since the year before Warren was born, so the family mood was generally sour. They yelled a lot, everyone in the family except Warren, who never said anything to anyone unless he absolutely had to. He claimed he hadn't talked at all until he was four years old, and Bob believed it. For the first week that Warren lived next door, Bob thought he was retarded or maybe deaf, but it turned out he was just careful. When it came to making up his mind, Warren believed in taking his time, but when he was good and ready, he talked to Bob all right, and after that he never stopped. He'd talk about anything: airplanes and death and car wrecks and the way his mother hit him with a slotted spoon once so hard that he had striped bruises for a month. Another thing about Warren was he ate dirt. He'd take up a pinch like fine candy and pop it into his mouth. He told Bob he'd always been a dirt eater. Bob couldn't see it himself. He tried it once, but it tasted like shit, plus he kept thinking of all the banana slugs that had oozed over it. He told Warren that, but Warren only shrugged and went right on eating dirt, a little every day.

Warren was the most beautiful person Bob had ever seen. His eyes were so dark they were almost black, and his hair was the exact color and sheen of a crow. He was pale, though, paler than anyone Bob had ever seen, which was saying something, all the people in Hubbard being pale from the never-ending rain. You could see all his veins winding around under his skin, headed for his heart, and he had a cleft in his chin and dimples when he smiled. The other boys said he looked like a girl, but Bob always thought he looked more like an angel. He'd never seen a dark-haired angel, of course, but he was willing to allow as how Warren might be the first, especially since he'd never actually seen a blond-haired angel either.

The two boys took to each other like salvation. Around Hubbard they were commonly acknowledged as strays, but since they didn't cause trouble and had each other for ballast, they were given a wide berth. They ate hot lunches for free thanks to the unspoken largesse of Bea Jones, the cafeteria cook, and were encouraged to wash their faces and hands in the boys' bathroom every morning by Mrs. Norris, the school nurse, who kept washcloths and towels there just for them. She also checked them regularly for head lice, which were found on neither of them or on both. A number of families left secondhand clothes for them with Mr. Deloitte, the principal of Hubbard Elementary in those days. Say what you would, Hubbard took care of its own.

Being neither missed nor mourned in their respective trailers, every summer the boys took to roaming the three hundred thousand acres of Weyerhaeuser timberland that stretched back of Hubbard into the low Coast Range mountains. At first all they found were unceasing fir trees, but when they were ten, they discovered a derelict homestead in a little valley choked with alders. There was a cabin, a fallen barn, leaning fences, and an overgrown pasture on a tiny stream they named Homesick Creek—the spare remains of lives that had guttered out or moved on ten or fifteen years before.

Warren was the first inside, pushing the cabin door open wide and slow, so if there were any ghosts in there, they could leave in an orderly fashion instead of running over the top of him and Bob. Warren claimed to have trafficked with a ghost or two, and in this, as in much else, Bob took him at his word.

Inside, the cabin walls were stained a rich tarry brown, the color in the bowl of a well-loved pipe, and rich with the odors of loam and smoke and dereliction. They found a primitive bedstead in the front room, its mattress ticking carefully rolled back and still stuffed with hay, though now old and rotten. The fireplace had been swept clean, as if someone had loved the place enough to leave it tidy even at the moment of abandonment. The roof was in better condition over the front room, but even so, daylight came through in dozens of places. Birds and rodents had made nests in the corners and low rafters of the place, and the windows were as empty as missing eyes. A quick search of the yard and overgrown kitchen garden yielded an old iron skillet, a kettle, and a stoneware crock, cracked but still watertight.

"Why do you think they left?" Warren said, standing in the

middle of the front room again, shivering in the gloom and the spookiness and damp.

"Something bad," Bob said.

"Bad?"

"Like maybe a wolf attacked their cow or something."

"Are there wolves here?" Warren said with apprehension.

"Well, coyotes."

"Coyotes can kill a cow?"

"Sure," Bob said.

"Can they kill people?"

"Nah, but they can gnaw your leg pretty good, I bet."

Warren shuddered. "Maybe someone came back here and killed everyone."

"Why would they do that?"

"Maybe there was gold."

"Maybe they all got sick," Bob said.

"Sick?"

Bob shrugged. "Could have. Smallpox, maybe, or yellow fever."

"So do you think anyone else knows about this place?"

"Don't look like it," Bob said. "I say it's ours."

"Can we do that?"

"Why not?"

Warren grinned. "Hey, we've got a house!"

"Except we can't tell anyone."

"I swear," Warren said gravely. If there was one thing they understood, it was the worth of a house.

"Me too," said Bob. "Shake."

They shook hands with great solemnity.

"So now it's ours?" Warren said.

"Yup."

And it had been. Many times in summer they stayed over-night, lighting a fire of twigs and branches, huddling together on the mattress ticking they'd made. In sleep they would often spoon up like puppies, Bob gratefully accepting the heat radiat-ing from Warren's perpetual sunburn. Sheltered from the ocean winds, they often shucked off their clothes and spent the days naked. It had been Warren's idea at first, but Bob had taken to it happily. They were Indians; they were heathens; they were in the Garden of Eden, where Warren usually consented to play Eve. But mostly they were settlers facing scarlet fever, crop failure, ax injuries, plague. By the end of August they both had perfected dying. Warren worked up to a series of twitches and spasms, as though he were being electrocuted or eaten alive from the in-side out. Bob's interpretation was less showy, involving massive paralysis followed by a single convulsive tic and the crowning touch, a trickle of drool out of one corner of his mouth.

It had all been so long ago and started so well.

Bob pushed himself out from under the Bloom minivan. He had found nothing wrong, of course, so he changed out filters and belts, not wanting to disappoint Faye. If he began to make up to her for all the cruel things the kids had done to her with this ad-mittedly small act of kindness, maybe God would look down on him with pity. It was a long shot, a very long shot, but it was worth floating out there. You never knew who might be watch-ing, God or even a lesser angel.

It was one forty-five. He was due at the health clinic at two.

He could hear his pulse hammering in his ears.

*Fuck.*

In the bathroom he cleaned his hands as well as he could and wiped down his face. The way he figured it, you shouldn't go to the health department in less than excellent condition. Otherwise you were giving them a chance to blame you for whatever it was they found wrong. Telling Francine he was taking a late lunch, he grabbed his jacket and walked the plank of the dealership parking lot to the Caprice. Fucking car leaked like a sieve; a new puddle mocked him from the passenger seat. Some mechanic he was, owning a car the color of a used sanitary napkin and worth about as much. Somehow the money just went, and the best he could manage was trading one beater for another. He knew Anita wanted a nice car, nice like Hack's LTD: landau roof, leather upholstery, radio that worked, power windows, power steering, seats as comfortable as old armchairs. It wasn't going to happen, though, not now.

At the clinic he was told to have a seat and someone would come out for him shortly. Why was it that government offices made you wait, often for a long time, even when there was just one other person in the waiting room? Did they sit back there and linger over an extra cup of coffee, just so you'd know they were better than you? He didn't keep people waiting at the dealership. It wasn't that hard to be on time.

He sat in one of eight molded plastic seats bolted to an aluminum frame—like anyone would steal the ugly pieces of shit if they were separated. Across the room, in a beat-up wooden teacher's chair, a young woman with stringy blond hair and a hooded sweatshirt two sizes too big rocked a screaming baby in her arms. Hell's lobby must be like this place, an ugly, down-at-heel room where they handed out faulty vaccines and notices of impending death.

"I didn't know if I should feed her before they gave her the shots," the girl across the room apologized to Bob over the screams of the baby, looking like she might start crying, herself.

A nurse appeared in the doorway. "Dorothy? Come on back."

"I didn't know if I should feed her before you gave her the shots," she said as she followed the nurse through the door.

Bob looked at his hands, back and front, at the broken nails, at the old grease that would never come off if he washed a million times with pure Comet cleanser, at the wedding band he hadn't taken off once in twenty-one years. He and Anita had picked them out at a jewelry store over in Sawyer: nineteen years old and getting married. Kids. He had still been boy-skinny, barely bearded, cock of the walk, marrying a girl he couldn't believe he'd landed.

"Bob?"

The woman who'd drawn his blood last week stood in the doorway in a white nurse's smock, wise-eyed and weary, her skin softly furred. It occurred to Bob as he stood that she might be the last person who would ever see him as a man with a future, as the person he had been and assumed he always would be. She knew his test results; she might already know that she was looking at a dead man.

He was scared. He was so goddamned scared.

They walked down a short hall decorated with posters from Al-Anon, AA, a breast cancer support group, the La Leche League. She showed him into a small, cluttered office and indicated that he should sit in the visitor's chair. She took her own seat on the other side of a beat-to-death old wooden desk.

"How are you?" She asked him as though she meant it.

Bob slumped. "Okay. You know."

"Good," she said, letting the lie pass, and opened a manila

folder in front of her on the desk. "Okay then, let's see." She extracted a slip of paper and smoothed it on top of his folder.

Bob wondered if he might vomit.

He watched her take a breath and fold her hands on top of the paper. "Here's the thing," she said. "Your HIV test came back positive. The lab ran it twice just to be sure."

Bob dropped his head. His ears began to roar, but inside his mind it was suddenly quiet, deadly quiet; deeper than deafness, absolute as a vacuum.

"Would you like a glass of water?" the nurse said.

"No."

"Would you like a minute to yourself?"

Bob shook his head.

"Then let's talk about what this means."

"My wife."

"Your wife?"

"Yeah." Bob jackknifed over his knees. "Does she have it?"

"Do you mean, is she HIV positive?"

"Yeah."

"Have you had unprotected vaginal or anal sex with her?"

Bob nodded. *Murderer.*

"Unfortunately, there's no way to know that without a test," the nurse said. "But just because you're infected, it doesn't mean that she is. For every time you had unprotected intercourse, she had a one-in-a-hundred chance of being infected. It's possible to beat the odds. But she needs to come in so we can find out. In the meantime I can't stress enough how important it is that you practice safe sex. Are you familiar with the term?"

"Rubbers." He could feel gummy spit building up in the corners of his mouth: fear spit, coward's spit.

"Condoms, yes, but there are also other sexual practices and alternatives that are safe. Mutual masturbation, fondling, protected oral sex. I'll give you some literature about it."

Bob licked his lips. "How long have I had it?"

"There isn't a test that can tell us that," the nurse said. "I wish there were. We'll need to find out how many T-cells you still—"

"I heard you can have it for years before you get sick. If I've had it for a long time, my wife has it too."

"Let's not jump that fence yet. Bring her in and let's get her tested. Then we aren't guessing."

"How?"

"How can you get her here?" the nurse said. "I'm sure we can arrange for transportation, if that's a problem for you."

"No, I mean how can I get her tested without telling her why?"

She looked at him compassionately, her voice low and even. "Honesty is usually best, though it's never easy. Is there any possibility that you might have gotten the virus from her and not the other way around? Has she had other sexual partners? Is she an intravenous drug user?"

Bob shook his head dumbly.

"Then you'll have to tell your other partners about your HIV status too," the nurse said. "That means anyone you've had unprotected sex with."

"He knows," Bob whispered. "He's sick. He's already sick."

"I see." The nurse leaned across the desk. "Listen. There are things we can do, that we can get started on right away, to prolong your quality of life, and your wife's too, if she's also HIV positive. We can't prevent this nightmare, but we can sure turn up the lights a little. There's a drug called AZT that's just been approved. It keeps your T-cell count from dropping as quickly—"

"Do you believe in God?"

The nurse sat back in her chair. "Yes, I do," she said evenly. "I didn't always."

"Why?"

"Why did I start believing in Him?"

Bob wiped his face on his sleeve. "Yeah."

"Three years ago my son was in a head-on collision. He was in a coma for two months. We were told he'd never walk again, never speak clearly. If you saw him now, if you talked to him, you'd never know anything had ever happened."

"And God did that?"

The nurse said softly, "I think He did, yes."

"My wife is going to die."

"You don't know that yet."

"I'm going to die."

The nurse looked away.

"What kind of a God would do a thing like that?"

"That's a question only you and He can answer. I'm afraid what I have to offer is more practical." She began pulling pamphlets and photocopied pages out of her desk drawers. "Let's go on. We have a lot to talk about."

"We got nothing to talk about."

"What?"

"Can you make my test negative?"

"No."

"Then nothing you've got to talk about is what I need to hear." Bob stood and circled the room, stopping in front of a poster about prenatal health care. He studied it for several minutes and then said, "Nobody knew about this shit when Nita was pregnant, you know? Hell, she ate pizza, drank beer, smoked a pack a day. She wouldn't have done that stuff if we'd have known."

The nurse watched him.

"That's the thing: We wouldn't have done it if we'd have known. But we didn't know," he said. "How the *fuck were we supposed to know?*"

"No one knew," the nurse said gently. "No one could possibly have known."

Bob stalled where he stood, looking out the window at the meaningless street, the pointless traffic, tears running down the panes of his face like rain.

The nurse said, "There's a support group through Sawyer Memorial for HIV-positive people and their families. They get together every week, on Tuesdays, I believe. I think you should consider going."

He kept his back turned. "And sit around with a bunch of dying faggots? No way."

"Homosexual men aren't the only people who get AIDS," the nurse said evenly.

"Yeah?"

"There are hemophiliacs, people who've had tainted blood transfusions or shared IV needles, family members like your own. And someone is usually there from the Sawyer Hospice."

"What does that mean, hospice?"

"A place where terminally ill people and the people who love them can find dignity and support," the nurse said.

"You mean a place where people go to die."

"Not only that."

"No way," Bob said. "No fucking way."

The nurse stood, seeing that Bob was leaving, but he paused at the door. "What's your name?"

"Gabriella," the nurse said. "Gabriella Lewis. I hope you'll come back in and talk to me when you feel ready. Or to your family doctor."

Bob smiled a thin smile. Bets used to read the Bible to him, so he knew that the archangel Gabriel delivered divine messages.

God Himself was fucking with him.

He walked out without another word.

From a pay phone outside the True Value, Bob called the dealership and told Francine he was sick and wouldn't be back for the rest of the afternoon. When she pressed, he said it was nothing, just a bad headache, sinus infection maybe, and hung up. He had no idea what he was going to do next, except that he couldn't go home, at least not yet. So he got back in the Caprice and drove. There were two orange triangles hoisted at the coast guard station: another gale coming in. For now, though, it was so still that the air itself seemed to be weeping.

As he crested Cape Mano, Bob found himself thinking about jumpers. When he was in high school, a kid had jumped off one of the cliffs, killing himself on the rocks nearly a thousand feet below. They said he died instantly, but how could someone know that? Maybe he'd been alive for a few minutes, too broken to move and feeling the advancing tide already licking his shoes. Drowning had always scared the shit out of him; that was one reason he'd never made much of an effort to fish commercially, though you could make a fortune at it. Boats went down, disappeared, were found with no one on board, drifting empty for weeks, sometimes months. He and Warren used to talk about it sometimes, Bob's morbid fear of the water. Warren said Bob had probably been in his mother's womb too long, and that's where it had all started, the business of breathing amniotic fluid when he was ready to be breathing air. Bob agreed the unconscious memory of sucking that thick fluid into his lungs could make a man nervous. Maybe that was it, and maybe it wasn't, but either way the ocean scared the hell out of him, and so did falling. Walt Disney movie characters always died by falling, as though it were painless, but Bob knew that was bullshit. You might die instantly at the bottom, but you were thinking all the way down.

Two miles south of Hubbard, he turned off Highway 101 onto a rough logging road leading inland. He'd never followed it before, though it had been put in a couple of years before by the Weyerhaeuser Catskinners, elite heavy equipment operators who could navigate a Caterpillar on a thirty-degree slope. Now he steered the old Caprice like an ark, wallowing in holes and rising up again on firm track, clinging to steep hillsides. The entire area had been clear-cut right after the road was put in, and there were snags and stumps everywhere. It used to take Bob and Warren two hours to hike in, but now, in just ten minutes, he was in their little homestead valley, the first time in nearly twenty years. He had assumed that when the area was logged, the homestead had been destroyed, but instead he found the alders still standing on the banks of Homesick Creek, providing a fringe of grace around the cabin. He shut off the Caprice and sat for a minute, listening to the gentle tap of raindrops on the car roof. It was so peaceful here, so quiet. The cabin still stood, patient as Methuselah: *I have seen some things, O Lord, and I have given shelter.*

Bob walked to the cabin and pushed open the front door that he and Warren had planed so it would shut behind them. From inside he could see that their childish repairs to the roof hadn't held; a lot of the shingles were missing, and the walls had new gaps and cracks where the boards had split and fallen away. It had taken nearly all summer when they were thirteen to patch the cabin together with old boards from the barn and nails they'd stolen one at a time from the True Value. But the bedstead was still there, and on top of it was the hay-filled ticking they'd made to replace the old one, a wild patchwork of scraps taken from Bets's fabric bag. Now it was worn too, but it held when Bob unfurled it and sat down, feeling the familiar crackle of hay. It was cold in here, but he didn't build a fire for fear the chimney was clogged with birds' nests and the accumulated booty of packrats.

He and Warren had brought Anita and Sheryl here just once, when they were eighteen. It must have been just before the Miss Harrison County pageant, because he could remember Anita fussing about not wanting to mess up her manicure. Miss Harrison County—my God, but that had been a night. Bob had been speechless with pride to see Anita dressed up so fine like that, with her gown and her matching pumps and satin sash. He had sat in the audience at the Elks Lodge, where the pageant was held every year, the grand elder's chair turned into a throne for just that evening, and stared and stared at this girl who had agreed to be with him when she could have chosen anyone. She had done her swimsuit promenade and runway turns like a movie star, and when it was over, he had held her coat and her champagne glass while she posed for picture after picture. They had stayed at the reception until the very end, both of them drunk, he on beer and her beauty, she on champagne and attention. Afterward they'd parked in a pullout on Cape Mano and traded in their virginity. He had held her in his arms in the tight backseat of his Buick and marveled at her softness after the hard planes of Warren. They coupled in the backseat twice, their blood rich and warm, their prospects bright and whole, because up until then nothing in their lives had gone wrong yet, not really wrong anyway. At eighteen they still held to the touching delusion that failure happens in catastrophic ways instead of by inches, from the inside out.

Less than a year later Anita had Patrick, his nursing mouth like a sucker pulling Anita's life toward him and away from Bob. Then, unable to make a living, Warren had moved to Portland. Bob stayed behind, failing at both jobs and sobriety, talking more, doing less, making his furtive pilgrimages to Warren four or five times a year, running up big phone bills in between, and then they got evicted from the house on Adams Street. Anita didn't think Bob had seen her crying as they picked up their things from the yard where they'd been thrown, but she was wrong; he'd seen her clutching the bag with her pageant gown; he'd seen it all, the terrible humiliation and the sadness.

He shivered, sitting on the creaky old bedstead in the gathering dark. For something to do, he picked up a loose board lying on the floor. Which one of their ghosts, his or Warren's, had put it down in that exact spot twenty years before, meaning to get back to it in a second that never came? He stroked the grain, remembering how much he'd loved the feel of wood in his hands, the dying gift of grand old trees. He and Warren argued once about whether trees have souls. Warren maintained that they did: the stronger the soul, the more resilient the tree. In Warren's mind, trees broke during windstorms not because of physics but fear. Bob had said that was bunk, but now he wasn't so sure. Maybe, after all, it took more than luck to withstand a high wind.

He picked a nail loose with his pocketknife, a square-headed nail that had been handmade by some settler dazzled with the good fortune of being here in this protected place, this sheltered valley. And to Bob and Warren too, it had been a sanctuary—

away from the molding, rotting trailers behind the First Church of God; away from Bets's temper, hardening over the years into bitterness; away from Warren's mother's suicide by hanging the year they were sixteen.

*Do you think they got lonely here?* Anita had asked Bob after looking the homestead over. *It's so far away.*

*Away from what?*

*Everything.*

*Life can happen anywhere,* he'd said. But evidently he'd been wrong.

A sudden gust chilled him through a broad crack in the wall beside him. Shivering, Bob picked up the board on his lap, and the square-headed nail, and found the old claw hammer he and Warren used to keep under the bedstead. He seated the nail and pounded it in. For a little while, at least, the patch would hold.

The last of the light had gone. Bob closed the door behind him tenderly and saddled up the damned Caprice. It was time to go home.

## chapter eight

*The Owl looked up to the stars above,*
*And sang to a small guitar,*
*"O lovely Pussy, O Pussy, my love,*
*What a beautiful Pussy you are,*
*You are,*
*You are!*
*What a beautiful Pussy you are!"*
—EDWARD LEAR, 1871

Sweating lightly, Hack hunched over the book of children's poems that Rae Macy had brought in while she read aloud over his shoulder in a light, clear voice. He should have been making sly innuendos, breathing in her nearness, her subtle perfume, and her heat. Instead he was trying to control his breathing as the return of memory thrummed in his veins like jungle drums.

*And hand in hand, on the edge of the sand*
*They danced by the light of the moon,*

> *The moon,*
> *The moon,*
> *They danced by the light of the moon.*

Rae pressed her hands together in delight and returned to her chair. "My mother used to read me that one. If she read it once, I bet she read it a thousand times, and I never got tired of it."

Hack closed the book cover he still saw sometimes in his dreams.

"Hack? Are you all right?"

"Yeah."

"Are you sure? You looked so pale for a minute."

"Must have been the poetry, princess," he said wearily. "I have a sensitive nature."

Rae looked wounded. "For a minute you had me fooled into thinking you liked these."

"Sure I like them. What makes you think I don't like them? Hell, I've *memorized* them."

"Have you?" Rae tucked the book under her arm protectively. "I don't know. You're the most confounding man sometimes."

"That's me, princess. I can found with the best of 'em."

"You're making fun of me."

"Absolutely not."

Rae pursed her lips and regarded him for a long minute. "Tell me about your sister."

"Maybe sometime."

"Not now?"

"Not now."

"Can I ask why?"

"No."

Rae flushed and rose.

"Can I borrow that book overnight?" he said, trying to keep his tone light.

"Only if you'll tell me about your sister when you give it back."

"Yeah, yeah," Hack said, figuring he'd get out of it somehow. The book was calling as powerfully as any love letter. He could feel the thick cardboard covers in his hands even after all these years, the top right corner buggered up where someone's baby had teethed on it, purchased for a quarter in an act of fierce pride at the annual Tin Spoon library sale.

Hack's phone rang, startling him badly. He needed to get a grip on himself.

"Hey," Bunny said.

"Hey." He waggled his fingers at Rae; bye for now. She left the book on his desk and walked out of the room, flushing a deep crimson. *Jesus*, the woman was sensitive. Her other half must have quite the challenge some days.

"I'm bringing Mom over to see the doctor," Bunny was saying. "We should be done around noon. Do you want us to pick you up for lunch?"

Shirl. God, but he wasn't in the mood for his mother-in-law right now, with her loud voice and thrusting bosom, but he knew how it would go if he blew them off. Bunny would sulk, and Shirl would sniff and tell Bunny that it looked to her like family didn't count for shit anymore. "Yeah, why don't you stop by at least?" he said. "I have a customer who might be coming in, but I won't know until later."

For years Bunny hadn't come over to Sawyer more than once a month, twice at most, to shop the Safeway specials, but now it seemed like she was here every other day to keep an eye on him, remind him he was hers, taken, claimed. Jesus, as though he'd forget. She'd come back from Fanny's a mess, though. He guessed she'd seen life through her sister's eyes, and it had scared the shit out of her. But Fanny had married a dick, a son of a bitch who fucked around every chance he got and treated Fanny like live-in help. Say whatever else you wanted about him, but Hack was no dick. He knew where home was, much as he liked his fun like anybody else. If Bunny didn't know that about him by now, there was nothing he could do about it. He wasn't going to pander to her, reassure her every minute that he wasn't having an affair with Rae Macy, goddamn it. He wasn't. He wouldn't. Mind you, he would've given a lot to see where they might go, him and Rae, but he was a man with a keen sense of reality, and the reality of the thing was that he and Rae Macy were pendulums swinging in opposite directions. They passed each other regularly and made a beautiful noise when they did, but that was all they were or ever would be. The rest was just so much mental masturbation.

Hack noticed that Bunny had hung up, so he must have said good-bye. He set down the receiver and rubbed his eyes.

The book throbbed in his mind like an old wound.

Katy had brought home their copy from the annual Tin Spoon library sale like a conqueror triumphant. The kid already loved to read, and she was only seven that year. She'd pleaded with Hack to take her.

"Come on, Buddy," she'd wheedled. That's what she called him, Buddy. "I've got some money."

"Where'd you get money? You didn't roll old Mr. Nelson again, did you?"

Katy put her hands on her hips. "Buddy," she'd said indignantly. Hack was always accusing her of the most heinous crimes against the frail and aged of Tin Spoon.

"So c'mon, tell me where you got it."

"Mr. Elliott gave me a quarter for holding open the door for him at the Thriftway."

"Honey, you can't block the doors like that until they pay you. It's against the law."

"*Oh, Buddy,*" she said, hands on small hips.

He even cracked himself up sometimes.

Still, people were always slipping the Katydid money, a dime, a quarter, even a couple of bucks sometimes. It wasn't pity money either; it was treat money, thanks-for-that-smile money, because Katy had the gift of delight, and it shone through everything she did. People smiled just because she was smiling, greeted her because it made her light up when they did. And he didn't just think that because she was his kid sister; people were always asking about her when he was in town alone, sending their greetings home with him.

So he'd given in and walked with her to the library sale on a scorching hot day when he would rather have been anywhere else. The library was a squat concrete building in the center of town, a WPA legacy with a frieze of heroic, thick-necked men and women parading across the front. They were presumably bound for glory on account of the knowledge gained from the books within. Privately Hack thought that was a bunch of shit; no one got anywhere sitting around reading. People who read went hungry. Work was the thing, and lots of it. He'd already had a job for a year, working as a bag boy at Howdy's Market six days a week. He wasn't supposed to accept tips, but if people slipped a little something into the pocket of his jeans when his hands were full, what could he do? When Cherise was in Las Vegas stealing and turning the occasional trick, he fed the Katydid from his own pay like a man.

That day she had marched into the library with her head held high; here was a discriminating buyer with money to burn. She'd agonized over her choices. Poems or fairy tales? Animal stories or silly riddles? She'd finally chosen the book of poems and grandly presented herself and her money at the checkout desk. The librarian slipped the book into a canvas tote usually reserved for people who spent fifty dollars or more, all proceeds going toward new book acquisitions, but she just gave the Katy-did a sly wink. Katy used that tote for years, for lunches, school-books, groceries. It was one of her most prized possessions.

She'd read him the poetry book all the way through that first night. That was the way they did it, her reading to him at bed-time because he was a lousy reader. She propped herself up in bed and read the way the librarians did, turning the book around importantly and panning it to show him the pictures every few verses, prouder than shit to be doing something he was no good at. She'd read him every single poem, more than an hour's worth. He'd started protesting halfway through: "Jesus, Katy-kid, you really go for this shit? 'The Owl and the Pussycat'? It'd never happen. In real life she would have done him in in about a minute flat and eaten him for lunch."

She'd said what she always said, her voice a masterpiece of world-weariness: "Buddy. It's poetry."

"It's shit, is what it is," he'd said, but mostly just to get a last rise out of her. He'd let her read him the entire book, and after that she'd read him at least one poem every night for years. One of the worst things of all, later, was hearing those verses in his head. It had taken Vietnam to shut them up.

Now the book lay within arm's reach and ready to detonate. He put it beneath his jacket, hooded until it was time to take it home.

With a supreme effort he distracted himself by making follow-up phone calls to prospective customers who'd come into the showroom in the last several weeks but hadn't bought. It didn't get him anywhere—it never got him anywhere; it was a sales technique proven to fail—but it made the morning pass. At twelve o'clock precisely Bunny came through the showroom doors, fluffing her hair and straightening her clothes in case she came face-to-face with Rae, smiling a showy smile at him.

"Mom's in the car. You coming with us?"

"Yeah, I'll come."

"Don't you want your jacket? It's blowing like hell."

"Nah."

He slid behind the wheel of the LTD. Shirl sat in the front seat beside him, smelling of mildew and gardenia and cigarettes.

"Hi, hon," she said, patting his thigh in sporty greeting. She took liberties with him sometimes, but he figured it had been years since she'd had sex, possibly even decades, so he usually let it go.

At the Bobcat he pulled out her chair for her and slid it back in, no mean feat since the woman weighed close to two hundred pounds. Then he did the same for Bunny, who always waited for him instead of just pulling out the damned chair herself and scooting it back in. Turned out he'd married royalty, only without the money.

"So what did the doctor say?" he asked Shirl, because he knew she was waiting for it.

Shirl shook her head. She was always shaking her head when she came back from the doctor. "It's not good," she said, and Hack could sense a long report coming. Shirl loved her visits to the doctor, and the worse the news, the better. "Blood pressure's up again, and so is the cholesterol. He said if I didn't get it under control, I'd blow out an artery like an old fire hose with a blocked nozzle."

"He said that?" Hack asked Bunny.

Bunny shrugged.

"Didn't Dooley have that?" Hack asked her.

"Nothing like as bad as me." Shirl sniffed.

"So what did he tell you to do?"

"Wait, that's not the half of it," said Shirl.

"No?"

"He told me my heart was no good, said I might need one of those pacemakers soon. He gave me some pills to take for now, but he's not hopeful."

"Yeah? Well, that's not so—"

Shirl held up her hand. "Then there's my bladder."

Hack looked at Bunny and saw the corners of her mouth twitching.

"Now, you know I've got incontinence. Well, he told me my bladder's real stretched out from having big babies." She reached over and patted Bunny's hand. "Don't feel bad, hon, it's not your fault."

"I wasn't feeling bad," Bunny said.

"There's gratitude for you." Shirl winked at Hack. "Anyway, so there's an operation he might get me to have, that kind of lifts and tucks things back where they should be."

"Sounds like a brassiere," Hack said.

Shirl slapped at his hand.

"So what are you going to do?"

"Wait and hope, honey. Wait and hope."

Their waitress came over and set down their food. "She'd be better off doing separate trays with the drinks and the food," Bunny said when the waitress had gone out of hearing range.

She always critiqued other waitresses' techniques. "I bet she spills a lot, being so off-balance like that."

It was true that Bunny was highly skilled at her trade. Nina Doyle at the Anchor didn't pay her a buck fifty above minimum wage for nothing.

Hack bit into his Monte Cristo. He always called them Monte Criscos when he ordered them, just to give the waitresses shit, but he loved the Monte Cristos at the Bobcat: ham, turkey, and Swiss, battered, deep-fried, and sprinkled with powdered sugar. They never scrimped on their portions. If there was one thing he hated, it was a restaurant that scrimped on its portions. You shouldn't have to go away from a restaurant hungry, but it had happened to him now and then, usually at some fancy restaurant Vinny had taken him to where you were given cloth napkins and water glasses with lemon slices floating in them and shit, and where none of the waiters spoke English. You shouldn't need an interpreter just to order off the fucking menu. That got his goat every time.

"You girls going home after this?" he asked, just to say something. He hated a quiet table at a restaurant.

"I told Anita we'd pick up Crystal at Head Start on the way," Bunny said. "You know Doreen's on day shift now. Plus they finally gave her thirty hours. Big deal, but still."

"Yeah," Hack said.

"That girl's a hard worker." Shirl picked a piece of food from between her teeth with a fingernail. "I've got to say that for her. Anita's done a real good job with her."

"It's hard, though." Bunny poured out more ketchup for her fries. "That house is too small for all of them, plus the roof leaks in Crystal's room, so they've got buckets everywhere. Nita's been asking Bob to do something about the roof for a week now, but you know him."

"He's not drinking, though," Hack pointed out. The women were always ragging on Bob about something, but that wasn't right. The man simply wasn't a high achiever, not like Hack, who'd made the most of what he'd been given. Bob lacked backbone, was Hack's private opinion. He didn't have Hack's flair either, but there was nothing wrong with that; not many people did.

"You didn't tell me he stopped drinking," Shirl said to Bunny. "When did that happen?"

Bunny shrugged, spooning soup; the Bobcat made a damned good bowl of ham and bean. "What, a week ago?" She consulted Hack. "Week and a half, maybe."

"Well, that's good," Shirl said approvingly. "Nita needs the support, what with Doreen back home and Danny locked up and all."

"They told her at the Lawns she might pick up some more hours next week," Bunny said. "That Mexican girl's taking a couple of days off."

"Goddamned Mexicans are taking over. What?" Shirl said to Hack. "I'm just saying what's true."

"Jesus, Shirl," Hack muttered.

Shirl shrugged loftily. "I'm not afraid to call a spade a spade, Hack, and you know it. There are more of them every year, and none of them speak a word of English, but they get the jobs just the same."

"Yeah, because they're damned hard workers, and they'll work for cheap without complaining."

"Well, you're entitled to your opinion."

"Anita says Bob's still been acting funny, though," Bunny said.

"Funny how?" Shirl said.

"I don't know. She says he's never home, but when she calls the Wayside, he's not there either. He won't tell her anything except she'll be able to see for herself when he's ready."

"Ready for what?"

"That's just it," Bunny said. "He won't say. Has he told you anything?"

"No," Hack said.

"Well, the man's always been shiftless," said Shirl. "Nice enough, of course, but shiftless just the same. Anita's had to be the man of that household. I just hope whatever he's doing is legal. He doesn't have a grain of common sense, and he never has."

When the waitress brought over their check, Hack was the only one reaching for it, like always. He dug his wallet out of his back pocket, flipping his Vernon Ford credit card on top of the bill. They'd talked about Bob, who was a Vernon Ford employee, so he was okay with using the company card; he didn't believe in putting too fine a point on his expense sheets, and Marv Vernon never seemed to care. He pulled back Shirl's chair and helped her up. More than a couple of people at nearby tables gave her hard looks. Hack was used to that. He just winked at a couple of them in collusion—she's my mother-in-law, what the hell can you do?—and let the rest go.

While he was waiting for the card to be run at the register, Shirl helped them all to toothpicks. She was a big one for dental hygiene, plus she took advantage of anything free just on principle. She walked out of the restaurant picking her teeth and leaving Hack to deal with the tip.

Sometimes, for the hell of it, he tried to picture her and his mother, Cherise, together. Jesus, it would be like the Roller Derby, two tough old broads biting and clawing in the ring. He didn't even know if Cherise was still alive, though. He hadn't talked to her in, what, nearly twenty years now. She'd tried to contact him two or three times in the first couple of years she was in prison, but she'd given up after a while, like he'd meant her to. He had nothing to say to Cherise, not a goddamned thing, and he never would. If she was broke and alone someplace now, whose fault was that? Not his. Not his, and not the Katydid's either. They'd been broke and alone in Tin Spoon, and she hadn't done a thing, not a single goddamned thing. She hadn't even had the balls to let them know she was leaving them. She just slipped out of town one day with her forger boyfriend. The last words she'd said to him were: *Looks like you're nearly grown up now, kiddo*. It had taken a month for him to figure out she'd been saying good-bye.

He'd just turned fifteen.

Once they figured it out, he and the Katydid never gave away to anyone the fact that Cherise was gone, the difference to them being somewhat academic since she'd already been mostly gone for years. For a long time they brought along some of Cherise's clothes when they went to the Laundromat. When the Katydid was out sick, Hack sent her back to school with notes he signed with Cherise's name, forging the signature of a forger being something that gave him a sense of grim satisfaction. They mussed up Cherise's bed some days too, and Hack dripped her cloying perfume around their apartment from time to time so if anyone came over, it would smell like she'd left only a minute or two before.

And for a while people did come by to check on them: Hack's

boss at Howdy's Market, who asked gentle questions and watched Hack with concern sometimes when he thought Hack didn't know it; Katy's fourth-grade teacher, who brought homework by once when she was out for a week with the flu.

Then, of course, there'd been Minna.

Minna Tallhorse, hipless and hard-bodied, perfectly erect, eyes as deep as outer space and ferocity crackling all around her like lightning, came into their lives four months after Cherise had left them. They'd found her waiting for them in a beat-up Volkswagen outside their apartment late one afternoon, the department of social services' answer to an anonymous tip that they were living without adult supervision. She shook Hack's hand hard like a man and followed him and Katy into their apartment with a long stride.

Hack had never seen anyone before who looked quite like Minna Tallhorse, dark and taut and somehow dangerous, as if she'd known things other people didn't. He stared openly as she sat on their old sofa, her heavy hair falling straight down on either side of her face until she seized it impatiently and tied it in a double knot at the nape of her neck. Mining her satchel for a notebook and pen, she finally looked them over and said, "Tell me about yourselves."

"You first," Hack said warily.

"Fair enough." She rested her elbows on her knees and frowned, her chin in her hands. "I grew up on a Blackfoot Indian reservation in North Dakota, was caught once stealing a steak, always wanted a dog but never had one, and my father is my mother's first cousin. Your turn."

The Katydid pressed a little closer to Hack. They were sitting side by side on the living room floor, the sofa being their only piece of furniture.

"What do you want to know? I'm Hack Neary, and this is Katy. I'm fifteen. She's ten."

"Keep going. I already knew that part."

"Our mother's out right now, but she should be back soon."

"How soon?"

"Soon," Hack said. "Anytime."

"Ah," Minna said. "So what did you have for dinner last night?"

"Hot dogs." The Katydid piped up, she being the cook in the family. "Macaroni and cheese and canned green beans."

"My favorites," said Minna, showing them her first real smile. She had beautiful long white teeth. Beside him Hack could feel the Katydid relax. "How much money is in the house right now, would you say?"

"Six dollars and twenty-two cents." Hack made a point of keeping current on their cash situation. "Why?"

"You should always have a little money around the house. You could need, I don't know, a cotton ball and not find one anywhere. If you have money, you can just go out and buy one."

"Why would you need a cotton ball?" Katy said.

"It's just an example," Hack said.

"Cotton balls can be very important." Minna crossed her arms and frowned thoughtfully. "You can put calamine lotion on a bug bite with one. You can clean goo off your stove, maybe, or blot up a nosebleed."

"Do you get nosebleeds?" said Katy.

"All the time," Minna said. "Don't you?"

"No."

"Well, you're lucky."

"Why is your name Minna Tallhorse?"

"The same reason yours is Katy, I imagine; my mother named me that. Minna was one of my aunts. I never met her, but I always imagined her as fat and with hairs on her chin. I would have preferred Augusta or Aurelia, but there you are."

"No, I mean the Tallhorse part."

"Ah. My great-grandfather was the first Tallhorse, as far as we know. I assume he owned a tall horse; we'll never really know for sure, but my family name has been Tallhorse ever since."

"I think it's a pretty name."

"Do you? Well, maybe so." Minna reknotted her hair and rose from the sofa like a Valkyrie. "I'd like to look around a little. May I do that?"

"Sure," Hack said. The Katydid hopped up and followed her. Hack trailed behind as the two of them poked around in closets and kitchen cupboards. Though the apartment was an absolute and undeniable piece of shit, with daylight coming through cracks in the walls and a bathroom you had to go around the outside to reach, the whole place was clean, cleaner by far than when Cherise had lived with them, the Katydid's being a tidy housekeeper. Soon they were back in the living room with its single ratty sofa balanced on three legs and a brick.

"Why did you steal a steak?" Katy asked, perching beside Minna.

"Ah, you remembered that, did you? My little brother Luther was terrible when he was hungry; he yelled and threw things from misery. I took the steak to shut him up." She leaned in close to Katy. "It wasn't the first one I'd stolen. I think the butcher knew all along. He would have let me get away with it too, but he wasn't working that day, his wife was, and she didn't like Indian girls very much."

"You have a brother?"

"Five."

"Five?" Katy brightened. "How old are they?"

"Oh, we're all grown up now. Three are younger than me. One's a year and a half older."

"That's only four."

"Sharp girl. My fifth brother died."

"How?"

"He had a hole in his heart."

"Did it hurt?"

"No, but it made him tired a lot of the time," Minna said. "And the bigger he got, the harder his heart had to work. After a while it just wasn't strong enough to keep up. He died when he was eight." Minna frowned. "He was my twin."

"But you don't have a hole in your heart."

"No?" Minna smiled a strange little smile. She turned to Hack. "I'd like to talk to you alone for a few minutes. Why don't we go outside?"

Reluctantly Hack followed her out into the heat and dust.

"What makes you tick, I wonder?" Minna Tallhorse said, folding her arms ruminatively and leaning against her beater Volkswagen.

Hack shrugged.

"Then tell me about Katy," she said.

"What do you want to know?"

"Anything. Everything. What's she like?"

"She's real smart."

"I already figured out that part. What else?"

There was a lot else, but Hack had no intention of telling any of it to this tall, prickly woman with a body like the flat, hard blade of a sword. He did not intend to tell her that the Katydid had nightmares all the time, screaming ones that woke Hack up in the middle of the night panting with fear until she sank down again into the hostile arms of sleep. He didn't intend to tell her that sometimes they got so mad at each other over stupid things like who'd finished the milk that three months ago she stabbed him in the hand with a meat fork and that once or twice he'd slapped her. And he had no intention of telling her the worst thing of all, that sometimes the Katydid cried for Cherise, and when she did, he yelled at her for it, screamed, *Shut the fuck up, just shut the fuck up.* To him it was all so much bullshit. If someone walked out on you like that, she was dead to you, ashes and bone. He'd never wept for Cherise, and he never would.

Minna was watching him shrewdly. How long had he been standing there with her sizing him up like that? "Is she hard to take care of?" she asked.

"The Katydid?" He tried to sound breezy. "Nah, she's easy. She pretty much takes care of herself. I mean, you never have to remind her about her chores or anything like that."

"What are her chores?"

Hack thought for a minute. "Well, she cooks usually, and she cleans. We both do the laundry because I don't want her around the Laundromat alone, but she folds better than I do. She keeps the grocery list."

"She sounds very independent."

"Yeah."

"And your chores?"

"I pay the bills and stuff, the rent and electricity and all. Plus I work."

"What's left for your mom, then? What does she do?"

Hack stiffened. Had he given too much away? "Oh, she does plenty of stuff. She takes care of us and all."

Minna held him with her eyes like an oncoming train. Hack forced himself to stare right back at her.

"And what about you?" she said. "Are you like your sister? Do you read a lot too?"

"Nah. Reading's boring."

"That depends on what you read. Are you a good reader?"

Hack shrugged. "I'm all right." He wasn't, though. He'd been the worst reader in his class since second grade, and he didn't write worth a damn either. The words he wrote looked okay to him, but his teachers said they were inside out or something. They got mad at him for not trying harder, but when he tried harder, he still wrote his words inside out, so what was the point?

"So what do you like to do? Sports?"

"Nah, I don't have time for that," he said proudly. "I've got a job at Howdy's Market."

Minna cocked an eyebrow. "A man on the rise."

"Yeah, I've been working there for four years already. I'm going to make cashier next year. You have to be sixteen."

"So you're paid, what, minimum wage?"

"Plus tips."

"Plus tips," Minna acknowledged. "How often do you get paid?"

"Every Thursday."

"What do you use the money for? Cigarettes? Taking girls out on dates?"

Hack turned scarlet. "Nah. I don't have time for that."

"What then?"

"I buy stuff with it."

"Stuff?"

"Yeah, food and stuff."

"Ah," Minna said.

"I'll probably stop going to school after next year," Hack blurted out. "I figure I'll know all I need to by then."

"Will you?"

"Sure. Plus I'll be earning good money."

"Let's talk about money," she said. "If I gave you forty dollars, what would you do with it?"

Hack frowned. "Forty dollars? I'd buy us coats. Then, if there was some left over, maybe I'd take the Katydid to a movie. Some Disney picture maybe. She hasn't seen that many movies."

"Have you?"

"Sure, I've seen plenty."

Minna nodded and folded her arms across her chest. "You and Katy live here by yourselves, don't you?"

He looked Minna dead in the eye. "No."

"If I asked Katy, would she say the same thing?"

"Yup."

"I guess she would." Minna regarded him for a long minute, deliberating. "Look. If you go hungry, or if one of you gets sick, or if you're in *any kind of trouble at all*, I expect you to call me," she said. "There are some rules I'm willing to bend, but that's not one of them. You break that rule even once, and I'll have you both in foster care so fast it will make your head spin. Do you understand?"

Hack nodded.

"I'm going to give you forty dollars and leave you a couple of phone numbers where you can reach me, at work and at home. I expect to hear from you every Monday without fail."

Hack nodded.

"And I'll stop by from time to time without warning. Also expect me every Thursday night for dinner. I'll cook."

"Yes, ma'am." Hack began to grin.

"Do you have any questions?"

"No, ma'am."

"All right, then, I believe we understand one another. Do we have a deal?"

"Deal," Hack said.

She extended her hand and shook Hack's hard. Then she folded herself into her tiny Volkswagen and roared away.

Bunny was already over at Joelle Burden's playing bunko, God be praised, when Hack got home from work. He didn't have the strength for Bunny right now, with her peering eyes and need to know every minute that he loved her best. The truth was, he didn't love anybody tonight, not really, not anyone he could summon up anyway. He felt like shit, what with the discovery of the book and all, as if his skin were on too tight, or he had cake crumbs under there like one of those *Just So Stories* the Katydid used to read him, the one about how the rhinoceros got his wrinkles.

He made himself a Dagwood sandwich and took it back to the garage. He and Bob had built a workbench there, and built-ins for storage, and a pegboard seven feet long for his tools. They had sealed the floors with gray marine primer and insulated and Sheetrocked the walls. Bunny got mad sometimes when he spent too much time out there, but hell, she had her damn sewing room and piano full of rabbits. He had the garage. Same thing.

He climbed back into the cab of the truck, set his sandwich on the dashboard, and picked up the *Golden Book of Children's Poetry*. Jesus, his heart was beating like a jackhammer. On the cover there was a drawing of kids playing ring-around-the-rosy. They looked so happy, and no wonder, there wasn't a grown-up in sight. The Katydid used to tell Hack two of those kids were them, him and her, when they were younger. Hack couldn't see it himself. He'd never been that young, had never played silly games where even if you won, you didn't get anything for it. He was all for winning, don't get him wrong, but only if there was booty at the end: good sex, money, a Caribbean vacation, new household appliances. His idea of a game was What's Behind Door Number Three. He was glad the Katydid had been more carefree, though.

He began turning pages, memories igniting and burning into ashes all around him. How she'd liked to wear one of his shirts as pajamas; how she'd tucked her feet under his leg when she read to him in bed. How she'd once read "The Puffin" eighty-nine nights in a row. How her hair had always smelled clean, even when all they had to use was cheap bar soap he'd stolen from Howdy's Market.

"What do you think real families do at bedtime?" he'd asked her once.

"We're a real family."

"Like hell," he said. "If we were a real family, Cherise would be out there in the living room. Not that I'd want her there."

"I would," Katy said. She had been almost twelve then, and Cherise had been gone for over a year.

"Why?"

"Because if she was out there, we'd know she thought we were worth coming back for. You know what Jane Sandrini told me at school today? She said, *Your mother's a whore, and she didn't want you in the first place.* Is that true?"

"Of course she wanted you," Hack said. "She had you, didn't she? She could have had an abortion if she hadn't wanted you. Hell, I even think she wanted me."

"If she wanted us then, how come she stopped?"

"Wanting us?"

"Loving us."

"She loves you," Hack said.

"If she loved us, she would have stayed."

There wasn't much you could say when someone was right. "I don't know, kiddo. Maybe there's just something wrong with her."

"Was she a whore?"

"Not by the time she had you." In fact Hack was hazy on the timeline of her retirement, but there wasn't any harm in tampering a little bit with the truth.

"She was one, though," Katy said. "A prostitute."

"Yeah, and Jane Sandrini's father is a goddamned drunk. He hits her; that's why she misses school all the time and wears so much makeup. I heard her father was screwing her too. She's not so great."

"Maybe we're not so great either, Buddy."

"You're great. You don't need to have Cherise to be great. You ask Minna Tallhorse. She'll tell you."

"Minna?"

"Yeah. She's your goddamned fan club."

The Katydid was always closer than he was to Minna Tallhorse. The woman scared the crap out of him with those fierce eyes of hers and her demands that he be honest with her even if it was about something bad. He didn't believe in total honesty now, and he never had. What was the point of telling the truth about little things that didn't matter when you knew it would land you in the crapper all the same? When he used to call Minna on Monday mornings from Howdy's, he always told her they were fine. Tonight, when Bunny came home from bunko, he'd tell her the same thing. It was easy to put a lie over on people when what you said was what they wanted to hear. He'd been getting away with it for years.

He finished his sandwich, closed the book, and looked through the windshield at his tools for a while. They all hung perfectly plumb, lined up with the outline he'd traced of each one on the pegboard. Unlike honesty, he set great store by order. Order kept things from flying apart—kept *him* from flying apart. He'd learned that after the Katydid had died, learned it the hard way, when there was nothing left of him but blood and bone chips and breakage, inside and out.

He opened his truck door abruptly and, leaving it gaping like an escape hatch, reached up into the rafters to pull down an old green army satchel. He rummaged around among the dog tags and compass and field knife and emergency supplies until he felt the cold metal touch of a bracelet. It had been a cheap thing to begin with, Indian silver, but the Katydid had loved it, never took it off. Hack turned it over and over in his hand, read its warped and twisted surface like Braille.

*In case of need or emergency, call Minna Tallhorse, (702) 555-3242.*

# chapter nine

Anita lay down in stages on the bed in room nine of the Lawns Motel and Tourist Cabins. First she stretched across to straighten the sheets, then to position the blankets, then to fluff the pillows, and next thing she knew she'd slipped under the covers and closed her eyes. It would be for only a minute, just for a minute. The place wasn't busy—it was only the first week in March—and anyway, Barb wouldn't care just as long as Anita finished her ten rooms by noon. Half of them were still occupied, and she'd finished the rest, all but this one. She still had hours.

When was the last time she'd been this tired? Maybe when the kids were little and had back-to-back cases of the flu; maybe not even then. She'd been feeling puny for a couple of weeks now, nothing much, nothing you could put your finger on; a little fever, a few swollen glands, a little diarrhea were all. That, and this crushing fatigue. She'd begun taking two of Crystal's Flintstones vitamins every morning with her coffee, but it didn't seem to be helping much. She should pick up some of those new women's vitamins next time she went over to Sawyer to see if that made any difference, but they were so damned expensive.

Maybe she should just squirt some of those iron drops into her orange juice like she did when Doreen had had anemia that time. The girl had been so washed out she'd looked like a ghost; even her blood had looked pale when they'd drawn it, though that might have just been Anita's imagination. Anyway, the iron drops had worked miracles. Anita had also read somewhere that cooking with a cast-iron skillet would do the same thing, and she could do that for free, just about, except for the cost of an old skillet at Goodwill. Bunny had been bugging her the last few days to go to the clinic over in Sawyer, but Anita couldn't see the point. She knew exactly what she had: a virus, same thing all of them got every spring. It would pass; it always did. The thing to do was just to ride it out in the meantime.

Suddenly the room phone rang, scaring hell out of her; Barb at the front desk must have tracked her down by the whereabouts of her housekeeping cart. Anita rolled out from under the blanket guiltily and picked up the receiver.

"Hon, call Bunny when you get a chance. She wants to know if you'll have lunch with her at the Anchor, her treat."

"Why didn't you just put her through back here?"

"I did, honey; I let it ring five times. You must've had the water running."

She must have been asleep. Lord. She hung up and called Bunny.

"You work too hard," Bunny said.

"I must have had the water running when you called. Barb said she let the phone ring five times, but I didn't hear a thing."

"So what time do you want me to come get you?" Bunny said.

"Why don't I meet you? Bob went in to work with Hack this morning, so I've got the car. What time is it?"

"Eleven."

"How about eleven forty-five. I should be done here by then."

"You sound beat," Bunny said.

"Whoops, I better go," Anita lied. "Guests just came back, and here I haven't even dusted yet."

"Okay. I'll see you there."

Yeah.


Thursday lunch at the Anchor in early spring was a very gloomy affair. No one was in the place but Anita, Bunny, and a lone family arguing about whether or not to go to the aquarium over in Sawyer. From what Anita could tell, they seemed to be split fifty-fifty. The husband and daughter said who in their right mind wanted to look at a bunch of fish in an outdoor facility in the first place, not to mention at this time of year in the rain. The son wanted to see sharks, though, and the wife said she'd heard the place had a great gift shop. "It's always about shopping with you, isn't it?" the man hissed. "It's always about spending money."

"There aren't really sharks there," Anita confided over her shoulder to the son, a kid about eleven with a mended harelip. "I mean, besides little ones. The biggest shark they have is probably three, three and a half feet long. It's not exactly *Jaws*."

The wife gave Anita a chilly smile that had *Mind your own damn business* written all over it. Ordinarily Anita steered clear of tourists unless they were in a position to tip her, but the daughter had wet shoes and a runny nose and looked like she could use having something go her way. She was maybe thirteen, a sulker. Doreen had been a sulker too. Anita felt for the wife even if she was a bitch.

Joelle came over to them and said, "So what are you girls having for lunch?"

Bunny said, "I'll do the clam strips if you tell Manny to make them extra crisp."

"You got it, doll," Joelle said, licking her pencil lead before writing. "Nita, what about you?"

"How much iron is there in eggs?"

"Beats hell out of me." Joelle frowned.

"Don't look at me," Bunny said. "They lie on those nutrition labels too, tell you what they think you want to know. Have you ever noticed how whether you're looking at yogurt or pound cake, the calorie count for a single serving comes out to about one eighty? There must be a study somewhere that says no one worries about a hundred eighty calories, but if it goes over two fifty, they'll put it back on the shelf. You think I'm kidding? Look at the portions on there. If it's something fattening, you get about a half a tablespoon, only nobody notices that. The calorie count's the thing, and as long as it's under two fifty, people are going to buy it. Then they eat a whole cup of the stuff because that's how much people really eat, and they wonder how come they're getting fat."

Anita and Joelle snickered.

Bunny shrugged. "Well, it's the truth, isn't it?"

"Yeah," Joelle said. "It is. So, are you doing an omelet, Nita?"

"I'm trying to find iron-rich food," Anita said.

"Liver and onions would be good, except no one eats that anymore, so we took it off the menu, what, Bunny, three years ago? Four?"

"Four," said Bunny. "Try broccoli. I heard that was high in iron. Or is that calcium?"

"I could ask if they have some in the back," Joelle said.

"How does a broccoli omelet sound?" Anita said.

"Disgusting," said Bunny.

"Yeah. To hell with it," Anita said. "I'll just go with a double patty melt and some fries."

"Good girl." Joelle thumped her on the back and went off to the kitchen.

"So what's with the iron?" Bunny said.

"I thought it might give me some umph. I feel like shit."

"You look like shit. Are you sleeping?"

"Like the dead, but you wouldn't know it by how I feel in the morning."

"You should go see someone," Bunny said. "You really should."

"Please don't start, hon. You know we don't have the money, and it'll burn itself out when it's good and ready. Viruses always do."

Bunny made a noise, but she knew when to change the subject. "So did Barb give you hours for the rest of the week?"

"Yeah, I'll work tomorrow and Saturday. Dominga has to have her uterus scraped."

Both women shuddered.

"Remember when I had those fibroids done?" Bunny said. "Jesus, I couldn't stand up straight for two weeks."

Anita shook her head. Bunny's female problems were legendary. By contrast, when Anita had had her hysterectomy she'd hardly been down at all; a couple of days, and that was it except for a weird, hollow feeling inside, like her other organs were dangling in the wide open space where her uterus had been. She had a high tolerance for pain, though; she always had.

"She should ask for Darvocet," Bunny was saying. "That way at least she'll have a little fun."

"No kidding."

Bunny shook her head. "Well, good luck to her."

"Yeah. So anyway, Barb gave me her shift."

"Lucky you," Bunny said. "You're a hard worker, Nita, that's for sure."

"Have to be. I've got kids to feed."

"Again."

Anita sighed heavily. "Yeah. Again."

"How long are her and Crystal staying?" Bunny asked.

"Doreen? I don't know. She's going to need a lot more hours at the hospital before she can pay rent again, I'll tell you that. There's this cute little apartment she's got her eye on over there in Sawyer on Thirteenth, that new complex, but right now she doesn't even have enough for the first and last, never mind the security deposit."

"It'll happen, though."

"Yeah. She's talking to some people at the community college this afternoon. She's thinking she might want to be a dental hygienist if she can get financial aid."

"Her grades weren't all that good," Bunny said. Vinny, on the other hand, had been an excellent student.

"Yeah, well, they don't go strictly on grades," Anita said. "They include personality and drive and all. Doreen's real motivated."

"Well, sure," Bunny allowed.

"I think it might be a good deal for her," Anita said. "People are always going to have dirty teeth. Dental hygienists and hairstylists are never out of work, you know? Hair's going to keep on growing, and teeth are going to keep on rotting."

"Yeah. So how's Bob doing? He still on the wagon?"

"Yup. Something's working on him, though. He's gone an awful lot, and he won't tell me a damned thing. He's got cuts all over his hands, and yesterday he smashed his thumb with something."

"Maybe he's going freelance; maybe he's doing auto repair at people's houses. Maybe he's going to surprise you with a new car."

Anita gave her a look: *Yeah, right.* "Anyway, we don't have any more damned money around, that's for sure. I can't even buy bread until next Monday."

Bunny tsked sympathetically. "You need a little something to tide you over? We've got a few extra dollars right now."

"Nah, thanks, hon, I'm exaggerating. I can afford bread. Crystal sure loves her cinnamon toast in the morning."

"She doing okay without Danny and all?" Danny had been convicted and sentenced to twenty months in prison; they'd sent him down to the correctional institution in Salem a couple of weeks ago.

"Oh, I guess," Anita said. "Of course she doesn't understand it, poor angel. We're just telling her Daddy's had to go away for a while to a camp. She thinks he's at Vacation Bible School."

Both of them chuckled. Kids.

Joelle brought over their food. The tourist family was getting ready to leave, and it looked to Anita like the husband's mood had continued to darken. He slapped down cash at the register and kept on going, leaving the family to catch up. The wife and kids followed him in a tight bunch. Bob never did that. Whatever else you could say about him, he never showed disrespect toward her or the kids, never humiliated them in public or tried to make himself bigger at their expense. She wished she knew what the hell was going on with him. His unwavering sobriety, much as she'd longed for it, was unnerving. She was proud of him, but it wasn't normal. Plus sometimes she caught him looking at her funny, like he'd seen a ghost. She didn't think he had a woman on the side. That wouldn't be like him. Then again, he didn't want to have sex with her that often these days, and when they did, he'd stop partway through and say he had to use the bathroom. Who had to use the bathroom in the middle of having sex? He'd go down the hall in the dark, and then he'd come back in the dark, and from what she could see, he seemed okay. She'd say, *Better?* And he'd say, *Yeah,* and then it was right back to business. It happened like that every time. She asked him once if he thought he might have a problem with his prostate or whatever, but he just said, *Leave it alone, Nita,* and she had.

The other thing she'd noticed lately was that Warren Bigelow had stopped calling. He and Bob always talked two or three times a week, and they had from the time Warren moved out of town years ago, but now, nothing. Anita had asked Bob about it, whether Warren was in jail or out of work or something, but Bob just said they'd been talking at work lately because Warren could use the phone at his job for free. Anita didn't buy it, though. Warren was always a stickler for the rules and wouldn't gab on company time; plus, she couldn't imagine any business allowing its employees to use the long-distance phone line for free. Maybe something was wrong with Warren's wife, Sheryl; she'd had a scare with a lump in her breast just last year. They'd told her it was benign, but maybe they'd been wrong and it had come back. That happened sometimes. You couldn't always trust the doctors. You could be dying, probably, and the doctors wouldn't tell you squat.

Bunny tucked into her clam strips. "Aren't you going to eat?" she asked Anita.

"What? Yeah."

"You were just sitting there."

"Oh."

"Look, just let me make you an appointment at the clinic—"

Anita shook her head stubbornly.

Bunny held up her hands in defeat. "When you end up in the hospital with pneumonia or something, don't say I didn't warn you."

Anita smiled a faint smile. "Doesn't sound half bad. Someone else does all the cooking and cleaning and laundry, and you get to just lay there. It sounds like a vacation."

Bunny shot her a skeptical look. Anita suddenly teared up. "Do you want to know the real reason why I didn't answer your phone call this morning? I fell asleep, right there in room nine on someone else's dirty sheets. Bob is never home, Doreen cries all the time, and no one has enough time for Crystal. I'm tired. I'm just so goddamned tired," Anita said, and then she started to cry.

Bunny jumped up and circled the table to put her arm around Anita's heavy shoulders. "Aw, hon, don't. You need some rest, is all. Do you want me to talk to Bob for you? He could help out more, you know he could."

She squatted at Anita's side, and her knees went off like gunshots.

"Ow," Anita said, laughing and crying at the same time. She and Bunny, it always seemed to come down to the two of them. How many crises had they weathered, one of them being the strong one, the other breaking down, and then switching so they could each have a good cry? Bunny's knees always cracked, and Anita always winced, and then one or the other of them found a Kleenex or a length of toilet paper to mop up with, and life went on. And inevitably, when they looked back on it all from a distance of weeks or years, it hadn't really been so bad, not really. Bob's drinking, Hack's infidelities, Bunny's female problems, the kids. Life went on even when it had looked like there was no clear path through it; somehow they always found a way to the other side. This too would pass, and she would look back from the safety of five or ten years and forget what exactly it was that had been so bad: the fatigue, the worry, the way they all needed her to take care of them even when she was too tired to take care of herself.

What she needed was a nap.

Bunny stayed beside her and rubbed her back, holding on like she was the only thing keeping Anita from rising and thinning like smoke. "What time do you need to pick up Crystal?" she asked.

"Two-thirty."

"Okay, then look. You go home and sleep. I'll call you at two and make sure you're up in plenty of time to get over to Sawyer. If you still feel like crap, I'll go pick Crystal up for you."

Anita nodded gratefully, too tired to bother even with her usual token protest against Bunny's picking up the tab for lunch.

Anita could remember Bob all the way back to the first time she saw him in kindergarten, a tiny kid with pants four times too big held up only by a wish and a piece of clothesline. He'd had the most aggressive cowlicks anyone had ever seen, big, thick, spiky ones that went everywhere but where they should: in a spiral at the back of his head, a pair of double buds on his head like horns. In most ways he was a sorry thing, but he had beautiful eyes, as though to make up for his lack of physical promise, God had given his soul an extrafine pair of windows to shine through. They were green, but they had brown flecks all through them and a black ring around the outside of the cornea, like the leading in stained glass. She had liked looking at him even that far back; she still did, even after all they'd been through, all the wear and disappointment and failure. She never doubted that he was a good man. Inept, yes, and a permanent stranger to success, but good in his heart. Maybe the rest came from being so poor. In elementary school when kids brought in candy or cupcakes for the class, Bob lit up like Christmas. Anita couldn't remember anymore how they'd gotten started, but her mother and Shirl had taken turns baking cupcakes for the girls to bring in on his birthday, since his aunt Bets maintained that she didn't have the time or money for that kind of nonsense.

When Warren Bigelow had come to Hubbard, Anita was easier in her heart about Bob and his having so little standing between him and abandonment. Bob had found a home at last in Warren's heart. Two boys, no matter how thin and pale, could take on the world if they believed in themselves, and Anita could see that together they did. Warren had been a girlish boy, delicate and pretty, but no one had teased him; that always surprised Anita. He was tough in his own way, tougher than Bob. When anyone said something unkind, he just sank down behind his eyes so far he couldn't hear a thing, and he stayed there until the trouble passed, even if it took days. She'd never seen anything like it, not before and not since.

Bob and Hack were good friends and had been since the day Hack slouched into town so many years ago, but it was Warren Bob loved. Anita knew that, although Bob thought she didn't. She knew, and she didn't mind. Everybody needed family, no matter how he came by it. Bob kept Warren grounded, was earth to his lightning. She remembered the two of them when they were still little boys, slipping through town in the rain, hair streaming, soaked to the skin, and there had been something feral about them, two wild, wiry souls fitting into the cracks of Hubbard life, accepting food and clothing when it was offered, expecting too little ever to be disappointed. She'd still been wary of them then, knowing that untamed animals bit when held or cornered.

But one day, when they were in high school, Anita was walking home from Bunny's and saw Bob and Warren up ahead, in the little park at the back of the harbor. They were crouched over Warren's bare foot, inspecting something, a barbed fish hook, as it turned out, that he'd stepped on and that was now embedded. It was a strangely intimate moment, and Anita felt she shouldn't be witnessing it somehow. Warren was crying—keening, really, in an eerie, high voice, the voice of a child, though they were fifteen years old. At first Bob spoke in a voice too low for Anita to make out the words, only that he was using soothing, soft, infinitely patient tones. But as she got closer, walking quietly, almost stealthily, she heard Bob say, *We're gonna do this now.*

*But it'll hurt.*

*Only for a minute, I swear. Come on, we've gotta do this, Warren. You know we do.*

*But I don't want you to,* Warren had wailed, but he left his foot in Bob's hand. A quick twist, a snip with a pocketknife's scissors, and Bob had pushed the fishhook through the skin and debarbed it. One more twitch, and he had the hook out and resting in the palm of his hand. Warren wept quietly, his forehead and Bob's just touching as they investigated the damage.

*It's okay,* Bob said. *You're gonna be fine. See how clean it came out?*

*That was so awful, Bobby. Couldn't you just feel it too?*

*Yeah. I could,* Bob said, rocking back on his heels. *It's okay, though. It's over. You're okay.*

*Do you think I'll get tetanus? Jesus, people die from that, Bobby—lockjaw, that's what tetanus is. I read about it once—*

*Nah,* Bob said soothingly. *You're not going to get anything.*

*Promise?*

*Promise.*

That was the day Anita first wondered what Bob would be like if she mothered him, held him close and kept him warm and dry. Would he run away? But no, he'd loved to nuzzle her bosom, settle in with both arms around her, holding her as close as he could and still breathe. He'd been surprisingly strong, wiry, and tensile. He had scraped together enough money to buy a huge old Buick from Buster Ludlow, and Bob liked to drive her way back into Weyerhaeuser land along the logging roads. They'd necked, of course, but they'd talked too; he'd talked anyway, and Anita had listened with her heart wide open. He'd talked about his plans for the future, the auto repair shop he'd have right there on the edge of town, next to the gas station Warren intended to buy. The two of them had ambition, boy, don't think they didn't. They were going to make money, buy themselves houses and fancy suits so they'd look sharp whenever the moment called for it.

Bob had never been a rebel, something that had always puzzled Anita. He was unfailingly polite to teachers and grown-ups, compliant when anything was asked of him. She guessed that to rebel, you had to be confident you'd have something to come back to when you were done. Bob hadn't had that, and neither had Warren—or Crystal. Maybe that was why Bob loved them so especially. Last week she'd overheard him telling the little girl, "Honey, you listen up now. No matter where you go, or how far away you get, if you need me, I'll always find you."

And at that moment, especially, Anita had loved him, loved him, and held him close to her heart.

Bunny called, as she'd promised, and roused Anita from her nap at two. Groggy but better, Anita declined Bunny's offer to go over to Sawyer for her, or at least to ride along, and headed to Sawyer alone and still in a light sleep. She'd come around when she had to; she always did.

The Head Start was in a dumpy old building on the far side of town, wedged in between a marine supply store and a fish market. They'd tried to spruce it up with bright paint and kids' art projects, but you could tell the cinder-block building had been no good to begin with, and even the best intentions could go only so far. Anita found Crystal in the little lunchroom, eating her snack: apple slices, graham crackers with peanut butter, a juice box. They tried to make even snacks filling here, knowing that for some of the kids this would be the only real meal of the day. All over the building kids were coughing and barking from various stages of flu and bronchitis, and you knew the place was crawling with germs despite the spray bottles of diluted bleach the teachers kept in every room and used obsessively on everything from toys to telephones.

"Hi, Grammy!" Crystal said, throwing her arms around Anita's legs.

"Hi, sweetie. How are you?"

"We did finger paints."

"I can see that." Crystal's fingernails were bright red, and there were telltale traces on her T-shirt, where she'd defeated her painting smock.

"I did a picture for Granddad." She pulled Anita over to a wall full of art and pointed to a chaos of red and orange. "That's mine. Right there."

"It's beautiful," Anita said.

"It's apples."

"Uh-huh," said Anita.

Crystal stood with her hands on her hips, assessing her work with the discerning eye of a master craftsman.

"Are you about ready to go home, honey?"

"Yes," Crystal said, slipping a sticky hand into Anita's.

"Go get your things then."

The child retrieved an enormous backpack from her cubby at the back of the building. She laid her coat upside down on the floor in front of her and, after inserting her arms, flipped it over her head. Another new skill acquired.

"Good for you, hon, you're getting to be so big."

"I'm ready now, Gram."

Anita signed her out.

"Bye, sweetie," one of the teachers called to her. "You were a real good girl today."

"Yes," Crystal said.

Anita buckled them both into the Caprice, and they drove all the way to Cape Mano in companionable silence. Then Anita said, "Once upon a time there was a little girl named Jewel."

Crystal clapped her hands. Anita didn't tell her stories very often. "Did she look like me?"

"Some," said Anita. "Maybe a little darker, though, and with green eyes. Oh, and she had real long banana curls that reached all the way to her waist."

"I don't have those."

"No, unfortunately you got your mama's hair. So anyway, because Jewel's family was very poor, everyone in the household had to work so they'd have enough to eat. Her mother's job was to raise vegetables and fruits so the family wouldn't go hungry, but her garden was a long way from the house."

"Why?"

"Zoning issues," said Anita. "Anyway, that meant that some days Jewel didn't see her mother until bedtime, and when she did, her mother was often cranky. She wasn't mad at Jewel, not at all; she was just tired from being bent over in the garden all day trying to make things grow."

"Did they?"

"Did they what?"

"Grow."

"Ah. Sometimes they did, but not always, and then she'd have to come home to Jewel empty-handed, which you can imagine made her feel sad even though she tried not to show it."

"Did she ever say, 'Damn it'?"

"Never."

"Sometimes Mommy says, 'Goddamn it, Crystal.' "

"That's just tiredness talking, honey."

Crystal nodded.

"Anyway, it was Jewel's grandmother's job to help Jewel learn to tie her shoes, and stay inside the lines when she colored, and keep the family's clothes clean, and cook, and read her stories at night."

"You read me stories."

"It's one of my favorite things, honey."

"What about the daddy?"

"Now, that's an interesting question. Unfortunately, the father and the grandfather both had to be away most of the time."

"Why?"

"Well, the grandfather fixed rich people's carriages, but to do that, he had to work far away. Sometimes he would have to stay away from home all day and all night for days."

"Didn't he get lonely?"

"Very lonely, honey. He missed his family all the time, especially Jewel, who he loved so much there aren't even words to describe it."

"Granddad loves me."

"He sure does, baby," said Anita. "As for Jewel's father, he had to be away from home even more. He made pots and pans that he sold in a land so distant that he'd be away from home for years."

"Like on the Home Shopping Channel."

Anita smiled. "Well, I guess a little like that. Anyway, people loved his pots and pans, and Jewel was very proud of him, even though she missed him."

"Did they have a pet?"

Anita frowned. "I think they had a cow. And oh, they had two goats and a donkey too. A little donkey so small that only Jewel could ride him."

"I'd like a donkey."

"Oh, I know, honey, wouldn't you just? So anyway, over the years Jewel and her mother and grandmother learned to be very self-sufficient; that means they learned to take good care of themselves without needing help from the father and the grandfather. That was the way they showed how much they loved them, by taking such good care of themselves that the men didn't need to worry about them."

"They still missed them, though."

"Like crazy, honey; that never stopped. But do you know what?"

"What?"

"It turns out that in one way, at least, that family wasn't poor at all; it was rich. Do you know why?"

"No."

"They had love. They had so much love between them that

sometimes after her mother or her grandmother had tucked Jewel in at night, she lay there just overflowing with love like a fountain."

"I like fountains."

"Well, and do you know what else? Even though Jewel's daddy wasn't in the room with her, he sent his love to her long distance every night. She couldn't see it or taste it or smell it, but she knew it was there just the same, all around her like a hug."

"Yes."

They had reached the outlying reaches of Hubbard. "I think Jewel and her family were a lot like us. Don't you?"

"No," Crystal said.

"No?"

"She had a donkey."

"Well, there is that," Anita conceded.

"I'd like a donkey."

Anita sighed and patted Crystal's leg. "I'm sure you would, honey. Look, we're home." She turned into Franklin Court. "There's nothing like a good story to pass the time."

She hauled on the emergency brake as hard as she could, and together she and Crystal flung open the car doors to the rain and made a run for the house.

Bob got home in time for dinner, and so did Doreen. For the first time in weeks they were all together for a meal just like a regular family. Anita spooned Hamburger Helper into a serving dish and passed around a bowl of creamed corn and a pan of scalloped potatoes.

"This looks real good, hon," Bob said, helping himself to ample portions. "Been a long time since you fixed this."

"It comes from a box," Doreen said.

"Don't matter to me," Bob said. "I like it anyway."

"So what did they tell you today at the college?" Anita said, spooning food onto Crystal's plate. "Did they like you?"

"It has nothing to do with liking me," Doreen said. She had way too much makeup on, as far as Anita was concerned. It made her look cheap and needy, but Anita knew better than to say anything. "It has to do with money," Doreen was saying. "They said they'd probably be able to give me some financial aid, but that I'd have to take out a student loan for most of it because my grades weren't good enough for a full scholarship."

"Hey, your grades are good," Bob protested. "Sawyer High gave you a diploma, didn't they?"

"Oh, please," Doreen said.

"You should go ahead and apply anyway, honey," Anita said. "At least it would mean you wouldn't have to wash sheets for the rest of your life."

"Are you kidding? I can't quit working. Who's going to support us, Danny? Yeah, right. I'm still paying on his goddamn truck."

"You should sell that," Bob said. "Hack's said he'd put it on the Vernon Ford lot for you and get you a good price."

"So what am I going to drive then?"

"Use the leftover money to buy something smaller, a Geo or something."

"Oh, right, a tin can."

"Then keep the truck, honey," Anita said. "You're the one who brought it up."

Doreen turned on her. "Are you going to pay for some of it?"

"You know we can't afford to do that," Anita said softly.

Bob kept his eyes locked on his food, eating fast.

"Yeah, well, that's what I'm saying," Doreen snapped. "I can't afford it either. So what am I supposed to do?"

Bob said, "Look. Me and Hack can drop you at the hospital in the mornings. Crystal's in Head Start anyway, and you can walk from the hospital to wherever your classes are." The college leased space in several buildings around town, mostly in the upstairs of retail stores and the Allstate insurance office. "Then you can catch a ride home with Hack and me when you're done."

"You mean, no car at all? No way."

Anita set down her cutlery. "Then what exactly is your plan?" she said evenly. "You're already living here for free."

Crystal stopped eating and put her hands in her lap apprehensively. Bob gave her a wink for courage.

"Yeah, well, it's not exactly the Taj Mahal," Doreen said.

"I only meant you need to make a budget of your expenses. Then you'll know what you can and can't afford."

"If you didn't want us here, you shouldn't have asked us to come home," Doreen said, and left the table crying. After grabbing her purse, she slammed out the front door and roared off in the truck.

Another meal gone to shit.

Anita jumped up and pulled Crystal onto her lap, but the child stiff-armed her.

"All right, honey, you can be excused," Anita said to Crystal softly. "It's all right, Mommy's just tired like Jewel's mother in the story. Why don't you see if you can find something on the Cartoon Network?" Anita had sent Bob in to pay up on their cable bill a few weeks ago, so Crystal would have something to look forward to in the evenings.

Crystal hopped down from the table and went off without looking at either Anita or Bob.

"What the hell?" Bob said.

Anita rubbed her eyes with the heels of her hands. "She's just got to grow up."

"Crystal?"

Anita gave him a look. "Doreen. We're not always going to be here to take care of her and Crystal."

Bob stared.

"Well, it's true," Anita said evenly. "I know it, and you know it too."

"Know what?"

"My weight? Your blood pressure?"

"Oh," said Bob. "Oh. Well, yeah."

"What did you think I meant?"

"I didn't know, that's why I was asking."

Anita pushed away from the table. "I wish I knew what was going on with you these days," she said, collecting plates.

"Nothing going on with me," Bob said.

"Like hell. You know this is the first night you've been home for supper in almost two weeks?"

"And look at the way it turned out," Bob joked.

"Honey, I'm in no mood for humor," Anita said, but she softened. He always looked like a little kid when she scolded him. "I'm so tired I fell asleep at the motel today."

"You're not sick, are you?" Bob said. "Are you?"

"I don't know, to tell you the truth. I'm sure run-down, I know that."

"If you think you're sick, though—"

"Something's been working on me, but I'm guessing I'm almost over it now. No fever today, and the diarrhea's almost gone."

Anita carried a big stack of dishes into the kitchen, and Bob followed with the rest. He shooed her aside and began to wash the dishes by hand. The dishwasher had been broken for going on two years. Anita picked up a dish towel and started drying.

"Where do you go anyway?" she said. "AA?"

"Mostly," Bob said, handing off the dripping scalloped potato platter.

Anita shook her head. "You aren't drinking again, are you?"

"Stone cold sober," Bob said. "Twelve weeks this Tuesday."

"Well, God does work in mysterious ways, His wonders to perform."

"I get a little credit too."

"Well, sure you do. I'm proud of you, honey. I hope you know that. I just can't figure out what turned you around."

"I love you."

"What?"

Bob stopped washing dishes, dripping water all over her clean floor with the sponge he still held in his hands. He didn't look a day over twelve. "I love you, baby," he said softly. "I always have, and I always will. I just want you to know that."

Anita's knees turned weak. Most days the man might as well be one more piece of junk in the side yard, but she loved him all the same.

That was the thing no one had figured out, not even Bunny. Even though he was skinny and scatterbrained, even though he was screwing up half the time, and drunk the rest, he still called her darlin' like he meant it.

Of that one thing, that single thing, Anita had no question.

# *chapter ten*

Last night, half crazed with insomnia, Rae Macy had had a waking nightmare of herself in black canvas kung fu shoes, polyester pants, and a self-collared pastel sweatshirt with big-eyed kittens on the front. It could happen. Not now, of course, not yet, but if she and Sam stayed in Sawyer for another ten or fifteen years, as Sam had lately taken to suggesting, she would take no bets. Just yesterday she had had to restrain herself from running to the Safeway in her sweatpants and one of Sam's old shirts. Why not? Everyone else here looked like hell. Still, let your standards slip, and the next thing you knew, you were shopping the sales rack at Sears.

At the bottom, though, her bravado was a brittle thing. She was lonely; she didn't know when she'd ever felt so lonely. Was there another person within fifty miles who cherished Chekhov the way she did? Sam didn't. God knows Hack Neary didn't. Rae wasn't even absolutely sure he could read.

Yet Hack Neary was the single thing she looked forward to each day with his secrets and sad eyes, his compulsive cheap seductions. Behind it hunkered some old tragedy or transgression. Could he have been an assassin in Vietnam? He refused to talk about the war except to say it had not always been the living hell you saw in movies, that not all his memories were dark. Rae had asked him if Bob had served there too, Bob lately having taken on the gutted look of a man who had seen more than he could live with. But Hack had laughed at that and said Bob was a charmed man; God had given him the flattest feet his draft board doctor had ever seen. Hack himself had had arches worthy of a ballerina.

Bob sometimes ate lunch with Rae and Hack in the showroom, unpacking two peanut butter and jelly sandwiches, a Hawaiian Punch juice box, and a Twinkie from a brown paper bag. It was the lunch of a schoolboy, no doubt a larger version of the one Crystal took to Head Start. Rae remembered the little girl in her pink plastic coat very well. Bob had brought her to the dealership several times since then, and she had played gravely until Bob or her mother got off work and could take her home. She rarely smiled outright, but Rae suspected it was the expression of a cautious nature rather than shame over her steel teeth. Plus she might not have had all that many reasons to smile. The mother was a laundress, and the father was a felon. Rae listened to Bob talk about Crystal and Doreen with appalled fascination.

"Hey, beautiful," Hack said from the doorway of her cubicle. She jumped.

"Hey," she said, flushing to her scalp.

"How about taking me to the Bobcat for coffee?"

"Now?"

"You too busy?"

He knew she wasn't too busy. She hadn't been busy since she'd started working here.

She stood, nearly as tall in her heels as he was, and swung her purse up over her shoulder. Hack watched her. As she passed in front of him, he put a hand on the small of her back, and it burned like fresh sin.

Francine looked after them with pure contempt as they left the dealership. Rae straightened her back, lifted her chin higher, and in the parking lot opened her own door and hoisted herself up into the cab of Hack's truck. She loved the muscularity of the pickup with its high running boards and stiff suspension, its toolbox in the back and deep, manly rumble. Hack pulled his door to amid a cloud of Brut aftershave.

As they pulled out into traffic, Rae tried to collect herself. She wasn't stupid; she knew what people were saying. They were saying she was having an affair with Hack. How did you deal with a thing like that? Yet she wouldn't give him up; she saw no reason to give him up. She was a writer, a thinker, an achiever, the wife of a successful attorney. Hack Neary was no part of that. He was an aberration, strong and fleeting as opium.

Hack pulled into the Bobcat's lot and parked right in front. When she opened her door, she slid out of the seat right into a puddle. She could feel the cold rainwater wicking up through her thin leather soles. Hack had already made it inside, smoothing down his hair as she struggled with the heavy door. By the time she got inside a waitress was already leading Hack back to a table.

The Bobcat's decor was Vintage Small-Town Sports. Bowling and softball league trophies lined the front windowsill and shelves behind the cash register; dozens of cheaply framed photographs hung on the walls, showing decades of Bobcat-sponsored teams squinting at the camera. On the wall by the restrooms a framed and autographed bowling shirt commemorated some three-hundred-point game.

After the waitress had filled cups of coffee for them and

taken their orders, Rae nodded toward the pictures. "Are you in any of those?"

"No."

"Why?"

"Knees." He stirred two packets of sugar into his cup.

"Ligaments?"

"Steel."

"You've had a knee replacement?"

"Let's just say I came back from Vietnam with a few extra parts."

"Ouch."

He shrugged. "So tell me about myself," he said, lifting the thick coffee mug with a foxy smile.

"Tell me about your sister."

"I don't have a sister."

"You said you read poems to her."

"I did."

"Then you have a sister."

"Had, princess." His face filled with something old and sad. He said softly, "I think you should tell me how wonderful I am."

Rae leaned in across the table. "What was her name?"

"Katherine. Katy."

"Pretty names."

"The Katydid was a pretty girl."

"Did she look like you?"

"Some people said so. I could never see it, though."

"Was she smart?"

"Real smart. Smart like you. She read all the time, everything."

"But not you?"

"Nah. I didn't have time for that. I worked. Anyway, the Katydid was the brains in the family."

"What was her favorite color?"

"Green." Hack smiled thinly. "You didn't see much green in Tin Spoon."

"Tin Spoon?"

"Nevada. Junky little cockroach town two hours outside Las Vegas. The town motto was, Glad you're here. Not that anyone was."

Their waitress slid their meals in front of them. Hack picked up half his Monte Cristo. Rae pushed waffle-cut fries around on her plate. She never had any appetite when she was with Hack.

"Why Tin Spoon?" she asked.

Hack shrugged. "Cherise ran out of money there."

"Cherise?"

"My mother."

"Oh."

"She was a whore," Hack said.

Rae gave him a look.

"Prostitution's legal in Nevada, princess. You don't believe my mother was a prostitute?"

"Sounds pretty unlikely."

"Only to you, princess," Hack said gently. "Only to you."

Rae didn't know what to say. She watched him finish his sandwich and wipe his mouth and beard neatly with his napkin. Say what you would, the man was fastidious. The waitress came around and freshened their coffee.

"You're bitter," Rae said when she was gone.

"Bitter? Nah. Why would I be bitter?"

"I don't know yet."

"Anyway, now it's your turn," he said, leaning back in his chair with his coffee mug. "Tell me about myself."

Rae shook her head in exasperation. "God, Hack. You're just

like a big kid who really believes this Christmas will be different."

"Maybe this Christmas *will* be different. Maybe you'll be under my tree."

Rae flushed. "That's not what I meant."

"I know it's not what you meant, princess."

"I wish you wouldn't call me that," she said.

"Why? It suits you."

"It's patronizing."

"It's a compliment. Where I come from, people like you are only on TV."

"Who are people like me?"

"Rich people," Hack said simply.

"Am I rich?"

"Sure. Fancy clothes, fancy lawyer husband, college education, condo on the beach. I bet your husband makes good money—what, fifty, sixty thou? I could do a lot with that."

Rae bridled. "It's not like it's just being given to us, you know. We've worked hard for everything we have, which isn't nearly as much as you think, and we both went to graduate school for years to get it."

Hack smiled, raising both hands in surrender.

Rae flushed and then deflated. "Francine gave me a look when we went out."

"What kind of a look?"

Rae shuddered. "Just a look."

"You want me to tell her not to look at you anymore?"

"You know that's not what I'm talking about."

"Yeah, I know," Hack said quietly. "Do you want us to not have lunch or coffee anymore?"

"I don't know."

"You want to stop?" Hack looked crestfallen.

Rae shook her head. "No."

Hack watched her. "We can, though."

"I know we can."

"Well, just so you know."

"I do. I know."

*"Fuck,"* said Hack.

"What?" Rae saw him looking over her shoulder at something in the front of the restaurant, and whatever it was, it wasn't good. She saw him straighten himself, straighten his shirtfront like he was preparing for combat.

Bunny slipped into the seat beside him.

Rae wondered if she would vomit.

"Hi," Bunny said exclusively to Hack.

"Hi," he said, his face a perfect mask. "What are you doing in town?"

"I had to pick up a prescription for Mom. I saw your truck."

"We were having lunch," he said. "Have you eaten?"

Bunny looked ready to detonate. Rae's pulse was roaring in her ears. "Look, I'd better get back," she said. "I can just walk."

Neither Hack nor Bunny acknowledged her or said a word.

"I'll just go then." Appalled, Rae fumbled in her purse, pulled out some money, and laid it blindly on the table. "It was nice to see you again," she said to Bunny lamely, ever the good girl. Bunny didn't even look at her. Neither did Hack.

Vernon Ford was four blocks away, and by the time she got there Rae was soaked. It didn't matter; she was stunned, reeling with guilt and humiliation. She walked past Francine blindly in her ruined pumps and her pointless suit, her eyes filling with bitter tears.

Hack got back half an hour later. His face was ashen.

He walked by Rae's cubicle without even slowing down.

Down at the public health clinic, Gabriella Lewis was getting impatient, but Bob couldn't help that. He had some questions, and he was going to stay until he got some answers, which was why he was sitting in this overheated little office with half-moons of sweat blooming under his arms.

"Look, it could be anything," the nurse was saying. "It's flu season, surely you've thought of that. Half the people in Sawyer are walking around in some stage of viral involvement. It doesn't mean they have AIDS."

"She says she's got lumps," Bob said stubbornly.

"Lumps?"

"Yeah, under her arms."

"Lymph nodes, you mean."

"Lymph nodes, yeah. Those."

Gabriella sighed. "That could be an early symptom, yes."

"Even if I'm not sick?"

"No two cases are alike. You know that; we've talked about that. You simply cannot measure your wife's health by your own condition. You might have years before you experience any symptoms. She may have only months. Or the other way around."

"So how the fuck am I supposed to know what's going on with her?"

"Her blood work, Bob. *Her blood work.*"

"Nope."

Gabriella Lewis threw up her hands. "For God's sake."

"She'd get scared, and there's no need for her to get scared. She don't need to know. I'll know for both of us."

"Has it occurred to you that you're depriving her of choices?"
Bob blinked at her. "What choices?"

"Say she's HIV positive but she isn't symptomatic yet. Doesn't she deserve to choose how to spend the time she has left, especially while she's still well? Maybe there's a place she's always wanted to see or a restaurant she's always wanted to try; maybe she has family—"

"Of course she has family."

"—that she'd like to reestablish contact with."

"What do you mean?"

"Maybe there are misunderstandings she'd like to clear up before she's too sick. Maybe she'd like to set her affairs in order."

"She's got no affairs except me and Doreen and Crystal. And Patrick, except he's halfway around the world and don't talk to us that often."

The nurse strained toward Bob across the desktop. "All I'm saying, Bob, is that yes, this may be the beginning of full-blown AIDS for her—or not. Maybe she isn't even HIV positive. You're depriving both of you of the right to know that and act accordingly."

Bob shook his head slowly. "It's not that simple."

"It's exactly that simple."

"If I tell her, she'll know about me and Warren. I can't have that."

"Don't you think she'd want to know?"

"That I'm going to die? What kind of a thing is that to know? Doreen's eating us out of house and home, and she's worried about Crystal, there's me and the drinking, and now you want her to know I'm dying? That's not love."

"It's honesty. They're often considered to be the same thing."

"With Nita and me it's different."

"You lie to each other?"

Bob worked a little piece of tobacco between his front teeth. "We spare each other things."

"Ah."

"What I'm saying is, I'll know for us both."

Gabriella sighed. "Look. Keep a close eye on her then, and keep me posted. Check her tongue and the inside of her mouth. If it gets white, she may have thrush, a yeast infection, but we can treat that. If she starts sounding gurgly deep in her chest or spikes a fever, get her in to see someone immediately, no matter what time of day it is. There is a rare kind of pneumonia we see in AIDS patients, and it kills. Do you understand?"

Bob nodded.

"And keep an eye on her weight. If she begins losing weight, she may need to go on food supplements. AIDS patients waste."

Bob cracked a tight smile. "She's always wanting to lose weight. She'd like that part."

Gabriella shook her head. Bob's smile failed. She watched him for a long minute.

"What?" Bob said.

"I'd like to check your T-cell levels."

"Yeah?"

"It will give us insight into your own state of health."

"My own state of health is that I'm fine."

Gabriella raised both hands high in surrender. Bob stood up and tugged his jacket straight. He had reached the door when she said softly, "I don't know if you pray at all, but if you do, this might be a good time to step things up a little."

But Bob didn't pray. He believed that people like him and Warren, people who'd strayed but not yet fallen, were too insignificant for God's full attention. If you were very bad, you got a bolt of lightning. If you were good—like Crystal was good, like Anita was—you got wings when it was over. But if you were Bob or Warren, damaged men of no particular accomplishment, you were overlooked by God and Satan alike. You were as invisible as a single drop of rain.

Bob didn't get back to the dealership from the clinic until three o'clock, but his service bay was as empty as when he'd left. All was right with the world, at least as far as cars went. Bob stuck his head in Hack's office and let him know that he was going out again. Hack maintained a no-questions-asked stance around the dealership as long as Marv Vernon wasn't around, and right now the old man was in Scottsdale, Arizona, playing in some old man's golf tournament.

"You want my truck?" Hack said.

"Nah. It's not raining anymore."

Hack lifted a dismissive hand, and Bob ducked out of the office again. Hack was a good man; God forgive Bob for any time he might have said otherwise, and there certainly had been times. But lately he'd come to find out Hack Neary understood that sometimes a man just needed to be left alone, and that was a rare quality. When he'd seen how Bob had stopped drinking and all, he'd loaned Bob his new dirt bike, no questions asked. Bob kept it stored out behind the used car lot. With the bike, he could get from the dealership to the homestead in ten minutes flat—less on a dry day when he could really open her up and fly. Rain gear took care of the rest. He was usually back at the dealership in time to hitch a ride home to Hubbard with Hack or Doreen.

Today he made it in just over nine minutes. He slowed down as he rounded the last turn, the one where the road wound down the valley wall like a ribbon of wonder, leading to the homestead he increasingly thought of as his. He and Anita had gone through dwellings like other people went through beater cars, running them down, using them up, moving on. Some had been livable enough. Not all of them, though. And Anita minded, he knew, though she hadn't talked about it since the eviction from Adams Street. She didn't need to. He'd seen her in Hack's living room, seen her face when she beheld for the thousandth time that goddamned baby grand and all those fucking rabbits. Yeah, he'd seen her.

Now, from his position on the hill, he found himself looking down upon bounty. The roof was completely mended with sound shakes he'd either split or harvested off the barn; the porch was propped up with a couple of two-by-fours, ready for more but stable in the meantime. He'd replaced all the rotten floorboards with barn salvage, and the windows were trimmed out with new frames. He figured he'd pay for a couple of windows out of the paycheck he'd be getting late next week.

The place was really beginning to look like something, goddamned if it wasn't.

He parked the dirt bike inside what was left of the barn—an old carcass of a thing now, whale bones left out in the open too long—and came through the newly weather-tight front door into the house. Dry as dry. He felt the unfamiliar thrill of pride. Warren would appreciate it. He had finally called Bob at the dealership late in the afternoon about three weeks ago, in the middle of February.

"Jesus, where the fuck have you been?" Bob said once Francine put the call through.

"Hell."

"Yeah, well, even hell must have a phone number and a mailing address."

"I'm in a place off Burnside."

"That's the part of town where all those bums are."

"Yeah. It's an okay place, though. I'm subletting it."

"Subletting?" Bob said.

"I'm renting it from the guy who's technically renting it, except he died, so now I'm him."

"You're renting an apartment as a dead guy?"

Warren sighed. "It's complicated, Bobby. This place is sort of a hand-me-down from one person with AIDS to another."

"Are you kidding? Jesus, Warren—I mean, *Jesus*. Sterilize everything. Get some Lysol or bleach. Do you have any bleach?"

"Honey," Warren said dryly, "it's way past time to bleach."

"Yeah, well," Bob conceded. "So, you know, are you okay?"

"Okay? Sure I'm okay. They fired me. Didn't I tell you they'd fire me? Well, they did. I have a KS lesion on my cheek now, so, you know."

"Shit," Bob said sympathetically.

"I'm going to try and get on as a checker or something at Fred Meyer. They have benefits."

"Yeah?" Bob said. He didn't really know anything about Fred Meyer. "So how's Sheryl doing?"

"I don't know. She's called me once or twice."

"You tell her anything?"

"At first I just told her I didn't love her anymore and that was why I was moving out, but Christ, Bobby, you should have seen her eyes." Warren's voice broke. "Hell, I figured the truth might actually come as good news, after that. So I told her the real reason."

"Yeah?"

"She said, *Oh*. That's all she said: *Oh*. I told her I didn't think we'd need to get divorced because she'd get everything as soon as I died, anyway, and we might as well save the legal fees."

"Fucking hell."

"Yeah," Warren said wearily. "So what about you, Bobby?"

"I went to the clinic a few weeks ago. I've got it too."

The line was quiet for a long time.

"Warren?" Bob said.

"Yeah. And Anita?"

"She doesn't know."

"Jesus, Bobby, you've got to tell her."

Bob's voice dropped. "The thing is, I'm fine, but she's got these lymph glands. Swollen nodes, or whatever."

"Are you sure?"

"Yeah, I'm sure. She's had them for a couple weeks now, maybe."

"Tell her," Warren said. "Bobby, you've got to tell her."

"Nah. I'll take care of her."

Warren's voice rose. "What about you? What about when you get sick, Bobby, huh? What are you going to do then?"

"Yeah, yeah. Listen, I'm working on the old homestead. No kidding, you should see it."

"What the fuck are you doing that for?"

Bob shrugged at the phone.

"Well, I guess that's good," Warren said.

"You should come down and see it."

"Jesus, Bobby."

"No, I mean it. Weyerhaeuser's put a road in through there. You can just about drive right up to it now."

"Yeah?"

"You should come back," Bob said quietly. "Come home."

"I've got to go," Warren said.

"Just tell me where to find you," Bob yelled, but Warren had already hung up. Bob started tearing up right there in his service bay. Jesus. He wiped his eyes on his coverall sleeve. Maybe he'd drive up there to Portland, find Warren, and bring him down. Maybe he just would.

Bob-and-Warren. They were closer than marriage, closer than brothers, than lovers. They were halves of the same whole, a unit indivisible. *One plus one equals one,* that's what they used to say to each other.

Warren had always been the smarter of the two of them, but also more scared. He was afraid of high winds, low bushes, loud noises, certain tones of voice, dying in his sleep. Fear was what had started it all, their spooning up at night when they first started staying over at the homestead. Warren was scared, and Bob was cold, so they started swapping body heat for courage. Bob wrapped his arms around Warren's skinny chest at night and found him no more substantial than a sheaf of twigs, of bird bones. Bob held on, and Warren whispered stories about princes and wizards, about wise men and saints. Love stories, though Bob didn't recognize them then. Spooned up like that on the crackling mattress ticking, his little pecker would bloom, and then Warren's would too, and it had felt good and natural, them playing; something lambs would do, something free and unimportant, like picking your nose. Warren and him, they'd had that secret between them all these years: the fact that they *did that* when they were alone. To Bob, *that* wasn't sex, not the hot, bottomless, black velvet well you could sink down into and die happy. Sex was Anita, the only woman Bob had ever wanted, though some others were nice to look at, even ornamental. And he'd look, sure, he'd look; he was a man, wasn't he? God had given him eyes. Yes, he'd looked, all right, but he'd never touched, and that was all right with him. Anita had been beautiful enough to last him, and not just when they were younger. She'd been beautiful all the time, even when her hair was messy and her eyes weren't made up and she'd put on some pounds. Not that he'd ever told her. Not that she'd believe him if he did. He had tried once or twice to tell Warren about her, about what it felt like to love her, but Warren had sulked.

"I don't know why you don't like her," Bob used to say, running his hands through his hair in vexation.

"I like her," Warren said defensively.

"Well, it sure doesn't seem like it."

"I just miss doing stuff by ourselves."

"What stuff?" Bob asked, because even then they were finding time to *do that*, even if it was only back in the woods at the end of Chollum Road.

"I don't know, go out to the homestead. Talk."

"We're talking now," Bob would point out, but Warren's eyes would get watery, Bob would chuff in exasperation, and the conversation would be over one more time. It only got better when Bob was able to convince him to date Sheryl Miller so Anita would have another girl to go to the bathroom with and Warren wouldn't feel left out. Sheryl, with her skinny legs and food allergies, so shy, so needy herself that Warren had seemed robust in her presence. Rumor had it that her father beat her, beat her mother, but she'd never talk about it when Warren asked. They'd coupled up like two broken things, gentle with each other in case they stumbled on something that hurt. It had been touching, seeing Warren pull out chairs for Sheryl, order a hamburger for her so she didn't have to speak in public. Sheryl had looked just like a doe with her big eyes and the true, trusting nature of a preacher's daughter. Anita used to say that even when she and Warren joined forces, the two of them could barely stand up in a medium wind; anything stronger, and they'd be blown across three counties. They went bowling together over in Sawyer sometimes, and Sheryl would use a child's ball, her hands were that small. Bob always remembered that about her, the way she looked rolling those black bowling balls so weakly they wobbled down the alley, bumped into the pins, and stopped. Warren had tried to teach her to be more forceful, to use at least an eleven-pound ball that could pick up speed, but she'd start to cry and Warren would look stricken and they'd end up huddled miserably in the gallery, waiting for Bob and Anita to finish and drive them home.

Sheryl. As Bob recalled, she'd collected thimbles. They were her single passion, which struck Anita, for one, as pretty damned sad. "If her father really beats her, you'd think she could find something to collect that would at least protect her better—I don't know, welder's face shields or baseball catcher's suits or fencing masks."

"Does he beat her?"

"That's what they say. She sure is funny about changing in the girls' locker room, I'll tell you that. She always goes into a bathroom stall. One time Bernadette walked in on her in the nurse's office, and she said she saw bruises all over her back." Bernadette—that had been before Hack changed her name to Bunny.

"Bernadette lies," Bob had pointed out.

"Sheryl lies. C'mon, everyone does. You never lie?"

"Not unless I have to."

"So when do you have to?" Anita asked. "To me?"

"Nah, come on, Anita. I wouldn't lie to you."

"Bet you would."

"Would you lie to me?" Bob said.

"If I had to, I guess I would."

"Why would you have to?"

"I don't *know*, Bobby, I'm just saying. And I bet it's the exact same way for you, only you're not honest enough to say it."

Well, she'd been right about that, the way she'd turned out to be right about most things over the years. That he drank because it was easier than trying; that he sabotaged things when they were going well. That he was a good man who'd never amount to shit, and that it was his own damned fault. But he was proving her wrong now, boy. He was sure going to have something to show her when the homestead was all done, her and Warren. Maybe he'd even take Hack Neary out there one day. Maybe he just would.

It was past dark when Bob finally got back to the dealership and parked the little dirt bike around back. He was startled to see Anita sitting perfectly still in a chair in the showroom, her face all puffy and pale, her hands folded in her lap like church. She stood up when she saw him.

"Hey, baby," he said, wiping his hands and face on a rag.

Anita waited until he was close enough to touch her. "Sheryl just called," she said. "Honey, Warren died last night. I'm so sorry."

*chapter eleven*

Nobody dies of pneumonia anymore," Bunny was saying to Anita. They were folding clothes at Anita's kitchen table and drinking coffee laced with Bailey's Irish Cream. "Nobody young and healthy anyway."

"I know," Anita said, matching socks. "That's exactly what I said."

"So what did Bob say?"

"It just made him mad. He said if Sheryl said it was pneumonia, it was pneumonia."

"Well, I bet she could sue that doctor," Bunny said, flicking a lint ball off a pair of Bob's work pants. "I mean, tell me the last time you heard of someone dying of pneumonia who wasn't eighty years old or a transplant patient or something like that. Name one person. See? You can't. I bet the doctor fucked up and gave him the wrong antibiotic or something. You should tell her, Nita."

"Maybe," Anita said.

"Are you going to the funeral?"

"They aren't having one. Sheryl said Warren told her once if he died, he didn't want any service."

"He said that?"

"Two months ago."

"Maybe he had a premonition or something," Bunny said. "You hear about that happening sometimes."

"I don't know, everybody says that kind of stuff. Haven't you ever told Hack where you want to be buried?" Anita said.

"Well, sure, but that's only so he won't put me next to Daddy. Can you imagine having to spend all eternity next to the bastard?"

Anita snorted appreciatively. She hadn't liked Bunny's father either. He had always stared at her breasts.

"Not even cemetery services, though?" Bunny said.

"No, he wanted to be cremated. You know him and Sheryl were separated, right? Well, she said why would he want to be around her, dead, when he didn't want to be around her when he was alive? So Bob had her send the ashes down here." Anita nodded in the direction of the living room.

"You mean that's him in there?" Bunny said, looking.

"Uh-huh."

Bunny shuddered. "It would give me the willies knowing that Warren Bigelow was sitting on my TV set in a jar." She went and picked up the green urn and turned it around in her hand, finally turning it completely upside down. "I hope she didn't pay much for this. I think it came from the Sentry Market. Remember when they were doing those giveaways, a free vase or serving dish or whatever for every place setting you bought? Mom picked up a couple just for the hell of it, she thought they were so pretty. They sure break easy, though; plus you just look at them wrong, and they chip." Bunny set the jar back down on the television gingerly and nudged it into place with a fingertip. "It was made in India," she said, returning to the table and dipping into the heaped laundry basket again. "You don't think of them making something like a jar over there, just those cheap bed-spreads you can't wash with anything else. We had one once that turned Hack's T-shirts completely pink, and you know Hack isn't going to wear a pink T-shirt even if no one can see it. I had to buy him all new."

Anita nodded, snapping towels straight and folding them. Every one of them had a frayed place in the selvage.

"Well, I guess you can't say no to something like that, though, taking someone's ashes and all," Bunny ruminated, pulling up a pair of Crystal's overalls from the clothes basket. "I mean, what if Sheryl would have just put them in the garbage or something?"

"That's the thing," Anita said.

"So how's Bob taking it?"

"Bad." Anita smoothed the stack of towels that was smooth already. "I went to put out the trash yesterday, and he was just standing there in the rain—no hat, no jacket, nothing, just standing there."

Bunny raised her eyebrows. "He drinking again?"

"No."

"You sure?"

Anita gave her a look.

"It just sounded like he might have been, doing something like that."

"Well, he wasn't." Anita folded a small pair of underpants. They were Crystal's favorites, the ones with a picture of Winnie-the-Pooh on the butt. Anita had bought her a set of them, one pair for every day of the week, a different character on each one.

"Let me see those," Bunny said, holding out her hand. Anita passed her a pair. "They're sure cute," Bunny said. "Where'd you find them? Fanny's granddaughter Maisy's crazy about Winnie-the-Pooh. Fanny said it's about enough to drive them all around the bend. She'd sure like these, though."

"Wal-Mart. They were on sale a couple of weeks ago."

"I'll have to tell her."

"Crystal can't wait for Wednesdays, because she gets to wear Eeyore," Anita said, taking the underpants back from Bunny and folding them. "She hasn't figured out that she can wear Wednesdays any damn day she wants to."

"Well, because the underpants police might tell on her."

"Yeah." Anita laughed softly. "I told Doreen to keep her mouth shut about it; this way it's good practice for the days of the week."

"Sure." Bunny brought over the Bailey's from the counter. "You want some more?"

Anita held up her hand. "I've still got some."

Bunny added some to her mug and screwed the cap on loosely, for when they wanted more.

"So anyways," Anita said, "Doreen got mad at me for buying them because she doesn't have the money to pay me back."

"Pay you back for what?" Bunny said, drinking.

"The *underpants*. I told her they were a gift, but she got mad anyway." Anita sighed. "That girl loses her temper at every little thing anymore, especially at Crystal. I feel like I spend half my time just keeping the two of them separated, I swear."

"Well, Doreen's got a lot on her mind," Bunny said, licking a dribble of Bailey's from the outside of her mug.

"Yeah. Did I tell you about Danny's divorce attorney? The boy is sitting there fat and happy in prison, contributing exactly zip to the family, and Doreen gets a call from his slimeball lawyer saying Doreen will have to turn over half their bank account to him."

"Is she going to fight it?"

"No, spend it. That way there won't be anything for Danny to get."

Bunny clucked sympathetically.

"They only have two hundred and sixty-six dollars anyway, and that's with her working two jobs." Doreen had taken a night shift at the Dairy Queen in Hubbard on top of her hospital job over in Sawyer. "She's working her ass off to keep her and Crystal going, and he's sitting there in that penitentiary in Salem getting all his food and clothes for free."

"Aw, honey."

"You know what she said? She said she should just go out and knock over a bank or something, and she'd be set for life. No kids, no bills, no husband holding his damn hand out."

"Well, she does have a point. Not that she should do it, but she's only nineteen, Nita," Bunny said, as though Anita didn't know it. "Is that Tommy Elliott still coming around?"

"He is, but Doreen won't have much to do with him. He has that cerebral palsy, and it makes him walk sort of herky-jerky. He's a nice boy, but she says it embarrasses her to go anywhere with him because people look."

"Doesn't his father own the Office Place?"

"Yeah. It's a good business. I pointed that out, but she just said, 'What, so he's going to give me and Crystal free pens and pencils for the rest of our lives?' "

"She's going to have to get a hold of herself, or she'll be nothing but a smoking ruin by the time she's twenty-five," Bunny said.

"You try telling her that, though. She just slams her bedroom door and won't come out until morning, not even to tell Crystal night-night. Me and Bob, we're going to end up raising that child yet, see if we don't. I told Bob so just last night."

"What did he say?"

"Nothing. He just gave me a funny look."

"He's probably worried about you."

"If he was worried about me, he'd stay home sometimes and help around the damned house."

"You look better, though, I have to say. Maybe it's burned itself out."

"Maybe so," Anita said. "I've felt better the last couple of days, but I didn't want to jinx it by saying anything, you know? God be praised."

"God be praised," Bunny echoed, and held up her spiked coffee mug to clink against Anita's.

Hack absently blotted water off the table at the Wayside with his Budweiser coaster. Shirl was half done with her beer already. Most women could nurse a beer forever, but not Shirl. She'd called him at work and asked him to meet her here for a beer and some talk. Well, she was talking, all right. "I'm saying keep your dick in your pocket. That's all I'm saying. What's between you and Bunny is between you and Bunny. Just keep your damned dick to yourself."

"Jesus, Shirl."

She looked at him shrewdly. "You think I'm just some old gal, don't you? Just some big old cow who's never seen the world—"

"I don't think that."

"—but I've seen a thing or two. I know you, and I know my daughter. If you're cheating on Bunny, she'll never be able to forget it, and she'll never let you forget it either. She's a tough nut. She hangs on. When she was a little girl, she used to sulk for days if she didn't get something she had her sights set on. For whatever reason, she has her sights set on you, and she has ever since she first laid eyes on you. You know what she told me that day? She said, 'I just met my husband.' That's just how she put it: 'I just met my husband.' She meant she'd seen you. She was crazy about you then, and she's just as crazy about you now. Maybe more."

Hack took a steadying breath. "Look, Shirl, I've always been straight with you. You and Bunny can believe me or not. This is the last time I'm going to say it to you, and I've already said it for the last time to Bunny: Rae Macy is an employee. That's all. I know where my goddamn dick belongs. But let me ask you something. How come no matter what I do, you and Bunny think it has to do with sex? Hell, I put on a new pair of briefs that *Bunny bought me* in the first place, and she starts sulking. Why does it always have to do with sex?"

"Because you're a man, son," Shirl said dryly, narrowing her small eyes in amusement. "Sex is your brass ring, your first-place ribbon, the hot fudge on your sundae. I know you, mister. I always have."

"Shit, Bunny gets all bent out of shape if I go to Portland to see Vinny, for chrissakes."

"Uh-huh. That's been a hard thing between you, all these years. Bunny's cried many a bitter tear about you and that child. She's a jealous woman, and it's a hard thing to be jealous of your own daughter."

"There's never been any funny stuff between me and Vinny, Shirl, and you know it."

"Course I know it, baby," Shirl soothed. "Did I ever say there had? But you have a powerful feeling for that girl, and Bunny's always been one to keep good things for herself."

"Yeah." Hack shook his head.

"How come you've never had kids of your own?"

Hack shrugged.

"Well, you've been a real good father to that child, better than that worthless piece-of-shit JoJo would've ever been. Man couldn't spend a month under one roof without turning mean—meanest boy I ever knew. We were glad when he took off. Good riddance, I told Bunny. Vinny, she didn't get anything of his bad nature, and I thank the Lord for that. That little girl always had the sweetest temper, sweeter than Bunny even, and Bunny was a sweet one when she was little." Shirl cracked a wicked smile. "Course, she's toughened up some over the years."

"Some," Hack said, grinning.

"Hell, I don't know, she always did feel she was getting a smaller piece of the pie than everybody else. I don't know why; never did. Maybe if she'd gotten more attention from her daddy, or maybe that's just bullshit, all that crap about how important it is to be the apple of your daddy's eye or whatever. I never have been able to make up my mind about it. When I was little, we were lucky if our daddy remembered our names, he was gone that much.

"My daddy never did forgive my mother for having us eight girls and just one boy." Shirl chuckled. "We lived way upriver in the woods, but every Sunday we kids came down here to church by boat. My mother didn't get to set foot inside that church for seven years straight one time, she was so tied down with the babies. There was no such thing as a crying room in those days; kids were expected to behave or stay home. Course, I was the youngest, and by the time I was old enough to remember, my mother was sitting right up there in the front pew regularly, belting out 'Rock of Ages.' The woman had feeling, but she could *not* carry a tune."

"You want another beer?" Hack said.

"Talked me into it," said Shirl, holding out her glass.

Hack supposed it was his lot in life to be surrounded by strong women. There was Shirl, of course, and Cherise, but there'd also been Minna Tallhorse, who was stronger than anyone he'd ever met, male or female.

The key to Minna's strength, Hack thought, lay in her ability to hunker down and take it when anyone else would have run screaming from the room. She was there the day Cherise came back, fifteen months after disappearing without a word. Hack had walked into the apartment to find Cherise drunk, the Katydid crying, and Minna Tallhorse towering over the living room like an avenging angel. Hack had already half prepared himself, having seen parked in front of the apartment the kind of flashy piece-of-shit car Cherise liked to drive, in this case a Camaro the color of freshly spilled blood.

When he came into the living room, Cherise was bearing down on the Katydid. One of Katy's eyes was swelling shut.

He didn't remember lunging for Cherise, but he must have. What he did remember was Minna Tallhorse clapping restraining hands on both of them and holding them apart until they'd calmed down. She pushed Cherise into a chair across the room and motioned for Hack to sit next to the Katydid on the sofa.

"Well, then," Minna Tallhorse said, "you must be the mother."

So she must have just come in a minute before Hack.

"Yeah," Cherise said. "And who the fuck must you be?"

"She's our friend," said Katy.

"Well, I'm back now," Cherise said. "You don't need a friend."

"My name is Minna Tallhorse. I'm a social worker. Your children have been under my supervision for the last eleven months."

"Yeah?" Cherise said, faltering but still shifty-eyed, looking for the angles. "Well, they're real good kids."

"I'm aware of that," Minna said.

"So you can go."

"What—and miss the fun?"

Cherise subsided.

"How come she hit you?" Hack asked Katy.

"I told her I wished she hadn't come back."

Cherise dug in her bag for a cigarette and lighter, making a production out of ignoring Minna Tallhorse. She picked a fleck of tobacco off her tongue and flicked it onto the floor, then walked across the room and fingered the cheap cotton throws Minna had bought for them to put over the battered sofa.

"Nice touches," Cherise said.

"What are you even doing here? This isn't your apartment anymore," Hack said. He could feel Minna's eyes burning behind him like coals.

"Is that right?" Cherise said.

"Yeah, that's right."

"Take a look at the name on the lease, kiddo. You know, you've sure turned out mouthy. She let you get away with that?" Cherise jerked her chin in Minna's direction. "Or maybe she's the one who taught you."

Behind him Hack could feel the Katydid's fingers latch on to his belt, ready to restrain him.

"She's helped us," Hack said.

"And I'm real glad. Now say thank you so she can leave."

"Isn't it fun to think it might be that simple?" Minna took a step forward. "The way I see it, you have a couple of chances to do something right. You can simply walk back out the door, which is the easiest thing. Or you can petition the state— through me, of course—to return the children to your care. Let's see, you'll need four consecutive pay stubs to verify your current ongoing employment, plus, of course, you'll have to prove that the state of Nevada's definitions of desertion and neglect don't apply in your case. Not to mention you'll have to convince me that you haven't been drinking, which I'll be legally obligated to include in my brief to the court, never mind the fact of your having struck your daughter. But if you feel full of vigor, by all means try it. You might even get a judgment from the courts before Hack turns eighteen, and if they turn down your request for custody, which of course they will, here's the beauty part: You'll have refined your communications skills, which may help you get increasingly responsible jobs in, say, the food service or hospitality industry. It's entirely up to you, of course, but in either case you should probably be thinking of which motel you plan to stay in tonight."

"I'm not going anywhere," Cherise said. "My name's on the fucking lease for this dump. I have the right."

"Well, no," Minna said. "Actually, you've pretty much done yourself in in the rights department."

Cherise looked at them all, dropped her burning cigarette onto the floor, slowly ground it into the linoleum, and stalked out of the apartment with her middle finger raised. A minute later they heard the Camaro roar off, its tires spinning in the gravel.

"Well," said Minna, "that was bracing."

"You were great," Hack said.

"Was it true, what you said to her?" Katy asked.

"Which part?" said Minna.

"All of it. It sounded true," said Katy.

"Yes," Minna said, starting to smile. "It did, didn't it?"

Hack watched Shirl tuck into her fresh beer.

All these years, and suddenly the past was leaching out of him like poison.

"What are you thinking about, baby?" Shirl said, watching him. "You're sure working something over."

"Nah. Just enjoying your company."

"Well, there's a pile of shit," said Shirl.

A week later Minna Tallhorse brought them gifts, small boxes wrapped in red—a powerful color, she told them, a lucky color. She'd been wrong about that, but of course they hadn't known it then. They'd opened the boxes with excitement, presents being a rarity. Hack pulled out a sterling silver dog tag on a chain, and the Katydid had a bracelet. Both were engraved with Minna's name and phone numbers.

They were odd gifts, if handsome.

"In case," she said, as though that explained anything.

"In case what?" said the Katydid.

"Just in case."

"You ready to go?" Shirl asked Hack. "Since you're not going to tell me any secrets."

"I don't have any secrets," Hack said, draining the last of his beer.

"Like hell, son," Shirl said, reaching across the table to pat his cheek. "Like hell."

As promised, Minna Tallhorse came over for dinner every Thursday. Hack liked to hear her stories. They often had to do with her family, as large as Hack's was small, though no less harrowing to live among. Most of her stories chronicled damage: wrecked cars, wrecked health, wrecked expectations and hopes. A brother who blew another brother's foot off with a shotgun; a cousin who got pregnant too soon and died in childbirth at fourteen, the fetus born dead, with cloven hands like hooves. Drunks, drug addicts, incorrigible losers, unrepentant slackers and wastrels and pests. The circle was broad, the familial bed roomy. Cousins bedded with cousins, and sometimes sons with daughters. From such blighted roots Minna Tallhorse had sprung, anomalously straight and strong. With that strength she blazed a trail for him and the Katydid right there in Tin Spoon, Nevada, a trail that led to school every day when otherwise Hack would have dropped out sooner; a trail to the cool interior of the public library, where the Katydid found salvation; to the market where Hack worked thirty hours a week humping groceries for a steady wage. Her legacy was a good and lasting one, and if she had ultimately failed to save them from harm, she had nevertheless managed to hold it at bay. For nearly five years in all, Minna Tallhouse had given them shelter, a wispy haven, a rickety, straw-built thing, granted, but nevertheless able to withstand almost five years of bad weather.

When Hack got home, Bunny wasn't there. He wasn't in the mood for silence, so he picked up the phone and called Vinny's apartment. She answered on the second ring. In the background Hack could hear girls laughing. "Hiya, kiddo. Sounds like you're having a party."

"Hack! When are you coming up to see me again?"

Her voice was high and light, the voice of a young girl. His heart lifted. "When do you want me?"

"Anytime, you know that."

"You working this Saturday?"

"Not at dinnertime."

"I bet you say that to all your dates."

"Only the ones with money." Vinny laughed.

"Oh, and that's me, Mr. Money?"

"Oh, Hack, you know I'm only teasing."

"Yeah, I know. So how's tricks?"

"Okay. They gave me more hours," Vinny said.

"Yeah?"

"I heard you get a raise at the end of six months too if they like you. My six-month anniversary's in three weeks."

"You want me to call and put in a good word for you?" Hack offered.

"Like that would help."

Hack laughed softly. He was always threatening to intervene on her behalf and really screw things up. He looked at his watch: just about time for the evening news. "Okay, Vin, I've got to go."

"Come up soon, though," she said.

"Soon," he promised.

He went into the living room, switched on the news, and awaited Bunny among the rabbits. She hadn't spoken to him since yesterday at the Bobcat. God, he was tired of her complaints about his imagined unfaithfulness, his inadequate passion for her, his dirt bikes and side buys, even though he'd gotten her the goddamn washing machine she wanted, a top-of-the-line Maytag that cost more than all the dirt bikes he'd ever bought, combined.

Hack had asked Minna Tallhorse once why she wasn't married. She'd said, "You've obviously never met my brothers-in-law." Even so, she'd probably found somebody by now. Women needed men, in the end, even when they pretended they didn't, even when men made them crazy, like they did to Bunny.

Even if Hack had been able to look down the road, he guessed he'd probably still have married Bunny. She was an okay wife. She loved him; he knew that. She loved him, and she wanted him to love her back, and he guessed it wasn't her fault that she wanted more than he had to give to her or anyone. Women didn't want to hear, *I'll love you as much as I can.* They wanted to hear, *You're all I'll ever need.* He couldn't help that. A leaky vessel couldn't hold more water than it could hold, and no amount of wishing was ever going to fix it.

Just before the weather report, Hack heard the door from the garage bang open and then shut. Bunny must have come in with a load of groceries, from the sounds of bags and cans landing hard on the kitchen counters. Hack pushed himself out of his recliner and went to help, something he didn't do except when he was in the doghouse.

"Hey," he said carefully, probing her mood like a wound.

"Hey."

They stacked cans.

"You left work early today," Bunny said. "I called, but they said you were gone."

"Yeah. I met somebody for a beer."

Bunny looked at him out of the corner of her eye. A muscle in her cheek jumped.

"Jesus, Bunny, lighten up," said Hack. Her jaws were so tightly clenched Hack could hear her molars grinding. "You know who I met at the Wayside? Your mother. She wanted to talk to me about my dick. Imagine my surprise. You probably know about that, though."

Bunny cracked open a Pepsi, slapped a cut of meat on the counter.

"I talked to Vinny today," he said.

"Yeah?"

"She thinks she's going to get a raise soon."

"That's good."

"She wanted to know when you'd be coming to see her. She's thinking you don't give a shit." He was lying, but somebody had to say it. "I just told her you didn't like driving in Portland."

"That's not true," Bunny said, stung.

"Yeah, well, what else am I supposed to tell her? You've made one visit, Bunny. One. What's the kid supposed to think?"

"She can come down here anytime she wants."

"The reason you won't go up there is you're busy spying on me. Imagine what it was like, defending my dick to your mother in the middle of the Wayside. I'm sick of this shit, Bunny. You hear me? *I am sick of this shit with you.*"

He saw Bunny's knuckles turn white as she gripped the countertop, but she didn't turn to look at him. It didn't matter; he was done. He walked out of the kitchen, into the sanctuary of his garage and tools. At least out there if something was broken, he stood a reasonable chance of fixing it.

He didn't come into the house until midnight, when he was sure Bunny was asleep. She'd been opening the Anchor all week. With luck he wouldn't see her awake again until tomorrow night, and even then he might just talk to old Marv and snag an evening's invitation to the Elks.

To hell with her. To hell with them all.

Sometimes Bob missed Warren like a fist clenched in his gut so hard it made him short of breath. But now, standing on the homestead road, there was only silence and the memory of those two little doll's-eye dots of cancer, too small to kill some-one. Hadn't they been too small to kill someone? But Anita said it couldn't have been pneumonia.

Whatever it was, Warren must have known what was coming. "Are you scared, Bobby?" he'd whispered over the phone in late February just a week before he died.

"No."

"I am. I'm scared all the time."

But Bob had heard a lifetime of that. He brushed it off.

"Will you get your T-cells checked at least?" Warren had pleaded.

"You and that nurse. I'll tell you the same thing I told her. I'm not getting the damned test because there's no point in it."

"What do you mean, no point? Of course there's a point."

"I'm going to die anyway, right? Isn't that what you all keep telling me? I don't want to know how fast I'm going down. I'm good right now. I don't feel sick. I don't look sick. Could be I'm *not* sick. Could be it's all a goddamned mistake. Who's to say no? Those doctors don't know everything. I figure I'm going to keep working on the homestead, I'm going to keep doing exactly what I've been doing until I can't do it anymore."

Bob could hear Warren breathing on the other end of the line, fast and light from high in his lungs. He whispered, "I love you, Bobby."

And because he'd been pissed off, Bob had said, "Yeah, okay."

Just fucking *Yeah, okay.*

It had been the last time they'd talked.

He hadn't gotten to say it back: I love you too. I love you like myself, like blood family—more than blood family. I love you, and I will keep you safe. He hadn't said that.

He'd meant to say that; he'd even thought it, loud and clear as a prayer. But he hadn't said it.

Now he could say it. Now that it was too late.

He guessed it was too late for a lot of things. Like the chance for him and Anita to get old in matching recliners they'd buy on credit at La-Z-Boy. Him and Anita, they'd joked about that for years, how they were going to get a pair of recliners and a fine TV and a fancy entertainment center to put it in, and they were going to get old right there in their living room with their feet up and their hands around ice-cold cans of beer, yelling at the sportscasters and the newscasters and the new generation of young people. Wasn't that what old folks did while the young bucks were screwing and having babies and making money? Of course, not everybody made money. Look at him; look at Warren. They'd provided the best they could, but that hadn't been saying much.

Until now. Now Bob was doing something worth crowing about. He had all the windows bought, and half of them installed. He had rebuilt the back porch out of salvage and sweat, roughed in a staircase to a new loft in the rafters. He had hewn broad-plank doors from windfall in the woods, built a lean-to for firewood, and cut enough wood to see them through a season. What he needed now were salvaged bricks to rebuild the chimney and the fireplace.

*Are you scared, Bobby?*

Not nearly. He was dying, and for the first time in his life things were looking up.

## chapter twelve

W arren and Sheryl and Bob and Anita were married in a
simple double ceremony at the Elks over in Sawyer, the
site of Anita's near triumph at the Miss Harrison County
Pageant, now the place of her culminating dreams. She and Bob
drifted down the aisle first, Anita woozy with sentiment and
morning sickness, Bob stiff in a rented blue tux. They passed
under an arch of pink and white balloons, along an aisle lined
with potted azaleas, to the spot they'd chosen in front of the
Grand Elder's chair, filled for the occasion with a huge spray of
pink roses and baby's breath. Anita had wept from start to finish,
spongy with sentiment and yo-yoing hormones, grateful she'd
chosen waterproof mascara. Halfway through the vows her
mother had tiptoed down the aisle and handed her a Kleenex, to
the everlasting amusement of all.

Warren and Sheryl, by contrast, swayed beside them in an
agony of embarrassment and reservation. Sheryl once told Anita
she remembered nothing about the ceremony, only the terrible
effort it had taken not to faint. She was still a virgin, though she
and Warren had tried hard to act as though they weren't, the two
of them having gone parking numerous times with Bob and

Anita, steaming up the windows of Bob's big Buick up at the Cape Mano lookout. Despite the opportunity, Warren had never done anything more than kiss her, and that had been chastely with closed lips. She told Anita it was years before she realized that that was not how other men kissed. Sex had been the same way, even on their wedding night. Warren was in and out of her like a rabbit, insisting on total darkness and the briefest possible penetration. Next door they could hear Bob and Anita humping like crazy, the headboard knocking on the wall between their two rooms at the airport Best Western all night long. Next morning they all flew off to Disneyland, where Anita spent four days vomiting on the rides and Sheryl anticipated with mounting dread the coming night, each one the same: the perfunctory kisses, the reluctant penis, the embarrassment.

Anita didn't know how Sheryl had stood it all those years. She told Bob what Sheryl had said, but Bob had only shrugged and said not everyone was as highly sexed as they were. Anita didn't know about that, but she let it drop. It was obvious that Bob didn't share whatever problem Warren might have. Patrick had been born seven months after the wedding, and Bob and Anita had had sex regularly right up to the birth and started again just one week later. It was only in later years that they'd slowed down, but that had been Anita's doing, not Bob's. She was tired from the kids all day, plus working at whatever job she could find—chambermaiding, clerking at gift shops, scooping ice cream at Passionetta's until she got tendinitis so bad that for months she could barely lift a spoon.

Mostly, though, Anita attributed her lack of lasting sexual enthusiasm to their living conditions: seven apartments in the first four years of marriage, all of them dumps. It was her belief that you could muster enthusiasm for scraping other people's dirt off floors and windowsills for only so long before your expectations started to dim. For Anita it had been a lasting struggle to keep her standards up. She'd bring Bunny over, and the two of them would scrub and scour all day while the kids played with pots and pans or watched hours of cartoons. But even with company there was only so much cheeriness you could fake before you had to acknowledge to yourself and to the world that you were living in a shithole.

Sheryl and Warren seemed to have better luck finding the apartments Anita never could, ones with cute window boxes or new carpets and curtains. After Sheryl and Warren had moved up to Portland, Anita only saw them once or twice. That had been all right with her. She was too damned busy to care, by then, what with the everlasting laundry and cooking and cleaning, with Doreen's croup and Patrick's recurrent ear infections. And since Sheryl and Warren never had kids—Anita privately thought that Sheryl, with all her food allergies and finickiness, was just the type to be barren—there wasn't really anything for Anita to talk with Sheryl about.

Warren never came down to Hubbard at all once they moved away either. Anita thought that was peculiar. How could you not want to come home? But then she couldn't imagine moving away in the first place. Granted, neither Bob nor Warren had a decent family, but what about your friends, your favorite spots? When she asked Bob once why they never came back, Bob just said, "Not everyone has roots like you do, Nita." Plus Warren got that job with the produce company and became an expert on lettuces or whatever, which probably took up a lot of his time.

She wished that Bob had Warren's drive. How many times had she suggested to him that he might need to get a second job? He never did, so she had had to, and that had been a wedge between them ever since, his inability to support them, her fatigue and frustration. As far as that went, the way they were living now—supporting Doreen and Crystal, trying to put decent food on the table—was nothing new. Anita took whatever work came her way. Lately she'd been helping out Marge and Larry Hopkins at the Seaview Motel.

Anita had thought of telling Doreen to pull Crystal out of Head Start for now and save the money, that Anita would look after her, but it was probably good for Crystal to have little friends to play with. She worried about Crystal. Doreen was mean to her, like Crystal was to blame for all her problems, even though she was only three. If Anita didn't cook a meal every night, Crystal would probably be living on nothing but peanut butter and jelly. You could probably get rickets or scurvy or whatever from that. So Anita made meat loaf and tuna noodle casserole, and if there wasn't anything else in the house, she fried bologna. On a good week, she bought Lucky Charms and a half gallon of whole milk instead of that low-fat watery shit Doreen picked up at the market to keep her weight down. Children needed fat and calories, Anita was sure. And Crystal liked Lucky Charms better than any food on earth. She was a good and loving girl despite living in an atmosphere that was damned thin on belovedness. She'd climb into Anita's lap when Anita was feeling low and tuck her small head into Anita's neck and rock until Anita would have tears running down her face. If Doreen took off for greener pastures once the divorce was finalized, and Anita was sure she would, she wouldn't take Crystal with her. That little girl deserved more than to be brought up by a worn-out old woman. Yet when Anita mentioned it to Doreen, Doreen didn't want to hear about it. She just said, "You're not old; you're fat. What do you expect when you're seventy pounds overweight?" Never mind that Anita had been overweight for years.

Everything was about weight, with Doreen. Everything was about weight, and nothing was her fault: Danny got her pregnant; Danny got arrested and slapped in prison; Danny was the reason she had to live at home again instead of in her own cute apartment. Anita guessed Doreen came by that quality through Bob, who could pass the buck better than anyone she knew. His bosses were idiots, no one was hiring, he was fired because he'd been set up, his talents were overlooked; she'd heard them all, over the years. In the end it didn't mean a thing. What meant something was that they never had money and never would.

Yet she'd known Bob's limited capabilities early in their marriage. She could have left him before Doreen was even born, but she hadn't. When Hack had first appeared like an apparition in the park, she might have gone with him if he'd picked her, despite already being married, but he hadn't picked her. But even if he had, she'd probably only have stayed away for a little while. There was something about Bob; there always had been. In Anita's mind he was Buster Brown, always spit-shined and eager to please even though he was holding nothing in his hands but air. Even now he had the look of a boy with happy eyes and a winning smile, and if it was all based on delusion, Anita still didn't begrudge him. Everyone had to get through the days, and that was just Bob's way. He'd never had a strong grip on the truth. If he had, he wouldn't have lasted past his boyhood, wouldn't have been able to tow Warren along behind him into calmer waters. But he had lasted, had brought Warren with him through childhoods so bereft that Anita often wondered how a just God could look away. He had looked away; Anita knew this, and in His absence Bob had done the best he could for her and for the kids and for Warren. Anita knew that too. If she was bitter now—and there were days when she was bitter enough to curdle milk—it was herself she blamed, not Bob. This was what she'd never been able to explain to Bunny or anyone: that Bob was not to blame for her life. And she accepted it.

She accepted it.

For as long as she could remember, Bunny had been sensitive about other people's appearances, especially when they looked better than she did. When people told her over and over how cute Vinny was, and later on how pretty, she'd considered it a mixed compliment. It wasn't that she minded Vinny's being pretty; it was that she minded her being prettier than Bunny had been. Bunny had never been what you would call a pretty girl exactly; it was her figure that got her the looks, small in the hips, long in the legs, and just busty enough to pull off any top. She took excellent care of her breasts, always buying bras that gave good support; plus she'd bottle-fed Vinny when she was a baby, so she wouldn't sag like those women in Africa who looked like they'd had their boobs sucked dry and then ironed. Those women were a cautionary tale, as Bunny had told Anita on more than one occasion. If it came down to it, Bunny would rather have a plate in her lower lip or a stack of gold rings around her neck.

Anita had never been much competition for Bunny. It was one of the reasons they'd done so well together all these years. Bunny secretly believed that she would have beaten out Anita at the Miss Harrison County Pageant if she'd entered that year. Anita had been voluptuous, full of curves and bosom, but she hadn't been pretty. LeeAnn Sprague, who'd won, hadn't been all that good-looking either. Bunny was sure she'd have turned heads if she'd walked down that runway, but Shirl had nixed it. Shirl had nixed a lot of things that year, hoping that keeping Bunny close to home would prevent her from running off with JoJo. A lot of good it had done. She hadn't run off with JoJo, but three years later she'd had Vinny. Shirl had just sighed and shaken her head when Bunny finally told her she was nearly five months gone. "I knew you couldn't let him get away clean," Shirl had said. "It's an old trick, hon, but it don't work, and it never has. You'd think after so many centuries girls would've figured that out."

It wouldn't have done any good to tell Shirl—and JoJo, if he'd given her a chance—that she wanted a baby about as much as she coveted a dead herring. No, Vinny was the product of a defective Trojan that JoJo busted right through one night in his orgasmic zeal. When he pulled out of her and she saw those shreds of rubber, she knew she was well and truly fucked. In Hubbard when girls got pregnant, they had their babies. They had their babies and they lived at home as long as they needed to—permanently, in more than a few cases—and year by year their color faded and their eyes got sullen and one way or another they took a 180-degree turn away from everything they'd once thought they'd be: a stewardess, a rich fisherman's wife, a telephone operator, a nurse. They weren't anything at all except somebody's mother and maybe the wife of someone who wasn't anything either. Bunny knew that her life was over the night her water broke all over her favorite chintz vanity stool. She endured thirty hours of labor with no one but Shirl and Anita in the waiting room, plus a torn perineum and stretch marks that lasted down the years no matter what she did with cocoa butter and baby oil. At least she hadn't had a cesarean section like Anita had had with Patrick and then Doreen, a big, ugly scar that said, *Open here*, like some kind of a party favor.

Yet Vinny had had the softest head, the most beautiful cap of curls when she was small. Bunny could still remember cradling that small pulsing skull in the palm of her hand and wondering how God could send down one of His most cherished possessions in such a fragile package. Vinny had been a sprite from the get-go, pretty and cheerful and eager to please. At first it was Bunny she'd tried to please, but then later it had been Hack. Vinny thought Hack hung the moon. If she was with Bunny and Hack together, she outshone Bunny every time, at least in Hack's eyes. She'd seen him; she'd watched. All these years that had been her special hell: to know he was in love with her daughter. A mother was supposed to be her daughter's best friend, but with Bunny and Vanilla it had never been that way, and Bunny didn't think it was all her fault. She and Shirl were close; Fanny and her daughter, Chantelle, were always going out shopping and to lunch or something. But Vinny was always out someplace with her girlfriends, and the few times Bunny had tried to set up something—dinner and a movie for just the two of them, or lunch together at the Bobcat over in Sawyer—Vinny always put it off until Bunny just gave up. That's just the way it was between them. They'd never meshed, and now they probably never would. Bunny could live with that except when Hack brought up that he'd been on the phone with Vinny or up there for a visit, like he was a better parent than her. He hadn't been the one who'd gotten kicked in the ribs so hard from the inside out that during her pregnancy Bunny had had to sleep sitting up for a month. He hadn't stayed up with her all night when she had colic in the beginning or when she got pneumonia and a double ear infection all at the same time. He hadn't scrounged for money or bought clothes only for her when there wasn't enough money to buy for them both. He hadn't done any of that, but somehow he'd turned into Mr. PTA anyway, the Good Dad, the perfect stepparent; that was what everyone always said about him. *Bunny*, people always told her, *you're the luckiest woman in the world to have found that man, but hey, you already know that.* It wasn't easy being married to a man who was better-looking than you, more likable than you, and who attracted women like iron filings to a magnet. There were always women, and there always had been, with Hack. It didn't make a bit of difference what he told her. She knew what she knew.

This latest girl, this prissy piece of merchandise, had been sitting in a booth at the Bobcat just two days ago like Queen Shit—and *in their booth*, hers and Hack's. Bunny made sure to keep Hack there long enough for the woman to get good and soaked walking all the way back to the dealership in the rain. Her perfume, some thick, sweet stuff that smelled like pastry, had stayed behind. Bunny could still smell it sometimes, even days later, like it had gotten wedged up her nose as a reminder. Hack could swear nothing was going on between them—and he did, over and over—but he'd gone white when he saw Bunny come in. Well, she'd caught him all right. She'd caught him, and now she was holding him, playing him out like a fish on a line. When she got hurt, it made her mean. Hack knew that. That's why he was being so sweet now, bringing her beers, watching TV with her. Same old same old, the way he always atoned for his sins. What would she do the day he no longer cared enough to bother?

If every day you thought about committing murder, did that make you a murderer, at least in your soul? If so, then Rae Macy was an adulteress, and no amount of protestation and hairsplitting would change it. Though she was only mentally wanton, this thing between her and Hack Neary, this love or lust, was so solid, so real you could walk across a bridge of it all the way to China.

She would have thought that such a great sin, such a moral transgression would at least return equal parts of pleasure and pain, but it wasn't so. The obsession went on and on, with none of the relief or release of consummated sex, but all the retribution. Bovine Francine, with her GED certificate and her grade-school handwriting, was now forgetting to pass along Rae's phone messages—all except the ones from Sam, which recorded the caller as *Sam, your husband*. Whenever Rae walked by Francine's desk, which lately was as infrequently as possible, Francine gave her a nasty smirk. In fact the only people at the dealership who did *not* seem to regard her with contempt were Hack himself and Bob. No, there was Jesús too, with his touching belief that there was such a thing as goodness. To judge by the stair step ages of their children, La Reina must have been pregnant during all but a few months of their marriage. She had a fierce Aztec face and the short legs and powerful build of a wrestler, a woman with corners instead of curves. Yet Rae had seen Jesús look at her with unqualified adoration when she stopped by sometimes to bring him lunch. How did a man develop such a love, the deepest desire of the soul as well as the body? When he and La Reina talked, he always put his head close to hers and spoke quietly, even intimately. What did he say to her? Rae imagined beautiful couplets, a continuous song of humility and gratitude. What would it be like, to be loved in that way, to have a man grasp and hold you with his eyes until he'd memorized every cell, every molecule? She would have liked to ask Jesús these questions, but her Spanish and his English were too poor, and besides, he was a simple man, a man in command of inarticulable truths: gladness, honor, joy. This morning he had shyly presented her with his latest pictures of *la reina y los niños* on the occasion of his oldest son's first communion. The child was dressed like a cheap lounge act, but he regarded the camera with serenity, a boy at peace with himself and his place in the world around him, a state from which Rae was increasingly a stranger.

She often dreamed now about leaving her house unclothed. Sometimes she arrived at Fred Meyer naked; at other times she was fully, elegantly dressed, but only from the waist up. When Sam was at work and she was not, she'd taken to driving blindly up and down the coast highway in a fug of stale longing and cheap sentiment. She'd put nearly a thousand miles on the car in three months.

Overwhelmed by misery, Rae had talked to Sam about how out of step she felt, about how she was being ostracized because she wasn't like everybody else, how neither her graduate degrees nor her sense of style seemed to mean anything to anyone in Sawyer even though those things *defined* her. Yes, she had perhaps ruffled some feathers by befriending men, but what was she supposed to do when these narrow Sawyer women would have nothing to do with her? She'd told him this as though Vernon Ford were teeming with high-spirited men with whom she glibly jousted and punned and discussed politics. "Honey, you're losing me. Exactly who is it that we're talking about?" Sam had asked mildly, trying to inform her vague statements with fact, and she'd whispered Hack Neary's name, and Bob's as a decoy, with a burning face.

Sam hadn't known what to make of it, of course, except to point out mildly that she'd always valued diversity, and Sawyer was nothing if not diverse, at least in socioeconomic terms.

Couldn't she learn from these people, put what she found to some use? But Rae didn't want to learn from these people. All she wanted, really, was to play out her tawdry little obsession in private. Not that she could say that, of course, and then it had gotten late and Sam had had an early court appearance the next morning, and the conversation hadn't so much ended as guttered out. Rae was left wondering what she might have given away that she would later come to regret. She was in the habit lately of replaying all her conversations and dealings with Sam. His mind was encyclopedic, a strangely efficient data storage system that indexed and cataloged even the most obscure information. One of his law school professors had said that Sam was the most highly evolved attorney he had ever seen, perfectly adapted to the dusty bins and endless shelves that were the law. Sam could recall in detail conversations that Rae couldn't even remember having, quoting as meticulously as though he was reading from a text. Yet he was at best only a fair judge of character. He could cite information chapter and verse, but he often missed the subtext. He was most at home with dry, bureaucratic matters: contested deeds, right-of-way disputes, articles of incorporation, contract law. There were times when Rae felt parched by the desert landscape of his mind, but she also had to admit it allowed her great psychic privacy. He could no more see inside her soul than perform miracles in the village square.

During her solitary drives up and down the highway, she sometimes thought that their relationship, hers and Sam's, was a mealy thing, without the glue and effervescence of bloodlust. There had been no wild nights, no weekends of sex from which they'd emerged groggy with pheromones, raw and stinking like zoo animals. Theirs was a gentlemanly, civilized affection that had developed during talks on many subjects. Sam had a lively intellect and the broad knowledge of a voracious reader; Rae always felt that she was a step or two behind him, the eager student rather than peer.

With Hack Neary, on the other hand, Rae gladly suffered ridiculous chatter about neighbors and dirt bikes and salmon bakes and sex, thinking all the while about how much she would like to run her tongue around the inside of his mind, lick it clean with her spit and adoration, then rebuild what she found there until it sang like fine crystal. She was reasonably sure he was not a stupid man. But where Sam lived all up in his head, Hack was a primitive, a throwback to times of brawn and guts and lustiness, where you seized what you would. He was Daniel Boone, Lewis and Clark, a pioneer pushing westward with two oxen and a bolt of cloth, weevily flour and a single Dutch oven. His instincts were highly developed. Sam did not have instincts; he had taste.

Six years ago they had been married in quiet elegance in the front parlor of his parents' exquisitely restored Victorian house in San Francisco. Sam's father was a retired history professor whose specialty was Victorian America. He had used his house as the central metaphor for a well-received book on Victorian values and the self. He was a man of beautiful manners and formal turns of speech, and just before the wedding ceremony was to take place, he had asked Rae to step into a small butler's pantry he used as his office, so that he could speak with her in private. She had had a spray of baby's breath in her hair, and when he lifted a hand to adjust its blossoms, she had misunderstood his intentions and turned away. Stricken, he said that he had only wanted to wish her, in private, happiness and long life with his son. My God, did she think he had intended to kiss her? She had stumbled through an agony of self-abasement and mortification, but they had never been entirely comfortable with each other again. And Sam was very much like his father, a man of ironclad morality and lukewarm lusts. Until recently they had made love comfortably, pleasantly, sometimes even wryly, as though their sexuality were a bit of evolutionary foolishness, the vestigial remains of their Cro-Magnon heritage. But for the last few months Rae had been repulsed by his touch, dreading the inevitable invitation that would come from beside her in the dark: *Would you care to share a roll?* They used to laugh about that silly turn of phrase, invariably asking each other the question in front of the baked goods section of the student union cafeteria, as their private joke. Now it made her flesh crawl.

So she drove her obsession north along the coast highway to Hubbard in hopes of catching a glimpse of Hack or even of his truck. Once she'd even driven by his home, a dangerous thing since he lived just two houses from the end of a dead-end street, and his wife would recognize Rae if she saw her. She had risked it, though, taking in with appalled reverence the chain saw bear carvings and climbing bear silhouettes in the front yard, the cheap frilly curtains and mailbox painted like a rabbit, its raisable ears acting as flags for the postman. It was a fussy house, a woman's house, Bunny's house more than Hack's, Rae guessed. She drove on with her heart pounding, terrified of being caught, knowing that this time she'd gone too far. As she turned around, she saw a pickup coming toward her up the hill, and for a minute she was sure it was Hack's truck, that he'd know she'd sunk to spying on him. It had turned out to be someone else, in a truck that looked nothing like Hack's, but she drove home deeply shaken.

If Sam had had an affair, or contemplated one, it would have made her feel better in some obscure way, but she didn't think he had the imagination for it, or the desire. She was the over-heated one of the two of them, with her secret thong panties and the lace teddies she bought on a trip alone to Portland on a day when she knew Sam couldn't go with her. She had gotten that far out of control. She waxed her legs every second Monday, wore an expensive perfume she had picked out and bought for herself. She experimented with cosmetics that enhanced her pale, fairy complexion until she looked like she was made of silk or marble, an acolyte offering up her immaculate beauty as part of some perverse cosmic contract with God.

She would not leave Sam if He would allow her to seduce Hack Neary.

## chapter thirteen

Hack hadn't sold a car in a week—a week and a day, to be exact, ever since he and Bunny had turned to shit at the Bobcat. He knew his sales patter was lackluster, his enthusiasm forced. People could read that plain as day and knew you weren't at the top of your game. You'd think that would make them zero in for the kill, but they didn't. It seemed unsportsmanlike. They were happy to kick your ass, *eager* to kick your ass, but they wanted you to be in peak condition when they did it. They wanted you to break a sweat, writhe in pain, cry out for mercy. Old Marv Vernon had been masterful, right down to the groans, the lowered head, the hangdog expression. *If all my customers were like you*, he liked to tell them, *I'd be waiting tables right now. God only knows what I'll tell my wife.*

What it came down to was, Hack Neary didn't bounce back like he used to. Bunny had whipped him good, and here was the thing he was beginning to think: If he was going to be hammered for having an affair, he might as well *have* an affair. It wasn't like the sex at home was any good anymore. And he was already paying the price of choosing the wrong company for lunch. It had been eight days since Bunny had found him with

Rae at the Bobcat, and when he'd walked by her sewing room last night, the machine had still been open full throttle, racketing along like a jackhammer. He pictured her feeding some poor Hack rabbit under the sewing foot without even slowing down, stitching him shut from his balls to his eyebrows. That's what he'd become, the Hack Neary Voodoo Bunny.

But—and this was the worst part, the truly depressing part— he didn't really want to have an affair. He didn't know what he *did* want, but it wasn't sex on the side, not even with someone as beautiful as Rae Macy. What the hell? He couldn't remember the last time a problem had been too big to be solved by sex. Sex was the answer to everything. You got your parts all slicked up and perky, and the rest just drifted away on a tide of slow orgasmic bliss. By the time it was over, you were too fuck-drunk to care.

He'd been dreaming about Cherise lately. In his dreams she showed up at his front door in Hubbard, wearing hot pants and four-inch heels. *Hey, baby doll*, she'd say to him. *It's Mommy.* And he'd tell her to fuck off, but he didn't really mean it, just the way he didn't really want to have an affair.

What was going to sustain him if it wasn't sex and rage? What did you have left when that was gone? Nothing. Absolutely nothing. You were as helpless as a newborn kitten in the bulldog-slobbery jaws of hell.

Hack couldn't remember anymore how Cherise had wheedled the police into coming to the apartment in Tin Spoon and waking him and the Katydid out of a sound sleep at one o'clock in the morning. Maybe she told them they were too young to be left alone while she was at the station; maybe she just told them the truth, that she was hoping they had enough money to post her bail. Whatever it was, Hack awoke to insistent knocking on the door. By the time he got there, hoisting jeans up over his boxers, the Katydid was padding out of her room in her night-gown, her hair going in a million directions.

"What the hell?" Hack had said when he saw a state patrol-man standing in the doorway.

"Are you Hack Neary?" the officer said, consulting a note-book.

"Yeah, that's me."

"Hack—unusual name."

"Tell me you didn't come here at one o'clock in the morning to say that," Hack said.

"Let him in, Buddy," Katy said, shivering. "It's cold."

It was cold, a February night in the desert, icy air leaking in through all the shoddy window frames and cracks in the floor-ing and doorjambs. Katy held her arms tight across her chest.

The officer tipped his hat. "Plenty cold. Thank you, miss."

Hack backed up and let the man through.

"Whew," the officer said, snuffling and stamping his feet.

"So?" Hack said.

Preparing for trouble, the patrolman set his feet while Katy shut the door behind him. He consulted his notebook again and said, "We have a Cherise Neary in custody over in Diederstown. She says she's your mom. That right?"

"Never heard of her," Hack said.

"That's right," Katy said at the same time.

"Well, we picked her up for solicitation and theft over there. She stole a couple wallets off some guys in a bar who weren't as drunk as she thought they were. Bail's seven thousand bucks."

"Pigs will fly first," Hack said.

"Pardon?"

"Buddy," Katy warned.

"She told you we have seven thousand dollars?" Hack said.

"Look, son, all I know is I'm supposed to bring you down to the station. If nothing else, maybe you'll be able to settle her down some." The officer cracked a rueful smile. "She decked the sergeant, landed a good one on him."

"I'll go. Let her stay here," Hack said, nodding toward the Katydid.

"I'm not staying, Buddy. If you're going, I'll go too."

"She doesn't trust me to keep my temper," Hack told the officer.

"That's because you *don't* keep your temper. He doesn't keep his temper worth a damn," Katy told the officer.

"Like we've even seen the woman in two years," Hack said.

"Doesn't matter," said the Katydid. "I'm going."

"Okay, look, both of you come then. You want to follow me?"

"Can't," Hack said. "Fucking car's in the shop again."

Two months earlier Hack had finally saved up enough money to buy them a car he hoped would run for a while, but it turned out to be yet another piece of shit, just a more expensive one. He'd bought it off an Indian Minna Tallhorse had warned him about, but the guy had promised Hack it was clean, and it looked clean, even to the boys in the garage. Yeah, right. In the first six weeks he'd owned it, he'd had to replace the carburetor, the timing belt, and now—for the second time in a month—the head gasket. He was fucking sick of piece-of-shit cars and being too broke all the time ever to buy a good one. His life goal, his dream, his obsession, was to have a new car, a white T-bird with porthole windows and red tuck-and-roll upholstery. Like that was ever going to happen. He was making only fifty cents an hour over minimum wage as a checker at Howdy's Market, and no one ever slipped tips to the checkers like they did to the bag boys. After expenses, they had fifteen dollars a month left over—unless they had to make car repairs, and of course they always had fucking car repairs because they could only afford a goddamn piece-of-shit car.

"I'll run you in," the officer said.

"Jesus," said Hack. "What if we don't want to go?"

"We have to go, Buddy," Katy said.

"Like hell."

"Well, I'm going."

"Fuck," Hack said, and pulled his jacket off the back of the couch. Katy put a poncho Minna Tallhorse had given her over her nightgown and they followed the officer out to his squad car. It was twenty minutes to Diederstown, and Katy nodded on Hack's shoulder. She was fifteen years old, but when she was asleep, she was still going on eleven. He smoothed out his jacket so she wouldn't have a big wrinkle mark in her cheek when she woke up. She always had wrinkle marks in her cheeks when she woke up; she had the kind of skin that was sensitive that way. He used to razz her about that all the time, told her she must have been a rag doll in her past life, the way she wrinkled up so easily.

"Yeah, well, if I was a rag doll, then what were you, one of those roly-poly dolls that you punch and they get right back up?"

It was true that he got into his share of fights, especially when he hung out at the Black Diamond Tavern, where someone was always spoiling for a fight. Hack was happy to mix it up, see what he could do. He was earning a reputation as a fighter. Lot of guys would back down before things had even gotten out of hand if they knew he was in the place.

So Cherise had decked a cop. He watched the sage go by in the moonlight and wondered what fucking ill wind had brought her back to them this time. Last time they'd seen her she'd breezed in like she owned the place and tried to leave some suitcase behind in the closet. Hack had jimmied the lock and found five Omega wristwatches, two Rolexes, a bunch of traveler's checks, a pearl necklace, and thirteen credit cards. He'd made her take the goddamn thing back. That was two years ago, and they hadn't heard a word from her since. If the cops had picked her up for theft, her timing must be off. Age did that to you, he guessed. Jesus, what was she now, forty-three, forty-four?

The patrolman pulled into the station lot in Diederstown.

"Out you go," he said, opening Katy's door for her. The kid was barely a kid anymore, and everyone still opened doors for her.

Diederstown was a dive, and so was the state police station, an old Quonset hut the government must have gotten cheap. There were only two cells, and Cherise was in one of them, carrying on a lively discourse with the duty officer—the sergeant, by the looks of him, all swollen up around the right jaw and making a show of ignoring Cherise and doing paperwork. Looked like it hurt. Hack had been hit there a few times himself, and he'd ended up sucking Cream of Wheat through a straw.

"You son of a bitch bastard no-good asshole," Cherise was saying. "You impotent pansy faggot. You're going to be so sorry—"

Then she saw Hack and Katy. "Hey, baby dolls," she said, turning sweet on a dime, like she always could. "Look what they've gone and done to your mama this time."

"Looks like a good place," Hack said.

"Are they treating you okay?" Katy said.

"Better than she's treating them," Hack said. "Look at that guy." He nodded in the direction of the sergeant, who glanced up at Hack wryly.

"Got that right," he said.

"So?" Hack said to Cherise.

"You don't sound glad to see me, baby. Aren't you glad to see your old mother?"

"Fuck you," Hack said.

"Well," said Katy, "at least we're starting off on the right foot. C'mon, Buddy. It's not going to help for you to get ugly."

"Listen to your sister," Cherise said.

"Fuck off," said Hack.

Katy shook her head and retreated to a metal bench against one wall.

"Let me get a good look at you, honey," Cherise wheedled, leaning on the cell bars. Even retired, she looked like a hooker: the hip-shot stance, the ridiculous flashy clothes and cotton candy hair. *Casino-wear,* she used to call her getups. *Designed to please.* "My God, but you've gotten big and handsome," she said to Hack. "How old are you now, baby? Eighteen?"

"Twenty."

"A man."

Hack shrugged, but some of the anger was ebbing away. Close up, Cherise looked so damn old. Her lipstick had bled into lines around her mouth that he'd never noticed before. Her eyes were bloodshot and red-rimmed, like she'd been on a bender. She didn't seem drunk now, though.

"What time did you pick her up?" Hack asked.

The sergeant consulted his log. "Call came in at ten oh six."

Enough time to get sober.

"I told them you'd come," she said. "Bastards."

"What do you want?"

"They're asking seven thousand for bail."

"And?"

"I thought you might be able to help me out, baby."

"What a joke. If we had that kind of money, we *wouldn't* have that kind of money because I'd have rented us a decent place with it and gotten a car that actually runs."

"So how much do you think you can come up with—a thousand, maybe, maybe two? They might go for that," Cherise said, talking fast. "Hey, would you go for that?" she called to the sergeant. "A couple thousand? I'd get the rest in the morning." Like she could be trusted to turn over that kind of money if she had it. The sergeant didn't even bother replying, just shook his head.

"C'mon, baby, think. Don't you know someone who could help us out? Honey, what about you?" she called to Katy. "Are you dating someone, maybe, someone with money?"

"No," Katy said flatly.

"Jesus," Hack said. "What's she supposed to do even if she does know somebody, say, *Excuse me but can I borrow seven thousand dollars to bail out my forger–pickpocket–thieving-whore mother?*"

"Watch your mouth."

"You watch it," Hack said. "This whole thing better be your idea of a joke."

"I don't know why you have to be ugly," Cherise said, fluffing her hair mechanically. She looked around the cell until she spotted a package of cigarettes. She looked inside, but the pack was empty. "Goddamn it," she said. "Honey, do you have a cigarette, by any chance?"

"I don't smoke, and neither does she," Hack said. "Look, this is bullshit. We don't have any money, and they're not going to let you out tonight without it. We're going home."

"Shit." Cherise balled up the empty cigarette pack and threw it across the cell. "I would've thought you'd want to help your mother."

"Why in hell would you have thought that?"

"You're my kids. I raised you."

"You raised us? *You raised us?* Ask her who was cooking dinner for her when she was five. Go ahead, ask her." Hack pointed at Katy, who was still sitting on the metal bench. Cherise turned her back. "Yeah, I didn't think so."

"I gave birth to you, I brought you into this world," she said, but the fight had gone out of her. "I did the best I could. I would have thought that counted for something."

"It doesn't count for shit," Hack said.

On the bench Katy raised her knees, folding her arms on top, and laid her head down. "How late is it, Buddy? God, I'm tired."

"We're going," Hack said, seeing her. "C'mon, this is garbage."

"You want me to give you a ride back home?" the patrolman asked. Hack had forgotten all about him, standing back there by the coffeepot.

"Nah. What's she driving these days?" He jerked his head toward the cell.

"Looked like a Camaro. It's down the block at the C'mon Inn, that's where we picked her up. You want to take it? She's not going to need it until she's arraigned. Least you'd have transportation."

"Yeah, we'll take it."

Cherise said nothing. The sergeant got her keys out of the property box and had Hack sign for them. "You mind?" he asked Cherise as an afterthought.

"Ask me if I even give a fuck," she said.

"I'll drive you down there," the patrolman said to Hack. "It's too cold to be walking."

Katy stood and went over to the cell. Cherise was still standing there with her back to the room. Katy stood staring at the hunched shoulders, the slack upper arms and sagging bosom, the tiny skirt and thigh-high boots.

"You have something to say to me?" Cherise said without turning.

"No," Katy said. "I guess I don't."

She and Hack followed the patrolman outside. "Jeez," the man said, rubbing his arms. "It's a goddamn icebox." He opened the squad car door for Katy and drove them three blocks south, to the C'mon Inn, a mean little building with blacked-out windows and asbestos siding. Cherise's Camaro was the only car in the lot. Hack unlocked it with the keys the patrolman handed him and slid inside. It stank of Cherise's perfume, but it was clean enough.

"You kids be careful now," the officer said, holding up a hand in farewell. "I'm real sorry about your mama." He got back in the squad car and headed up the street.

"Yeah," Hack said to no one in particular.

The engine turned over smoothly, and there was half a tank of gas, more than enough to get them back to Tin Spoon. Hack ran through the gears a couple of times, checked the brakes, and peeled out of the empty parking lot.

"Nice car, Buddy," said Katy.

"Yeah. Maybe we should keep it."

The Katydid looked at him.

"C'mon, I'm only kidding," Hack said.

They drove for a while in silence. Fog had clamped down over the desert, and it was hard to see.

"Buddy? What do you think she wanted to be when she grew up?" Katy finally said.

"Cherise?"

"Yeah."

"A whore."

"I mean it. Do you think she had dreams once of being something? I mean, nobody wants to grow up to be a prostitute."

"How do you know?"

"Come on, Buddy. It's a shit job. It's demeaning, and it's dangerous, even if it is legal. It doesn't even pay that well."

"How do you know?"

"I asked Minna once. She said Cherise probably made about as much money as an experienced waitress."

"Yeah, just hold the sauce," Hack said.

The Katydid shook her head. "I can't talk to you. When did you get so mean?"

"C'mon, I'm not mean."

"Bitter then."

"Not me," Hack protested. "Me?"

"Just drive," said the Katydid. "Let me know when we're there."

She pulled her poncho over her eyes, laid her head back against the seat, and put her life in Hack's hands, the way she had thousands of times before.

Last Christmas Vinny had given Hack a desktop toy, six steel ball bearings suspended on monofilament from a wooden frame. You picked up a few balls and let them drop against the rest, and they set up a complicated ricochet rhythm—tak TAK tak TAK TAK tak tak tak—until eventually the damned thing got fainter and slower, like someone losing his conviction. Hack was sitting at his desk watching the balls go back and forth when Rae walked by—tock tock tock—in her high heels and pure silk stockings that had been spun by pedigreed silkworms in the Shanghai province or some damned thing. She stopped in his office doorway, one hand climbing the doorjamb, the other on her hip in a classic come-on.

"Hey," she said softly.

"Hey," he said, stopping the balls from swinging before they left a maddening rhythm in his head.

"You busy?"

"Very busy."

"Oh—" she said uncertainly.

The woman was pretty insecure for someone who could afford to cover her legs with pedigreed silkworm spit. "I was being sarcastic."

"Oh."

"Jesus, doesn't anyone kid anyone else where you come from?"

Rae sighed. "Not the way you do, no."

"What way then?"

"Never mind. I don't know. I'm probably wrong."

"Ah," Hack said.

"So are you okay? You don't look okay."

She was always asking him if he was okay now, ever since the Bobcat.

"I'm fine, princess, just a little low on motivation today," he said. "I've been thinking about taking a little road trip." Actually, the thought hadn't crossed his mind until that very moment. Why would he want to go anywhere?

"Really?" Rae perked up. "Like to Eugene, maybe? Isn't that funny because I was thinking about going to Eugene this Saturday. Sam's got a lot of work right now, and I don't expect him to be home this weekend much, so I was thinking of getting out of town, maybe going shopping or something."

Hack hadn't heard her talk that much in days. She hadn't had a lot to say lately.

"That right?" he said.

"Maybe you have something you need to do there too, and we can drive together." She was turning scarlet, but he had to give it to her, she kept on going. "Maybe you'd like to come with me—you know, save on gas by taking one vehicle. Or something." She finished lamely. "I was just thinking that. I don't know."

"Shopping? Like at Mervyn's or something?"

He saw her flinch. "Well, maybe Nordstrom or Frederick & Nelson. Kaufmann's."

"That where rich women shop?"

He could see her struggling for composure.

"Sorry, princess. I'm not trying to pick on you," he said. "So you'd do that when, Saturday?" Today was Thursday.

"Well, then. Or Sunday."

He could see her chest rising and falling, rising and falling, like she'd run a mile. When she took her hand from the door-jamb, it left a damp mark. But her eyes were locked onto his with complete conviction.

"Sure," he heard himself saying, and it sounded to him like he was talking in slow motion. "I could probably do that."

Bob was feeling real steady these days—steady and calm and re-sourceful. He had some things to do at the homestead, and he would do them: shore up the front porch for good, try to make the pump work in the kitchen sink, maybe install a new toilet seat in the outhouse. One day he might even put in a septic sys-tem and a real toilet right there in the house. Jesus, but the place was looking good. He liked to imagine sometimes that the original homesteaders would come back and see it and thank him for turning his love on the place like a hose, raining affection and handiness over the whole thing until it sparkled like new. There was love there, he knew, in the walls and the floorboards and the very nails that someone had made all by hand. Dehydrated love, that was what all the dust was. Dehydrated love and desiccated hope, now reconstituted with Bob's sweat and conviction. He'd never known such a thing before, had to stop himself from gathering pocketfuls and bringing them home, he felt that rich. As he sat at a back table at the Bobcat, waiting for Doreen, he actually felt himself glow.

"Where's Mom?" Doreen said to Bob, looking around the restaurant. "She in the bathroom?"

"No," Bob said, flipping open a menu, as though he didn't already know everything that was on it. "I thought it would be nice for just us to have lunch. Just me and you."

Doreen looked at him suspiciously. "Why? You haven't heard from that lawyer again, have you? That son of a bitch better not be—"

"Nah, nothing like that. Can't we have lunch?"

"Yeah, I guess."

"Okay. So what do you want to eat?"

"Burger, I guess. A burger and a chocolate shake."

"Tell her, not me," Bob said mildly, nodding at the waitress who'd arrived. He'd been saying, *Tell her, not me*, to Doreen since she was eight or nine and old enough to speak for herself. Bob was mindful that someone who was shy—Sheryl, for instance—was at a disadvantage out in the world, not being able to talk for herself. He hadn't wanted Doreen to grow up shy like that. He probably didn't need to worry, though. The kid had an edge on her, an edge and a mouth. She'd say anything that came into her mind, even ugly things, hurtful things. He didn't know who she'd learned that from. Anita didn't talk ugly, not even when things were bad. She got a little cranky from time to time, but that was understandable, what with his drinking and so little money and all.

"How about a burger and a chocolate shake?" Doreen was saying to the waitress.

"Same for me," Bob said, clapping the stiff menu covers together.

The waitress winked at him. "Seems like she was just in kindygarden, this one," she said to Bob.

"Yeah. It sure goes fast," Bob said.

"So what's Mom doing?" Doreen asked when the waitress was gone.

"Dunno," Bob said. "Working, probably. She's got some hours at the Lawns this week."

"Is she going to be able to pick Crystal up this afternoon?"

"Far as I know," Bob said mildly.

"Because I can't. I told her that, that she'd have to pick Crystal up herself, at Head Start."

"Then she will."

"You know what she said to me this morning?" Doreen asked.

"Mom?"

"Crystal. She said, *Gram sleeps a lot.* I don't know why she said that."

"Mom's been kind of tired lately, what with her working some extra hours and all."

"She's only been working about fifteen hours a week."

"Well, yeah, but she's been taking care of Crystal."

"Is Crystal giving her any trouble? If she's been giving Mom trouble, I'll beat her butt. She's gotten real sassy with me a couple times."

"Nah, nah, she's a good girl."

"Well, she better be." Doreen subsided, tapping the sugar packets into an even row in their little dish. "You know what she said the other day? She asked if Danny was coming home soon. I said no because he'd been sent to a place where bad people go until they can be good again. She wanted to know if Danny'd been bad, and I said yeah, he'd done some real bad things like lying and playing with someone's toys without their permission and messing up their house. She wanted to know if when you go to the bad place, mommies and daddies can go too, and I said nope, you had to go all by yourself, and it might be years before they'd let you come home."

"Aw, now, what did you tell her that for? The poor kid. Now she's going to worry all the time about what if she's bad?"

Doreen sulked. "I figure she needs to start knowing the truth about Danny."

"She's three."

"She's almost four, and she could start hearing stuff from the other kids at Head Start about how her daddy's a criminal and all."

"I don't think she's going to hear that from the other kids."

"Well, she could, though."

Bob methodically drank an entire glass of water. "Speaking of Crystal," he said when he was done.

"Here it comes," Doreen said. "I knew there was something."

Bob thought carefully about what he wanted to say. "I just think you shouldn't count on leaving Crystal with us, honey. To raise and all."

"I never said anything about that. Have I ever said anything like that?"

"No, but you've been thinking it."

Doreen said nothing. The waitress brought over their food and set it in front of them. Bob slowly opened his burger and added ketchup. He'd become very careful with ketchup. You could ruin a perfectly good burger in seconds if you let your attention wander.

"Will you please just tell me what the hell is going on?" Doreen narrowed her eyes at him. "Because *something's* sure going on. You and Mom aren't splitting up or anything, are you?"

Bob looked up, shocked. "Why would we do that?"

Doreen shrugged, took a bite of her hamburger, then opened it up on her plate. "Shit," she said. "They put pickles on it. I hate when they put pickles on your hamburger." She picked the two offending pickle slices off with the very ends of her fingernails.

Bob carefully poured out some ketchup for his fries. "You've got to tell them that, honey. You can't expect them to read your mind."

"So are you saying that me and Crystal can't live with you anymore?"

"Nah, nothing like that. But Mom gets tired sometimes."

"Yeah, well, if she'd lose sixty or seventy pounds, she wouldn't."

"That's not nice," Bob said.

"Well, it's true." Doreen was pounding down french fries like she hadn't seen food in days. The child had always eaten when she was unhappy.

Bob put down his hamburger and chewed thoughtfully for a full minute or two. "I wish you could have seen your mama when she was your age, honey," he said. "She was so pretty; she was the prettiest girl in our class. You'd spot her across a room, and her face would be shining like an angel's. She had skin that was the envy of every girl there; she's never had a pimple, never in the whole time I've known her, not one. And she had a real womanly figure, none of that stick figure stuff like everyone wanted back then, like that Twiggy had. Anita, she was ample, you could say; real curvy—like Marilyn Monroe, someone you could get a hold of. And she was never stuck up either, not even when she was in that Miss Harrison County Pageant and came in first runner-up. You'd have thought that would go to her head, but it didn't. She was real nice about LeeAnn Sprague winning, even though she was prettier and all. I sat in that audience, and I thought I would bust, I was that lucky to have her as my girl-friend. I looked at her up there—and I swear, you've never seen somebody as beautiful as she was in her gown and all—and I thought I must owe God a pretty big debt for giving her to me."

"Jesus, Dad," Doreen muttered.

"That's what she looked like, Marilyn Monroe. Spitting im-age."

"She's not even blond."

"Don't matter."

Doreen raised her eyes to the ceiling.

"I thank God every day for giving your mother to me," Bob said gravely. "Every day. Plenty of people wouldn't have put up with me, with my drinking and all. Plenty of women, they'd have shown me the door, given me the boot. Don't think I don't know it. I know it. Your mother, she never locked the door against me, not once, and there were plenty of times she could have. You don't think I know that, but I do. I know. It hasn't been easy for her."

"Then why'd you do those things?"

"It's complicated," Bob said.

"Yeah?"

"There've been reasons. Let's just leave it at that. There've been reasons."

"Are you crying? Jesus, you're not crying, are you?" Doreen looked at him, appalled. "Stop it," she hissed.

"I always meant to do right by Nita, that's the thing. I always wanted her to be proud of me, to see me as a man who could accomplish things, you know? A capable man. But it wasn't so easy for me."

"Why are you telling me this anyway?" Doreen said. "Because I really don't want to know this."

"I just think you need to be nice to Mom right now," Bob said. "She deserves it. That's all I'm saying."

And then lunch was over. He went up and paid their bill and got a toothpick from the dispenser, confident that he'd expressed himself clearly for once. He'd said what he had to say even if it wasn't what Doreen wanted to hear.

# chapter fourteen

Hack had always hated Eugene. Everyone seemed to be connected in one way or another to the University of Oregon, shuffling around in their Birkenstock sandals and socks and tie-dye T-shirts like they'd fallen into the 1960s and couldn't get out. Plus the place was always fogged in, as though it were permanently cupped beneath the sullen, clammy hand of God. You couldn't see shit, not even with good fog lights, which Hack always made sure he had, on whatever vehicle he was driving. In fact, it had been foggy almost all the way over from Sawyer, ever since they got out of the Coast Range and hit the Willamette Valley. He negotiated Highway 99E with care.

Rae Macy sat beside him with her hands clasped tightly in her lap. Earlier he could have sworn she was crying. What was she crying for? There were at least three feet of space between them in the truck cab; he hadn't laid a hand on her, hadn't so much as said an improper word the whole way, and they'd been on the road for an hour already. Plus they'd met at the old Georgia-Pacific mill outside Sawyer, which was derelict now and had been for years. Rae had left her car around back, where you certainly couldn't see it from the street.

"Princess," he said gently, "we're only driving. That's all. Nobody ever turned into a bad person from driving, at least no one I ever heard of." He couldn't help cracking a little smile. "*Parking*, yes. Driving, no."

With his peripheral vision he could see her nod. As scared as she looked, she might as well be wearing a chastity belt. Chastity belts: Now there was a screwed thing. What kind of person had invented those? Probably someone like Bunny, someone jealous, only male. Suddenly it didn't seem funny anymore.

"You okay?" he said.

She nodded again and cleared her throat.

"So tell me a story," he said.

"What story?"

"Hell, I don't know. You're the writer. Make something up."

"It doesn't really work like that," she said.

"No?"

"No."

"Oh."

They drove for a while.

Hack said, "You know, old Luther Newton went into that creek one time when it was foggy like this." He nodded at the muddy water licking its upper banks beside the road. "He was seventy-five years old, and it scared him so bad he never did get behind the wheel again, made Hattie do all the driving, and all of Hubbard knew Hattie couldn't drive worth a damn. Turns out the creek was only three feet deep there, but old Luther didn't know that when he went in. Took the paramedics fifteen minutes and a pile of Valium to get him to stop yelling so they could get him out."

"Luther Newton?"

"Yeah. Funny old guy, lived in Hubbard all his life. He's dead now."

"Oh," Rae said, and went back to looking out the window.

Hack sighed and planted his hands more firmly on the wheel. This could turn out to be one long goddamn day.

Before Hack had gotten even five miles from Diederstown and Cherise and the police station, all he could see was the double yellow line down the middle of the highway. Tiny fog particles were flying toward him in the headlights at the speed of light, millions of them like he was traveling through intergalactic space. Luckily, it was nearly three-thirty in the morning, and no one else was on the road. The only sign of life was a single brilliant light moving far away through the fog—odd since there were no roads in that direction, but the desert in nighttime played tricks even on a clear night. The Katydid was fast asleep with her poncho over her face, snoring gently from inside its folds. He liked to give the kid a hard time about keeping him awake with her snoring, but it was a peaceful sound, the sound that a healthy body makes repairing and improving itself in the night. He'd listened to her snoring more times than he could count when he was awake and worried about money, which was mostly all the time. His idea of paradise was a place where everything was free and no one could ever take the last one of anything.

He marveled at the Katydid's ability to shut herself off, no matter what the circumstances were. He couldn't have slept right then if you'd offered him a million bucks. He was too pissed off. Cherise had some balls, trying to hit them up for money. They were the kids; they were supposed to hit *her* up for money. Isn't that what parents were supposed to do, accuse you of costing them a fortune and give you a hard time about staying out too late? He'd said that to Minna Tallhorse just the week before.

"How quaint," Minna had said, patting his arm. "Do you also believe in the tooth fairy?"

"So then what's it like to have parents?" Hack said. "You had parents."

"Sure. One was a drinker, and the other was a drunk," Minna said. "Tell me, kiddo, when are you getting out of Dodge? Have you got your bags packed yet?"

Hack just shook his head. She asked him that question every single time she saw him now, ever since he'd dropped out of high school, and he always answered it the same way: not now, not yet. In three and a half more years the Katydid would have graduated, and that was when he would leave Tin Spoon. Minna insisted that Katy could come live with her right now and finish out high school there, but Hack didn't go for that. It wasn't that he wanted to stay in Tin Spoon any longer than he had to; he'd even told the Katydid what he'd do when he drove away for the last time. "I won't say good-bye, nothing like that. I'll just hold up my middle finger and floor it."

"Oh, Buddy, it hasn't been that bad."

"Sure it's been that bad."

But even with all that, here was the thing: Minna Tallhorse couldn't unconditionally guarantee that she could keep the Katydid from harm. Hack himself was the only one he trusted to make that promise. As long as he was there, the kid would be all right. In his soul he knew it.

"Do you want to go home?" Hack said to Rae after another five miles of silence. "Just say so, and I'll turn around right now."

Rae looked stricken. "Do you want to?"

"I'm not the one who's shaking."

"I'm fine," Rae said, folding her arms more tightly across her chest. "I'm just a little cold."

"Ah," said Hack.

Neither one of them moved to turn up the heat.

The Katydid was determined to attend college, planned to go to one in California, maybe, or even New York. She was always reading some ten-pound book or other. She'd try to describe the story to Hack, but he could never follow them. He was more practical. He liked cars, car engines, car styling, all that. Maybe he'd end up in Detroit working for Ford or something. Maybe he'd end up in Los Angeles dating beautiful women to whom he'd sold Mercedes-Benzes. Who knew? He was good enough looking; he had something on the ball too. He was a hard worker who earned every dime he got. Other people slacked off, did a shoddy job, but he was the genuine article, a man who could put his head down and get things done and done right. Minna Tallhorse was always telling him he should cut himself a little slack, relax a little bit, but that wasn't how you got ahead. Hadn't he been the youngest person Howdy had ever made a checker? Didn't he close the market regularly now, night after night and all by himself? His register had never been short, not even by a penny, in all the time he worked there. He knew the meaning of responsibility. Even in Tin Spoon, Nevada, he was on his way up. Nothing but good things awaited him. Three years from now he might even have enough extra to give the Katydid a few bucks toward college. Him, from a family with a college graduate. Wasn't that a hoot.

They had reached the outskirts of Eugene and were traveling fast through flat, ugly fields and lumberyards and mills. "So do you have any brothers or sisters?" Hack asked. Not that he really cared, but the silence was getting on his nerves.

Rae roused herself a little, made herself brighten. "Just an older sister."

"Yeah? She smart and beautiful like you?"

"PhD, summa cum laude, from Berkeley. She teaches women's studies at Humboldt State."

"Huh." Hack didn't know why they taught shit like women's studies. He had never met a woman yet who didn't know perfectly well how to be a woman on her own; women came fully equipped at birth with all the know-how they'd ever need and often more than was necessary or fair. Even dykes were plenty good at being women, just women of a different flavor. He had nothing against that: whatever got you off. In the end, sex might just be God's way of compensating for all the shit He planned to send your way.

"Hey. I brought your book back." He nodded in the direction of the toolbox in the bed of the truck. " 'The Gingham Dog and the Calico Cat.' " He shook his head. "Jesus, you'd think they wouldn't want little kids hearing something like that."

"I've always thought that poem was a sociological metaphor for the violence between disenfranchised groups of have-nots. Like gangs; like *West Side Story*."

"*West Side Story*?"

"You know, 'I Feel Pretty'?"

"Do you?"

"No, I mean, that's the name of the song. 'I Feel Pretty,' " she said.

"Oh. So anyway, I brought your book back," he said.

"Thank you."

They fell silent again.

"This isn't working out very well, is it?" Rae said.

"No," Hack agreed. "Not very."

Minna Tallhorse was really the one the Katydid talked to about her books and shit. She'd read a book by some Russian guy, and then the two of them would talk about why the book was written and who the author was and what symbolism made it go. Hack didn't know where Minna had learned all that: She was a social worker and an Indian, for God's sake. But she and the Katydid would go on and on for hours sometimes. Hack was glad the Katydid had someone to talk to, though. If Minna pushed her a little, and she did, what she taught the kid might be her ticket out. People didn't leave Tin Spoon all that often. It wasn't as easy as it sounded. You had nothing, you knew nothing, you offered nothing a million other people didn't offer too. That was the fucker of it; that was the real world. In the real world you were from a dirt town in the middle of nowhere, and that's where you were likely to stay. Except for him, of course; except for the Katydid.

"Did your folks read to you much as a kid?" he asked Rae. *Your folks.* He loved that.

"My mother did. She has a beautiful reading voice. We'd go from one book to the next; there was always something wonderful to look forward to. Of course in the beginning they were just young kids' books: *The Wind in the Willows, Alice in Wonderland, Winnie-the-Pooh,* all of those. But as soon as I turned eight, my mother started on *The Hobbit.* I have wonderful memories of that book. You know, they've made it into a movie, but I've never wanted to see it because I could already visualize the characters so clearly in my head and I didn't want that spoiled. What did your mother read to you?"

"*The Valley of the Dolls.*"

"You're kidding."

"Well, she wasn't much of a reader. She liked that writer, though—what was her name, Suzanne something."

"Jacqueline Susann."

"Yeah, her. I guess the Katydid was the only one of us with what you could call book ambition. Kid started reading Shakespeare in the sixth grade. She told me once she was pretty sure that William Shakespeare, not Jesus, was the son of God, because how else could you explain how one person could know so much about human nature?"

Rae laughed. "I like that. I wonder if she's right. Did she have a favorite play?"

"Hell, I don't know, that was a long time ago, and anyway, I could never keep them straight. Couldn't understand them either. She tried reading them aloud to me, but I'd just fall asleep. She'd punch me and say, *Wait, Buddy, just one more part, you've got to hear this part*, and then she'd read me some more drivel and I'd start snoring and she'd get mad. She used to tell me all the time that just because we were from a hellhole, it was no excuse for having narrow horizons. I told her she could have broad horizons for us both because I had to work the late shift again tomorrow and I needed my beauty sleep. I sure could rile her. Jesus, I made her so mad one time she stuck a meat fork through my hand. It wasn't really her fault, more of a spur-of-the-moment thing."

"What had you done?"

Hack shrugged. "Hell, I don't remember anymore. It could have been almost anything."

He did remember, though. They had been fighting about food stamps. The Katydid wanted them to enroll in the program, but Hack wouldn't do it. He had a job, didn't he? He paid their bills on time, didn't he? The Katydid had said pride was stupid and nobody overcame fucked-up roots by turning away help, especially when it came to money. And if it was offered to him now, Hack would probably take it. But then he couldn't stand pity. *It's not pity, Buddy; it's just a leg up, that's all*, the Katydid had said, but it smelled like pity to him, and he said so, and that's when she'd given a roar of frustration and stabbed him. She'd been very solicitous afterward, and from then on they'd had this thing they used to say to each other if it looked like they were headed for another stabbing. One of them would say, *How could you do such a thing?* in this hoity-toity voice, and the other one would say, *Fuck if I know, honey.*

Hack smiled to himself. *How could you do such a thing? Fuck if I know, honey.* God, he'd almost forgotten about that. The Katydid had had a bunch of fancy things she liked to say. *Oh, my dear*, and *I beg your pardon?* and the one that always killed him most, *May I?* instead of *Can I?* like she was some society debutante.

*May I?*

Well, God had sure as hell given her the big *No, you may not.* Hack earnestly hoped that up there in heaven or wherever, she'd been given the chance to say it again and hear *Yes.*

He'd asked Minna Tallhorse once what she thought happened to dead children's souls. She said, "They become all the things you think are beautiful. Full moons, just the right shade of purple, perfect lawns. They aren't the things themselves, just the extra bit that makes them beautiful. Like MSG on Chinese food."

He held on to the steering wheel and sliced open his memory like a vein.

• • •

When he came to in the hospital, the first thing he saw was Minna Tallhorse sitting in a vinyl chair beside his bed, breaking the back of a book in her lap.

"What the hell?" he said.

"Hey there," she said softly, rising from the chair.

As the room came into focus, Hack realized his head and gut hurt like nothing he'd ever felt before or could have imagined.

"Hi, sweets." Minna came to stand beside him.

"Jesus, Minna. What the hell? You look like shit."

Minna smiled a wan smile. "Just wait till you get a look at yourself, sport."

"Is there water?"

She poured some from a plastic carafe and put a paper straw in the glass. "How do you feel?"

"Like shit. Did you do this?"

She shook her head. "No. Go ahead and drink."

She held the glass for him while he swallowed a couple of sips.

"What day is it now? What the fuck are we doing here?" he said.

"It's Tuesday. You've been unconscious for a couple of days. You have a bad concussion and a ruptured spleen. There was an accident, kiddo."

"An accident?"

"You tangled with a train." Minna rested her hand lightly next to his on the sheet, where they touched like a whisper. "You were on your way back from Diederstown."

Cherise. They'd been to see Cherise. He remembered that.

Jesus, his head hurt.

"Okay," he said.

"It was very foggy when you drove home. They figure you never even saw the train coming. It hit you broadside."

The Camaro. He'd been driving a Camaro. Cherise's Camaro.

"What about the Katydid?"

Minna's hand twitched just slightly, but she kept her eyes steady. "She's gone, kiddo. I'm so sorry."

"No, listen, she was sleeping. She had on that poncho you gave her, and she was sleeping."

Fiercely, Minna cradled his eyes in hers. "She died instantly, Hack. She never knew a thing."

"Are you all right?" Rae asked, alarmed. "Hack? What's happened? Something's happened. Is it me?"

"No," he said. "It isn't you."

He'd argued with Minna then, and when she refused to change her story about the Katydid, he lost his temper. His own best guess was that Katy was in the next room, but didn't want him to see her for some reason. All right, maybe she'd been badly bruised or even disfigured; an accident with a train, that would be bad. She'd probably made Minna promise to tell him some malarkey until she felt more presentable and could spring like a conjurer through the curtain around his bed: *Fooled you!* It was a stupid joke, and his head hurt too much to play, but Minna insisted on sticking to her same cock-and-bull story. Then he was yelling something, and she was crying—Jesus, what was she crying for?—and a nurse came in and did something to his IV, and he fought to stay conscious and lost.

He and Rae were moving fast through railroad sidings and lumberyards and sodden pastures.

"How old was she? Your sister, I mean."

"Not quite fifteen."

"That's not very old."

"No," Hack said. "It wasn't."

Rae sat quietly for a moment, evidently gathering breath and courage. "Would you like to kiss me?" she asked.

"Not really."

It might have been the first completely honest thing Hack had said in twenty years.

For the first week Hack had drunk broth, peed blood, and hurt like hell. That was okay with him. The pain and the headaches kept him from spending too much time up there in his brain, where only bad things happened. At all times of the day and night he welcomed open-armed the nurses with painkillers. On gusts of morphine he drowsed outside himself among the clouds. Cherise was up there sometimes, looking like he hadn't remembered she'd ever looked, a young woman, not much older than he was now, smoking a long, thin cigarette and laughing at him splashing in some little kid's wading pool in a low-rent motor court. How old was he? Two? Three? He didn't even know he had memories that went that far back. Cherise didn't look so bad: cotton-haired and bleached, but with a nice smile. She must have lost that smile a long time ago because it didn't even look familiar. Happy. She looked almost happy. Happy with him in his little sunsuit, his face all screwed up but taking the sunshine on the chin like a man.

He also saw Minna Tallhorse, felt her cool flat palm on his forehead as she soothed and whispered to him, surrounding him with words like fragrant bubbles. *You couldn't have helped it. She wouldn't blame you. Nothing else you could have done.*

But mostly it was the Katydid he felt sitting in a chair in his room with one of her ten-gallon books and talking on and on.

*Come on, Buddy, get moving. You've got things to do.*

*Don't want to.*

*Nobody wants to. That's a thin excuse.*

*I hurt.*

*So?*

*You don't know what I feel.*

*Sure I do, Buddy. Sure I do. I know what you feel, and I know what Minna feels too. Let me tell you, she's the one who's hurting.*

*I hear her crying sometimes.*

*Only when she thinks you're asleep.*

*Yeah.*

*You should feel what I feel right now, Buddy. It would help.*

*Why? What do you feel?*

*Lighter than air, like a helium balloon, maybe. I can see out over everything.*

*You see Cherise?*

*Nah.*

*Do you miss her?*

*You're the one who misses her, Buddy.*

*I never missed her.*

*Baloney. You've missed her a lot, all these years. Don't think I don't know it. You know what you do? You talk about her in your sleep.*

*What do I say?*

*Mommy. You say Mommy.*

*That's all?*

*Mostly.*

*It's not much.*

*I didn't say it was much.*

*What do you say?*

*Me? I don't have to say anything. You're there, Buddy... you and Minna. I could care less about Cherise. You're the one who cares.*

*Stop saying that.*

*Okey-dokey, Buddy, but it's true. You should look Cherise up when you get out of here. You and Minna.*

*Nope.*

*Well, there's nothing I can do for you then.*

*Wait. Don't leave.*

*I've got to. I've got things to do, Buddy, things that won't wait.*

*Like what? What do you have to do?*

*That's a stall tactic, and it won't work.*

*Come on, I really want to know. What's so important?*

*Everything,* she said. *Everything's important, Buddy, and all of it's beautiful. Remember that. It's beautiful.*

Like hell.


Rae was staring at him across a restaurant table.

"It happened a long time ago," he said.

"Yes, but how do you live with a thing like that?" she said.

Hack just looked at her. "You don't."


A state highway patrolman came to the hospital several days before he was discharged. Hack recognized him as the patrolman who had come to get him and the Katydid at their apartment that night and driven them to Diederstown. He clapped his hand into Hack's in a meaty handshake.

"Were you there?" Hack asked him. "At the accident? Did you see anything?"

"Yeah, I went out there."

"And?"

"It was a bad one, son. I've never seen worse. You were real lucky to come through it."

Hack said nothing.

"I was sorry to hear about your sister. She was a real sweet girl; she had a lot of life in her."

"Yeah."

"I brought you something. I thought you'd want it." The patrolman pulled a twisted piece of metal from his jacket pocket and handed it to Hack.

"What is it?" Minna came over to see, then turned away. It was what was left of the silver bracelet Minna had given the Katydid, buckled and scorched.

"A couple of our boys found it a quarter mile or so down the line from where you got hit, son. Must have got caught on the train's undercarriage. They thought you'd like to have it."

Hack turned the bracelet over in his hands like shrapnel.

"You know, there's no rhyme or reason to what you find at an accident scene," the patrolman said expansively. "You can have a vehicle completely demolished, and right there beside it a lady's compact will be sitting on the road without so much as a mark on it. It's best not to try to make sense out of it, son, is what I'm saying. Best you can do is keep going. Honor your sister's memory, and keep going, that's the main thing."

Hack stared at the bracelet.

"You have any plans for when you get out of here?" the patrolman said.

"No."

"Well, then that's what you need to put your mind to, son. Isn't that right, miss?" He looked at Minna.

"Yes."

"You need anything?" the patrolman asked her. "I heard you were spending a lot of time over here."

"I'm fine," she said. "Thank you for coming to see us, and for bringing the bracelet."

"Ma'am," he said, putting on his hat. "Son."

"Wait. Does Cherise know about the accident?"

"Yeah. I heard she was real broken up."

"Fuck that," Hack said.

Minna stepped toward the bed.

"Yeah, yeah," he told her.

"I shouldn't have asked you that," Rae said as they drove home. "About kissing me, I mean."

"It's okay."

"I'm very embarrassed."

"There's no reason to be."

"I love you."

"Don't," said Hack.

After he was released from the hospital, Hack stayed with Minna in her apartment. She had already packed up their things, his and Katy's, what there was of them: a few clothes, some cheap dishes and pots and pans. The Katydid's books, which Minna kept in her own overloaded bookcase. Hack rarely left the apartment. In the evenings they said very little to each other, and what they did say was polite, as though they were strangers. But every night he slipped into Minna's bed, curled up to her long, hard body and found shelter. There was no talk then, only a crashing together of the two of them. She held him fiercely, sometimes all night when the trembling wouldn't stop, vigilant in the darkness, tiger-eyed. They never talked about this. There was nothing to say.

Once he asked her why she'd given him and the Katydid the jewelry engraved with her name and phone number.

She said, "Just in case."

"Did you know this was going to happen to us?"

She looked at him from the vast and bottomless blackness of her eyes.

"I don't know."

Hack resigned from Howdy's Market by telephone. They tried to talk him into staying, but he couldn't go back there again. He couldn't go anywhere in Tin Spoon. Tin Spoon was over and so, in many ways, was he. He joined the army as soon as he was well enough, and after basic training found himself in Vietnam. A month after he shipped out he got a letter from Minna saying she had taken a job back on the Blackfoot reservation in North Dakota. He never found out exactly what she did there; maybe he never asked. Over the years her letters came less and less often, and Hack answered fewer and fewer of them, until eventually they stopped coming. He assumed she had remade herself the way he had, out of scrap cloth and baling wire. He wasn't a real person at all anymore, but people mistook him for real. At first it was awkward being new like that; it was like being a puppet you didn't know how to work very well. But you got better and better until, after a while, even you forgot the difference.

## chapter fifteen

Funny how?" Shirl said.

"I don't know—just funny," said Bunny. "Like he was up-set or something, except when I asked him he said he was fine, which is what he always says. He wasn't fine. There's something going on."

"Well, he's not cheating on you, honey, I can tell you that. I had a little talk with him day before yesterday. If there's something going on, hon, it's in his mind, not his dick. But listen to me—are you listening? You're going to lose him if you don't back off. There's only so much even a good man can take."

"Lose him how?"

"Hell, I don't know how. There are lots of ways you can lose a man—booze, fishing, sports TV—without his even having to take a single step from home. I'm just saying you're going to drive him away if you aren't careful, honey."

They were sitting out on Shirl's little deck, watching fog as thick as cotton roll in and out of Hubbard Bay. It did that all summer, and it always stopped right across the street from Shirl's house, a two-story pile Bunny's father had built in sections over a span of more than twenty years. None of the siding matched, and all the windows were different—whatever he could get for cheap down at the building supply store in Sawyer. The deck was nice, though. Hack had built it for Shirl a couple of years ago so she could get some sunshine between her toes the few times each year when it was warm enough to take your shoes off.

"How's that girl of yours doing?" she asked Bunny. "I sure miss seeing her around here. She brightens up a room."

"She's good, I guess. She doesn't call much."

"And your fingers are broken?"

"Don't," said Bunny.

"I'm just saying," said Shirl.

"I call her."

Shirl lifted the lid of the little Igloo ice chest she'd stocked and dragged out on the deck a couple of hours ago. She extracted a fresh wine cooler for herself and held a second one out to Bunny, who declined.

"You keep drifting off someplace," Shirl said, sitting down with a grunt and squinting at Bunny. "I'm sitting here looking right at you, and you might as well be over there in China or someplace."

Bunny sighed. "I heard Sheryl Bigelow, Warren's wife, is getting remarried."

"No. So soon?"

"Nita told me."

"Well, she'd know, close as they all were."

"They weren't really that close."

"No?"

"No. Just Bob and Warren."

"Well, now I didn't know that." Shirl took a long pull on her wine cooler and looked out over the bay. "Honey, isn't that Jimmy Creech's boat? What's she called now, the *Angel III*? They rechristened her, you know, after that boy was killed on her. College kids are a menace, I'll tell you that. Many's the time your father came home cursing the air blue over some smart-ass summer kid who got tangled up in the gear or the nets. Over there, now isn't that Creechy?"

Bunny peered through the fog. "I think so."

"Shit, I didn't even know Creechy took the boat out anymore," Shirl said. "But no one crosses the bar like he does, with that sort of sideways sidle. Man will be one of a kind even in heaven or wherever. I think the good Lord broke the mold after seeing the way Creechy come out."

Bunny looked through binoculars hanging from a rope nailed to the deck. "Yeah, that's him, all right. Windbreaker with the hood up and tied tight under his chin."

Shirl chuckled. "Yup, Little Red Riding Hood, people used to call him. I heard his kids got together and talked him into deeding the boat over to them. Old bastard's got to be, what, eighty-five?"

"Something like that."

"He'll just drop one day, you watch," Shirl said with satisfaction. "So you talk to Fanny lately?"

"Couple of days ago, three maybe. She sounded okay."

"You must not have been listening then."

"Why? Is she bad?"

"Yeah, she's bad," Shirl said. "Frank told her she can keep the furniture—"

"That's bad?"

"—because he's getting married."

"Uh-oh," said Bunny.

"Uh-huh. He's marrying some woman it turns out he's been seeing on the side since forever."

"She never told me that."

"Well, she's got her pride," Shirl said.

"Even so."

"She probably didn't want to upset you, honey."

"Why would that upset me?"

"It's not exactly a secret you're on edge about Hack."

"Does she know something? She knows something, doesn't she? See, I *told* you there's—"

"She don't know a goddamn thing," Shirl snapped. "Christ almighty, Bunny. She just knows you're jumpy, that's all. That's *all*. And you are." Shirl stood up and pulled at the crotch of her knit pants. "I'm going to get something to eat and pretend we never talked about this. You want something?"

"No."

"Suit yourself." Shirl tugged open the sliding glass door that led into the kitchen, slid it shut behind her, then yanked it open again. "Mark my words, Bunny. If that man ever leaves you, you'll be the one at fault. There comes a time when you just have to believe in someone. You hear me?"

"Yeah, I hear you," Bunny said.

"No, you don't, and you never have. I don't even know why I waste my breath anymore." Shirl slid the door shut with a decisive thunk and disappeared inside.

Bob was having linoleum dreams. Every night it was a different pattern, but the rest was pretty much the same: He measured and cut and laid down the adhesive in big swirls with his trowel and then pressed down the flooring like he'd done it a million times. The glue went on like butter, and it all fitted exactly perfect.

In actuality, the stuff he had was vinyl, not linoleum, a pretty beige and blue in a tile pattern. Larry Hopkins was putting down a new floor in the Sea View Motel office and said he'd give the old stuff to Bob for free, just for hauling it away. It was in real good shape too, except for a couple of cigarette burns and a gash like someone had tried out new ice skates on it. Bob had been able to hide the damage under cabinets he'd salvaged from a house that was being torn down. He'd also scavenged a clawfoot bathtub for the bathroom, a heavy cast-iron thing that would last forever.

Not that he needed it to last forever.

He'd even found an old push lawn mower at a garage sale and mowed a little yard out of the weeds and wild grass. The place cleaned up so pretty. He couldn't imagine why anyone would ever have let it go.

"Bob? Come on in." Gabriella Lewis summoned him from the clinic waiting room. He tugged at his ball cap as he followed her down the usual corridor of posters and handbills. He thought she had a pretty nice backside for an archangel. You wouldn't necessarily expect that.

He sat in his schoolboy chair by her desk. She took her seat, folded her hands in front of her, and looked at him expectantly.

"I wanted to ask you about that pneumonia," he said.

"Pneumonia?"

"That one you said goes with AIDS."

"*Pneumocystis carinii* pneumonia, PCP. Why? Do you have a fever? You look well."

"Not me, my wife. She's been under the weather."

"What do you mean, under the weather?"

"Oh, just real tired and that. She got better for a while, but now she's not feeling good again."

"Fever?"

Bob frowned. "Yeah, probably sometimes."

"Is she coughing?"

"Maybe some."

"Look, surely you don't expect me to diagnose something from a conversation like this."

"Nah, I wouldn't ask you to do that. If she did get that pneumonia, she could die, though. Isn't that right?"

"You know that. I've already told you that how many times. PCP is swift, and it's deadly, especially in someone with a T-cell count under two hundred. Look at me." Abruptly the nurse reached across her desk, put her hands on either side of Bob's head, and turned him to look at her. *"Take your wife to the doctor."* She dropped her hands. "You're never going to do it, are you? And for the life of me I can't figure out why."

"Well, sure," Bob said, drifting along on his own thoughts.

"You haven't heard a word I've said."

"Yes, I have," Bob said. "I have."

He stood up and straightened his chair. It reminded him of being in school, those heavy chairs that made a noise like the rending of heaven when you scooted them. He'd always sat toward the back of the classroom, him and Warren, so they'd be overlooked for questions. Not that they were ever called on. Mostly teachers and parents looked right through them, their being so poor and often raggedy and all. Plus they didn't always smell good. People thought they didn't know it, but they did. It's just that it wasn't so easy getting to a real bathroom with a

shower and all. There had been a lot of times when he and Warren had gone out back of Eden's View into the woods with a
bucket of water and cleaned themselves that way, in the freezing
cold and with rags for washcloths. Of course, once they were in
high school they could shower to their hearts' content in the
locker room. They washed their clothes in the sinks until Coach
found out and offered them the school washer and dryer, which
was real nice given that neither of them had gone out for a sport
in their lives or ever would. By then Bob was wanting to date
Anita so bad it made his toes tingle. Warren had told him a million times that she'd never go out with someone like him, but
he'd been wrong; Bob had proved that. She'd come with him the
first time he asked her out toward the end of eleventh grade.
That was the first time he'd been able to summon up the
courage, her being so pretty and all. By then he'd had his big old
Buick; suddenly he was a man with transportation to offer. And
he guessed he was good-looking enough, though sometimes
people mistook him for Mexican with his skin tone and black
hair and all.

When he asked her out that first time, he'd put his car keys
into a little box he'd made in wood shop and had her open that.
It was a good way to break the ice, even if Warren had told him
it was silly and wouldn't ever work. She'd laughed and looked
him full in the face and said if he was asking her out for a drive,
why, she thought she'd accept. Now what other girl would do
that for a trash heap boy like him? You could have carted him directly off to heaven that day and he would have believed he'd
been granted his wings. Warren had slipped into a funk for a
week, but he pulled out of it eventually, like he always did. If Bob
had gotten a nickel for every one of Warren's bad moods, he'd
have been rich as a king by now. Warren was—had been—the

moodiest person Bob ever saw. Not that he didn't have some damned good reasons why. Jesus, imagine wanting another man the way he wanted Anita. How could he have stood it? Warren never had to drink when they *did that,* like Bob had to. And now that Bob thought back on it, Warren had had crushes on boys all through high school, though Bob didn't recognize them as crushes, of course, not back then anyway. He'd thought Warren's attentions were fueled purely by envy, especially since he admired their clothes as much as the boys themselves.

"Look," he'd whisper to Bob, and point out somebody's sweater. "Do you think it could be cashmere?" As though either one of them would know cashmere any more than they'd recognize a Rolls-Royce. What they did recognize, mostly, was clean instead of dirty, big enough or small enough instead of a bad fit. Even in high school they wore secondhand clothes they got at a place over in Sawyer. It didn't bother Bob much, but Warren was mortified. He'd cried bitter tears more than once over the outdated cut of a jacket or the wrong-way taper of a pants leg. Bob did the best he could to keep Warren's spirits up, but it didn't always work, and then he could count on hearing silence for days on end. Not that Warren would stay away from him; neither of them ever stayed away from the other one. No, Warren would just clam up, wade through the days like he was hip-deep in mud and working like hell to reach more solid ground. Bob wasn't moody himself, but he didn't hold that against Warren. He knew Warren wouldn't be like that if he'd had a choice, especially after his mother committed suicide by hanging herself off an old broken-back pine way up near the top of the windward side of Cape Mano. No one had ever figured out how she got there or why she chose that spot. Hell, no one even found her for more than a month, and that was just by accident when Julius Otten pulled over to take a leak on the way home from a Sawyer tavern. Scared the holy bejesus out of him, he was fond of saying; peed all over his own shoes when he saw that body dangling in open space over a nine-hundred-foot drop straight down to the ocean. Rocks down there too; big ones. How had she known the tree would hold her? What if it hadn't, and she'd plunged all the way down there and busted herself all up? They'd talked about it for weeks, all over town. All but Warren. He hadn't had more than maybe ten minutes to say about it all together, and that was mostly spent explaining how he'd been expecting it all along. Still, he had his mother's eyes, and when the heebie-jeebies were on him, he'd say, *Bobby, you know that look she'd get in her eyes sometimes, like things had gone all crazy in her mind? Sometimes I think I'm going to get that way too. God, Bobby, I think about things—things I shouldn't. Please don't let me do what she did, die all alone like that in the woods at night in the wind. It doesn't matter if you're dead. You're still you, and you're still alone hanging over a whole lot of nothing off the thin end of a pine tree.*

Bob would promise, of course, and if it got really bad, he'd take Warren to the homestead and lie down on the mattress ticking and hold him for hours in the gathering dark. And no matter how old he was, Warren would ball up and tuck into him just like a boy. They didn't *do that* then; never then. Bob would sing, sometimes; or they would talk. Mostly, though, they just *were.* And that was all right too.

Hack was sitting at his desk nursing the dregs of a migraine when Bob pushed open his office door and came in. It occurred to Hack that he hadn't seen much of the man in a long time except to hand over his truck keys from time to time. Jesus, he looked reborn: sunburned, bandy, bouncing up on his toes the way high school kids walked when they believed in themselves. Things must be going better at home. Hack hadn't asked in a while. There was only so much bad news you could take, and Bunny kept him apprised daily of the deepening shit that Anita had fallen into. The latest thing was some kind of skin problem or something; Hack hadn't been paying much attention. With Bunny, you couldn't.

"You busy?" Bob said, shifting from foot to foot in the doorway.

"Nah, just sitting here looking at the backs of my eyelids for a minute. You don't have any aspirin or Tylenol or whatever?"

"No."

"Yeah," Hack said regretfully.

"Ask Francine or Rae, maybe. Girls always have stuff like that in their purse."

Hack tried to rally. "So what can I do you for?" It wasn't much, an old joke, a real groaner.

"Do you have time to help me with something? It won't take long."

"Yeah? Will it cure a migraine?"

"Don't know about that," Bob said.

"Well, go ahead and try me anyway."

"I have this project I've been working on."

"You finally going to tell me what it is?"

"Aw, it's nothing much. I've been fixing up this place, is all. There's a bathtub I got to move in, but the bastard is cast iron, and I can't lift it by myself."

"You going to pay for my hernia?"

"What?"

"That was a joke. Yeah, I'll help you. You've got me curious now," Hack said. "When, this weekend?"

"Nah, I've got to get it in now, pretty much. How about I ask Francine for some aspirin or maybe some of those pills they take for the cramps, they'd probably help a headache, and then we can just go out and do it?"

What the hell, it beat sitting at his desk pretending to read sales reports. "Tell her to give me double the normal dose," he called after Bob, who'd taken off so fast he damn nearly left a contrail behind him like a cartoon action figure. And Bob wasn't the kind of man to move in a hurry normally. Hack was still fishing around in his pocket for his truck keys when Bob returned with a fistful of white pills and a Dixie cup of water. Whatever they were, Hack put four of them in his mouth and pocketed the rest for later, pounded back the water, and crushed the cup in his hand to take his mind off the rush of pain and nausea. If he made no fast moves, no abrupt changes in direction until the drug kicked in, he might just live.

"So where are we going exactly?" he asked Bob as he unlocked the doors to the truck.

"I'll show you as we go."

The cab was warm inside, and clean, smelling of wax and Armor All. Hack had detailed it from top to bottom over the weekend. "North or south?" he said.

"North."

Hack pulled out into traffic, heading north on Highway 101. "Remember those road rallies we used to go on, thirty-six checkpoints in four states in two days?"

"Yeah."

"That was fun. Maybe we should do that again sometime," Hack said.

Bob said, "Make a right turn up there."

"Here?"

"Yeah."

"This is Weyerhaeuser land."

"Uh-huh."

Hack shrugged and turned onto a gravel logging road that twisted and wound back into a valley he'd never seen before.

"There," Bob said suddenly, and there was a note of excitement in his voice that made Hack look a little harder. Down below them he saw a broken-down barn and an old cabin of some kind—rustic, but some people liked stuff like that. Him, he was all for his creature comforts, his recliner and his remote control and his occasional finger of scotch. He looked over at Bob. What the hell?

Bob hopped out of the truck before it had even stopped, looking like he was going to bust wide open with excitement. He trotted over to an old cast-iron tub resting upside down in the grass by the cabin door. "This is it. This is a real good old tub. They don't make them like this anymore. Problem is, I can't get it inside by myself." He grinned at Hack. "It's really something out here, isn't it? Isn't it just something?"

Hack pushed open the cabin door and walked inside. The cabin had only two real rooms, a front room and a back bedroom, plus a loft, a kitchen—or what Hack assumed was a kitchen, because he could see a sink through the doorway—and a bathroom. It was primitive but tidy and scrubbed and snug, with freshly sealed walls, a fire laid in the fireplace, and a green jar placed carefully on the mantel. Someone—Bob, evidently— had brought in an old rocker, a cane-bottomed chair, a primitive wooden bed, a bureau, a blanket chest, and a couple of old paintings, scenes of mountains and rivers. The bed was made up with soft old linens and a faded quilt.

"Holy shit," Hack said, impressed. "Did you do this yourself?"

"Yeah," Bob said proudly.

"Why?"

Bob stood in the doorway, considering. "Anita and me, we haven't been doing so good lately. So I thought, you know—" He opened his arms, taking in the cabin, the land, possibly the entire valley.

"So?"

"So I never gave her a nice house before," Bob said. "I always meant to."

"How in hell did you find this?" Hack said.

"Me and a friend used to come out here all the time when we were kids. It's been that long since anyone lived here. Never used to be a road until lately."

"It's Weyerhaeuser land, though," Hack pointed out.

"Yeah."

"They're going to find out, Bob. It might take a while, but sooner or later they're going to find out, and when they do, they're going to boot your ass."

Bob waved a hand dismissively.

Hack's head hurt too much to be having this conversation. "All right, look. Let's just hump the son of a bitch inside and get going. We're trespassing. Tell me at least you know we're trespassing."

"I know that," Bob said.

"All right, that's all I'm saying."

They grunted and lifted and twisted and squeezed through the door and fell into the makeshift bathroom on the back porch that Bob planned one day to plumb and outfit with a toilet and a sink, as well as the old clawfoot tub. A neat vinyl floor had been laid with precision. Hack was impressed in spite of himself; he'd never thought of Bob as the kind of guy who could pull something like this together, but maybe Hack had been underestimating him all this time. Maybe he was more than just an alcoholic screwup. Go figure.

"Did you see a lot of people die over there in Vietnam?" Bob said as they were catching their breath.

"What?"

"Vietnam."

"Yeah, I saw a lot of people die."

"I've never seen that."

"You're lucky then," Hack said.

"Is it bad?"

"It sure ain't good."

"Yeah. I've never seen it."

"I don't talk about that stuff," Hack warned, because he didn't. Ever.

"Nah. That's okay. You know it when they're dead, though, huh?"

"Yeah, you know it when they're dead." Hack picked up the green jar on the mantel, for something to do. "Heavy thing, isn't it?" he said.

"Yeah. It's somebody's ashes, a friend of mine."

"No shit?" Hack looked at the jar with interest, then put it back on the mantel.

"Yeah."

"Young guy?"

"Like us."

"Young. So what did he die from?"

"AIDS," Bob said.

"Shit," said Hack.

"Alone," Bob said. "He died alone."

"Huh."

"That shouldn't happen."

"Yeah," Hack said.

"It shouldn't."

"No. I know."

Both of them got quiet. "Was he a fag, or what?" Hack finally said, to lighten things up a little.

"No."

"Because I heard that most of the people who get AIDS are fags."

Bob shrugged.

"So you must have been good friends, though, to keep the guy around on your mantel."

"Yeah. I knew him from when we were little kids."

Jesus, was he crying? Bob had turned his back and put his head down. Hack looked closer, and sure as shit, Bob was crying. They must have been mighty damn close friends.

Hack walked over to one of the windows and looked out to give Bob some privacy. He said, "You lose someone, and it's like their dying is a thirty-five-pound undershirt you can't ever take off. It's the heaviest goddamn undershirt you've ever heard of, but after a while you get used to it. It's always there, but after a while you won't notice it so much."

Bob pulled up the bottom of his T-shirt and wiped his nose.

"Come on, sport," Hack said, clapping him on the shoulder. "Time to go."

"Yeah."

Bob closed the door carefully behind them, waiting for the latch to take. "So you like the place?" he asked. Vinny used to fish for compliments the same way.

"Yeah, man, I do. I like the place a lot."

Bob drew a deep breath, and then they climbed back in the truck and drove home.

Bunny was folding a heap of clothes at Anita's kitchen table. She'd come over first thing in the morning to see how Nita was doing. She'd called Bunny last night, crying, and said she was feeling like shit all over again. When she arrived this morning, Bunny saw a mountain of laundry four loads high in the back bedroom that Crystal and Doreen shared, and from the smell of it, it had been there for a while. It wasn't like Nita to let things go. She might not have much, but she took care of what there was.

Bunny had called and looked in every room, but no one was home. She loaded up all the laundry and took it to her house and ran it through her new washing machine with hot water for both the wash and the rinse cycles, along with a double dose of Spray 'n Wash. It was a splurge, especially the hot-water part, but from what Bunny could see, it might be the only thing that would get Bob's coveralls clean after sitting for so long with grease and muck all over them, front and back. The man must sit directly in the pools of oil and fluids on the garage floor, to get that filthy.

Anita was home when Bunny humped the clean laundry back. She was sitting at her kitchen table, perfectly still and perfectly silent, scaring the crap out of Bunny, who didn't even see her at first.

"Jesus Christ, Nita. I mean, whew, you nearly gave me a heart attack sitting there."

Anita pushed up from the table. "I'm sorry, hon. I was just—" She gestured vaguely around the room, but Bunny didn't see anything that would indicate activity of any kind.

"You all right, Nita?" Bunny said.

"Oh, sure. Sure."

"I brought you clean laundry," Bunny said carefully. "It looked like it might be getting ahead of you there in the back room."

"Was it?"

"Well, four loads. Is your machine still broken?" Anita had the oldest Maytag on the planet.

"Yeah. I asked Doreen to do our things at the hospital laundry, but she said she couldn't use it for personal."

"Well, I could see that."

"I didn't want to bother you."

"You could have."

"You do enough," Anita said. "I'm going to sit."

She was already sitting. Bunny said again, "You okay?"

Anita looked straight at Bunny for the first time. "No. I don't think so. What do you think this is?"

She tugged up her knit top and pointed to a purple spot the size of a quarter just above her left breast. When Bunny moved in closer for a good look, she noticed that Anita's bra fitted loosely. That was odd.

"A bruise?" Bunny said. "It doesn't really look like a bruise, though."

"See, that's what I said. I noticed it a couple days ago, but it doesn't hurt."

"Allergic reaction maybe?"

"I've never been allergic to anything," Anita said.

"Well, it doesn't look like a wart. Doesn't look like much of anything exactly."

Anita shrugged and lowered her top.

"Honey, you've lost some weight," Bunny said carefully. "Have you been dieting?"

"No. It's just happened. Not that I'm complaining."

"It doesn't seem right, though."

Anita sighed. "Well, I'm too damned tired to think about it anyway. I don't remember when I've been this tired."

"You running a fever again? You look like you've got one." Bunny laid her hand across Anita's forehead. "Maybe a little one. You're not real hot, though. When's the last time you took your temperature?"

"Nineteen eighty-six."

"I really think it's time you went to a doctor, Nita. This has been going on too long. It's been, what, three months maybe?"

"Off and on. I was better." Anita dipped into the laundry basket. "Well, I'll figure something out," she said. "Next Monday's payday, plus I've got money coming from the motel."

"I wish you'd let me take you. I'd loan you the money, you know that."

"It's only a few more days. I'll be fine."

Bunny didn't think so, but she let it drop. You could only push Nita so far, and then she dug in her heels and brayed like a mule. It didn't mean Bunny wouldn't worry, though. She'd worry all right. She thought she'd talk to Hack, get him to give Bob a hard kick in the ass. Bunny had never met anyone so oblivious. Anita had deserved better all these years, and that was a fact. Bunny couldn't see what she saw in Bob, never had. He was a skinny, lazy, worthless man who never seemed to get things right, at least not where Anita was concerned. The night Anita had had Patrick, Bob had picked up a bottle on the way to the hospital. By the time the baby arrived he was three sheets to the wind and on a bender that lasted, off and on, for a year.

"I've got me a son," he'd tell Bunny whenever he saw her, "and I got to be a father to him. How am I going to get that right? Huh? I never had a father; Warren never had a father, at least one who was worth a goddamn. You tell me how I'm supposed to get it right."

Of course Bunny was trying to deal with JoJo, and that made her surly, but even discounting her circumstances, she'd have had no patience for him. Bob was trash; he always had been, he always would be, and he was going to drag Anita down with him. She'd told Anita so even on the eve of her wedding; threatened to tie her up and kidnap her until her good sense kicked in, but of course she hadn't. There'd been many a time over the years that she wished to hell she'd gone through with it. This was one of those times, this rainy afternoon that oozed like a sore, as she watched Anita go down without so much as a struggle. But if there was one thing she knew from her years with JoJo and Hack, it was that you couldn't make someone do squat if they didn't want to. Nobody listened to anybody else and they never had, at least not in her experience. The most you could hope for was that they'd lip-read from time to time.

## chapter sixteen

Rae Macy was nervous; that was the first thing Hack noticed. The second thing was, she wasn't wearing perfume. He liked her perfume. Sometimes he could still smell it when he went to bed, like it had crawled up through his sinuses and taken root in his brain. She didn't have it on today, though.

"Can I talk to you for a minute?"

"For an hour, princess, if you want to."

"It won't take that long." She ran her palms down the sides of her skirt. It was a denim thing, more casual than what she usually wore. That was the second thing he'd noticed. "I wanted to let you know that I'm resigning."

"What?"

"I'm giving my notice." She handed him a plain white envelope. Her voice was steady enough, but her hands were shaking.

"Why?"

"My husband has asked me to head up his election campaign. He's decided to run for state representative."

"Your husband?" What was that shit? As though Hack were some stranger.

"Sam," she said, flushing. "Yes."

"You think he'll be any damned good at it?"

Rae bridled. "I think he will, yes. He has the right training, and he cares about people."

"You?"

"People. Me. Yes."

"You sure never said that before." He watched her flush.

"You know, you're not making this any easier," she said.

"Was I supposed to?"

"It would have been the generous thing to do."

"Then I'm not a generous man." He was all off-balance, like someone had hit him hard on the back of the head with a brick. He lifted up three of his desktop toy's six steel ball bearings and then dropped them sequentially. THOCK thock THOCK thock thock, THOCK thock—

Rae caught the ball bearings in her hand. "I'm sorry, Hack. I just can't do this anymore," she said quietly.

"Do what?"

"You."

"Why not?"

Rae just looked at him. It had been five days since they'd come home from Eugene.

"All right. Look," he said. "You don't have to quit, though."

"I think I do. Plus we've been talking about having a baby. I'm twenty-nine. I've always wanted children. A small town's a good place to raise a baby."

"Is it?" said Hack.

"Isn't it?"

"Depends."

"On what?"

"Whether you love somebody there."

"I love my husband," Rae said.

"Oh," said Hack.

"I'm just trying to do the right thing."

"So am I supposed to feel happy?"

"No, but look at it this way." She smiled a sudden, tight little smile. "You can score some points with your wife. Tell her you fired me."

"Hell, she doesn't believe anything I tell her," Hack said bitterly. "If I was the Virgin Mary, she'd accuse me of screwing the stable boy."

Rae stood up and laid a wrapped gift on his desk. "I thought you'd like to have this," she said. "It seemed to mean something to you."

He knew what was inside. It was the poetry book.

"I'm going now," she said. "I think it would be best if I make this my last day rather than work the two weeks."

"Best for who?" he said, but she was already gone.

He couldn't remember the last time things had felt this fucked up.

He picked up the wrapped book, grabbed his jacket and keys, and told Francine that he would be at an out-of-town meeting for the rest of the day. Five minutes later he was speeding north on Highway 101, his head so full of junk he could hardly see.

While Hack was holed up in Minna Tallhorse's apartment, the district attorney paid him a call. He was a greasy bastard, the kind of john Cherise had liked to service because they came fast and paid full price anyway. Hack and the DA sat on Minna's stove-in couch for hours with a tape recorder turning on the coffee table. Hack talked on and on, words tumbling out of him. He only came up for air when the DA had to change tapes.

"Slow down, son," he said, fumbling to thread a new reel of tape. "We've got all the time in the world."

There was no point in telling him that time had already run out. What was left wasn't time; it was purgatory. Instead, as the tape fed through, Hack talked, naming names, dates, places, events, a banquet of facts all served up from the excellent oven of his memory. When Hack was finally done, the DA wiped his face with a handkerchief and said, "Well, it's quite a story, son. Now, I have to ask you again whether you personally witnessed or had direct knowledge of everything you've told me. Do you under-stand that family quarrels have no place in the courtroom? What's between you and your mother is between the two of you."

"Yeah, I understand."

"And you're prepared to testify under oath to everything you've told me?"

"Yes, sir."

The DA scratched his head. "Mind my asking why you came to me with it?"

"There were reasons."

"I imagine there were." The man packed up his pens and tablets and tape recorder. "Well, whatever they are, the state of Nevada is grateful to you."

"Yeah."

At the door the DA turned back. "I'm sorry for your recent loss, son." He shook Hack's hand. "Real sorry." Then he'd taken his tape recorder, tapes, pens, pads, and briefcase and packed them into a snappy new Chrysler and driven away.

Hack washed his hands as soon as he closed the apartment door, used up half of Minna's bottle of Joy before he stopped.

*Oh, Buddy.*

*C'mon, she's a whore, a liar, a cheat, and a thief, and she has been for years.*

*It was nobody's fault, Buddy. See it for what it was. It was an accident.*

*You think we'd have been out on that road at three-thirty in the fucking morning if it hadn't been for her? That's bullshit. That's bullshit.*

*You're so angry.*

*Yeah, I'm angry.*

*You always get into trouble when you're angry.*

*Hey, you heard him. He said the goddamn state of Nevada would thank me.*

*Oh, Buddy.*

The next day he went down to the local recruiter and joined the army. They deposed him overseas and wrapped up the trial in just four days. Cherise was given the maximum sentence allowed by the state of Nevada. He heard that a year before her prison time was up she came down with liver cancer, but he didn't know whether it was true or not. Either way, it didn't matter to him. He could not, by then, have given a single goddamn.

Hack arrived on the outskirts of Portland at the height of rush hour. He could never see what the big deal was about living in a city. It didn't seem like much of a life to him, spending an hour in traffic to go twenty miles. Vinny sure seemed to love it, though. He drove by her house, but no one was home, so he battled his way downtown to see if she was at work. No, the other girls at the department store told him, she wasn't scheduled to work that day. No, no one knew where Hack might find her, but they'd be glad to give her a message when she came to work tomorrow afternoon.

Screw that. Hack put the gift-wrapped poetry book on his dashboard, where he could see it, and went across the

Willamette River again, inching along in traffic, cursing out loud until he lost patience completely and pulled into an AM/PM minimart just to get the fuck off the road for a few minutes.

"Where are you?" Bunny said over the phone. "It's late. I was worried."

"I'm here in Portland."

"Portland?"

"I came up to see Vinny," Hack said.

"Why?"

"No reason. I just thought I would."

There was silence on the other end of the line.

"It was a pretty day for a drive, so I just...drove," he said.

"You could have stopped here on the way," Bunny said. "I would have come with you."

He hadn't wanted to stop. He hadn't wanted her to come with him. "Yeah, I guess I didn't think you'd want to," he said.

"I would have, though."

"Well."

"So is she there?" Bunny said.

"I don't know. I'm stuck in fucking rush-hour traffic."

"How do you know she's even home?"

"I don't, Bunny. Call me crazy, okay? I just thought the kid might like a visit. That's all."

"She's a young woman now," Bunny said. "She's not going to want you up there all the time."

"I'm not up here all the time."

"You know what I mean."

Hack didn't say anything. He didn't want to know what she meant.

"What will you do if she's not there?" Bunny said.

"I'll drive home."

"And if she is there?"

"I'll take her to Elmer's or something and *then* drive home."

Silence.

"Look," Hack said. "I called you, didn't I?"

Bunny sighed.

"So, anyway," Hack said, "I'm getting off the phone."

"Wait, wait a minute. I went over to Anita's today. I think something's wrong."

"Here we go again."

"No, I mean, really wrong. She didn't seem right. She's got this, I don't know, this rash or something. And she's lost a lot of weight."

"Hell, throw a party."

"It wasn't like that," Bunny said. "I was going to ask you to go by there and see what you thought. I guess that's out, though."

"She's forty, for God's sake. She's a big girl."

Bunny wrapped the noose of recrimination around his neck. "I should have known you wouldn't understand," she said.

"Fuck that, Bunny. Just *fuck* that, you know? You think you've got me by the balls like some giant kite, like you can give me so much string and then—yank!—you can reel me back in again? Well, just fuck that. Fuck that, and fuck you too."

He slammed down the phone.

Now he'd gone and done it.

*Oh, Buddy.*

Yeah.

Vinny's car was parked in the driveway when he got back to her house. He pulled up to the curb but didn't turn the truck off right away. He watched through the living room window as Vinny walked through the room with a towel wrapped around her hair. Even years ago she was the hair-washing queen. She was dressed, though, so she'd probably put her head in the kitchen sink, not showered. She did that sometimes.

He turned off the truck and picked the wrapped book off the dashboard. She answered the door immediately, as he'd known she would.

"Hey, Vanilla Sundae," he said.

"What are you doing here?"

He couldn't tell whether she was pleased or not. "I ran away from home," he said.

"Does Mom know?" Still standing in the doorway, she took off the towel and shook out her wet hair.

"Yeah. She just chewed me a new asshole."

Vinny rolled her eyes. "Well, come on in."

"Is it okay?"

"You're here, aren't you?" She closed the door behind him. "God, the thing is, though, it's a mess. I wished I'd known you were coming. I mean, everyone's been real busy." She gestured broadly at the room, with its unfolded clothes and dishes and glasses and empty soda cans. Neither of them sat down.

"You eat yet?" Hack said in what he hoped was a light tone.

"The thing is, I'm going out in a couple of minutes. Someone's coming to pick me up."

"Oh."

"Yeah. So what are you doing in Portland anyway?"

"I had an errand to run for the dealership," he lied.

"That's a pretty long way for them to make you drive for an errand," she said.

"So anyway, I brought you something." He held out the gift-wrapped package.

"Oh, how sweet!" She tore the wrapping off. Inside, as he'd suspected, was the book of children's poetry.

Vinny looked up uncertainly and then brightened. "Oh! I know—was this one of my favorite books when I was little or something?"

"No," Hack said.

"I don't understand."

*Oh, Buddy.*

He made up something about getting two gifts mixed up—hers had been a new chemise, but he must have left that at home—and in minutes he was back in his truck, shaking so badly it took several minutes just to get the key in the ignition. As he pulled away from the curb, a car pulled into his place and a boy jumped out: a kid about the age Hack had been when it had all come apart. Vinny's date.

*She wasn't me, Buddy. She was never me.*

*You think I don't know that?*

*I think you didn't know it. Now you do.*

*Yeah. Now I do.*

*So what will you do?*

*I don't know.*

*It's cold here.*

*Yeah.*

It was one o'clock in the morning, and Hack was sitting at the overlook near the top of Cape Mano, looking at the halogen lights of the fishing fleet winking like stars out to sea. Jesus, he was cold. He'd started shivering halfway back from Portland, and he hadn't stopped since, not even after he'd cranked the heat up to high. Shit, maybe he should just light a small fire on the floorboards and warm himself that way. He could use the poetry book to get it started. Then he'd go ahead and add his marriage license and his house keys and his electric garage door opener. He'd toss in Bunny's Hack Neary Voodoo Bunny doll and a bunch of her other rabbits, and then maybe he'd add the goddamn piano no one knew how to play, and how about their bed, while he was at it? Now, that would be a thing to see. He got some satisfaction from picturing the refuse from all those years going up in a single whoosh and tower of sparks. A conflagration, one of the Katydid's thousand-dollar words. *Why do you talk like that, use a word no one but you can understand?* he used to ask her.

*Because it means what I mean.*

The Katydid always knew with crystal clarity what she meant. He used to envy that.

Hack thought about Minna Tallhorse. If she were here, what would she tell him? To buck up, probably; to pull himself together and move along. She never had had any patience for sloppy thinking or self-pity. She and the Katydid had had that in common. Thursday night dinner conversations with them were like sparring matches, requiring muscle and agility.

*You should find her, Buddy.*

*No.*

*Maybe she could help you.*

*The only thing we ever had in common was you.*

*That's not true.*

*Sure it is. You should have seen us, after—After. You weren't here. You don't know.*

*I couldn't help not being here, Buddy.*

*Yes, you could have.*

*How?*

*I don't know how. Somehow.*
*Is that really what you think?*
*Yeah, that's really what I think.*
*Oh, Buddy.*

Then he was sitting in the front seat of his truck at two o'clock in the morning, sobbing.

Bunny was afraid of the dark. She'd never admitted that to anyone, not even to Shirl, but it was true. Whenever Hack was away, she slept with the hall light shining in her eyes like a beacon. Tonight even that wasn't enough. She lay in bed as clenched as a fist, rigid with despair. Hack wasn't coming home, and he might never be coming home again. She'd tried to prepare herself for this moment for sixteen years, more strenuously in the last six months, and here it turned out she still wasn't ready.

If she'd kept her mouth shut this afternoon on the telephone, would it all have worked out differently? Probably not. Even if the blowup hadn't happened now, it would have been soon. He'd been coming apart for months; she'd seen it day by day. His step was a little heavier, his smile a little tighter, even sex was a little flatter, like he'd lost the joy of it—and it had always been his joy, even in bad times. When he was younger, he used to whoop like a rodeo rider when he came, lusty and transported to someplace where Bunny couldn't follow but didn't mind, because he was inside her, and that was worth something too. She used to come home all the time with abrasion burns from the thin, starchy sheets at the Patio Courts over in the Valley when Hack was especially keen, but she hadn't minded that, either. As long as she could do that for him, he would stay. When had she first forgotten that? Jesus, how could she have forgotten something like that?

Without Hack, who would she be? Who had she been, years

ago, before Hack, before JoJo even? She'd just been Shirl's kid, Fanny's little sister. She was nobody at all, a student who wasn't good enough or bad enough to be noticed in school, nobody's girlfriend for the longest time, until nasty little JoJo started to come around, and even that wasn't worth much. The night Vinny was born, JoJo never even showed up, so Bunny had had the baby alone except for a pair of mean obstetric nurses and a doctor who'd arrived after the show was over. Maybe he'd been drinking at the same bar as JoJo. He'd stunk of whiskey, shoved his hand up inside her like she was some kind of cow, and withdrawn it only when one of the nurses cleared her throat extraloud and told him the child had already been born.

And Jesus, having Vinny had hurt. Bunny had pushed and pushed and pushed against this stranger who hadn't wanted to leave, who'd wedged herself in Bunny's birth canal for the longest time, hours and hours. *Push*, the nurses kept snapping at her, like it was all her fault, and she pushed, and they told her, *Push harder*, and she pushed harder, but it was only when she started cursing JoJo at the top of her lungs that the baby had finally uncorked herself and shot from between Bunny's legs like a cannonball.

That was the last time in her life that Bunny had really been in the limelight. Right from the get-go, Vinny had been prettier than Bunny ever was. Shirl told Bunny that; Shirl's mother, Mayette, told her that; Bunny's father, Jack, told her too: *God almighty, girl, your head looked just like a squash when you come out of Bigger, there. I never saw anyone living or dead who looked uglier. Course, after a while you got better.* Vinny had been everyone's darling, a pleaser who learned early how to ask for things and get them. Bunny had always had to fight like hell for what she wanted.

At one o'clock in the morning she got up, turned on all the

lights in the house, and went into her sewing room. She was working on a fairy godmother rabbit, one with spectacles and a white mohair wig and a little magic wand. It was a variation on a figure she'd created over and over, a kindly soul whose job it was to fix other rabbits' problems. Who knew? Maybe it was God Himself in disguise. Bunny didn't know much about God, and none of that firsthand, but she certainly believed in some force that was out there granting incredible good fortune to people with flimsy prospects. How else did you explain why some people won the lottery, beat terminal cancer, reunited with long-lost twins or parents, stumbled upon fame? Call it magic or luck or Jesus, but it was real. She pieced the rabbit together with tiny stitches and the greatest skill she could muster, the muslin parts trembling in her hands like living things. She stuffed the limbs, rouged the cheeks, looped the wire spectacles behind the bunny ears, and as she worked, she offered up a fervent prayer: *Allow me to keep my life, O Lord, and I will put joy before envy, adoration before need, and love before judgment.*

At six o'clock in the morning, the telephone rang. Bunny nearly came out of her skin. She'd fallen asleep with her head on her sewing table, a rabbit arm still grasped in one hand to keep the stuffing from coming out. She picked up the wall phone in the kitchen, her heart in full flight.

"Do you know where Mom and Dad are?" It was Doreen, and the girl sounded panicky. "They aren't here. I don't think they've been here since yesterday. Did they tell you anything?"

"I haven't heard from them, honey," Bunny said, coming instantly awake. "I saw your mom yesterday morning, and she didn't say a thing about a trip."

"Well, they're gone," Doreen said, and started crying. "I can't take this. First Danny and all his crap and now this."

"Are you sure they didn't leave a note?"

"I'm sure."

"You looked everyplace? Did you look in the refrigerator?" Anita had left a note for the girl once inside the refrigerator, put it there when she was assessing groceries and then forgot to take it back out.

"Everywhere. I've looked everywhere."

"Is the car there?"

"No. They better not be gone. If they're gone, I'm going to just lose it. I am. What am I supposed to do with Crystal? It's Saturday. There isn't even Head Start. I have to be at work in an hour."

"Is Crystal still asleep?"

"Yeah."

"Okay. I don't work today, so I can take her if your mom's not back when you need to leave. I'm sure it's nothing serious."

"*Shit*," Doreen said, and hung up.

Bunny set the receiver in its cradle gently and sat down at the kitchen table, where she noticed that she still had a rabbit arm clenched in her fist. Maybe the whole world had just gone crazy.

Two hours later Bunny heard the garage door open. She held her breath until she heard Hack's truck come all the way inside and the garage door close behind him. Crystal was watching *Sesame Street* on television and didn't even look up when Bunny left the room.

She and Hack reached the kitchen at the same time, each from a different door. He looked like hell, and so did she. They both stopped just inside their doorways and stared at each other across the no-man's-land of the kitchen floor.

"Looks like a shoot-out at high noon." With the greatest effort, Hack managed a smile.

"I don't see any guns."

"Well," said Hack, "it never was about guns."

"No?"

"No."

"Then what was it about?" Bunny said, feeling her way.

"Ghosts," Hack said. "It was about ghosts."

## chapter seventeen

Bob had taken it slow yesterday, steering the old car down the logging road at fifteen miles an hour to avoid the ruts and potholes. It had been late afternoon, the time of day when a drunken man could forgive himself his lesser sins, knowing he still had hours to drink away the greater ones. Anita slumped on her side of the car, wrapped in an afghan she had made a long time ago, during one of the kids' bouts of chicken pox or the flu. It was a soft and stretchy thing, shapeless after how many years and knitted with odds and ends of yarn bright as a carnival. He remembered her knitting it, sitting in a chair by the window— which window? which house?—listening to her children breathe in the night. He recalled the click of the needles in the darkness—she knitted by feel and sound alone—safe in the knowledge that she was watching over them.

Now she was precious cargo, breathing heavily in the seat beside him. He'd told her he had a surprise for her, and at first she'd protested, but he'd worn her down. He fed her toast and aspirin and bundled her into the car. He'd found an old spool-turned rope bed at the thrift store just the day before yesterday, and a mattress with hardly any wear that fitted it just right. The house was ready at last to receive her.

When he rounded the final turn in the logging road, he whispered her name, but she'd fallen asleep, and he had to shake her shoulder gently to bring her around. Her forehead and cheeks and chin were livid pink. Her fever was on the rise.

"Nita," he said again, and pointed. The homestead was laid out below them like a dream, neat and tidy, half of it still glowing with sunlight, the other half already in the shadow of the steep valley wall.

"Where are we?" Anita had said, groggy with fever and sleep.

"Home," Bob said. "We're home."

"No. This?"

"Yup," he said proudly.

"What?"

"I've been working on it for months, darlin', just for you. Me and Warren fixed it up some when we were kids, but not like this. Not finished like this." Bob's voice caught with emotion. "It's yours."

Anita just looked at him with fever-dulled eyes. This wasn't the reaction he'd anticipated for so long and so often, but he'd show her the inside, and then she'd recognize his accomplishment. He pulled into the yard, rounded the car, and helped her out, looping the extra length of the afghan over her arm like the train of a wedding dress.

"I'm so sick, honey," she said. "Take me home."

"I have."

"I don't know this place."

"You will, though." Bob opened the front door for her and led her in. She saw now; he watched her see.

She looked at the furniture he'd found, and the walls and floors and windows he'd whitewashed and sanded and cut and installed with so much love, and said, "We aren't supposed to be here."

"Sure we are."

"It's Weyerhaeuser land."

"That's the beauty part." Bob lied nimbly. "I told them this homestead had been in my family for seventy years, and they said in that case we could just go right ahead and live here as long as we wanted."

Anita bought it. She walked through the front room, the kitchen, the little bathroom—not fancy but adequate, judging by the fact that she closed the door gently and peed into the sickroom commode he'd brought in just yesterday. Bob listened to the sound and felt a lump rise in his throat. He had done this. He had done all this for her, and now she was here.

"Please take me home," she said, with him again. The afghan had slipped off all but one shoulder and was dragging on the floor. He draped it more securely and led her into the bedroom by the elbow. "We don't have to," he said, and patted the bed invitingly.

"Please."

"You can lie down right here."

"Does Doreen know where we are?"

"Sure." He lied again. "Course."

"I'm so sick, honey," she said, and pressed the flat of her hand to her chest.

"I know," he said softly. "I know you are, darlin'. It's going to be all right, though. Papa's going to make it all right."

"I have to lay down, honey."

"I know you do."

"I guess I better see somebody tomorrow if I'm not better."

"Sure," he soothed, turning back the quilt and top sheet on the bed he'd made up with so much care. He helped her take her shoes off and pulled the covers over her once she lay down. "Now, isn't that nice?"

She closed her eyes.

"You like it?"

"It's real nice, honey," she whispered.

"A house of your own."

"I'm so tired. Maybe you can call Bunny and ask her to come get me. I've never been tired like this before."

"It's okay, though," Bob said. "I'll pour you a cup of tea."

He opened the Thermos he'd brought, but by the time he'd poured a cup Anita was asleep, breathing heavily. He could feel the heat rising off her. Should he wake her up and give her more aspirin? She seemed peaceful enough, though. And it wasn't like she was going to get better. She could go very quickly, Gabriella Lewis had said. That would be the best thing. Maybe in her final sleep she'd dream of him: a joyful dream, a love poem. She'd be young again and wearing her gown, but in this dream she would be Miss Harrison County herself and not a runner-up, and he would lead her down the aisle on his arm, the satin sash across her bosom, the tiara of brilliants threaded through her hair. She would be weeping, leaning against him in the momentary weakness of her joy. And he would steady her.

He pulled up an old cane bottom chair with a broken leg and ran his index finger over the pale veins in the back of her hand, veins he knew like a road map home. It was just the two of them now, him and Anita. It had never been just the two of them before. There had always been someone, Warren or Patrick or Doreen or Crystal. She hadn't admired the place as much as he'd pictured, but she'd appreciated it in her own way, he was sure. She'd appreciated it and gone to sleep knowing him as a man of achievement. No one could take that away now. Once you knew something, you knew it.

As he watched and stroked and settled more deeply into the weary old bones of his chair, Anita passed into a deepening fever sleep, and her lungs sounded like they were full of dish-washing detergent, bubbly and thick. He pressed her hand to his lips, stroked her forehead gently now and then. He sat and watched the shadows gather in the room and thought about him and Warren and Anita and all that had gone wrong, and all that had gone right, and it seemed to him that it had mostly been good.

Anita was suspended in a well so dark and so deep she couldn't tell which way was up, only that it was hot where she was, and airless. She sensed that she was drifting, but she wasn't frightened by it, or even curious. She was working too hard to breathe.

She heard Bob talking. What was he doing down here? The man had never been reliable, and now he was saying things that made no sense. *It won't be long before I'll be there too, darlin'. And I'm thinking it's going to be a nice place, all white, maybe, and clean and new and where all the walls and ceilings and floors meet without caulking, and the plumbing's brand-new and the windows fit absolutely perfect. You think that's how it'll be, maybe, all white like that?*

Then Bunny was in the well too, or at least her voice was there saying the same thing over and over: *Oh, my God.* Anita would have liked to open her eyes, to ask Bunny what she was doing in this place, but she couldn't seem to lift her eyelids she was so tired. She could hear, and she could breathe, but that was all, and the breathing was getting harder. It was like the atmosphere was turning to glue. Why would she be down there in a hot, airless well full of glue?

Someone laid something cool on her forehead, cool and wet like paradise had arrived here on earth. Bunny. Bunny always knew what to do; her and Hack. So capable. So successful. You knew it just by looking at them. Not Anita, though. Not Bob. People like them had to struggle all their lives and still ended up in a dark, hot well, and she knew now that there wasn't a damned thing she could have done to prevent it. She could have met Hack a thousand times over, and he would still have chosen someone else. She understood that from the time you were born you were given one thing to become—a great doctor, say, or a king. In Anita's case, she was meant to love, even in the face of great trial. And so she had: She had loved Bob with all her might, through anger and disappointment, through famine and bitterness. She had done that for him, that one thing he needed so much. But she was finished now; she had been released in order to keep breathing. She heard someone weeping and felt the glue thickening in her lungs and fought for every single breath.

She fought and she fought, and she failed, and she was so sorry.

Then there was nothing. Nothing at all.

Bunny stood at the foot of the bed, tears coursing unchecked down her face. If she and Hack had come earlier, right after Doreen's phone call, they might have been able to save her.

Should Bunny have sensed just how much trouble Anita was in? If a signal had come, it had been too weak for Bunny to hear over the din of her own troubles. Doreen had been frantic, but she'd been frantic before over things that meant nothing. It had been afternoon before Bunny finally asked Hack if he knew where Anita and Bob might be. To her surprise he seemed to know just where to go, and in minutes after dropping Crystal with Shirl, he and Bunny had been at the door of a small cabin way back in a lonely valley. She looked at Hack for an explanation, but he didn't say anything, just pulled up next to Bob and Anita's old car and, knocking, let them in the front door.

Bunny could hear Anita's terrible breathing the minute they were inside. She must have already been in a coma by then, though Bunny didn't know that at first, only that Anita's skin was pasty, hair soaked and oily against the pillow.

"*Jesus,*" Hack had said, rushing to the bedside, pressing past Bob. "She's drowning. Sit her up." He pulled Anita up and propped pillows and rolled bedding under her. She moaned and slumped to one side without regaining consciousness.

"Oh, my God," Bunny said. "Oh, my God, oh, my God."

Bob stayed exactly where he was, rocking himself gently in a little three-legged chair by the side of the bed, watching Anita sink.

"Cool her down," Hack told Bunny. "Wet anything you can find. I'll go find a phone and call an ambulance."

Bunny pulled the quilt off the bed, rushed into what passed for a tiny kitchen, and pumped the hand pump in the sink. The water came out clear and cold. When she laid a heavy swath of wet cloth over Anita's forehead, Anita's eyes flickered under the closed lids. Bunny whispered, "It's okay, honey. I'm here."

But it wasn't okay. When Bunny moved the wet cloth to put a

new, cool length on Anita's forehead, Anita twitched convulsively. Bunny jumped away, frightened.

"I believe she's going," Bob said quietly. He stood, lifted one of Anita's hands to his lips, and whispered, "Honey, you make sure you save me a place, 'cause I'll be there soon myself."

Bunny laid her hand over Anita's brow, as though she could will Anita to fight. For every labored breath of hers, Bunny drew three, fast and shallow until she started feeling faint. She held Anita's free hand and keened a voiceless prayer: *Let her stay here with me.* But it was no good. Anita exhaled a convulsive breath, and her chest never rose again. Instead her eyes flew open, staring at Bunny. "Oh," Bunny cried out. "Oh, no. Oh, my God."

Hack came around Bunny and closed Anita's eyes with gentle fingertips. For the first time in years Bunny had no idea how long he'd been in the room.

Hack leaned against the cabin doorjamb, his back to the room and his arms folded tightly across his chest. He'd stood beside Bob for a minute, then pressed his shoulder hard and walked away. In a world ordinarily filled with his own noise, he didn't have a thing to say.

High up on the logging road, a siren wailed. Hack had stopped at the first house he'd come to and called 911.

Now Bob fussed over Anita, crossing her hands over her bosom, turning her head slightly as though she were listening to celestial voices, straightening her legs. Bunny watched until she couldn't stand it anymore. "Jesus Christ, Bob," she hissed, "can't you leave her alone? Just leave her the *fuck* alone."

"Bunny," Hack warned, coming back into the room ahead of two paramedics wheeling a gurney.

She walked out of the house and across the scrubby lawn to the little creek—Homesick Creek, Bob had called it. *When someone dies, the angels sing to guide their spirit home,* Shirl used to tell her when she was little, as though death were no more than a trip to Disneyland. Bunny knew now that that was a crock. No expression of wonder had filled Anita's face, nor any glimmer of joy at being received at the Lord's heavenly gates. Anita had simply left them, without drama, without moment, without recognition of her impending death. She died the way she had lived, underrecognized and without gratitude or celebration.

It was June and warm. There was a fog bank looming like a solid wall just over the hill, but it wouldn't reach this far back in the valley. Bunny slipped off her shoes and stepped into the creek, gasping at the cold. Underwater her feet were white and pretty, the toenails painted bright red just that morning. Anita had always admired Bunny's feet. Her own third and fourth toes were fused together and she'd always kept them covered no matter what the circumstance or weather. Bunny hadn't thought they were so bad, but Anita held on to that one vanity even after she'd gained so much weight and let the rest of herself go. Bunny should say something to somebody so Anita was buried with her feet covered. Whom did you tell about something like that, that Anita wouldn't want to go through all eternity with her toes showing?

The cold-water pain in Bunny's feet was terrible, but she made herself stand it and stand it until the pain became unbearable and moved straight up into her heart.

"Are you riding in the ambulance?" Hack asked Bob.

"Yeah, I'll ride." He smoothed the sheet back over the bed. It had been tossed aside by the medics when they'd moved Anita onto the gurney.

"Doreen called us," Hack said, watching him. "She was afraid something had happened to you."

Outside, an ambulance door slammed.

"You want us to tell her?" Hack said.

"Yeah, you could tell her."

"Do you have some way of getting hold of Patrick?"

"What? Naw, Nita's got something somewhere about that."

One of the paramedics appeared in the doorway. "We're ready, sir."

"Yeah, okay."

Hack clapped Bob on the back as he passed in front of him, thinking he'd never noticed before how small a man he was.

Bob followed the paramedic to the ambulance. He was young, maybe Patrick's age. What would Patrick and Doreen say when they heard Anita was gone? Doreen would be annoyed, probably, the girl not being one to see farther than the end of her own nose. Patrick now, Patrick might be different. The boy would suspect. He had seen Bob and Warren together once, in the woods where they'd gone to play. They'd been done and were cleaning themselves up, but Bob was sure Patrick had figured it out, his being eighteen by then. He'd stopped twenty feet away, stricken. Bob hadn't said anything. What was there to say? The boy had fled without a word, blindly snapping twigs and tripping over ferns and roots. Next day he'd told Anita he'd enlisted in the army. Yes, when he heard about Anita, Patrick might figure things out. If Anita hadn't already written to Patrick that Warren had died, Bob would keep it from him.

Patrick didn't need to know right now. Bob couldn't have him knowing.

What had Gabriella Lewis said? *I don't know if you pray at all, but if you do, this might be a good time to step things up a little.* Well, all that was past now. Bob would have to stop by and see her one day, let her know that Anita was out of danger. He figured she'd be glad.

Hack wondered how many deaths he had witnessed. Dozens, certainly. In Vietnam, death had waited around every bend in the road, in every jungle clearing, every town and field and paddy. You could kill with the most basic technology: a can of nails, a canister of fuel, a trip wire attached to a forty-year-old grenade. He once saw a soldier sheared in half by a spinning saw blade. Even the smallest child could carry a bomb.

*Death doesn't hurt, Buddy. You should know that.*

*It doesn't?*

*No.*

*Well.*

*It was brave of you, offering to tell the daughter like that.*

*I figured it was my turn. Minna had to tell me.*

*She loved you.*

*Did she?*

*Yes, Buddy, she did. Too much. It scared her. She'd never loved anyone like that before.*

*Like what?*

*So much it was hard to breathe after we were gone. Like being on the moon without a spacesuit.*

*She never forgave me.*

*She never blamed you in the first place.*

*No?*

*No. Only in your mind, Buddy.*

*I don't want to talk about that.*

*She used to say people don't mourn death; they mourn their inability to prevent it.*

*Is that true?*

*What do you think?*

Bunny watched Hack step out the cabin's front door and come to her as she stood in the creek.

"Are you all right?" he said when he reached her.

"No."

"No," he said. They went back to the cabin's front door and sat side by side on the sill with their knees drawn up. Hack drew lines in the dirt with a twig. "Would it help to know that she wasn't in pain?" he said.

"How do you know?"

"I've seen people die in pain. That's not what it looks like."

"Do you think she knew what was happening to her?"

"I think she might have."

"Was she scared?"

Hack ran a blade of grass over the toe of his boot, tracing the decorative stitching. "I don't know. No."

Bunny drew a deep, shuddering breath. "I keep thinking I could have done something. I should have done something."

"Like what?"

"I don't know. Known, or something."

"Listen to me. No one could have known about this," Hack said. "It happened way too fast."

"But what if we'd looked for them sooner?"

"Don't."

Bunny looked directly at him for the first time, imploring, her eyes swollen and her nose running.

"Don't do that," Hack said. "What if."

"I can't believe she's gone." Bunny dropped her head into her arms. Hack leaned against her, pressed into her a little more deeply with the length of himself.

"Say something," she said after a while.

"You want a Kleenex?"

Bunny gave a half laugh, half sob and held up a sodden tissue she'd held balled in her fist. "God, what I must look like."

"You look okay," Hack said. And she did.

"Everyone's leaving," she said.

"Leaving?"

"Leaving me." Bunny turned to him bleakly. "Anita. Vinny. You."

"I'm right here." Hack patted the doorsill.

"That's not what I mean."

"I know it's not what you mean."

"You're in love with that girl," Bunny said. "You don't need to tell me."

"Look." Hack pulled away from her. He could feel her stiffen beside him, lock her eyes on her shoes, fortify herself against more bad news. He pressed his thumb and index finger into his eyes.

*Tell her about me, Buddy. Tell her about me now.*

"There are some things you should probably know."


Anita's body had been secured and covered with a sheet on the gurney inside the ambulance. That was all right with Bob. In death the body was nothing, not Anita or anybody else. He thought about telling the paramedics that, but it was too much of a struggle to find the words. As they climbed the valley wall— no siren now, everything so still, so *over*—he knew he would never come back to this place again. The memories were that perfect.

## chapter eighteen

Hack sat in Gabriella Lewis's office at the public health clinic, relaxed and expansive. It was two weeks before Christmas, and he was feeling good, all things considered. There was no official reason to keep her informed about Bob's case, but he had found her insights comforting in the past, and she always seemed glad to see him.

"He's not eating. Drinking, yeah, but not eating. You think that's going to bring the AIDS on?" Hack asked.

"I don't know. It could. Or not. Even HIV positive people can die of other causes. He certainly doesn't appear to be symptomatic."

"No. He ever tell you how he got the thing in the first place?"

"We discussed it briefly."

"He said he got it when he gave blood a couple years ago, remember that, when the blood banks were so low?"

Gabriella started to say something and then evidently changed her mind, saying simply, "Yes, I remember."

"He says you're an archangel. Do you know what that's all about?"

"He's thinking of the angel Gabriel, I suppose." The nurse's face was as soft and worn as chamois. She regarded Hack with some amusement.

"*Are* you the archangel Gabriel?"

"No, I'm afraid not." She smiled at the thought.

"Well, don't tell him that, because he thinks you're keeping an eye on him and Anita."

"I suppose that's harmless enough."

"You think this whole AIDS thing might be God's way of getting back at us for fucking things up?"

"I'm afraid I don't have an inside track into the thoughts of the Almighty. For what it's worth, I think it has more to do with viral mutation. The granddaughter—how is she?"

"Good—she's good." Hack had told Gabriella about Crystal, even brought her in one day so the nurse could meet her. "She and my wife have gotten real close, closer than she ever was with Vinny."

"People change."

"Yeah, I guess they do. That's not what everyone says, though."

"I don't think it happens all that often."

"Yeah."

"It must be making things a little easier for Crystal, having Christmas to look forward to. After all those losses."

"Oh, man," Hack said. "Bunny has presents hidden all over the house for her. She's getting a Barbie car. Can you believe that? Her first set of wheels at four."

"You're very generous."

"Nah. We just have the money to spoil her a little, is all. People always pretend they're buying stuff for their kids, but don't believe it, we do it for ourselves."

"Even so."

Hack stood and patted down his pants pockets for keys. "Yeah. Well, I better get going," he said. "Listen, you have a merry Christmas."

"Thank you." The nurse stood too and held out her hand. Hack grasped it warmly. "I hope your family has a wonderful holiday too," she said. "For what it's worth, I think you've earned it."

Hack raced the rain to his truck, thinking that if Gabriella Lewis *was* an emissary of God, He had made a good choice. She reminded him of Minna Tallhorse, about whom he'd been thinking more and more lately, though he wasn't sure why. On pure whim he turned into the parking lot of the public library. The Katydid would have been appalled that he'd never been inside it until now, not once in all these years. Now he asked a reference librarian how he could find telephone area codes in North Dakota. She found them in a reference directory on the first try. Hack borrowed a pencil stub and a slip of paper and wrote down the numbers. He wondered if Minna's hair still hung to her waist, thick and coarse and strong as horsehair and gleaming like armor. It had been a long time since he'd seen her face even in his dreams, but suddenly there she was, as perfectly rendered as a hologram in his mind's eye. And she was so young, much younger than he was now. He'd never realized how young she was when she took them on, him and the Katydid. The last thing she'd said to him before he left the safety of her apartment for good was: *I love you. Remember that. It might help.*

He folded the slip of paper in half and stuck it in his left breast pocket.

Most Thursday afternoons before dinner Hack took Crystal to visit Bob, who still lived at the house on Franklin Court, now a sorrowful place with its thick layer of grime and prevailing odors of cheap beer, machine oil, and rust. There hadn't been a scrap of toilet paper in the house in weeks, and Anita's plants were all dead, blackened and upright in their pots as though seared by a sudden blast of hellfire. The smallest tap, and the leaves would shatter.

Tonight Crystal fidgeted under Hack's hand, which he'd rested on her small shoulder for whatever reassurance it gave. She held a stuffed rabbit in her arms, a Grammy doll Bunny had made for her after Anita's death. At first Crystal had looked for Anita anew every time they went to the house, but it had been six months now, and she seemed resigned to Anita's absence even if she didn't understand it.

"How's my favorite baby girl?" Bob said too heartily, reaching for her and pulling her into an unsteady embrace.

Crystal pulled away. "You don't smell good, Granddad."

"No?"

"Pee-yew." She held her small nose between her thumb and index finger with elaborate conviction.

"Kid says I smell bad," Bob announced to Hack, as though he hadn't been standing two feet away. "You think I smell bad?"

"Yeah." Bob had on his oily Vernon Ford coveralls, which he'd been wearing for more than a week straight, even though he hadn't worked in much longer than that. His real profession now was drinking, which he dedicated himself to with singular cunning, energy, and purpose.

"When's the last time you ate something?" Hack asked him.

"Now, that's a tough one." Bob frowned. "Coulda been yesterday. Day before, maybe. Some of that flank steak Bunny fixed—I had some of that."

Hack sometimes brought their leftovers by. If Bunny didn't

exactly sanction it, she didn't stop him either. "That was last week."

"No kidding? And see, it stayed fresh and delicious that whole time. She's a fine cook."

Hack sighed. "Look, you need to eat. How about coming home with us and we'll rustle up something?"

"Bunny don't like my being in the house. She thinks I don't know that, but I do. Woman can't even look me in the eye," Bob said.

"She's doing her best." Bob was right, though. Bunny didn't want him around, though she tried to treat him civilly—not for his sake, as she told Hack, but for Anita's.

Bob gave Hack a sly look. "So, hey. You got a little beer money for your old friend?"

"Nope."

"Cheapskate," Bob muttered. He dug an empty peanut butter jar out of the back of a cupboard and regarded it dolefully. "Nita and me, we always kept our change in here. Usually had enough for a beer or two. Someone musta taken it, though."

"You did."

"No kidding?" Bob frowned. "Coulda, I guess. Nita, she always got so mad when I took money out of there. Our nest egg, that's what she said it was. Saving up for when we got old." Bob leaned in and stage-whispered, "Don't need to worry about that now, though, huh?" He chuckled. "Nope. No need to worry."

Crystal slipped a hot, damp hand into Hack's.

"Look," Hack said. "You think you can make it to work tomorrow? The old man's on my case, says he could hire some young guy who would cost less and be more reliable."

"Aw, hell, I don't know." Bob gave Hack an earnest look. "You could tell him I've got some medical problems. Need a little time."

"He doesn't want to hear that anymore."

"No?"

"No."

"Well, what the hell can you do anyway?" Bob said sympathetically. "Man's put you in a tough spot, all right."

Hack shook his head. Crystal gently tugged on his hand. "Time to go, kiddo?"

"Uh-huh."

"Hey now," Bob said, "you just got here. Don't you want to spend some time with your old Granddad?"

"No," Crystal said.

"No?"

"No," she said firmly.

"Well, kid's got a mind of her own, and I say that's good," Bob said with some dignity.

"Look—" said Hack.

"Nita, she'd say so too." He leaned in again and said, "You know, she's seeing all of this from up there." He lifted his face to the ceiling, lost his balance, and stumbled backward. "Don't matter if I can't see her." He pulled his filthy coveralls straight. "She's up there all right."

"Bob—"

"Her and Warren, they're up there smilin' down."

Hack gave up. "Listen, sport, we've got to go."

"Well, course," Bob said. "And tha's okay too. I got me a houseful anyway."

Hack looked up from retying Crystal's shoe. "Houseful of what?"

"Souls. Whatever."

"Oh. Right," Hack said, but he'd already moved on. "Look. To-morrow the old man wants to talk to me about you. You sure you can't come in? He's a pushover; he'll keep you if he thinks you're trying." The truth was, Hack had already been stalling Marv Vernon for months, telling him Bob would come around if they just gave him a little more time.

"Naw, tha's okay. Man's gotta do what he's gotta do."

Hack couldn't tell if Bob was alluding to himself or to Hack. He guessed it worked both ways: Bob wouldn't come to work, and Hack would have to fire him. There wasn't any point in put-ting it off anymore; even Hack could see that. Bob was a smok-ing ruin by the side of the road. He and Bunny would bring over food more often, slip Century 21 a couple of months' rent, pay the electricity, pay the phone bill so Bob could call if he needed them. There wasn't anything more they could do. As Hack backed out of the driveway, Bob lifted a hand in farewell or benediction. Every good-bye now looked like forever.

"You okay there, peanut?" Hack asked Crystal. "Granddad didn't look so good, huh?"

Crystal nodded in vigorous agreement. "He was stinky."

"Well, he's not feeling too good right now."

Crystal nodded solemnly. Hack wondered what went on in her small head. So many separations in such a short period of time, and it hadn't only been separation from Danny and Anita. After her death Bob had plunged alone into a bottomless sea of beer, and a month later Doreen had moved up to Portland alone to live with Vinny and work at Meier & Frank. But maybe that was for the best. She was appalled by Bob's HIV status, which she had discovered when the medical examiner's report showed

that Anita had died of AIDS-related *pneumocystis carinii,* and refused to see him. She'd lost ten pounds since moving and had a
boyfriend now, a nice boy, not like Danny. He wasn't thrilled at
the idea of having a kid around, though—he was only twenty
himself—and anyway, day care was too expensive to afford on
Doreen's wages.

It had been Bunny who'd suggested that Crystal live with her
and Hack. With Vinny gone, they had the space. Rather than give
Crystal the back guestroom with its one small window and stale
air, Hack had cleaned out Vinny's old room one day when Bunny
was at work. Bunny hadn't known about it until she came home
and found Vinny's things boxed and ready to take to a storage
place over in Sawyer, the room itself as empty as a blown egg. He
and Bunny hauled the things over to Sawyer the next day, ar-
ranging everything neatly with an aisle down the middle and the
boxes stacked and labeled high on either side, orderly enough
for eternity. Bunny had made Crystal new curtains, a new dust
ruffle, and a bedspread, cheerful things with, what else, rabbits
all over them. That's when Bunny had made the Grammy doll
too, to keep Crystal company when she felt lonesome. She told
Hack she hadn't been able to bring herself to make a Granddad
doll to go with it—the bastard was still alive, for one thing—and
on her own Crystal had never asked for one.

As soon as they got home, Crystal raced to her room and
brought back a new rabbit dressed as Santa Claus. "Look what
Bunny made me."

Hack frowned. "I give up. Who's it supposed to be?"

Crystal put her hands on her tiny hips. "*Santa.* Santa Claus."

"Boy, you'd think the elves would be missing him, though,

huh? It's their busy season and everything. Maybe you better send him back."

From the sink Bunny shot him a look. Crystal held out the doll to Bunny uncertainly.

"What's she doing?" Hack said.

"Sending him back."

Crystal had started to cry. "Oh, no, honey," Bunny said, folding the doll back into Crystal's arms. "Hack was just teasing you. He's yours for keeps. He's not the real Santa Claus, he's just Santa Bunny."

"Shame on you," she said to Hack once Crystal had stopped crying, accepted a juice box from Bunny, tucked the rabbit more firmly under her arm, and gone off with considerable dignity to watch *Sesame Street*.

"Jesus, I never expected her to take me seriously," Hack said. Vinny had always loved to be teased and could give as well as she got. "Poor kid."

"I don't think anyone ever teased her before," Bunny said "You know, I don't think she got that much attention, period. I'm sure Nita did the best she could, but you can tell she had her hands full just keeping Doreen's feet on the ground."

Hack leaned on the kitchen counter, watching Bunny wash lettuce.

"So how was Bob?" she said, giving him a sideways look.

"Blotto."

"I figured." Bunny took a tomato out of the vegetable bin in the refrigerator and cut precise wedges with a knife she kept lethally sharp. Lately Hack had found it comforting to watch Bunny prepare food. She had a sure hand and moved around her appliances and cutlery with an athletic grace. It surprised him that he'd never noticed it until recently. The Katydid had been all business when she was in the kitchen. Minna, on the other hand, had been a slovenly cook for their Thursday night dinners, gesturing with a loaded spoon to illustrate some point, cutting meat and vegetables into large chunks and then cursing at the stove when they failed to cook through. On Thursday nights they always said a mock grace: *God help us eat this food.* It cracked up the Katydid every time.

"How soon till dinner?" Hack asked now.

"Fifteen minutes. Maybe twenty."

"All right. I'll be done by then," Hack said.

"Done?"

"Phone call." He waved the slip of paper he took out of his breast pocket, went into the living room, and called directory assistance. Minna was listed. His hands were trembling faintly as he punched in the number. He listened to two rings, and then he heard that voice—a little deeper, a little huskier—shoot like a burning arrow straight into his gut.

"A friend of mine killed his wife the other day," he said. "I don't know why, but it made me think of you."

"Ah," she said dryly. "Well, it's always nice to be remembered."

"How are you?"

"Older," Minna said. "I assume the same is true for you?"

"Yeah. Smarter too. Not a lot smarter, but smarter."

"That generally happens to people who listen well. Do you listen well now?"

"I'm learning. So what about you? Are you married?"

"No. There have been some people, but no."

"Good people?"

"Most of them."

"But no one stayed?"

"They stayed. I didn't. It's a skill I've learned," she said. "How to leave. I do it all the time now."

"So, that's not good."

"No, not very," she agreed. "Why did your friend kill his wife?"

"So she wouldn't find out he had given her AIDS."

"We have some cases on the reservation already. Drug users mostly."

"He didn't use drugs."

"It's sad, isn't it, the things we sometimes leave hanging in our closets?"

"He didn't want her to find out. He said he wanted her to be as in love with him when she died as she'd been when they got married."

"So he killed her?"

"He fixed up a house for her, the thing she'd always wanted most, and then he took her there and watched her die."

"A bit twisted, wasn't it?"

"Yeah. Not to him, though. To him it was perfect. For a while it looked like my wife was going to press manslaughter charges, but she let it drop at the last minute."

"So you have a wife."

"Yeah—Bunny."

"Please don't tell me that's why you chose her."

"What's why?"

"Her name. You have a certain history, shall we say, with animal names."

"Nah," Hack said, cracking a smile. He'd forgotten what a strenuous business it was, talking with Minna. "I just call her that. It isn't even her real name. Her real name's Bernadette."

"And does Bernadette know everything there is to know about you?"

"She didn't," Hack said. "Now she does. It took me some time to get ready."

"Katy was the only one of us with a knack for wearing her soul inside out. No lies, no secrets. It's why people always took to her."

"They did, didn't they?" It had been years since he'd talked to anyone who'd known the Katydid. He'd forgotten how good it felt.

"The two of you were so damn fierce about each other," Minna was saying. "I used to think if one of you fell off a mountain, the other one would jump off right after just so you'd be together when you hit bottom."

"Yeah. It didn't work that way, though, did it?"

"No."

"Do you think about her?"

"Quite often."

"I dream about her all the time." Hack gave a hollow laugh. "And she's usually giving me shit about something."

"That would be Katy. A girl who knew her worth."

"Yeah." From the kitchen Hack could hear Bunny clanking plates, setting the table. "So, listen, Bunny's got dinner ready. But it was good talking to you."

"Yes, it was," Minna said.

It was only after he'd hung up that he realized he hadn't given Minna his phone number, and she hadn't asked him for it. It didn't matter. When he felt like talking to her again, he'd call her. He had found her once; he could find her again. He knew that whenever it was, she would be there waiting.

Bob lay on his back in bed, watching the rain stream down the small window in his room. He slept in Doreen's old room now.

No one else was going to be using it. The kid would barely even talk to him anymore. Nita wouldn't have put up with that kind of disrespect. Doreen had always been pretty much of a little shit, though. Not that he'd have ever said that to Anita. If he had told her, Anita would have thought it was her fault. Bob wasn't one to lay blame or take it, but Anita was always doing it, blaming herself for things no one could have prevented—things like Doreen's thin hair, Crystal's steel teeth. The only thing she didn't blame herself for was their succession of piece-of-shit houses. She blamed Bob for those. Not anymore, though. He'd shown her he could provide her with something wonderful, and he bet she was up there remembering that about him right now.

A single Christmas decoration hung from the power pole outside his window, and the rain blinked red to green to red. Anita used to decorate the whole house for Christmas. Construction paper bells, angels with tinsel hair, Advent calendars, homemade wrapping paper Doreen and Patrick made from paper bags, and stamps Anita helped them make from potato halves. She'd bake and cook and blow money they didn't have on gifts they didn't need until it was actually Christmas morning, and then it was over just like that. Anita was always so disappointed. The presents were nothing more than themselves: a new pair of hunting socks wrapped in green tissue paper, a new matching hairbrush and comb. You could tell it all came from the sale bins at the Ben Franklin. Some years Anita's post-Christmas funk would last until Easter, a fresh annual reminder that dreams and reality made damn poor bedfellows.

Warren had loved Christmas too. Every year the First Church of God had collected Christmas gifts for charity, and he and Bob always got at least one present apiece. Sometimes the gifts were used things, a scuffed-up basketball, maybe, or a pair of roller skates with a wobbly wheel. Sometimes they were given new things—usually clothes in sizes the church had announced to the congregation ahead of time. You could map the economic health of Hubbard by the gifts Bob and Warren were given over the years.

He watched the rain and drank his last two beers, ones he'd stolen from the Quick Stop after even Dooley Burden had refused to lend him any more money. He hoped Patrick would be sending another check soon from over there in Germany. He was a good boy, his son, but he acted like Bob embarrassed him. He'd come home the week after Anita died, but he stayed only a couple of days and went back to Germany early. There hadn't been much to say. Anita, not Bob, was the one who'd always found things to say.

He lay back and felt his mind get cloudy. That happened sometimes now. Then he must have dozed, and when he woke up, he thought he heard footsteps in the kitchen. Anita must be fixing something to eat. Why was everyone always trying to get him to eat all the time? Anita was probably making stew, his favorite thing. But no, she was dead. She was dead, and Warren was dead. How could he forget something like that? God, but he wished Anita could come back to visit him, or Warren. He was too drunk to be horny, but it would be enough just to see their faces and to hear them say they loved him.

Hack opened the door for Shirl just as Bunny set dinner on the table.

"Hooey," she cried, shaking water off her plastic rain bonnet. "It's raining like a son of a bitch out there. Coast guard's posted storm warnings again. Winds to a hundred miles an hour on the headlands."

Hack hung her wet jacket on a coat hook behind the door.

Crystal hid behind his legs; Shirl still scared her. Nevertheless she held out her Santa Bunny for Shirl's inspection. Shirl fell heavily to her knees for a better look.

"Well, will you look at that. Now isn't he a fine one?"

Crystal nodded solemnly.

"You think he's ready for Christmas yet? It won't be long now."

Crystal watched her, transfixed.

"Are you ready for Christmas?"

Crystal nodded emphatically.

"Well, sure you are, honey." Shirl patted Crystal's cheek and then held out her hand so Hack could hoist her up off the floor. "One day I'm going to get down there and never get up again," she puffed. "I swear to God."

"Come eat," Bunny called. "Crystal, if you'd like to set a place for Santa Bunny, you can. Get a plate from your tea set, and we'll put a little dinner out for him."

Crystal fetched a china plate the size of a half dollar that Bunny had bought for her when she first came to live with them. Most of the toys Anita had gotten at the Goodwill were broken or soiled, and even though Bunny knew Anita had done her best, she hadn't been able to bring herself to keep them. Now she spooned two peas and a shred of pot roast onto the tiny plate. "Do you think that's enough?"

"Yes."

Bunny spooned some pot roast and vegetables onto Crystal's bigger plate. "Now, you need to set a good example for Santa Bunny by staying right here and eating all your dinner before you get up." They'd had some trouble getting her to sit at the table until she finished her meals. Bunny figured she'd always been fed in front of the television, off a TV tray, eating and wandering as she pleased. They'd made progress, but it was slow, especially on days when Crystal wasn't hungry to start with. Bunny and Hack had been talking about getting her evaluated by the children's services people to make sure she was okay. The staff at Head Start had told them she seemed to be coming along more slowly than they'd expected with her letters and coloring. Bunny thought Crystal knew more than she was letting on, but still, Doreen had drunk a lot more than she should have when she was pregnant. Anita had always worried about that. Now Bunny was worrying about it.

Shirl hitched up her chair to the table. "This looks real good," she told Bunny. "I always was one for pot roast. Your daddy couldn't stand it, but I always fixed it on the night he left. You remember that?"

"Yeah." The nights when her father went back to the boat after being home for a month or two were always celebratory, even though Shirl and the kids would never say as much out loud. They'd have pot roast, hot buttered rolls, and vanilla bean ice cream, just like a party.

Shirl smacked Hack's forearm. "So what's the latest? You see him today?"

"Yeah."

"He still bad?"

Hack looked pointedly in Crystal's direction: not in front of the child.

"I was just asking," Shirl said huffily.

"Yeah, he's still bad."

"So you think he'll get that AIDS soon too?"

"Jesus, Shirl," Hack said.

Bunny gave Shirl a look across the table and turned to Crystal pointedly. "Honey, if you eat nine more peas, you can be excused from the table. Can you count them?"

Together they counted. Those Head Start people could say what they wanted about her letters, but Crystal knew her numbers all right.

"How about one more for good luck?" Bunny proposed. Crystal ate one more pea. "Is Santa Bunny done with his food? All right, then you can both go watch TV. You did a good job."

Crystal hopped down and left the room with her doll tucked firmly beneath her arm, giving Hack a baleful look as she slipped past.

"You're doing a fine job with that little girl," Shirl said to Bunny. "I want you to know that."

"It hasn't been easy," Bunny said. "I could just take her m-o-t-h-e-r and shake her sometimes."

"Well, she's young," Shirl allowed. "And with that Danny and all."

"Shhh," said Bunny.

"She couldn't hear that."

"Even so," said Bunny.

The table fell silent. After a while Shirl said, "You know, I've thought about it over and over, but I still would never take him for a fairy."

"He says he got it from giving blood," Hack said.

"And you believed that?" said Shirl.

"Well, if he is, he never told me or anyone else," said Hack. "I'm just saying."

"I read the papers," said Shirl. "All those little fairies in San Francisco are getting sick just like Anita did, dropping like flies."

"Mom—" Bunny said.

"You think you can get it from the public john?" Shirl ruminated. "I've worried about that. I can tell you I always lay toilet paper down first now."

"You can't get it from a toilet seat," Hack said.

"How do you know?"

"I asked the nurse. She said it didn't work that way."

"Well, I'm not about to take any chances. Those people don't know everything, for your information."

"Hell, Shirl, it takes up to ten years before you even get symptoms," Hack said.

"You saying I'm too old to worry about catching AIDS? Well, my life's still worth something to me, mister, even if it isn't to you," Shirl said hotly. "Anyway, it's easy for you men to say don't worry. You know why? Because you don't have to sit down, that's why."

Bunny shot a look at Hack, barely suppressing a smile.

"Will you listen to that wind," he said.

Lately Bunny had begun to understand that when she'd missed Hack over the years—when he'd gone so far away from her that he only brought his sex drive home—she hadn't missed him so much as she had hoarded the scraps of him he'd left behind in hopes he'd come back for them someday. With Anita, she'd never wanted anything more than exactly what Anita had had to give her, even including Anita's caustic temper. Grief, in Bunny's experience, was like quitting smoking. You reached for a cigarette you could no longer have before you were even aware that you were longing for one, and every time the dawning understanding came as another small death, another awful parting.

It had taken Bunny nearly a month to decide not to press charges against Bob for neglecting to provide Anita with adequate medical care. Hack had been the one to convince her. If you loved someone once, no matter how long ago or under what circumstances, that had to be worth something. If you couldn't do them good, you could at least decline from doing them harm. He said he hadn't always known that, but he knew it now.

Tonight he went to bed before Bunny. That had been happening more and more often lately, when before it had always been the other way around, and not just when she had to work the opening shift down at the Anchor either. She'd become a regular night owl, and at her age. Now she sat in her sewing room, listening to the rising wind rattling the birdhouses in the trees, thinking that if any birds actually took shelter inside them, they'd be knocked silly by morning. The birdhouses were one of Bunny's projects with Crystal. The True-Value had had a special on unpainted pine ones, two for nine bucks. She and Crystal had painted six of them in a rainbow of colors and decorated them with hand-drawn birds (Bunny) and stick figures (Crystal). Crystal painted two kinds of people, tiny ones and huge ones. The huge figures were grown-ups, bulbous and looming. The tiny figures were Crystal, stem-thin and brittle. It didn't take a lot to figure out who was the victim here.

Now, in the warm light of her sewing room, Bunny brought out a last Christmas gift she was making for Crystal, a family of rabbits. Almost as soon as she began working, though, she heard Crystal wake up, as she often did, crying in the dark with an odd, dry, hopeless keening that Bunny took to be grief. She dimmed her work lamp and padded down the hall that always looked different in the dark, as though she'd never made the trip before. She lifted Crystal gently and settled them together in a big soft chair Hack had bought on sale at Meier & Frank for a steal. Crystal tucked her head under Bunny's chin and, slumping, fell deeply asleep again, a warm, damp, breathing weight safe in Bunny's arms.

As she had been doing lately, Bunny closed her eyes and listened to the hundred small sounds of her household. There were the obvious ones like the refrigerator's hum, Hack's light snores, Crystal's tiny sighs, the rasp of numbers turning over on the cheap digital clock at her elbow. But beneath those noises there were others that were older, fainter, vestigial: the thousand remembered sounds that Vinny had made within these walls; the whistle Anita used to make when she blew cigarette smoke out of the side of her mouth; the curses and jokes that Bob and Hack had made over sixteen years of work on cars and trucks and dirt bikes in the garage. The remembered sounds of Bunny herself as she had moved through her empty house, trying in all the wrong ways to fill it. And now she had become this woman who used her belly and arms and bosom to keep from harm a little girl who was not her own; who was somehow more than her own. Vinny had always reached out and taken what she needed, secure in the knowledge that in most things she came first. Crystal had none of Vinny's strength or confidence. Crystal had learned very young what it was like to be left out, left behind, left alone to coax her own pale green shoot from parched and barren ground.

*Honey, there are two kinds of people in this world, whole people and damaged people. People like Bob and Warren, they're the damaged ones. God made them take on more than was fair, and I don't claim to understand why. I just know that they're laboring under a mighty load of scars and shortage. And here's the thing, Bunny, that nobody ever gets: The damaged ones, the ones like them, work at love the hardest.*

Bunny was getting used to hearing Anita here in the dark.
*Hack?*

*Hack, yes.*

*You never told me.*

*Would you have believed me if I had?*

*I don't know. No.*

*And now?*

Crystal stirred, pushing free of Bunny's encircling arms.
Bunny tucked her into bed again with a goodnight kiss she
would never remember receiving, her small head damp and
smelling of Barbie shampoo. Bunny closed the door softly and
went back to her sewing room, picking up where she had left
off an hour before. She loved this part of the work, pairing up
legs and arms and seeing the small bodies take final shape in her
hands.

*Do you believe me about Hack?*

Bunny thought. *That he's damaged?*

*Yes.*

*I do now. I didn't, before.*

*Then you weren't ready before. Or he wasn't.*

*It's an awful story.*

*They're always awful stories. That's why they're hardly ever told—
sometimes only once in a lifetime, sometimes never. You have to be ready to
hear them, and they have to be ready to tell them.*

It had taken Hack nearly two hours on the cabin steps beside
Homesick Creek to tell her about Cherise and the Katydid and
Minna Tallhorse, and half that time he hadn't been talking at all,
only thinking he was talking; Bunny could tell it from his eyes.
And the whole time he never looked at her once, not really, not
until he was finished. Then he'd looked at her all right, and his

eyes had been like holes in the universe, places where you could drop all the way through to oblivion if you didn't hold on, and then it was over. But in that time Bunny had seen things she'd never dreamed of and would never forget. Pain, suffering, re-crimination. Rage, not all of it spent. She had knelt in front of him, wrapped her arms around his head, and said, *I'm so sorry. God, I'm so sorry.* He had held on to her like someone afraid of dy-ing, scaring her so badly she had had to get up and go pee, and when she came back, it was over and they'd gathered their things, closed up the cabin, and gone home.

*See? You think you know all there is to know about someone, and then it turns out you didn't know a damn thing.*

*Nita, all those years, and it was never about Vinny at all.*

*Evidently not.*

*I should have known. Shouldn't I have known?*

*No, because he didn't want you to know, honey. People protect their se-crets like birds incubate eggs. Bird spends all her time sitting and waiting, making sure so no one can get at them until it's time. Well, it wasn't time.*

*I feel like a fool.*

*You're not a fool.*

*I miss you, Nita.*

*I know you do, honey.*

*I love you.*

*Well, that's how it begins.*

*How what begins?*

*Everything.*

How many times had she and Anita sat here together laugh-ing about some dumb thing while they sewed Halloween cos-tumes and cheerleading skirts, baby quilts and holiday crafts, the two of them peering like blind men through cigarette smoke so thick it made them cry? In this room they were the best they ever were, making things for people they loved, no matter how imperfectly. Now, enveloped at last in a silence as deep and pure as forgiveness, Bunny leaned alone into a pool of light, stitching together a family with a million pieces of love and remembrance, stuffed only with soft things, pliable things, things that could cushion a fall.